MANIX

GRACE MCGINTY

ALSO BY GRACE MCGINTY

Hell's Redemption Series

The Redeemable/The Unrepentant/The Fallen

The Azar Nazemi Trilogy

Smoke and Smolder/Burn and Blaze/Rage and Ruin

Dark River Days Series

Newly Undead In Dark River/Happily Undead In Dark River/Pleasantly Undead in Dark River

Black Mountain Mates

Hunting Isla

Eden Academy Series

The Lost and the Hunted (Prequel)/Heart of the Hounded (Prequel)

Rebels and Runaways (Book 1)/Sweethearts and Savages (Book 2)

Stand Alone Novels and Novellas

Bright Lights From A Hurricane

The Last Note

Castle of Carnal Desires

For Raewyn,
Who climbed aboard the crazy train voluntarily. That will
teach you for having such good grammar.
Choo-choo!
- G x

MANIX

1

This parking lot smelled overwhelmingly of vomit and dried bodily fluids. How the outdoors, with all this fresh mountain air, could have such overwhelming scents was truly a miracle of nature. The crumbling building, lit only with flashing neon signs, sat in the center of a lot filled with pickup trucks. To the left of my group, a couple were fucking down a side alley and the male sounded like a boar with a hot poker up its ass.

I realized why it smelled so much like puke when I stepped into a small puddle of it, and it splashed up onto the laces of my boots. Humans were fucking disgusting sometimes. I lifted my hand to motion us forward and we walked into the club, which was devoid of security at the front door.

The establishment vibrated with too much bass,

like a tribal drumbeat, and it had whipped the crowd into a frenzy. The smell of sweat and lust permeated every corner, and we tightened our formation around Raiden.

The distressed scent of an unfamiliar Omega had me growling low under my breath, and the humans who lingered too close quickly moved away. Not because they could hear the growl, but because they could feel the coiled violence that rolled off my Pack.

Finlo stepped closer to me, leaning in to be heard over the ear-shattering noise of the music. "Are we sure this is the place? Perhaps Seven's nose is broken?" the other Alpha asked.

Seven scowled, baring his teeth at Finlo. Seven was a Beta, but he was a strong Beta. Too strong. It was a generally held belief that a strong Beta would resist orders and cause problems. And it was true, Seven did cause issues at times, especially when given orders. But our Pack weren't hardcore traditionalists when it came to hierarchies. I treated Seven the way I'd treat any other Alpha—hell, any other Manix—with respect and understanding. In return, Seven was grateful to even have a Pack, even if it was one filled with misfits. He was loyal and loved, and that was worth something too.

"My nose didn't lie. There is an Omega here, one that is close to heat."

Ellar hovered over Raiden, practically glued to his

side. "I trust Seven's tracking. His nose is his best trait. Goddess knows, it isn't his winning personality," he joked, making Raiden chuckle. Unlike Seven, the family's other Beta was like me. A half-blood Manix. He'd had no other choice than to join us, because no one else would muddy their bloodlines with a half-caste.

This was us. A tiny, ill-formed Pack, except for our one crowning jewel—our Omega.

One of the last male Omegas left, he'd chosen us to be his mates. When an Omega comes of age, he is allowed to choose which Pack he joins. No one had been more shocked than us when he'd chosen ours. Until Raiden, we'd been a rag-tag bunch of mutts on the outskirts of Manix society.

I looked over my shoulder at Raiden, whose soft expression met mine. Just a look from him shored up my resolve. Although our natural instincts wanted to protect and coddle Raiden, he was a warrior in his own right. Maybe that's why he picked us. He didn't want to be pampered and adored. He wanted to fight and fuck, which was wildly un-Omega like. Despite the fact that I *knew* he could defend himself against humans, my Alpha instincts insisted that he be protected at all times. He was the heart of our Pack after all.

I scanned the crowd, but the overwhelming conflicting scents muddled everything. "We'll split up. Raiden will come with me. Trust Seven's nose," I warned Finlo.

Finlo was my childhood best friend, and had chosen to build a Pack with me rather than join one of the more prestigious warrior Packs more suited to his bloodlines. I owed him everything.

He nodded and split off, the two Betas following behind him. I tucked Raiden closer to me as we waded further into the club. There were stages dotted around the room, each lit up with a different color. Blue, red, purple. On each stage, a woman danced, spinning around a pole. I'd been born in human society, raised here until I was eleven, and I knew what a strip club was. But Raiden didn't, and his eyes almost bulged out of his head. He shook his head at me as he grinned.

"My sire was right, the only place you could take me is into the gutter," he teased.

Yeah, not everyone had been overjoyed that Raiden had chosen my Pack. I nudged his shoulder with mine, despite the fact that I wanted to reach out and place a kiss on his temple. "Admit it, you like being dirty down here in the gutter with me."

He laughed, reaching down to squeeze my hand as we parted the crowd. "Wouldn't be anywhere else."

We were getting a few weird looks, and that was another reason we needed to split up. Together, we seemed inhuman. Ridiculously tall and broad, we looked like the warrior race we'd once been, before we were killed off and forced to flee to the mountains of

Montana, forever separate until we were slowly dying out for other reasons.

Manix. We were the real reason the word manic entered the English language. It was the way early humans described the rut, where we thirsted for blood or sex, and wreaked havoc. But now there were barely two thousand of us left. Of that, there were less than a hundred full-blooded female Manix. Only twenty-five Omegas, but none of those were female.

We were dying out at a rapid rate. Which is why when Seven said he'd scented an Omega female on the wind, we'd come on this wild goose chase. I was happy to chase a wild goose if it gave my Pack a chance at a real future.

I stayed at Raiden's back, my eyes trawling in front of us for threats. "Scent anything?" I asked, despite the fact it galled me. I was half-blood, the result of a Manix male and a human female. Mating with humans was frowned upon, and according to the Manix Legion, little better than lying with a beast. As a result, I was little better than an animal to the upper crust of Manix society.

I pushed down the residual rage I felt toward the Legion and searched the crowd. Raiden tilted his head, his pupils blowing out wide. "That way," he said softly, his feet taking him in the right direction before he'd even lifted his arm. If I'd had any doubt about Seven's nose, it disappeared at that moment. I kept my hand on Raiden's belt as he moved through the crowd with single-minded focus. He might have been the smallest of us, but he was still over six feet in height, tall in comparison to a human.

He stopped in front of a small platform, bathed in blue light so it appeared like it was in the depths of the sea. Raiden's eyes went wide and his knees nearly buckled as he looked up at the girl on the stage. Finally, her scent permeated my duller senses.

And when I scented her? My dick went rock hard.

She danced in heels that had to be six inches high, her movements easy as her body swayed to the music. She kept her eyes closed, like she could block out the world if she just deprived herself of the sight of these salivating humans.

She was small, tiny in comparison to a Manix female. Her body curved sharply though, her figure like an hourglass of old. Given the overwhelming smell of lust that hung like a cloud around us, she had a body that men would bankrupt themselves to have just a touch.

Wearing basically nothing, her scent was like a caress, followed by a slap to the face. I could feel the Omega presence, scent her oncoming heat cycle. I cast a worried look at Raiden, whose whole body was taut with the urge to rut.

Breeding in Manix society had historically occurred in one of two ways. A female could be impregnated by a single Manix male, and would usually give birth to a solitary offspring. Or, a female and male Omega could mate during a heat cycle, and the male Omega would draw the viable eggs into himself. Afterwards, the pack would lie together during the rut and all the eggs had a chance to be fertilized. It was animalistic, feral sex that would leave the entire Pack drained and weak.

This is why the heat in a female would send us all into an insane rut, but especially Raiden, as our Pack Omega.

I noticed my Packmates on the other side of the stage, also looking up at her like she was a gift from the Goddess. She was definitely the one, and I would make her ours. Raiden was all but shaking with need, and I moved him toward the back wall so we could watch her and be obscured by the shadows a little more.

Her hips swayed with exaggeration to the music. She hooked her leg around the shiny metal pole in the center of the stage, swinging in a slow loop, her left foot barely scraping along the floor. Her breasts were barely contained in a tiny little bikini which matched the barely-there thong that both covered her intimate flesh and attracted the gaze of the audience to it.

As I searched the crowd, watching the hungry eyes of the humans, smelling their lust and violence, my Beast rose up in my chest. They were looking at what was mine, or at least, what would be mine. I looked at the red lever beside me, secure behind its safety glass from accidental knocks. The fire alarm.

Looking over at Finlo, I lifted my chin toward the girl. Finlo would know what to do. He nodded back, so I pushed through the safety glass and pressed the fire alarm. Within seconds, there was a loud whooping noise that blared across the music, the interior fire sprinklers opening the metaphorical heavens.

Panic ensued, and there was a mass exit for the door, people pushing and shoving as they nearly trampled others to make their escape from nothing. As people turned and fled, the girl jumped off the stage, but Finlo moved incredibly fast. He gathered her up into his arms and walked out the rear exit, the girl over his shoulder, Seven and Ellar at his back.

Raiden whined as he lost sight of the other Omega, and we moved with the tail end of the panicked exodus. The rest of our Pack would get her where we needed her to be. I would just take care of Raiden.

An Omega pair... Could we really be that lucky? Raiden whined low under his breath, his hand gripping mine. "She's close, Gat. So damn close. Maybe a week? It's making my skin itch."

Female Omegas had been the first thing to die out. There were no Omega pairs left. Back when they'd found out the Omega females were dying out, we'd tried the Omegas of different species, but while they might be hierarchically the same, they weren't physiologically similar enough for there to be an Omega bonding. That had led to an uprising against us by shifters, because the Manix of the past didn't exactly ask for the Omegas nicely, which drove us further into the Mountains, isolating us even more.

It had been a bleak time in our history. Because we weren't like shifters, or other supernaturals. We were different completely, an entirely different genus. That was why the girl we'd just pulled off the stage was such a miracle, a true gift from the Goddess.

She was going to save our Pack, and then maybe, our species. But first, we had to get her to like us.

2

NAJA

I was in the middle of my set when chaos erupted. The sprinkler system kicked in, soaking the ground and all the clientele. I didn't mind really; I'd been running a fever for a week and the water felt blessedly good on my overheated skin. But my heels weren't made for wet weather, and I slipped across the stage. I was about to scramble down, when my heel went out from underneath me completely, sending me flying.

I screeched, but strong hands caught me around the waist, pulling me upright. I looked up at the man who'd caught me. And I do mean up. He must have been close to seven feet tall. And he was handsome, literally steal your breath handsome.

"Thank you—oof!"

He hauled me over his shoulder and pushed his way into the staff hallways toward the back entrance.

"Hey, asshole! Put me down. I can walk," I screeched, ignoring the fact that I'd nearly fallen on my face moments before.

That's when I noticed the other two. They closed ranks around the other guy, and fear began to replace my outrage. Shit. Fuck. I was being fucking kidnapped. I hammered at the guy's back, shrieking obscenities and god knows what else, both in Spanish and English, but none of them seemed to pay me any attention.

No one could hear my calls for help over the wailing of the alarm, and my panic turned to icy fear in my veins. Everything they'd ever told me in self-defense classes came roaring to the front, such as never let them take you to a secondary location, and go for the soft bits. But over this guy's shoulder, with his arms banded around my leg like a vice, and his back impervious to my nails and bites, I didn't know what my self-defense instructor would have wanted me to do. There were no soft bits back here.

I was going to be a statistic, going to my death in only a fucking thong.

My kidnapper stopped outside a black minivan and one of the other guys zipped around to open the trunk. Oh hell no.

"Let me fucking down, you cocksucking piece of

shit asshole!" I screamed, twisting my body up to grab at his hair and yank hard. He hissed, but I swear to fucking god, he grinned at the pain. He went to put me into the back of the van, but this fucker probably thought I was a human. He couldn't have been more goddamn wrong. As soon as my ass chafed against that cheap auto carpet, I twisted hard, putting my ridiculous heel into his stomach. He flew back with a grunt, and I was out of the car and sprinting across the parking lot back toward the building. I'd take my luck with the fucking fire and lock myself in the boss's office.

I made it a few more steps before I slammed into a wall. Or at least, it felt like a wall. When a set of arms wrapped around me again, my stomach sank. I craned my neck to look up into a gorgeous face, the kind with high cheekbones and a sharp jaw that made a person look cruel. This guy definitely belonged with the other group.

I opened my mouth to scream, but another set of arms yanked me away from him. The new guy was shorter, but still towered over me. He looked down at me with the softest blue eyes I'd ever seen. "It's okay, Omega," he whispered, and my entire body went lax. It was like someone had shot me with an overdose of Xanny, making my body languid and chasing away the terror.

He picked me up in his arms, and while my brain

wanted to run from the other predators, I found myself snuggling into this one's arms. The hell?

"Ah, little one. You must be so uncomfortable. Let us take care of you," he cooed, and I wanted to cry. I wanted to tell him how sick I'd felt the last few days, how exhausted I was all the time. But at the same time, I wanted to claw out his eyes and run away as fast as my stupidly tall heels would let me. As if he could sense my thoughts, he tutted his tongue. "We mean absolutely no harm, Omega. We couldn't hurt you if we tried." He stared down into my eyes, finding a truth there that I desperately wanted to remain hidden. "How hard it must have been for you."

I sniffed, realizing I was crying and also now in the back of the fucking minivan. Goddammit. What an epic fail.

But one thing was clear—these guys were some kind of supes. "Not an Omega," I said groggily, fighting the pure calm that was radiating from the guy currently holding me. "Shouldn't take me. I'll bite off your dick."

One of the guys in the back of the van laughed. "Some of us might like that." When the guy holding me tutted, the other one bowed his head. "Apologies, Omega."

Whatever effect the designated nice guy was having on me was beginning to wear off, and I rolled off his lap and onto the seat beside him. Unfortunately, that put me nearly in the lap of another giant. How the holy hell did they all fit in this freaking van?

He smiled down at me happily, his head brushing the roof. "Hi. I'm Ellar."

"I don't care."

His face fell, and I tried not to feel bad. Step one of feminism: you did not have to be polite to people who were trying to abduct you in nothing but a thong. Maybe that should be steps one through five. There was a lot there to unpack.

The nice guy—the one who made me feel like he could cure all my problems—grabbed for me again but I shuffled closer to Ellar. At least I could think around him. I toed off my stupid shoes, just in case I got a chance to run.

"It will be fine, Omega. Once we get you up the mountain, we can take care of you how you deserve." It sounded wonderful when he said it but in reality, it was creepy as fuck. Pretty sure that's what someone would say before they wore your skin as a suit.

Then his words began to sink in. Back up the mountain. No. We couldn't.

Panic raced down my spine and I launched myself into the front of the car, grabbing at the wheel.

"No!"

The driver swore as he swerved all over the road. We were lucky it was reasonably late so there was no oncoming traffic, but still, I kept trying to drag us off the road and onto the shoulder. If I could get out of the car, I could run.

I'd always been fast. I just had to get out of the car.

Strong arms grabbed me and dragged me to the passenger side, arms like steel vices. "Omega! Calm!" a voice commanded, and my body reacted of its own accord. I went entirely limp like a rag doll.

The fuck? I inhaled, though my senses were weak for a shifter. But what I scented was definitely Alpha.

"What our Omega said was true. No injury will come to you while you are with us; I swear this to you on my life." The pledge was murmured softly beside my ear, his tone calm.

"Can't guarantee that if you are trying to crash us into a fucking tree though," the driver snarled, obviously a little rattled.

The Alpha who currently had me clutched to his chest let out a rumbling growl. "Finlo…"

The guy huffed. "Apologies, Omega."

I looked at the guy, Finlo, with his strawberry blond hair and sharp jaw, and decided he was actually sorry. Also, they still actually thought I was an Omega.

I looked up at the Alpha holding me, at the small dimple in his chin and soft gray eyes staring back at me. I had a feeling they weren't always soft though, because there was something about the lines of his face that spoke of bitterness.

"Look, I meant what I said. You guys have snatched

the wrong girl. I'm a half-breed tiger shifter. We don't even have Omegas. I can't even shift forms, for fuck's sake. I just wanna go home, and I promise to forget this ever happened." The guy just shook his head, so I went to Plan B. "I have a kid. You can't steal me. Who will look after her?"

Well, that got their attention. The whole car went dead silent. I mean, there wasn't a single rustle or exhaled breath or anything.

The guy driving looked at me. "You already have a mate?" There was an actual whine in his voice, like he felt pained by the thought. "How did Seven's nose miss a mate?"

I interrupted the other guy before he could speak. "Yep, I do, and he's a Navy Seal. Real badass. I've watched him kill a man with nothing more than a yellow pencil." I blurted out the lie. "He'll look for me, with all his buddies. They're wolf shifters, good noses. They'll definitely rescue me. Better you let me out here and go and find your Omega. I promise I won't tell a soul."

I silently apologized to the unknown Omega.

All eyes turned to the guy in the back, who just scoffed. "There's nothing wrong with my nose. She's definitely an Omega, and I don't smell any other supernatural scents on her. She is days from her heat. We can all scent that. If she had a mate, he wouldn't have let her leave the house."

I gasped. "Excuse me? I don't need a mate who tells me what to do. Uh, Frank lets me do what I want. He respects my choices, and doesn't try and kidnap me."

The guy in the back with the nose—Seven, I think they said his name was—scoffed. "Uh, Frank doesn't exist."

I gritted my teeth and tears burned my eyes. "Okay, so no mate. But I do have a kid. Luisa. She needs me." I implored the Alpha who was still holding me tightly, but it had started to feel more reassuring than restraining.

The guy with the Xanny essence cleared his throat. "I believe her. We cannot steal her from her young."

The whole car was silent and the guy holding me was stiff. "Fine, we will return to her home. She would be more comfortable there during the heat anyway."

"What?" I squeaked. "No fucking way. I'm not telling you where I live." I wasn't taklng them home to the place that was a refuge for Luisa and I.

There was rustling in the back, and Seven chuckled softly. "I grabbed her bag on the way out. Her scent was all over it." I looked between the seats as he pulled out my purse and read my address off my drivers license.

I would have to run again. Luisa was still too young to understand, so it would be fine. She wouldn't hate me, despite us already setting down roots here, and me promising that things would be better now.

The Alpha's arms tightened. "Hear us out, and then

I promise, if you want us to leave, we will. We pose no threat to you or your young. You hold all the power here; you just don't understand yet. But I promise, you will."

I nodded in defeat. I'd have to play it safe, especially as they now knew where I lived. I was gambling with both mine and Luisa's life for the second time in a year, but there was no other choice.

"If you hurt her in any way, I will skin you alive," I growled under my breath, and he made a humming noise of agreement.

"And I will hand you the knife. I vow this."

3

SEVEN

Her scent threatened to drown me. Being in an enclosed space, where all I could smell was the beginning of her heat, and then under that, her own natural scent... well, it was killing me. Or at least killing my dick. My cock was so hard, I was pretty sure it was going to explode like an over-filled water balloon.

The car had fallen silent since Finlo had done a U-turn on the freeway and headed back through Missoula toward Lolo. Made sense why she would live out of Missoula, and separate her two lives, especially if she had a kid. Guess she didn't want anyone to know she was a stripper, but it made sense to me. Even humans were susceptible to the kinds of pheromones she was throwing off right now. If we hadn't hit the fire alarm, she would have made a bucketload tonight.

A little guilt snuck up on me, but then I remembered that if everything went well, she'd be ours and we would make sure she never needed a damn thing ever again. Both her and her offspring.

My nose twitched, and I second-guessed myself. I had a highly sensitive olfactory sense, or at least that's what Ellar said. Better than most other Manix, which was why I was able to pick up this female's scent from the mountains.

It was better than most Alphas I knew. Hell, I was stronger than *every* Beta in Maxton, which was why it had been so hard for me to find a Pack that would take me, despite my good bloodlines. The only ones who would even consider me were this ragtag bunch of half-bloods and misfits, and I'd never been more fucking thankful that they'd looked past the attitude and the hierarchy than I was at this very moment.

It was because of my annoying nose that I was wondering if there even was a kid. I could smell information about people—which sounds fucking weird, and I guess it kind of was. But I could scent that this female had never bred. I didn't mention it though, because one, I'd already put the pretty Omega offside... uh, twice now. Two, because there was the scent of young on her stuff; I just didn't think it was *her* young. Better to see what it was all about before I made any sweeping statements that got me even further up the shitlist.

She seemed content in the Alpha's arms up the front, and a pang of something—not jealousy, but something like it—hit me in the chest.

Unworthiness, maybe?

I hadn't been good enough for a Pack, so why would I be good enough for the last female Omega on the fucking planet?

"Seven," Raiden said softly, looking over his shoulder. His eyes were soft, and I reached out a hand to touch him.

"I'm fine, Omega," I whispered softly. His eyes narrowed like he was going to call me on my bullshit, but he resisted. Thank fuck. Ellar, the other Beta in our Pack, sent me a worried look too, but kept his mouth firmly shut.

We rolled through Lolo, and it looked like a cookie tin picture of a small town in the Montana mountains. Finlo didn't ask for directions, which meant he was probably getting them off his cellphone. We might live isolated from humans, but that didn't mean time had passed us by. Honestly, I couldn't have gotten through the last decade without video games.

I grabbed the Omega's oversized tote, and found a sweater dress and some flip flops.

"Alpha," I barked, passing the clothes to Ellar. "The Omega might be more comfortable arriving home dressed in more than a thong."

The Omega's eyes met mine in the rearview mirror

as she snatched the clothes from Ellar. "I wouldn't be in a thong if you hadn't abducted me. Pull over," she demanded, turning to glare at Finlo.

Surprisingly, Finlo complied. Watching her like she was a rattlesnake, we let her step out of the car, and shuck the dress over her head. She paused, eyeing the distance for a moment, before climbing back into the car again. With agility that was only really granted to short people, she maneuvered into the middle row of seats, sitting between Raiden and Ellar again.

The silence this time was almost deafening. She'd voluntarily—or at least pseudo-voluntarily—got back into the van, which didn't mean anything really. But it felt like it meant something.

The silence, as always, was too much for Ellar. "May we know your name?" he said softly, his entire body language non-confrontational. As a half-blood Beta, he'd been even worse off than Gatlin. But where Gatlin had had to forge his path, he'd taken Ellar under his wing almost immediately, protecting the softer Beta from the harshness of Manix life.

The girl looked at him but stayed silent, and I could see his little Beta heart breaking.

We eventually pulled up in front of a squat house painted bright pink—so pink I could see it in the dark. "Can I convince you guys to stay outside?"

Gatlin looked over his shoulder, and gave her a single shake of his head.

She huffed. "Can you wait until I send the babysitter home before you come in then? I'd rather the good folk of Lolo didn't think I was running a fucking brothel out of my rental."

There was a tense silence, and Raiden huffed. "Of course, Omega. You aren't a prisoner. We request that you listen to our plea, but then if you wish, we will leave and go back to our home."

She gave him another narrow-eyed glare, but it vanished nearly immediately. Raiden was very disarming. I had the opposite effect though.

She climbed out over his lap, holding her hand out for her tote bag. I hefted it between the seats to her, and she stomped off toward the front door. We sat in the darkness, not even a street light illuminating the interior of the car.

"She could be calling the cops," Finlo said.

Gatlin shook his head. "No, I know her type. She won't call the cops. She might run though."

The disquiet that ran through the car at the thought was nearly a living thing. "She can run, but I will find her again," I said confidently, and Ellar snorted.

"Show off." He frowned. "I don't know how you're still walking. Just the faint hints of her heat and I'm choking on air," he whispered, and I decided to play it tough and pretend I wasn't ready to fuck the tailpipe of this Mom-Van.

Gatlin made an uncomfortable sound from the front. "No one pressures her. If she kicks us out, we leave. We aren't our brethren of old. We are better. A willing Omega or no Omega."

Raiden nodded. "Of course, Alpha. But if Seven can smell her heat now, eventually those with less impressive noses will scent her and come down from the mountains. We both know that not all Packs have our beliefs."

A low growl rumbled in my chest, and I tried to squash it down out of habit. No one would beat me down for my dominance in this pack, but old habits died hard.

"Then we stay and protect, warn her about what might be coming, and then when her heat is over, we leave. She'll know the dangers she faces then if she stays here. She'll probably move on."

Raiden whined, and Ellar pulled him into his arms. We slid back into silence as the minutes dragged on.

I was beginning to worry that Gatlin was correct about her running when the blue front door opened and a teenage girl walked out, sliding into a beat-up car that whirred like bees caught in a bottle as she sped away. The door opened again, and the Omega was there. She eyed the van like she could set it on fire with her mind, but eventually she lifted her chin, motioning us into the house.

We were stealthy, protecting her reputation as

much as possible. Luckily, despite our size, Manix were actually built for stealth. It was what made us such good warriors. Semi-shifting, a light coating of fur slid down our skin, making us blend with the darkness.

We slipped through the Omega's door like shifting shadows in the night, and she closed it gently behind us.

Finally, she stank of fear. "What the fuck are you guys?"

Finlo looked down at her—hell, she couldn't be more than five-two—and grinned. "Manix."

4

———————

NAJA

"Manic? Like maniacs?"

Who the fuck had I just invited through my front door, with Luisa in her bed in the next room?

The calming one stepped forward, making a soothing noise. "No, not maniacs. We are a breed of supernatural called Manix. We have all but died out, except for a small colony of us in the mountains."

I screwed up my face, but it did explain the weird camouflage thing they'd done a minute ago. It was like they'd just disappeared before my eyes. "Never heard of you."

Ellar gave me a sad smile. "Not many have."

I kinda felt guilty again for being a bit of a dick to the guy who'd only been polite so far. I chewed my lip as I looked up into his nearly gold eyes. "Naja. My name is Naja."

The smile he gave me was dazzling, and made my body clench like it was a caress. Every single one of them snapped to attention, their eyes lingering on me like I was prey. I curled my lip in a snarl and they all looked away.

The big one, Finlo I think his name was, dropped his eyes until he was looking at my toes. "Excuse us, Omega. But your scent calls to us."

I sighed, because they were still carrying on about me being an Omega, and ushered them into the tiny living room. How they'd all fit among the giant pile of clean laundry and the warzone of Luisa's toys, I didn't know, but I perched myself on the armchair and let them spread out where they would. One big guy sat on the couch, with another leaning against the door frame. Ellar sat on the floor, his back resting against the couch, and the calming one pressed against the big one's side. The surly one with a big mouth rested against the wall in the corner, frowning.

"You better tell me your names. I can't keep calling you 'scary ass fuckers' in my brain."

The guy on the couch pointed to himself. "I'm Gatlin." Okay, Gatlin with the gray eyes and the incredible jaw. I could remember that. "You know Ellar, he is a Beta. Raiden, our Omega male." He pointed to the calm guy whose eyes were warm and imploring, though I didn't know what they were imploring me about just yet.

The guy holding up the doorframe pointed to himself. "Finlo. I'm an Alpha like Gatlin, and this is our second Beta, Seven. He's the one who found you."

I raised an eyebrow at Seven. "Like the number?"

He just shrugged. "Probably."

I looked back at Gatlin as he explained, "We're a Pack, a bonded group."

I tipped my head. "Like wolves?"

Ellar snorted. "Not like wolves." Well, I sensed some tension there. "More like family."

Now it was Seven's turn to make a rude noise. "A family who all fuck, maybe."

Woah. Hold the fucking phone. Back that truck right the hell up and dump that load of what-the-hell right at my feet. "You what now?"

Raiden tensed. "Seven makes it sound more sordid than it is. We are lovers, true, but it's more than that. We took vows to protect and care for each other, and sometimes that care comes in the form of..." He seemed to grapple for words.

"Making each other come?" I offered.

He grinned and nodded. "Exactly."

I knew I needed to move on from this bomb they'd dropped, but my brain seemed to be stuck on taking a visual snapshot of each one, and then adding him to a sordid mental fantasy of them all fucking one another.

The broad, muscular chest of Gatlin pressed against the lithe muscles of Raiden, or fuck, Finlo grabbing the shaggy blond hair of Seven as he bent his powerfully built body over the couch while the slimmer built Ellar kissed him. Shit, that was hot.

I swallowed hard as my vagina gave a hearty round of applause.

Everyone shifted uncomfortably, and I pretended not to see the blown out pupils and the giant fucking salami that Finlo was packing in his jeans.

Gatlin cleared his throat. "Uh, as we were saying, we are a Pack. It's the system of relationships in Manix society, where there are few female births, and we are now all but extinct. There are even fewer male Omegas like Raiden, and they are revered in Manix society."

Raiden screwed up his nose. "He means suffocated and coddled until we are fucking useless for anything but sex and happy feelings." I could almost taste his bitterness on my tongue. Gatlin wrapped an arm over his shoulders, tugging him closer to his body. Raiden sighed, taking the comfort easily.

My eyebrows drew together in a frown as I watched their easy affection. Had I ever had that level of quiet comfort with anyone, except Luisa? I didn't think so, and once again, I was incredibly sad. I wasn't one to sit in the corner and think about how shit my life was, but one day, I'd like to have someone I could depend on. Someone who would reassure me that everything was okay. I didn't have that with my parents, that was for sure, and I was fairly sure I was too broken to accept it anyway, but hey, a girl could dream.

Suddenly, there were arms around my shoulders and I was pressed hard into a chest that vibrated lightly. It was kind of like a purr, but without the noise. Just a gentle thudding against my cheek. It was nice.

Too nice.

I tugged myself out of the arms that felt way too comforting, and looked up into the face of Ellar.

"Beta," Gatlin warned, and Ellar's face fell.

"Sorry Alpha. Omega. I couldn't help myself. The scent of her sadness hurts my heart. It is harder to resist comforting her than it is to resist the call of her need."

Gatlin gave him a patient look. "I understand, but I don't believe Naja is at the level where she is comfortable with physical contact. We must respect that, no matter how difficult."

I felt like I'd kicked a fucking puppy with the way Ellar's face fell. I grabbed his fingers as he turned away and squeezed. "Thank you for the hug," I said softly, and he gifted me that smile again.

Then the rest of his words finally rattled through my consciousness. "Wait a sec. What the hell did he mean by the 'call of my need?'" I needed a lot of things —a new furnace, a dishwasher, a million bucks. I didn't think these guys would give me those things though.

Gatlin cleared his throat again. He was obviously the Alpha of the Alphas, or maybe Finlo just wasn't a big talker. "While male Omegas are rare, female Omegas have been non-existent for decades."

Finlo finally stepped forward. "Until you."

Ah. I was beginning to see how the whole cloak and dagger, 'let's kidnap her' thing seemed like a good idea to them now. But boy, were they wrong.

"You aren't listening. I'm not an Omega. Tiger shifters don't even have Omegas. I'm a tiger shifter who can't even shift. You're wrong."

Seven frowned. "Not wrong. Your scent is unmistakable to us. To Raiden, you are like a balm to his soul and a Viagra to his dick."

Raiden flushed bright red. "Seven!"

He shrugged. "It's true. She's—"

Finlo growled from the doorway. "She has a name, Beta."

Seven huffed. "Apologies. Naja is obviously a halfblood. If her Manix half is the latent half, how would she even know?" He turned to me. "You didn't grow up in our society, learning our rules, experimenting with your abilities. But my nose, it's not wrong about this. I swear it to you. You are the last female Omega Manix on the planet."

It was hard not to be swayed by how sure he seemed. I looked around at them again, each one earnestly sincere. I walked over to the bookcase, pulled out my copy of the bible and grabbed the small bottle of tequila from behind it.

I had a feeling I was going to need a drink for what came next. "Say I believe you, that I'm the last Manix Omega female blah-blah. What does that even mean for you guys? For me?"

Finlo sauntered toward me until I was nose to chest. "It means you can impregnate our male Omega."

Say what?

Naja took a huge step away from Finlo. "Woah, no one is impregnating me, Gigantor."

Finlo's lips twitched. "I didn't say anyone was impregnating *you*, Tiny. I said *you* could impregnate Raiden."

I watched her eyes grow real wide, and slow blink. "I'm not sure I understand what you're saying here. That's not how nature works. Maybe you guys have spent too long in the mountains surrounded by dicks all the time, but pregnancy is usually a female thing."

I shook my head at her, stepping closer, drawing her attention. "Not with Manix. It is why we are all but extinct. Females do give birth, but they can only give birth to one offspring every nine months. Their biology is similar to that of humans really, one egg once a month. But female Omegas, they can produce up to ten eggs during a heat cycle. They do not have the strength to carry that many offspring to term at once though. That's where male Omega Manix come into the picture. Our physiology is different; it's stronger, better equipped to carry the load that half a dozen cubs would be."

She was still frowning. "But you don't have a vagina." She paused. "Do you?"

This was simultaneously embarrassing as hell and funny as fuck. I never thought I'd have to explain this to someone outside our society. It sounded preposterous, and even to the younger members of Manix, it was an urban legend. "Uh, no. I don't have a vagina. I have a secondary urethra that extracts the eggs, and a womb for gestation."

She swigged down more tequila. At this rate, she was going to be shitfaced by the time we got to the real issues. "Then how do you give birth?"

"In the olden days, it was a ritualistic thing performed as a Pack, involving daggers and stones and blessing chants to the Goddess. Today, we would just call it a Caesarean section."

She was shaking her head softly, over and over, like she couldn't stop. She slumped back onto her couch. "I still don't understand."

Seven huffed. "It's not really that hard if you stop being so fucking human. You two fuck during the heat.

He steals the eggs with his super sucker dick. We fuck him and fertilize the eggs in what is one very long and dirty orgy. He grows some cubs. In four and a half months, we cut him open, deliver our young, and we are finally a family."

Gatlin growled. "For fuck's sake, Seven."

She was silent for a long time, and I could see the information bouncing around in her head. Damn, she smelled so good, she made my mouth water. My dick ached and she wasn't even in full heat yet. It would be unbearable then.

She finally slid her eyes to Seven and gave him a sour look. She was looking a little more chilled out—all the tequila probably. "I get the logistics, asshole. I don't understand what my part in this is. Do you just want me to donate eggs? I mean, I don't think I have this heat thing that Seven mentioned."

There was an audible grunt in the room, and Gatlin stood. He sauntered over in that way he had that made my dick impossibly harder, until he was standing in front of her, slightly stooped so he didn't look like he was looming.

"You are nearly in heat now, Naja," he murmured softly. "You'll know because your skin feels hot and tight, and nothing cools it down. Your body clenches in need, and no matter how much you touch yourself, it doesn't ease. The sound of my voice right now is making you so wet; we can all smell it. You're responding to my Alpha pheromones, and Raiden's Omega scent. You don't ovulate like other humans, or even other shifters. It will come only once a year and it is excruciating and bloody and you feel like you want to die. Mating during the heat eases the pain and duration."

She swallowed hard, and I saw goosebumps spread across her warm skin like wildfire. "Irregular periods are a sign of trauma. It wasn't that unusual."

My eyes whipped to Finlo, and he mouthed, "Trauma?" as I felt my hackles rising instantly.

Gatlin quelled his Alpha response to the little Omega's statement, which was exactly why he was our unofficial leader. He kept a cool head when he wasn't dealing with the Legion, and he saw things from alternate perspectives. He shook his head at her. "No, it is because you are Manix. And an Omega at that. Something we were so sure was gone from the world that you may as well be a unicorn."

He stepped away, but she followed him like she couldn't help herself. I resisted the grin because I knew what that meant. We had her, at least physically. Now we just had to convince her head and her heart that we were the best option for her. We could do it.

This bunch of ruffians had convinced me easily.

She looked back at me, and I was once again floored with how beautiful she was. "So, what? Me and

Raiden have sex, he steals my eggs, and you guys go away?"

Gatlin lowered his chin in agreement. "If that's what you wish, yes. It's not the ideal scenario, but if that was your decision, we would accept it."

She clenched her jaw like she was preparing for a fight. "And if I said I wanted nothing to do with this whole twilight zone scenario?"

Gatlin dropped his eyes. "Then we would accept that as well. However, you would need to move on from Montana. My Pack will protect you for this heat cycle either way, but if you stay here, other Packs will eventually scent you and come down from the mountains. Some may be less... polite with their invitations."

I snarled at the thought of anyone doing anything to Naja against her will, and it made her head whip toward me.

"They'd rape me?"

Gatlin inclined his head solemnly. "Perhaps. The heat can make us crazy and some Manix are from a more barbaric school of thought than ours. But even if they have complete control over themselves, you are something that hasn't been seen in many decades. They will take what they can from you, with or without your permission."

She looked like she wanted to crumple, but instead, her shoulders went stiff like she was injecting her spine with steel. "They could try." She looked over at Seven. "Who'd have thought that you guys, with your abduction, would be the polite option?"

She screwed the cap back on the tequila, settling down on the couch beside Ellar. I hid my smile as the soft Beta didn't move a single muscle so as to not frighten her. I loved that man. "Say we do this, and I give Raiden my eggs. You guys leave, and then what happens next year when the, uh, heat hits again? Are you going to try and breed an army of tiny Manix out of Raiden?"

I shook my head vigorously. "Oh no. Not for many, many years after the birth of the cubs would we even consider doing this again."

She nodded her head. "Understandable. So next year, when I go into heat again, and my milkshake brings all the Manix to the yard, what then? I'm on my own?"

Finlo rumbled low in his chest. "You will be the mother of our cubs. We would never abandon you to that fate."

I winced when her face went pale. Until Finlo had opened his big mouth, she hadn't thought of the eggs in terms of being actual children. I knew, looking at her, that she wasn't the kind of person who would happily abandon her kids into the care of others, even if I did birth them.

She held my eyes as she asked, "And what would be the ideal situation?"

I couldn't help but move closer so I could touch her, reassure her. "The ideal situation would be that over the next few days, you would get to know us. When your heat hits, we would spend our time making love in the hope that we ease your suffering through the heat, and that we would be well on our way to having a large bounty of beautiful cubs. Plus, you know, a countless amount of wonderful orgasms." I grinned. Her lips twitched, so I soldiered on. "Then, if you decided you liked us, and wanted to pursue something more permanent with us, we'd move you back to our home on the mountain where we could protect you properly. We would take care of you. You'd never have to be scared or unhappy again."

Her lips parted as her eyes grew so wide that I knew I was selling her a dream right now. I knew in my very soul that she'd never felt completely safe or happy in her life. I could give her that. Hell, I would do nearly anything to give her that.

As if Fate knew how close we were to getting everything we ever wanted, a cry from the other room pierced the silence.

I watched as she took a shuddering step away, building her walls back up, letting go of the dream I'd presented. She turned on her heel and moved further into the house, leaving us all staring pensively at her back.

6

NAJA

Luisa was awake, probably roused from her sleep by the voices of the men in the other room. She was a good baby, but the sound of men still upset her. I didn't know if it was a throwback from her beginnings or it was just a pitch that she didn't like, but the only guy she'd ever let hold her without wailing down the entire neighborhood was the man who'd smuggled us out of Mexico in the back of his beat-up old car.

She held her arms up to me sleepily, still whimpering. "Hey, baby. Bad dream?" I said softly, grabbing her out of the bed. She clung to my neck with her chubby little arms.

I hugged her tightly to my chest, like just the smell of baby shampoo could help me keep my head in the hot soup of pheromones and sexy men occuring in the living room. She continued to fuss, and I felt around in the darkness for her pacifier, tensing as I suddenly picked Raiden's scent behind me.

"Would you like me to try to settle her? I have a way with kids. Comes with the designation." He walked over, brushing a finger along Luisa's sleepy cheek.

"Sorry, she doesn't like men…"

As if to prove me wrong, Luisa held her arms out to Raiden, and he looked at me for permission before pulling her into his own. He murmured softly to her in another language, and I saw the gentle vibration of her cheek. He must have been doing that purr thing that Ellar did. Whatever it was, it put Luisa back to sleep almost instantly. That would have been a handy trick to have when she was a newborn.

He laid her back down in her crib, and we both snuck out of the room. When we got back to the living room, everyone had shifted around like they'd been pacing. Raiden gave me a loaded look. "She is beautiful. Looks like you."

I smiled tightly at him as I moved back to my chair, thankful that they'd left it for me. "Thank you."

He looked at me appraisingly. "She's not Manix though. She can't be your daughter."

Seven fist pumped the air. "I knew my nose wasn't broken. You've never had children," he crowed, and Ellar slapped him on the back of the head.

"Not now, dumbass."

I look around at them, fear clutching my heart. Like the walls had ears and if the wrong people heard about my life, they'd take Luisa away. "She's my sister."

I begin to shake, the long-held demons of my past rising up in the darkness of the night. I looked at the clock on the wall. Witching hour. That would be right. All my ghosts were coming out to play now. I should be dancing, bringing home money to give Luisa a better life, not baring my soul to a bunch of strangers.

The odd rumbling sound reverberated through the room again, and I realized they were reacting to my stress. To appease them—or at least that's what I told myself—I went and sat beside Ellar, close enough that he threw an arm over my shoulders and held me tight. If I sat this close to Raiden, his Omega aura would disarm me completely. At least with this Beta, I could maintain my wits a little, even while he chased away my fear.

He rested his cheek on my hair. "Where are her parents?" he asked softly, but there was no accusation in his tone. Just mild interest.

"Her, I mean, *our* mother is dead. Her father, if the Goddess has any sense of justice, is dead too."

Flashbacks of swinging fists and dark closets, of blood and broken bodies assailed me before I could stuff it back down into the box where it belonged. Ellar groaned, dragging me into his lap and surrounding me with his body. This time I didn't fight it because it did feel nice. I'd believed Gatlin when he said that if I said no about this, that they would just leave. It might be stupidly naive to believe him, but I had to hold out hope that some good survived in the world, otherwise I despaired for the society Luisa had to grow up in.

No one chastised Ellar this time either. His chest thrummed and I let it lull me. "Will it be a problem for you, that Luisa isn't Manix? Because she is my first priority always. She's the only family I have left. There's no one to stand between her and the monsters, other than me."

Ellar stroked my back softly. "And us, if you consider us. We'll stand between you both and anything that may come for you."

God help me, I was considering it. What they were promising, these near perfect strangers, was a scenario I could only consider an impossible dream. But my experience with dreams was that they always turned into nightmares. I didn't even have to promise them forever. I just had to promise them a week for safety. For time to move all my things and find somewhere else safe for Luisa—preferably somewhere that I wasn't some kind of supernatural catnip.

Exhaustion swept over me like a wave. "I need to sleep."

Gatlin and Finlo both stepped forward, but it was Finlo who spoke. "Of course, Omega. We will be around just in case any other Packs have caught your scent on the wind, because you smell fucking delicious. If you are not considering our offer, I implore you to stay indoors and keep the windows closed, until this passes at least."

I looked between the two Alphas. So different, yet so alike. They both held themselves with authority, like they knew they were the strongest people in the entire room. Finlo was lithe and fair, his body lean yet muscular. He looked like some kind of sleek predator. Gatlin was like the dark side of Finlo's moon, with a beard that had to be a couple of days old creating a shadow across his cheeks. He was a touch shorter, but broader across the chest, and gave off the vibe of being an immovable wall.

I was kind of glad that they were deciding on civility, because if they hadn't? I couldn't have fought them off. Their ominous warnings reverberated in my head, along with my headache.

"Thanks. I'll keep everything locked up tight." I tilted my head at the door, and they all converged toward it.

Each one of them brushed my hand softly as they passed me on the way out the door, and it seemed almost reverent somehow. Maybe my brain was trying to make the fact that I was stuck between a rock and a hard place a little more pleasant, but as they disappeared into the darkness, I didn't even feel scared of them anymore.

Which was fucking insane.

Shaking myself hard, I told my brain to stop listening to my damn lady parts and get its shit together. Keeping my promise, I closed and locked all the windows, and double deadbolted the front and back doors. I curled up on the toddler bed in Luisa's room, just so she was closer. The Manix had me freaked out, but what they said made sense.

I could feel this so-called heat coming on. It was like a bad flu, compounded by an epic period. I should have known that life would kick me in the crotch while I was down.

The exhaustion hit me like a wave again. I needed to sleep for a week, but somehow I didn't think I'd get the opportunity. The loss of tips tonight would mean I'd have to try and pick up an extra shift at the flower market tomorrow, which meant I'd have to ask Tamsin if I could bring Luisa, which meant I'd have to be up early to make sure I have everything, which meant I'd probably only get a few hours sleep, which meant... It went on and on. It wasn't that Tamsin wouldn't let me bring Luisa, but working all day and caring for a toddler at the same time was not easy. Tamsin was amazing about it though.

I slid beneath the blankets and tried not to think of the Pack that was probably sitting in their van in front of my house right now. Tried not to think of the things they'd offered me, the promises they'd made. And I definitely tried not to think about the fact that my entire body had wanted to fuck every single one of them in every dirty, deep way I could manage to stretch myself into.

Closing my eyes, I drifted into a sleep filled with hot tongues and hungry hands.

FINLO

We drove around the block and then parked in a dark copse of trees just at the end of the Omega's street.

Gatlin climbed out of the passenger seat. "Take Raiden to a hotel. He looks exhausted."

Our stubborn Omega stuck out his chin. "I'm fine."

Seven rolled his eyes at him. "Dude, if your dick gets any harder, you are going to pass out. Naja's heat is draining you, and the longer you're around her without giving into those urges, the more exhausted you'll be. Go to the hotel room, let Ellar suck your cock, and relax. The female will agree to our offer. I can feel it."

Ellar flushed, but I could see the desire in his eyes at the thought. We were all high on the pheromones, and I knew if we didn't have to put someone on Naja's block to watch the house, we'd all be back in the hotel, paying homage to our bonds.

And by homage, I meant fucking in one huge sexfest.

Raiden crossed his arms over his chest, and I'd fuck that attitude out of him later. How we ended up with the biggest brat in the universe as an Omega was a weird twist of fate, but one I loved. "Come on, we basically ran down the side of a mountain. I'll fuck you until you can't remember your name, we'll take a nap and later, we'll come up with a plan to lure the pretty Omega to our nest forever."

Raiden finally grinned. "My name has only two syllables, Finlo. I don't think your skills are quite that good that I'd forget two syllables."

I growled and pretended to hold myself back. "Challenge accepted. Prepare yourself, Omega."

I saw the shiver run over his skin and grinned to myself.

Gatlin rolled his eyes, but he was smiling. "Try and get some sleep so you can relieve us at dawn." I saluted him, and he just shook his head as he faded into the darkness.

Gatlin and I weren't lovers, not the way we were with the other members of our Pack, but we were best friends. I would lay down my life for him without thought, and I knew he would do the same for me. For any one of our family.

Ellar climbed into the seat that Gatlin had vacated, still looking starry-eyed about the female Omega. I pulled back out onto the road and drove us to the small motel that we'd seen this morning on the outskirts of town. It had said vacancy then, so hopefully that was still the case. Raiden wasn't the only one with a bad case of blue balls.

Ellar looked over at me, his straight black brows pulled down in a frown. "Do you think Seven is right? Do you think that Naja will say yes?" The hope in his voice was nearly heartbreaking, but I shrugged. In her position, I'd run as far and as fast as I possibly could.

"Maybe."

We all fell into silence, thinking about what our future could hold. It could be everything or nothing, and it all rested on the shoulders of one tiny, curvy little stripper.

I pulled beneath the portico of the hotel, thankful to see the vacancy sign still lit up. I mean, why anyone would stop here outside of ski season was beyond me, but there must have been a reason. It would have been pretty enough, I guess, if I hadn't been raised in the mountains, surrounded by landscapes that had never seen human feet. Vistas that had never been seen by human eyes. It was isolating, but there was no doubting the human footprint had a negative impact on nature.

I looked at Ellar. "Stay with Raiden."

He nodded, though I wasn't sure who would be protecting who if they were attacked. Raiden had come from a long line of fierce warriors, the best the Manix had. His brothers were all high up in our army, and his only sister had married the Manix equivalent of a General. The fact that Raiden had been born an Omega had shocked his father halfway into the grave. So he'd just treated him like the rest of his sons, training him in hand-to-hand combat, as well as close-range weapons. I knew for a fact that Raiden was an expert with a sniper rifle.

Ellar, on the other hand, had been dumped on the mountain's doorstep, like so many before him. A half-blood teenager, he was a weak Beta and basically considered prey in our society. That was, until Gatlin had pulled him into our Pack like a mama hen. That was Gatlin though—crusader for the weak. Because despite the fact that he was a half-blood too, he was strong. As strong an Alpha as me with all my damn fancy pedigree, and that irked the Manix upper class more than anything had for the last century.

I pushed open the door, and there was a small electronic beep. A woman stuck her head around a curtain, and I could hear a movie playing in the back room. "Need a room?" She sounded like she was offering me a blowjob the way she purred the words, but I ignored it.

"Two. Adjoining if possible," I said, and her eyes

went real wide. It happened when women heard the timbre of my voice. It was low and gravelly, and Raiden said it was like auditory foreplay.

"Uh, yeah, umm, sure. We should have..." She trailed off as she opened and closed drawers. "We have a self-contained apartment at the end, if that would suit better."

I gave her a wide smile, and she blinked at me slowly, her face a little slack. "That would be perfect. Thank you."

She thrust the key at me, and then escaped into the back room. Well, okay then. Guess I'd pay up when we checked out.

I walked back to the car, and I wasn't surprised to see Ellar and Raiden cuddled up together in the back. I climbed in and drove to the designated spot, right down the end of the long line of rooms. I was glad to see there weren't any cars in the spots for the five rooms next to us. It would make it easier to be alert without some human beside us moving around all the time.

Hopefully we wouldn't have to be here long. Maybe Naja would let us take her back to our Pack house. As much as Raiden wouldn't admit it, he wanted to be by his nest. Naja's heat was really bringing out his Omega instincts, if the way he was dry humping Ellar in the back was any indication.

I wrenched open the back door and ushered them

inside, getting our stuff from the rear of the van. When I walked into the room and switched on the light, they were already half-naked, their hands running over each other's bodies. I dropped our crap by the door, reaching into the pocket of my duffel for the lube before leaning back against the door to enjoy the show.

Watching Ellar and Raiden was one of my favorite pastimes. They were fucking beautiful together, like a symphony. The warm gold of Ellar's skin was even more burnished against Raiden's pale tone, and they were a similar height, like they were made to each be one half of a matching pair. Raiden had always refused the purported weakness of his Omega designation, and Ellar was all heart, more like an Omega than a Beta. Neither was who they were supposed to be, but they drew strength from each other, and that was perfect.

Ellar fell to his knees, peeling Raiden's skinny jeans down, which were holding his dick painfully trapped. Raiden kicked his feet frantically, trying to get his pants off and his dick in Ellar's mouth, but he was swaying wildly, completely off balance. I was behind him in an instant, running a palm down his spine, making soothing noises.

"It's okay, Omega. Ellar is going to get those off and give you some relief."

Raiden was already panting. "Fin, please. I need the knot."

Well, fuck. I couldn't say no to that, even if I wanted

to. My dick throbbed at the thought of knotting my sexy Omega, and I purred against his ear, making him shiver.

"Mmm, but what do you say?"

"Please, Alpha."

"Good little Omega," I growled, and Raiden slumped against me as Ellar sucked down his cock. I looked over Raiden's shoulder at Ellar's plump lips sliding up and down his shaft. His eyes were on mine though, and I smiled at him. "Make our Omega feel good, El. I'll do my bit back here."

I unbuckled my jeans, shimmying them down my thighs. Pulling the lube from my back pocket, I squirted a good portion on my hand and on my cock. Then I slid my fingers between Raiden's cheeks, feeling him buck back against me as I pressed my fingers against his tight hole. He gasped as I worked them in, spreading him to readiness.

But my greedy Omega wasn't having it. "I'm ready Alpha, now," he choked out as Ellar swallowed his dick.

I lined up my cock and then slid slowly inside him, all of us groaning. As my hands steadied his hips, I felt Ellar's hands on the back of my thighs, anchoring himself to us. Fuck, I loved that guy, and not just because he ate cock like a champion. No, Ellar was a giver, and in a society of takers, he was a fucking gift. I looked down at him over Raiden's shoulder again, seeing his eyes flick up to me. "Love you, El."

He hummed, making Raiden's knees go weak, and my own turn to jello as he clenched down on me. I slid faster and harder, Ellar setting the pace with my thighs, legit topping us both from the bottom—cheeky fucking Beta.

Still, I slammed into Raiden harder, bending him over until he was almost resting on top of Ellar, and I felt my knot swell.

"Oh Goddess, oh fuck, oh fuck," Raiden chanted. "I'm so fucking close."

That was definitely my cue. I made love to him until our bodies were a sweaty, slick mess, my knot growing and swelling around the base of my cock. When Raiden shouted, gripping the curly dark hair of Ellar, his hips jerking as he came, I knew it was time to move. Ellar scooted out of the way, and I took Raiden to the floor on his hands and knees. I shoved myself inside him to the hilt, my knot locking us into place. I watched as Ellar grabbed his own dick and stroked it in time to my thrusts, like it was him fucking our Omega. Raiden's ass milked my knot, and wave after wave of my cum released inside him. My muscles no longer able to hold us up, I gripped his hips tightly against mine and rolled to the side, pulling him into my body and curling around him protectively. At this moment, we weren't Finlo and Raiden. We were Alpha and Omega.

Ellar came to my other side, curling around my back. I gripped his hand and put it on Raiden's hip, placing my palm on top of his hand and lacing our fingers.

He nuzzled my neck and I thrummed, the deep purr-like vibration emitting from my contented body and through my Packmates. We weren't just physically satisfied; we were fucking happy. We were missing a piece, but if Naja chose not to join us, we'd still be happy.

I answered Ellar's earlier question again. "I think she'll join us. How could she not want this?"

Raiden hummed low, his body drifting off to sleep even with me locked tight inside him.

Ellar kissed between my shoulder blades. "She doesn't know what's missing yet, but we'll show her."

Yes, we would. We'd woo the little Omega with the promise of love and safety that would endure anything life threw at us.

8

NAJA

No sane human being could function at four a.m. especially when they were only functioning on three hours sleep. But here I was. Travel mug filled with the strongest coffee known to man, a whole bag of snacks, and breakfast for a hungry toddler, and I was set.

I loaded up the car, leaving Luisa asleep in her crib for as long as possible. Then I grabbed a groggy but still sweet-as-pie little girl, and strapped her into her carseat. I'd strap her to my back for the morning, and we should be done by eleven. Then we could come home, curl up on the couch, and watch princess movies for the rest of the day. At least until I had to head to the club tonight.

I sighed, already exhausted. I hit the remote on the

garage door, and when it rolled up, a figure was standing there. I jumped, squeaking out a screech of surprise before the figure stepped into the garage.

Gatlin.

"Jesus fucking Christ, asshole. It's four in the morning. You scared the shit out of me."

He bowed his head. "Apologies, Omega. I was just checking that you were okay."

I narrowed my eyes. "I have to go to work, because some assholes robbed me of an entire night of tips last night. So now I have to be up at the asscrack of dawn, working with a toddler, because you guys decided you needed me so you just took me."

Yep, I was fucking pissy when I hadn't had coffee.

"I apologize again," he said, and I huffed.

Striding toward the driver's seat, I just growled. "Whatever. Stop apologizing. I just need to get to work."

Gatlin did an elaborate whistle, and then Seven appeared, silhouetted by the street light. "We shall come with you," the Alpha said, and I froze.

"Uh, no. Thank you." But Seven was already sliding into the back seat with Luisa. "You guys don't do 'no' very well, do you?"

Gatlin stared down at me, his face unreadable. "Your scent is nearly unbearably strong now. If there are any hunting parties lower down in the mountains, they will scent you. I would feel better if you were protected at your workplace."

"I'd feel better if she just stayed home with the doors locked," Seven said, but he said it in a high-pitched cooing voice as Luisa, suddenly wide awake, babbled at him incomprehensibly. He looked toward me. "I think she likes me."

I groaned and started the car, backing out of the garage. "Fine, but you guys loiter out of the way. I don't need my boss knowing you guys are stalking me, and then getting it in her head to call the cops or some-thing. Even better, pretend you're florists or some shit."

Seven snorted but no one argued. I looked at them in their jeans and tees, and I had to agree with him. No one was going to believe that they were florists.

We drove up to Missoula, and the early morning traffic was non-existent. I sipped my coffee, feeling less murderous by the second. But with the caffeination came the scent of the guys, and by the time we pulled up to the markets, I was actually sweating.

Grabbing my tote bag and the baby carrier, I reached into the back of the car for Luisa who had been wooing the gruff Manix the whole way here. Knowing the drill, she moved with me as I slipped the harness around from the front to the back. I reached into the bag and gave her a yogurt pouch, and looked up to see both men staring at me.

"It's time for you two to make yourself scarce," I pointed out. Gatlin looked between me and the baby carrier on my back.

"We can watch your cub for you, if you'd like?"

I scoffed, picking up my tote and swinging it over my shoulder. "Gee, should I leave my toddler with two strange men? That's a tough one. Uh, no." I walked toward the market's rear entrance. "I finish at eleven, then I intend to go home and nap on the couch until the sitter gets there at nine tonight. Then I've gotta go to the club. So you guys can, I don't know, clock out or something. I promise no one's going to steal me from the middle of the flower market."

Gatlin narrowed his eyes at me. "To insinuate we would do anything to your child is abhorrent. A child's life is worth more than ten adult lives in our society. They are the future. Years of potential. We would lay down our lives for her protection."

My heart thudded in my chest. "Luisa isn't Manix, remember?"

Gatlin shook his head once, viciously. "Doesn't matter."

I paused at the doorway. "Sorry, I didn't mean to offend you."

He waved a hand. "You didn't know. Not just humans have innate cruelty to their young. Even shifters can be vicious with children."

I swallowed hard, pushing back memories. "You have no idea."

I disappeared inside the doorway, closing it softly and taking a breath. Walking quickly to Tasmin's stand, I saw she was already busy unloading her trolley of flowers from the back of her truck.

She smiled when she saw me. "Hey, girl. Hey, cutie," she cooed at Luisa. "Big delivery today. Some high society wedding up in the mountains. Their florist is coming to pick us over so I brought the best blooms I could find. I want to beat out that dickhole Henry's peonies. We both know mine are better than those sickly little plops." She waved a few of the aforementioned blooms like a scepter.

I grabbed them and put them in a bucket. "Well, we better get the rest of this unloaded then," I prompted before she could start a rant about Henry the flower farmer. Or as Tamsin liked to call him, Henry the flower fucker. Which was good alliteration but not exactly anatomically possible.

We worked for the next hour, loading up Tamsin's stall and making it perfect. She'd gotten the inside scoop that the bride wanted pink and white blooms, so that's exactly what we were, a sea of taffy-colored confection.

Then the doors opened and there was no more time to think as I got to work, taking money, talking to customers, and feeding Luisa. I was so lucky that she was happy to just watch the bustle of the morning market with its bright colors and noises. Eventually, she fell asleep against my back, exhausted from the early morning and the constant activity. It wasn't the first time I'd brought her, but I preferred not to drag her around if I could help it. Once again, I was so fucking grateful for her. She made it hard, but she also made life worth something. I'd be lost if I didn't have her, or if we were still stuck in Mexico with *him*.

It was about nine a.m. when I felt eyes on me. I searched the market, but it was bustling, just like Tamsin promised. I tilted my nose to the air and I could smell them. Manix.

As if the action was an invitation, Raiden appeared in front of me. His pouty lips were turned up in a smile, and even his eyes were smiling. He was happy to see me, and though I would never admit it, I was kind of happy to see him too. "Naja."

Tamsin stopped, whistling through her teeth. "Are you here to check out the flowers or the girl?" she asked, but there was no accusation in her tone.

Raiden grinned, and even I could admit it was enough to make any red-blooded woman swoon. "The girl. I'm trying to convince her to come on a date with me."

Tamsin fanned herself, but I noticed Raiden left out that the date would probably turn into an orgy. Actually, no. That would only encourage Tamsin more.

My boss just nodded. "Fair enough. She could use some fun." Then she walked away to serve another customer, the traitor.

I rolled my shoulders, the weight of Luisa on my back starting to make my muscles ache. Raiden's blue eyes watched the movement carefully, his brows drawn together in a frown. "I can hold her. I promise I'll stand just there where you can see me, and it will give you both a break." He pointed to the little stool where we normally sat and had a rest in the mornings if things slowed down. I hesitated, but he was right.

A part of me inherently trusted Raiden—hell, trusted them all. And that was part of the reason I was so hesitant. You *couldn't* trust people, no matter what your gut said. Prepare for betrayal and hope for the best.

Luisa squirmed, and I knew she wanted out. A two-year-old wasn't meant to stay still for so long, and her legs needed a break. I chewed my lip a little more, weighing up whether it was worth the risk. In the end, Luisa made the decision for me, squirming and reaching out to Raiden, this perfect freaking stranger to her.

He grinned at me, shrugging. "It's an Omega thing," he said, and I sighed fin defeat.

"Fine. But just there. You don't move anywhere else with her. Got it?"

He crossed his heart and held out his hands. As I

unclipped her, Luisa launched herself into Raiden's arms. He laughed and tossed her in the air, catching her easily but still making me want to scream. She giggled too, and something in my heart shattered. I didn't play with her enough. It was all work to keep a roof over our heads and food on the table. Paying the sitter. Keeping the heat and electricity on. There was never enough time to just play.

I was a shit mother.

"Hey, stop." Raiden was looking at me now, his hand halfway to my face like he'd forgotten he wasn't supposed to touch me. "You're doing the best you can, and that is enough."

I swallowed the lump in my throat and blinked rapidly. Huh. Pollen must be bad today.

Nodding at Raiden, I went back to work, keeping half an eye on him. He'd gotten her a snack from my tote and was feeding it to her, listening to her babble a million miles a minute, her little hands flailing as she jumped and bounced wildly.

I got through a few more sales, straightening haphazardly strewn flowers, until another scent stopped me.

Manix. But not one I knew, not that I was an expert on their scents or anything. I looked up, and continued looking up. The man in front of me had to be close to seven feet tall, and he was just as broad. He was like a mountain, craggy and rough like one too.

His lip had a scar—or maybe it was a sneer—pulling it up.

"I thought my Beta was lying, but here you are. I can scent you myself. A female Omega. An impossibility."

Raiden was in front of me in a second, thrusting Luisa into my arms and pushing us both behind him.

"You aren't wanted here, Wilkie," he growled, and it was kind of impressive.

But the big Alpha—because there was no doubt to me that this monster was an Alpha—laughed in his face. "No one asked you, *Omega.* Though, I wouldn't mind a two-for-one if I can. Save your sister from having to take so much cock all the time."

Raiden paled but his jaw tensed. "Not if you were the last fucking living being on the planet, you Neanderthal."

Just as suddenly as Wilkie had appeared, so did three other Manix I didn't know. I jumped as gentle hands grabbed me from behind. "Come, Naja," Ellar whispered, and I went with him. I was relieved to see Gatlin and Seven appear from between the flowers.

I looked over at Tamsin, whose wide, confused eyes held fear. I could never come back to this place, to this job. I was relieved to see Henry the flower farmer in front of her though, protecting her with the huge bulk of his body. He wasn't as huge or as powerfully built as a Manix, but he was fit and strong for a human. It was a weird thing to fixate on as Ellar hustled me out of the market.

They'd been right, and I'd been too arrogant to see it.

"A little further, Omega. It will be okay," Gatlin murmured from behind me, and I nearly jumped out of my skin. Raiden rested a hand on my spine as they led me to my car. "Seven, take the van with Ellar and head back to Naja's house. We will meet you there. Raiden, in the front with me. Finlo in the back with Naja and the babe."

No one questioned him, everyone just jumping to do what they were told. Even me. I strapped Luisa into her seat, noting that she'd gone silent and still. It was a throwback to our old life, and I fucking hated it. Hated everything about it, and I wanted to scream.

I slid into the car, belting myself in as Finlo slipped in the other side. Gatlin and Raiden slipped into the front, and seconds later we were tearing out of the parking lot of the market. I wanted to cry but I held my shit together—I would cry later when I was alone, and no one would see my weakness. Finlo looked behind us, his eyes taking in everything, but eventually they settled on me and then Luisa.

He reached out a hand and placed it on her tiny body. She looked like a newborn in comparison. I could feel the swell of his Alpha power, the one that promised protection, and her tiny stiff body finally relaxed.

So did mine. He reached across the carseat and grabbed my hand. "It truly is okay, Omega. Wilkie is an arrogant fuck, but he won't chase us down. He might try to steal you, but he won't break the rules to do so."

That was not as reassuring as he thought it was.

9

GATLIN

I hated Wilkie. He was everything that was wrong with Manix society. A purist, and an asshole to boot. He believed Omegas were made to breed with and that was all. I knew he'd made a move for Raiden back when he was selecting a Pack, but Raiden wasn't a fool. He knew that Wilkie was a sadist. He was also high up in the echelons of the Manix army, but so was Raiden's father. When Raiden's sister had bonded into Wilkie's Pack instead, Raiden had been devastated. Me? Not so much. Raiden loved his sister, but she was a fucking bitch. Wilkie and Susannah were a good match in my opinion.

When we pulled up to Naja's house, something like panic hit me. We were so close to having everything. I didn't want to pressure Naja, but she wasn't safe here by herself. I hated that she wasn't in our nest where we could protect her and Raiden. I hated that they were so vulnerable.

So many things I hated right now, and it was driving my instincts wild. I wanted to bundle her up and drive her up to my mountain. Show her the amazing nests that Raiden had created around the big house. Show her the kitchen and the group shower. We could convert a room into a nursery, first for Luisa, and then for all our young. I was getting ahead of myself, but it was hard not to rush ahead.

I hit the garage remote and pulled inside, closing it behind us straight away. At least I could secure her here. She wouldn't be in the open. But her scent was insane. Wilkie wasn't going to be the only one. More would come for her, and I didn't know what to do. I slammed out of the car, breathing deeply through the possessive rage.

Raiden came up and wrapped his arms around my waist, infusing me with his calm. "We'll figure this out, Gatlin. Our happily ever after is within reach. Don't lose it now."

I turned, grabbing him up into my arms, kissing him hard. He kissed me back, his hands gripping my shirt. He was feeling it too; I knew we all were. He was right though—I needed to keep my shit together. "I'm so thankful that you didn't choose Wilkie."

Raiden made a rude noise. "Not even if hell froze over. Overbearing asshole."

Finlo had bundled Naja and Luisa inside, and I could scent our Betas on the wind. We could hunker down here for a couple of days if Naja permitted it. It wasn't as good as the Pack house, but it would do.

I grabbed Raiden's hand and led him inside after Finlo and Naja. I let the Betas in the front door on the way past, and Seven locked it behind them. I found Finlo and Naja in the living room, Luisa playing at her feet.

Seven paced around the room. "We should be up in our own territory. Fucking Wilkie prowling around is like ants crawling across my skin."

I clapped him on the back as he strode past again, my eyes flicking between the Beta and Naja. "Wilkie being here is a problem, but we can protect this place enough to get through the heat. Unless Naja okays returning to our territory with us? I promise you'll be safe there. We have everything you'll need." Before I even finished, Naja was shaking her head. I couldn't blame her really. What we were offering was an impossibility to her. I could see the fear in her eyes, and knew that she'd been hurt in the past. My Beast knew too, could sense the injuries that festered inside her. I ached to make them better.

"No. I'm not leaving. I don't know you guys any

better than I know that fucking Monolith that was pretending to be a human."

"Manix," Ellar corrected softly, coming to wrap his arms around her once more, dragged toward her by her pain. I envied him the ability to take her in his arms without feeling threatening. Never thought I'd want to swap with a Beta till now.

She rested her face on his chest, and exhaled. I saw the tension run from her body, and spotted Raiden stroking her back. Ellar and Raiden together were like a drug, but one that made you chilled out and happy. I was glad they were turning that effect onto the strung-out Omega female.

"I realize that we are still strangers to you, and that you only have our word telling you that we are nothing like Wilkie, but what does your gut say?" Finlo asked softly, and she sighed again.

"My gut lies. It doesn't warn me people are evil until it's too late." There went the trauma of her past again. One day I'd get to the bottom of what happened, but we'd deal with the problems at hand first. Her heat was a day away, two max, and then we'd all be in a rut. No one would have our backs and we couldn't lock this place down tight enough to satisfy me. Wilkie wouldn't leave town now he knew there was an Omega female here.

Couldn't take her home. Couldn't stay.

We were fucked.

"It's fine, we'll figure something out," I said softly to the room. "Will you allow us to stay? We can protect you better if we are here."

She only hesitated briefly before nodding. I could see Ellar's smile widen as he looked around the room at us all. His eyes said, *See, we're making progress. Just a little further and she'll be ours forever.*

Yeah, except we had to make her like us enough to want to be with us for even a little while. I held myself tall as I said, "You won't be able to go to work tonight." I put a touch of Alpha into my voice, and she narrowed her gaze at me. Ellar gave me a 'you're fucking this up' expression, but it needed to be done.

"Obviously. I'm not an idiot," she hissed. "I can't ever go back to today's job either. How would I explain nearly a dozen oversized fucking giants turning up at a damn flower market to fight over me? How am I meant to explain running out of there like I was some kind of damsel in distress? How am I going to explain any of that?"

Sweat was starting to bead on her brow, and her scent was going wild. Fear mixed with lust, mixed with the scent of the beginning of her heat-slick—it was all sending my Alpha insane. I looked helplessly at the Betas, because one look at Finlo told me he was no better off than me, and quite frankly, Raiden looked just as rough.

Ellar proved once again that just because he was

physically the weakest member of our Pack, didn't mean he was the weakest link. "Come on, Angel. I'll run you a bath. You need to relax, little mama. You're all stressed out and that heat is riding you, I can tell." He scooped her up into his arms, his chest thrumming with the purr, and she nuzzled straight in. She wanted comfort—I could see it in every line of her body, but her brain wouldn't let her take it.

Soon. Soon we could see to her needs.

She murmured something into his chest, and Ellar nodded. "Seven, grab Luisa. Naja would be more comfortable if she could see her cub."

My chest cavity cracked open. She still didn't trust us with the baby, but I got it. She didn't know us. But it felt like we were beating ourselves black and blue on this brick wall that surrounded Naja.

Ellar's eyes warned us all from commenting, and Seven scooped the baby into his arms, holding her high in the air. I could imagine the stubborn Beta with our young. He'd be a great father, that near Alpha stubbornness would make him protective, but the underlying Beta of his nature would make him a nurturer too. He just didn't know how wonderful he was going to be yet.

Once they were out of the room, I turned to Finlo, squishing Raiden between us. It soothed the Alpha a little, protecting the Omega with our bodies, even if it wasn't this Omega who had been in harm's way.

"What do we do? We don't have time to properly fortify this place for the mania of the rut—"

"Which she still hasn't agreed to," Raiden added.

"Indeed, which she still hasn't agreed to. And with Wilkie and his Pack in town, we are sitting ducks, literally with our naked asses in the air for him to take a shot."

I nuzzled into Raiden's neck. "Maybe he'll respect that the Omega has made her choice."

Raiden growled low in his throat, making it vibrate against my nose pressed there. "When has Wilkie respected anything from anyone lower down on the food chain than himself?"

Raiden had a point. But I didn't have any answers. "Outside of reinstating Plan A and abducting her back to our territory, we just have to do what we can. Maybe try and sit out this heat from the outside."

They both groaned, and I didn't blame them. It would be torture for us all, including Naja. We were hardly equipped to let her suffer, but I would if I had to, if that's what she chose.

Finlo slapped my shoulder. "Let's show her how easy we could make her life; that we'd make a good Pack for her and her young. As Ellar would say, we'll woo the fuck out of her until she comes to the Pack house willingly. Then we can court her properly."

I mean, it was a sound plan, but I didn't think it would be that easy. I could already tell that Naja wasn't going to be won over by cooking her food and giving her foot rubs. No, she had to decide we were worthy, and it was going to take some extreme trust building to get there. We could do it though; I knew it.

And the first step was food. I kissed Raiden softly. "Food is a good start. Raiden, work your culinary magic. Finlo and I will try and make this place as secure as possible so we can all rest a little easier."

Raiden nodded, sliding from between us and moving deeper into the house. Where they'd taught us how to fight as Alphas, they'd taught Raiden how to cook, like he was just some wishy-washy Omega with nothing else better to do than to cook food and lay on his back. He'd proved the system wrong, but his love of cooking had endured.

Both Finlo and I watched him go. "I don't like it, Gatlin."

I nodded. "We can only do what we can."

Finlo huffed. "Stealing her is back on the table."

I laughed and shook my head. "Having met her, do you really think she'd be okay with that?"

Fin sighed. "You make a point. I'll do the back of the house."

I watched him go and then moved to the front, checking windows and reinforcing doors. We'd make this place as safe as possible and then we'd go back to wooing the Omega female. I found the house already had bolts on all the windows and doors, and it made me wonder once more where this pretty Omega female, this unicorn of the supernatural world, had actually come from, and what drove her to lock her house up like it was Fort Knox.

10

———

NAJA

I'd told Ellar that I didn't have a bath. I had a shower and a tiny sink, and that was the extent of it. Honestly, this place was too small to house five huge men. What was I thinking, letting them stay?

As if my body was reminding me of the exact reason *why*, a fresh wave of heat-related torture rolled over my body. It was like the sensation of a phantom sneeze, like something was just there waiting for you but you couldn't quite grasp it. On top of that, my skin felt like it was on fire. It was hot and tight along my bones, and every hair on my body was so sensitive it was like there were bugs crawling on me. Add that to the insane cramps that I knew would come and then the blood, and I could see why the Manix only did this shit once a year.

Yeah okay, so the guys might be useful, if I let

myself go. Let myself do what all my instincts were screaming at me to do. And if it had just been me? I'd have climbed Finlo like a tree in the car. I looked at the jabbering toddler on the floor as she played with a container of bath toys. Ellar had held me even as he'd set the water temperature to perfect, Seven protectively holding Luisa. When Ellar had been happy, he'd set me on my feet, kissed my temple and left. Seven had put Luisa on the fluffy bath mat without a word, grabbing the rubber ducky from the basket and handing it to her on the way out.

Both so damn thoughtful; it was getting hard to think of them as possible threats. The whole thing should have felt weird but it felt just right, and that scared the shit out of me. I peeked around the glass shower screen.

"What do you think, Lu?" She waved her duck like it was the cure to all the world's problems and I sighed as I leaned back under the water, letting it run over my body, soothing me. It was the perfect temperature to cool my skin without freezing me to death. I rested my head against the tiles and pretended I was a normal twenty-year-old. I'd be in college somewhere, probably here in the US, because that's where Mom had been born. We'd never have gone to Mexico. I'd be studying something ridiculous and frivolous, while I tried to decide what I wanted to do with my life. I'd be going to parties; maybe I'd have a handsome boyfriend.

Instead, I was a stripper with a toddler and a room full of hot paranormal guys who wanted to *breed* with me.

I banged my head on the tiles and turned off the taps. Stepping out from behind the glass, I grabbed a towel and tucked it around myself, scooping up Luisa who had somehow fit most of the duck's head in her mouth. I gently pried it out, and she gave me an indignant look.

"We don't try to stuff too much in our mouths. That's how we choke," I chastised her gently, and thought maybe I could take my own advice. When I stepped into the hall, it was empty. I could vaguely hear them in my kitchen, so I snuck down to my room.

I knew I'd run myself down to near exhaustion over the last few months. It was especially apparent when underneath all the panic about how I was going to pay the rent this week, was the feeling of relief that I could just put on my yoga pants and an oversize t-shirt, and curl up on the bed.

Sure, I was ignoring my problems, but I'd face them soon enough. I couldn't remember the last time I wasn't cramming too many things into every single minute of the day.

Luisa took the opportunity to blow raspberries on my face. We both giggled, and I realized I wouldn't give her up for all the normalcy in the world. Not for an average, safe life. Not for a college education and a boring vanilla boyfriend. Luisa was worth all my sacrifices.

She grizzled, and I knew she was probably hungry. "Time to face the wild beasts, huh?" I asked her, and she grinned.

"Yeh!"

I snorted and put her on the floor, letting her run out of the room ahead of me. I wasn't really worried that the big guys would hurt her. They looked at her with that softness and protectiveness that made my ovaries beat faster. My tigress might be practically non-existent, but she was wildly protective too. She didn't want to rip their faces off, and that was a good start.

As for Luisa? She had no fear of them at all, and in her short few months of life, she'd seen the worst of humanity. She knew evil, which is why she'd gone so... blank today. She'd sensed the badness of the other Manix Pack.

She weaved between legs, grabbing onto jeaned calves and all five of the huge Manix looked down at her indulgently. She stopped at Gatlin, raising her arms.

"Up."

Gatlin looked between us, pausing. "May I?"

I nodded, and he bent down and hauled the little girl into his arms. They locked eyes and stared at one another for what seemed like a long, silent moment.

Then Luisa poked him in the eye.

"Argh," he mouthed, not shouting so he didn't scare her, but he needn't have bothered. Finlo bent over and roared laughing. Which made Luisa giggle and try to do it again.

I clicked my tongue. "No, Lulu. Gentle hands."

Seven was laughing now too. "Telling the toddler to be careful with the Manix Alpha," he chuckled. "The irony."

I looked around the room and noticed Raiden was missing. I frowned, and Ellar came over to hug me to his side. "He's cooking. It's Raiden's happy place. Don't tell him it's because he's an Omega though, or you will get a knife through the thigh. Ask Seven."

The man in question scowled. "You're going to convince her that we are bloodthirsty assholes. We both know it was because Raiden was going through the yearning and I opened my stupid mouth." He switched his eyes to me. "If you come to live with us, Raiden would never go through the yearning again. He's much more pleasant when we aren't flipping off Mother Nature."

I didn't say anything, because Mother Nature was flipping me off in return at that moment, making my body cramp. Desperation made me ask, "So how would this work?"

Gatlin was still juggling Luisa, so it was Finlo who answered. "It works however you want, really. You call the shots. From our point of view, just, uh, copulating with Raiden during the heat would be a blessing. Anything more than that would be a miracle we would be completely thankful for." He rubbed his palms down the front of his jeans, and I ignored the bulge there. Well, kinda. "As for you, we can ease the suffering of the heat, but as you know, it involves a lot of sex. And orgasms. It's basically a week-long orgy."

As if my body knew what we were talking about, it cramped again, making sweat breaking out across my skin and my fresh underwear grow damp. Gatlin rumbled low in his chest, handing Luisa off to Ellar, and walked out the front door.

I looked at Finlo, who was gritting his teeth. "Don't worry about him. It's your need. We can scent it, almost see it. It's making us a little... distracted."

I nodded, because it was distracting me too. "What do we do about the other Pack in town while we are having this marathon orgy? Or about Luisa? Toddlers aren't something you can stick in a room and forget about while you're having a good time," I growled, and they all looked horrified. Again.

"Traditionally, the Betas care for the young, as they don't usually get the option of creating young in a Pack, especially during a heat. But we aren't a usual Pack, and we believe that all members should be able to express their, uh, desire during the heat. Besides, believe it or not, all six of us will not be creating the world's longest conga line. There will always be someone who is around to care for Luisa. She will not be neglected as we see to your needs." His body tensed and he stared at the door. "As for Wilkie and his Pack, well, we can fortify this place, always be on guard, and hope that he respects the boundaries." He didn't sound convinced though.

This was fucking insane. Absolutely bananas. It was too much and I wanted to run away screaming.

As if he sensed my distress—which hell, maybe he did because I knew nothing about Manix Omegas—Raiden appeared in the doorway to my kitchen. He smiled at me and it made my chest feel weird. Too full, like I was having an anxiety attack, but like, a happy one?

"Dinner's ready."

Thank god. I was starving, despite the painful cramps, the multilayered worry, and the gut-clenching anxiety. It was official. The heat was like PMS sent straight from Satan.

11

ELLAR

I wanted to feed Naja by hand. I wanted to lay her across the table and lick the lemon cream pasta sauce from her body. I wanted to crawl under the table, bury my face between her thighs, and ease the ache that I knew was plaguing her right now.

I kept all those thoughts off my face as I ate Raiden's signature dish. Handmade pasta, a lemon sauce with seared lemon rounds and whatever green stuff he could find for color. In this case, it was asparagus, which tasted amazing. Naja was already on her second bowl and even baby Luisa had spread it right around her face. I knew Naja was carb loading, her body unconsciously preparing her for the gruelling—or amazing—week ahead of her. Only Naja could choose which one it would be.

Goddess, I hoped she chose amazing. Luisa flung a

long piece of fettuccine, and I whipped my hand out and caught it before it could hit the wall. Then I put it in my mouth and slurped it down like a worm, making the little girl giggle.

Gah, I was clucky as hell. We all had our biological roles during the heat, and a Beta's job had always been as a caregiver. We'd take care of the Omegas, of the young. We'd make sure everyone remained fed and hydrated, and be the first line of defense in case of attack. It meant our nurturing instincts went into overdrive, which was why Seven was sitting between Naja and Luisa like he could protect them both from any unseen attack. He'd hate to admit it was his Beta instincts; no one resented their designation like Seven.

Me? I loved it. I loved caring for everyone, giving comfort, without all the posturing of an Alpha or the vulnerability and expectation of an Omega. Sometimes being perfectly ordinary was freeing. Seven didn't see it that way, but that was okay. There was a place for Seven and his strength in the Pack too.

All that being said, I felt kind of sorry for the Betas in traditional Packs because if I had to resist Naja right now, to leave satisfying her up to the Alphas, I'd go crazy. We weren't a traditional Pack though.

I snorted. We were anything but a traditional Pack.

Naja was making this happy moaning sound as she ate pasta, like any normal being, but it was making my dick twitch. And by the looks of the strained faces around the tiny kitchen, I wasn't the only one.

There was no dining room in Naja's house, and obviously she and Luisa usually ate at the tiny two person table underneath the window. No matter how I searched, there didn't seem to be the influence of any other males in the house. No male scent lingered on her sheets. I was glad she'd been in the shower and hadn't seen me sniffing her blankets like a damn weirdo.

We were all squeezed into the kitchen, Raiden sitting on the bench with his bowl of pasta in his lap, Seven at the end of the tiny two person table, with Naja and Luisa on each side. I rested my bowl beside Raiden's thighs, and Finlo and Gatlin leaned against the wall either side of the door. This house was too tiny for a Pack, and it made me yearn for home. But we couldn't go back without Naja. I knew it in my bones.

But first, we had to woo her. I broke the strained silence.

"How long have you been in Lolo?"

She swallowed hard. "About a year. We came up from Mexico."

I could tell, she still had a faint accent. Barely there really—one, or both, of her parents had been American, that much was obvious.

"Illegal?" Seven asked, and she whipped her head toward him.

"Why would you ask that?"

He shrugged. "You're jumpy. Suspicious. Evasive."

She pointed her fork at him. "I'm crammed into my house with five huge strangers who could literally tear me apart. You'd be jumpy too, asshole."

Seven frowned, like her words physically hurt. "We'd never."

She shrugged. "I'm beginning to believe you. But so far, I've only had your word for it."

We kept circling around and around back to this point. "What can we do to convince you?" She shrugged again, and I sighed. "Do you want to know a little about us?" I'd bare my soul to her if it got her to accept us. Just cut myself open and let her poke around at my insides until she decided that we were suitable mates for her.

She gnawed at her lip, but nodded. "Sure."

I looked around the group, but none of them seemed like they wanted to take the leap and go first. Honestly, whoever said Betas were the weak ones had never tried to get an Alpha to open up emotionally.

"Hi, I'm Ellar, Beta Manix of Pack Huxley-Grey."

"Huxley-Grey?" she asked.

I cast a look over my shoulder at Finlo and Gatlin. "The Pack takes the surnames of the Alphas who join. If another Alpha were to join, we'd add it to the Pack name." She nodded, her face thoughtful as she considered that, so I continued. "Up until I was sixteen, I was raised in a normal suburban house on the outskirts of Denver. When I started manifesting my Manix traits around puberty, my father—who obviously wasn't really my father—freaked out. Realized I wasn't his. Gave an ultimatum to my mother, who'd accidentally conceived me when she was on a business trip to Missoula. It came down to me being sent away or they'd get a divorce."

Shit, the hurt of the kid I'd been was still raw. "My mother stuck me on a bus and told me I was going to boarding school, but at the other end, a huge guy who said he was my biological dad collected me from the bus station in Missoula. He took me back to the Manix colony in the mountains and told me to fend for myself."

I shivered as I remember those first few weeks when I was lost and confused. I'd gotten the shit kicked out of me every single day until Gatlin arrived, beat down all the other Alphas and claimed me for his Pack. Back then, the Huxley-Grey pack had just been Finlo and Gatlin, but it wasn't long after me that they'd taken in Seven too. I'd lived happily with them for five years before I'd worked up the courage to kiss Gatlin one day. When he'd kissed me back, it was like everything had fallen perfectly into place. They'd thought that because I'd been raised human, perhaps I stuck to the ideals of human gender norms.

Oh, they'd been so, so wrong. The next few years were a sexfest.

A throat cleared. "Might want to skip to the next part, Beta." Finlo sounded amused, and I realized I'd been saying all that shit out loud. Whoops.

My cheeks flushed as Naja's eyes bounced around to all of us. Seven had told her that we all had sex, but I guess she didn't really believe it until now. And if I wasn't mistaken, there was more than a little lust in her eyes.

"Uh, so next. That part is more Raiden's story, but I guess there isn't a happily ever after until we get there, so if he doesn't mind...?" I looked up at Raiden, and his eyes were soft and filled with love. He leaned down and kissed me, nipping my lip as he pulled away. And that was Raiden in a nutshell, really. Softness with a hint of pain. Like the stroke of a palm across your ass before it came down in a heavy blow.

I cleared my throat and mentally told my cock to behave. "So, when an Omega turns twenty-five, he leaves his parents' nest and chooses a Pack of his own. Packs try to woo him like he's a Victorian era debutante. It's kind of gross."

She looked between us all. "You guys petitioned for his hand in marriage?" Amusement colored her tone, and she was laughing at us politely. I guess it would be weird to think of us sitting around eating finger sandwiches and drinking tea as we tried to convince him we were his best option.

I shook my head. "Hell no. Our Pack wasn't considered... suitable for an Omega."

She frowned, her jaw growing tight. "Why the hell not?"

Was she outraged on our behalf?

It was Seven who answered. "We are misfits. Gatlin and Ellar? Half-breeds. I'd been kicked from two Packs already, and Finlo..." He trailed off. "Actually, Finlo would have been a perfectly fine option, except he'd formed a Pack with a bunch of cast-offs like us."

Now it was Raiden's turn to frown. "Don't talk about yourselves like that. You're the only worthy Pack on that damn mountain and you know it."

Seven gave our Raiden a soft look. "We are now that we have you. Sorry, Omega."

Raiden shook his head, and I knew he'd fuck the idea of unworthiness from Seven's head as soon as he could.

Naja huffed. "I don't know what the rest of the Manix are like, but if they're anything like the other Pack from the flower market, then I agree with Raiden."

I bit my cheek to stop myself grinning widely. She was starting to like us. *Keep it together, Ellar. You've got this.*

"Seven is right—we were considered rejects. Anyway, Seven was a hot head, and got into a bar fight. This other guy was badmouthing Omegas as being weak and spoiled, a waste of space on the mountain, and good enough only to fuck. Like a pretty ornament to sit on the Pack house mantlepiece. Anyway, Seven, being the passive fucking Beta he is, fights this guy, yelling the whole time about how Omegas were the heart of Manix culture, how they were the glue that held us all together, and so on. All the while, he's throwing punches. And, I mean, it was a brawl. It took Finlo and Gatlin to pull them apart. Turns out the guy badmouthing Omegas was Raiden, an actual fucking Omega."

Seven flushed. "The tequila burned out my nose. Never touched the stuff again." I couldn't tell if he was embarrassed at his fighting or his subpar sniffing skills.

Raiden threw back his head and laughed. "Apparently, one of those hits shook something loose inside my head, because I decided then and there that they were the Pack for me."

I grinned, and when I looked around, the rest of the Pack was smiling too. One day we'd tell that story to our young.

Probably leave out the tequila and swearing though.

Speaking of young, Luisa was nodding off in her highchair. Naja stood, wiping her down, and then bundling the baby out of the seat. "I'll sleep in Naja's nursery. You guys can fight over the bed or sleep on the couch. There's extra blankets and pillows in the closet." She grabbed her plate, but Seven stopped her, stacking it up with his own.

"I've got it, Omega."

She blinked down at him slowly, before shuffling tiredly toward the door. She paused just over the threshold, looking back over her shoulder.

"Give me tonight. I'll have your answer in the morning, one way or another."

All the air in my lungs whooshed out as she disappeared. It wasn't a yes, but it also wasn't a no. The waiting game was on, and I just hoped her scent didn't send me crazy before then.

12

NAJA

I nestled down in my blankets, pretending to still be asleep despite the fact that Luisa's gurgling had woken me about fifteen minutes ago. I'd been awake all night, tossing and turning, going over everything in my head. I even made a pros and cons list, in between the hot sweats that wracked my body as my heat got more intense. Pro: they'd end this fucking torture in the best way possible, with orgasms. Con: they were huge and what if everything was in proportion? I'd seen what Finlo was packing in his skinny jeans and I honestly didn't think that was going to fit. Pro: I would be making all their dreams come true. Con: what if they were some kind of cult of perverts and I was just handing over my biological children to them?

And that was the sticking point really. If it had just been sex, it would have been fine. But a little piece of me, or several little pieces if Raiden was to be believed, would be with them forever. These near-perfect strangers.

If I was honest with myself—and three in the morning, when your body felt like it was crawling with fire was a good time to be honest with yourself—I trusted them. It was insane, of course. But I saw that desperate longing in Raiden's eyes when he talked about carrying cubs, and I got it. I could make him happy. I could make them all happy, as long as I didn't overthink all this shit.

Luisa started to grump more. "Up!"

I sighed and stood from the small bed that was in Luisa's room. One of Tamsin's friends had given it to me for the time when Luisa outgrew her crib, but it worked well enough for me. For a night at least, because my feet hung over the end and I had to sleep curled up in a ball.

Pro: I'd get to sleep in my own bed, when we weren't having mind-blowing sex.

I grabbed up Luisa, changed her diaper, and walked hesitantly out to the living room. Unsurprisingly, everyone was awake. I put Luisa on the floor with her toys, switching on some crazy kids show that was probably created by someone on acid. Raiden appeared with a bowl full of cut up fruits and a little pile of eggs and some chopped up sausage beside it. He handed it to me for my inspection. "I researched what two-year-old humans can eat. It said they should eat from the major food groups. I figured it would be the same for tiger infants." He handed me a sippy cup of milk. Yep, that would do it. He'd hit all the food groups.

I gave him a relieved smile. Anyone who's ever been a parent knows that life's a constant juggle of making food. Breakfast, snack, lunch, snack, dinner, snack. To have someone take that responsibility away even once was amazing. Two meals in a row was basically a holiday.

I put Luisa in a high chair but kept it in front of the TV. Sometimes I needed to breathe, and if a talking pig could give me that for ten minutes a day, I'd take it. When I turned around though, Seven was sitting on the couch, his elbows on his knees, watching the infants show just as intently.

"Are they shifters?" he asked me, and I snorted. When he frowned, I schooled my features.

"Uh, no. They just talk."

"And wear pants."

I nodded.

"And live in social groups."

I nodded again. Okay, I could see what he was getting at. "Okay, yes. They're shifters. Do you feel better now?"

He nodded, his grin smug, and I shook my head. Looking back at Raiden, I saw the warmth in his eyes as he looked at the engrossed Beta. I walked toward the kitchen, but I paused on the threshold.

"Seven?" The Manix turned to look at me. "Could you, uh, watch Luisa? Make sure she doesn't choke on her food?"

The silence in the room felt weighty, but he nodded. "Of course." Then he turned to watch the baby chew with single-minded focus.

I shook my head and followed Raiden. I purposefully ignored the hopeful light in his eyes. "Where are the others?"

They weren't in the house. It was too small and their presence too big to be hiding indoors.

Raiden handed me a breakfast burrito. I took a bite. Cheese and egg oozed out, and I might have moaned a little.

"They are patrolling, but after that noise, I think they'll be back in five... four... three... two...."

The front door banged open and the three of them were suddenly there. I looked at Raiden with wide eyes, and he just grinned.

"You guys have super hearing, don't you?"

He shrugged and nodded. "Sorry?"

I swiped a hand down my face as the guys moved into the kitchen. As if my heat could sense them, my body cramped up and I threw them a wild-eyed look, clutching my stomach. "Fuck," I breathed.

Ellar was in front of me in a flash, dropping to his knees. He pulled up my shirt, ignoring Gatlin's warning noise, and laid his lips over my abdomen. Just like that, the cramp eased.

The hell...?

Gatlin made another growly noise of warning, and I waved him away. "No, leave him. Damn, that feels better," I whispered.

I looked down at Ellar, who was still placing little sipping kisses all over my stomach. It should have been weird, but the relief was undeniable. "Thank you," I said softly, before half-joking, "How do you feel about doing that for the rest of the day?"

He grinned up at me. Gone was the sweet Beta, and in his place was someone who made my body flood with lust. His pupils blew out as he inhaled my scent, and shuddered. "I'll gladly spend the day on my knees for you, Omega."

Oh boy. Warmth crawled along my skin, and I ran my fingers through his beautiful curls. His eyes closed, and he nuzzled against my stomach again, his kisses turning to slow, sinful sucking of skin. He kept his hands locked behind his back, and I wondered if he was a sub for one of the guys. I flicked my eyes to Finlo, then to Gatlin. Their eyes all but glowed with need, and instead of feeling intimidated being under the heavy gaze of two gigantic Alphas, I just felt needy.

Ellar nipped my skin, and I fisted my hand in his hair, tugging him closer. Oh god, I wanted to push him between my thighs so he could chase away this ache. He made that purr against my stomach, and I swear, it went straight to my clit.

Oh god.

How could a man just kissing my stomach make me so damn wet? I felt like I was going to come and we were still fully clothed. The heat was pain, but at the back of that sensation, there was a promise of pleasure unlike anything I'd ever known. I was getting too weak to resist the call of that promise.

Gatlin strode forward, grabbing Ellar's chin, tilting it up until he was looking at his Alpha. "That's enough, Beta. You are confusing things, and we need her to decide with a clear mind."

I was panting a little, but the mention of the decision I had to make brought me back a little clarity. Ellar reluctantly stood at the prompting of his Alpha, but he leaned forward and kissed my lips lightly. A mere promise of a kiss, but it was enough. I wanted to chase his lips as he pulled away.

"Omega." Finlo's voice snapped me out of my horny trance. "We need your decision. Things are getting a little... out of control." He tilted his head. "Seven?"

The other Beta's voice was strained from the other room. "I'm feeding the young. I can hear Naja's decision from here."

Because they all had super senses. This was it, though. The moment. The decision felt huge—hell, it *was* huge—but for the first time in nearly a decade, I went with my gut.

"I'll do it."

My knees went weak. It was lucky that I was beside the counter, because I used it to prop myself up. She was going to do it. It was something I hadn't even dared to let myself hope for, because it had seemed improbable. I heard Seven's whispered "Thank fuck" from the other room, and I smiled.

I pushed down the Omega urges that roared to the front of my brain, and then leapt toward Naja, dragging her into my arms. I hugged her tight, like I could show her what this meant to me with this one embrace alone. Finlo cleared his throat, and I reluctantly withdrew. When I turned, everyone was watching her with a guarded, yet hopeful expression. Even Seven was there, holding Luisa in his arms.

Gatlin cleared his throat too. "We should be specific. What is it you are agreeing to?"

She eyed him seriously. "I'm agreeing to you guys staying here and helping keep the other Packs at bay and helping with my, uh, situation."

"Your heat," Ellar clarified.

She nodded. "Yes. In exchange, Raiden can extract my eggs and you guys can do... whatever it is you need to do."

There was a long silence, and then Finlo nodded. "Sounds good." There was lust in his eyes as he looked between us, like he knew what this whole conception thing was going to entail and he just couldn't wait. That look didn't help the ridiculous hard-on I'd been sporting for the last two days. If blue balls were actually a thing and not a ridiculous concept made up to get women to put out sex, I'd have them.

Gatlin nodded too. "Sounds fair. If you won't come to our territory, we'll fortify your house a little better before things get too heated."

"And we lose our goddamn minds," Seven added, bouncing Luisa up and down in his arms without thought.

Ellar held out his hands. "I think the little princess wants to come to me," he told the other Beta. "Do you want to come to El, Little Bit?" he said in a high-pitched voice, and Luisa held out her arms happily.

Naja shook her head in amazement. "She usually

hates men. She hates the butcher and the postman. She hates the guys at the drugstore and the grocery store. Either Lolo is a mecca for bad people, or she just really likes you guys." Ellar grinned like she'd given him the biggest compliment ever.

Just then, there was a knock at the front door, and everyone froze. Gatlin stepped in front of Naja, and Finlo edged me slightly into the corner.

Seven lifted his nose to the air. "Human. Smells of flowers."

Naja groaned. "Shit, Tamsin. She's probably coming to check on me. You guys stay here so I don't have to explain you all."

She wandered toward the door, and despite what she said, Finlo half-shifted and slunk into the shadows around her doorway. When a minute went by and there were no voices, I started to worry. Then there was the pungent scent of her fear, and I was moving before I even consciously thought about it. I ignored Gatlin's yell to stay back until I was crowded around a pale-looking Naja.

She was holding a black box, a single happy yellow flower inside. There was no note, nothing I could see that would cause that kind of response. Finlo had her in his arms, dragging her backwards and shutting the door, locking all of the deadbolts. He didn't understand what was upsetting her either—I could read the confusion on his face—but he was always an act first, ask questions later kind of guy.

He bundled her back into the kitchen, and we closed ranks around her. Well, they closed ranks around us both, Ellar handing me Luisa so he could guard my left. I thrummed softly, the deep purr instantly calming the baby.

"This isn't necessary," Naja said softly, pushing gently at Finlo's chest. "It's just a flower." It sounded like she was trying to convince herself, but I could still smell her fear. This close to the heat, there was no way the guys were going to back the hell up. No, this was going to make their protective instincts go wild.

Gatlin was still glaring at the door like marauders were about to break in, but as soon as Seven whispered there was nobody near the front door, he spun so he was facing Naja. "It's not just a flower. A flower doesn't give you that kind of reaction. What is wrong?" Naja shook her head, which just made Gatlin clench his jaw harder. "I said to tell me what is wrong, Omega. What has you so fearful?" He added a lot of Alpha oomph to that, and I almost had the compulsion to confess all my deepest, darkest fears.

Naja swallowed hard, but threw him a defiant look. "Don't Alpha me, asshole."

He visibly softened as he took a step forward, grabbing her face softly so she'd look at him. "Apologies, Naja. Your fear makes my Alpha crazy. We want to protect you, but we can't if you don't tell us what is hunting you."

She shook her head again, but she eyed the flower in her hands once more. She jerked like she'd forgotten it was even there, before walking to the trash can and binning it. "Is the offer of taking me back to your territory still on the table?" She met Gatlin's eyes and stared him down.

Finally, he nodded his head slightly. "Yes."

"Good. I'll go pack." She held out her hands for Luisa. I passed her over, and we all watched as she slunk out of the kitchen, looking smaller somehow.

"The fuck?" Seven whispered, and I nodded. I had to agree. What the fuck indeed.

Gatlin was still looking at the door she left through. "She's running from something."

Finlo grunted. "That much is obvious. There are like fifteen locks on every window. She's scared right now, so scared that the scent of the heat has almost receded behind the scent of her fear. You saw the baby yesterday—it was like a petrified doll. Domestic violence?"

Ellar growled low in his chest, and I put out a hand to soothe the normally easygoing Beta. I looked back at the guys. "Seems likely. She's too young for it to be anything else. Plus, she's caring for her sister like she's her own child. Something has gone wrong in her Pack."

Seven raised a brow. "Not an ex-boyfriend?" I could see the barely contained violence in my Beta warrior, and I rubbed his arm.

"Doesn't seem to be, but I'm sure there is someone we can punish for making her feel that way." I walked to the garbage and pulled out the flower. "It's a marigold. Why would that evoke such a response?"

Seven had his phone out and was googling. He made a low rumbling noise which could have been a growl or a hum. "Mexican marigolds are a symbol of grief and despair, and are often used in the Day of the Dead rituals."

Ellar frowned more. "Someone is sending her death flowers?"

Seven nodded, and we all looked toward the door one more time, as if the threat would show itself. Or maybe like the grim reaper would stroll right through it. I didn't like anyone threatening her, and the sooner we got her back to our house, the better. We'd purposefully fortified the land, and there was nothing that could get in or out without us knowing. On top of that, the whole place would be locked down for the rut.

Ellar stepped toward the hall. "I'm going to help her pack. The sooner we are out of here and back home, the happier I'll be."

He wasn't the only one.

y hands shook as I stuffed all of Luisa's clothes into a suitcase. He'd found us. Found me. I would have to run again, but staying with the Huxley-Grey Pack in the mountains for a week was a good start. I could plan, set all my ducks in a row. Maybe I'd run to Canada. The guy who'd smuggled us out of Mexico said there was some kind of supernatural refuge up there. But I needed time to come up with a back-up plan and to shake off this debilitating heat.

He definitely couldn't find me now, while I was like this. No way.

It all made sense now, with the whole Manix revelation. His interest in me. His anger at Luisa. The death of my mother. It made sense, and I was so scared.

Maybe I should leave Luisa with Tamsin, or maybe the Pack, when I ran.

They'd look after her, protect her. It wasn't Luisa he wanted. It was me. Always me. He'd just used Luisa to keep me in line. I thought some more, thought about how the Pack had treated Luisa. I'd leave her with Raiden and their future offspring. They'd raise her well, and she'd still have a family. Still have blood. The cubs that Raiden would birth would be her nieces or nephews. Weird concept.

"I don't know what you are thinking about, Omega, but you're breaking my heart."

Ellar's soft voice behind me made me freeze. I looked over my shoulder, meeting his soft eyes. "I don't wanna talk about it, Ellar."

He nodded, coming into the room and wrapping his arms around my waist, pulling me back against his chest. He rested his chin on top of my head, and I was basically cocooned in his warmth. I instantly felt better, like his very nearness was soothing. "Tell me what needs to be done, Naja, and we will do it."

What needed to be done? That was the problem—I didn't know either. So I just focused on the *next thing*. And then I would do the *next* next thing. And then the one after that. One step at a time.

"Luisa will need her toys. They're in the little tub by the TV. And the food, no need for it to go to waste." Once you'd been starved, you didn't waste food. You squirreled it away in places like wardrobes, and chimneys.

Ellar nodded. "I'll put it all in the van."

While he was gone, I put the rest of Luisa's stuff in the suitcase. Her blankie, her teddies, diapers, sippy cups. Everything. Luisa was never coming back here. When her suitcase was full, I moved to my room and did the same. Well, kind of. I left a lot behind, but it was just stuff. Luisa was the most important thing, and I could always get more stuff. Everything I considered irreplaceable fit into a battered backpack. I threw in some extra clothes, my stash of cash, and a few pictures of my mom, and Luisa as a baby. That was it. The sum total of irreplaceable objects in my life.

I needed to get out of here. He was probably watching the house, and he'd love the smell of my fear. And if he could smell my fear, he could smell all the males in here. It was probably the only thing stopping him from waltzing in right now and taking what he wanted.

A part of me wished he would. That same part wished that Gatlin would grab his head and tear it clean off his shoulders. Maybe bowl it down the street. Something visceral and graphic, so I'd know once and for all that our nightmare was over and my personal boogeyman was dead.

Ellar was back, and this time Raiden was with him.

They both looked at me with concern, and I figured I must look like absolute shit.

"I'm okay, really. Just eager to be gone."

Raiden's nose twitched. "That's only partly true."

I shrugged. I could give him pretty lies, or he could have silence. I wasn't ready to hand them my truth yet, every ugly, heinous minute of it. "That's all I can give you right now."

Ellar wrapped an arm around my shoulders and nodded. "That's okay." He picked up my backpack. "Is there anything else you need?"

I shook my head, and sank into the side of his body. He kissed my temple and it wasn't a lecherous gesture. It was pure comfort. Raiden stroked his hand down my arm, his eyes filled with something I wasn't going to analyze too hard.

Seven appeared with Luisa on his hip. She was clutching her stuffed bear, talking to it like it was talking back. He paused. "Do you want to take her?" he offered softly, and I knew it wasn't because he was sick of holding her, but because he wanted me to be comfortable.

I shook my head. "She looks happy." That grin spread across his face again. Fuck, he was hot. He had these dirty blond good looks, like every boy your mama should have warned you about. I mean, not my mama because that would have been hypocritical. But he had short hair that bordered on too long, so it fell across his forehead and he was constantly combing it back with his fingers. Piercing blue eyes that just burned with emotion, though what that emotion was varied. Right now, it was somewhere between pride and lust.

And that body...

Raiden cleared his throat. "We need to get on the road," he said, sounding pained, and I saw him palming his dick behind his jeans.

Boy, was he right. The sooner we got to safety, the sooner we could all let go.

I followed Seven out into the living room. I took one last look around before walking through the front door and out into the front yard where they'd parked the minivan. The irony of five huge supernatural warriors in the back of a soccer mom van was not lost on me. I watched the curtains across the road twitch as my neighbors tried to figure out what the hell was going on.

When I noticed the carseat in the van, I frowned. Finlo came around, his face passive like he was ready for an argument. "Don't be mad." Well, that was never a good start but I stayed silent, giving him my best *don't fuck with me* stare. "The last part of the trip to our place is inaccessible by car. We have ATVs. It's better for the safety of our Pack. Ellar will run up to get the ATV and collect us from the base of the mountain, and then Seven will return the rental." He stepped closer, his lip caught between his teeth. "Splitting up the Omegas would be too much for my Alpha right now. We need you both together so we can protect you. I promise you won't be trapped though. I'll give you the keys to your own ATV as soon as we get there."

I felt like alarm bells should be going off in my head, because surely this was a way to get permanently abducted. 'Come to my inaccessible mountain home, where there'll be no possibility of rescue. I promise we'll be good.'

However... "Okay. That should be fine."

Honestly, normally I would have run screaming in the other direction, with images of being chopped up and buried in the forest for wolves to eat later running through my brain. But inexplicably, I trusted them. And what awaited me here? Way, way worse. The idea of being inaccessible was actually kind of reassuring, which was obviously the true indicator of how fucked my life really was.

They all eyed me like they'd expected me to blow up, and my lack of response seemed more concerning than having to talk me into a van. Seven was strapping Luisa into the carseat, and now Norma up the road was standing on her front lawn unapologetically staring at us.

"Uh, Omega. You might have to kiss me so your neighbors don't call the cops," he joked, but the heat that pooled in my belly at the suggestion was no joke. I stood on my toes, placing my hands on his chest. Even on my toes, I was nowhere near his lips. His huge hand rested on my lower back as he stooped down, taking my lips in a soft kiss that made my whole body tingle. I grabbed his shirt and held him to me as I deepened the kiss, running my tongue across the seam of lips, making him moan.

A throat cleared. "There's a difference between convincing them she's leaving willingly and a live porn show on the front lawn, Finlo." Gatlin's dry baritone ran over my skin like an actual caress, and I shivered.

Raiden groaned. "Let's go before we have an orgy in the front yard and Naja can never return."

I froze, but stepped around Finlo toward the car. I couldn't return, ever. They didn't know that, but given the looks on their faces, they at least suspected. I climbed in beside a contented Luisa, and Finlo climbed into the back row of seats beside Ellar. Raiden sat on the opposite side of the car seat, and Gatlin was in the driver's seat, Seven beside him.

I looked at the little pink house that had been my refuge for a year now, and couldn't help but feel sad. Which was stupid. It was just a house, and not even my house. But I'd had some of the first happy moments for Luisa there, when she'd smiled and laughed and hadn't been terrified all the time.

As we pulled away from the curb, away from the house, I reached out and grabbed her hand, which she gripped like she had the strength of ten men and not a toddler. Hell, anyone who's ever tried to get something off a toddler will know that bodybuilders and toddlers have the same hand strength.

Raiden reached over, his huge hand covering both of ours. "This is a good thing, I promise. We will treat you like the queen you're supposed to be, Naja. I swear it."

I gave him a weak smile. I didn't need to be treated like a queen. I just needed us to be safe. And I had a feeling that our ordeal was far from over. The guillotine was hanging in the air, and I just didn't know when it would fall and end us all.

15

———

SEVEN

The Manix people were once the fiercest warriors. One Pack of Manix could take out a whole settlement of shifters. We were trained in armed combat from the time we could walk, in ancient weapons such as the sword and bow, and in more modern weapons like firearms.

But it was just tradition at this point. No one was coming for the Manix, and the enemy that was killing us off wasn't one you could fight with a sword or a gun.

The Legion, the ruling council of the Manix, were proud and traditional to the point of fucking us all over. They believed that the solution to our slowly dwindling numbers would come in the form of divine intervention or we'd just die out, whatever the Goddess' will would be. At no point should we ever sully our bloodlines by finding mates outside of the

Manix. Oh no, if we were going to die out, we were going to die out pureblooded. Idiots.

I looked in the mirror at Naja, who had her face turned to look at the scenery rushing past. Normally I would have called out the Manix ability to stick its head in the sand and ignore any problem that couldn't be solved by fists or firearms, but Naja seemed a lot like divine intervention to me.

The Manix lived in a heavily warded section of mountains, somewhere just over the border of Montana in Idaho, in a valley between two giant mountains. My Pack lived as far away as we could damn well get from the other Manix while still being inside those protective wards. We avoided Maxton, which was the main Manix-populated town, as much as we possibly could. If we had to go into town for supplies, normally Finlo went. His parents were well-respected, plus he was an Alpha, which already commanded more respect than the rest of us.

Didn't mean Finlo liked it, at all. He hated the trips, hated the people, and when he got back, he was usually sullen for a day. I got it.

Manix society was archaic. Low-ranking Betas were ignored. Half-bloods were basically kick toys for every-one. It was nepotistic and backward, and definitely contributed to the fact that we were almost extinct.

Sometimes, a little part of me wondered if we shouldn't let nature take its course—adapt or die was the very fundamental principle of nature. But then I looked at Raiden, who rebelled against his society-given role. And Naja, a gift dropped in our laps by fate herself.

Maybe the next generation could make better choices and save us all.

We turned off onto a fire trail, bouncing alongside the river for nearly twenty miles. Luisa had woken at the first bump, but she was having a great time, screaming and flailing like we were on an amusement park ride.

Finally, we reached the end of the road, and also the edge of the ward. My Beast felt like he could relax now that we were so close to home. I'd been stressed out since I first caught Naja's scent.

Ellar climbed out of the car, his grin wide. I could tell he was over the moon to have the Omega on Manix land, and soon to be in our house. Ellar liked to make nests almost as much as an Omega. He said it was natural to want a cosy little spot, and people had been making nooks for centuries. The guy had a knack for it, and honestly, it made him happy, so I'd order all the fluffy throw pillows online that he asked for.

And there were a lot.

We all climbed out and stretched our legs as Finlo turned the car around so I could take it back to town. I'd drop it down in Hamilton, and the hire company would come and collect it. Then I'd run back, and once

I hit the privacy of the woods, I'd shift. I was damn fast as a Beast. I'd be back by nightfall, quicker if they left me a bike at the trailhead.

There was a slow running creek down under a small wooden bridge that had been put there over a century before but remained sturdy, and it was a warm enough day to splash around. I sidled up to Naja, still trying to figure out how to even talk to her. Every time I opened my mouth, stupidity fell out.

I cleared my throat. "The creek is clear and slow moving, if you want to let Luisa play in it?" I asked softly. I just had to control my natural instincts to dominate, which had come from years of trying to be the best, until I'd realized the best made me completely unappealing to Manix society. Because Betas weren't meant to be the best. We were the back-ups. The support for the Alphas, as we propped up *their* greatness.

Not in our Pack, of course. Gatlin didn't buy into that crap and neither did Finlo.

She smiled and nodded, handing me the baby as she pulled off her own shoes. The small dirt trail to the water had been worn smooth by animals, so it was easy for Naja to pick her way down the embankment. I tossed the baby in the air, and she loved it, completely trusting that I would catch her when she came down.

That was a heady kind of feeling. Unlike the rest of the Pack, I hadn't been fussed about whether we had cubs or not. I was happy; I had a Pack that respected me, a home that was filled with love, and I had Raiden. We didn't need cubs to be happy, but if it made everyone else feel complete, I was fine to go along with it. Plus, the baby-making part would be a whole lot of fun.

But babysitting the little tiger cub these last two days had made me, well, clucky I guess. There was something inherently joyful about her musical laughter. The unconditional trust she put in me made me want to protect her from everything. Honestly, babies were weird and so was biology.

Naja turned her face to the sun. "It's so beautiful out here. Like you're the only person on the edge of the world, and it's paradise."

I made a noise of agreement, taking off Luisa's shoes and passing her down to her mother. Because she might biologically be her sister, but she was a mother to this baby in every single way that mattered.

The baby splashed and stomped while Naja held her by the hand, and I sat back up on the bridge, looking at the perfect picture they made. I wanted to paint them, or photograph them, or somehow immortalize this moment forever because it was really something. When I looked over at the guys, I noticed they were all surreptitiously watching the pair too. Having them here, so close to our territory, was like a dream.

"How far up the mountain is your house?"

"About ten miles, give or take. We own everything down to this bridge though."

Luisa got distracted by throwing rocks in the water and watching them splash, and Raiden came over to play too. Naja let them play together and came to sit on the bridge beside me. I tried to hold myself as still as possible so I didn't scare her off. Didn't help that being in a car with her, a literal day away from her heat, had made my logical brain go haywire. I was achingly hard, but then we all were. I'd permanently tucked my dick under my waistband.

"Tell me more about being Manix. I'd never even heard of you."

Ah, geez. She should have asked one of the other guys. I wasn't the best person to give a Manix history lesson, but I'd try.

"Uh, so we were really prevalent around the 1700s; there were as many of us as there were Lycanthropes. Unlike most other supernaturals though, we have three forms. Human, mid-change and full change. We call it the Beast. In full change, we are, well, the closest I can think of is feline-like. It's like the thrumming is similar to a purr."

"Thrumming? Is that what you call the vibrations in your chest?"

I nodded. "Yes. Also, our mid-forms are furred and have a camouflage pattern similar to a tortoiseshell cat."

Nothing says fearsome like being a giant housecat.

"We basically melt into the darkness, we move with stealth unheard of in any other supernatural. We can block our scent. We have razor-sharp claws and protruding canines. It made us natural assassins, and we were often used as such."

She was nodding as she lay back in the sun. God, she was beautiful, like a curvy angel come down to torture my dick.

"And there aren't many of you left?"

I shook my head. We were mere decades from an extinction event, but I didn't want her to feel pressured so I kept that direness to myself.

"Will you show me your fully shifted form?"

My chest felt full. "Of course. When we are back inside the wards and in our territory, I'll shift. We have scales and fangs. It's a whole thing. I'm kind of impressive, if I do say so myself."

Raiden laughed up at us. "I'll back that."

She chuckled low, which made her boobs jiggle a little. Yeah, I looked. I couldn't help it. Then she sighed. "I wish I could shift, but I'm not enough of either, really. Not enough shifter to have a tiger form. Not enough Manix to shift. I'm trapped as a human."

I leaned back so I could see her eyes properly. "Up until a few days ago, you didn't know that Manix was even an option. You can try again, if you want. We'll help."

She shrugged. "Ellar said he shifted by accident. If I could shift, it would have happened at some point already. I've had enough stressful situations to force it."

I growled low, making her pop open an eye, and I swallowed my emotions down. "You never know. But you are perfect how you are. We should be able to at least teach you how to hide your scent. It will give you more freedom."

She smiled at me, her eyes meeting mine from under her lashes. "You aren't so bad when you're not pacing around being sharp-tongued."

I flushed, and it made Raiden laugh again. "She's not wrong." He spun Luisa around in the middle of the creek so her toes were just skimming the surface of the water.

"Apologies, Omega. Being out of my territory stresses me out. I'll try and be better."

I smelled her guilt almost immediately. "Sorry, Seven. That was bitchy of me."

I grinned. "It's okay, Omega. I'll bury my face between your thighs later, and you can tell me how you like my tongue then."

I swear, it felt like the whole forest went silent as her scent flooded the air. Both Alphas took a step toward her as her heat notched into overdrive. Jesus, I was going to have to run home with a hard-on. Sounded uncomfortable. Thank god we were purposefully downwind of Maxton so no one should pick that up, unless they had a nose like mine.

And no one had a nose like mine.

Finally, Ellar reappeared with the ATV, and there was an audible sigh of relief.

Gatlin cleared his throat. "Let's load up. It's time to go home."

Thank fuck.

Naja's gasp as we reached the house made me grin. I loved this place. Gatlin and I had built it with our own hands, because it was our Pack house, our home. I was proud of what we'd accomplished.

"Guys, this isn't a house! It's a flipping mansion."

I could see how she'd think that. It had a huge square footage on a gentle slope, with a full wrap-around porch. The whole lower level was made up of small glass windows which looked out over a small garden and down to the private lake we had. The top floor was all the bedrooms, as well as an office. The attic was a nest for Raiden. It was rustic, made entirely of logs and stone from the area.

As Ellar pulled us up at the front door, I helped Naja

out, shifting the baby onto my hip so Naja could get her bearings. She was just looking around in utter awe and I couldn't help but preen. Gatlin prowled around the perimeter, checking that no one had stepped foot onto our territory while we hadn't been home.

I unlocked the door and lifted my nose, but the inside didn't hold any foreign scents. Despite what Seven had said about Manix being able to mask their scent, it was very hard to mask it in someone's home. I knew how it should smell, and even the tiniest disturbance would have been like a giant red flag. Eventually, the smell of home would include Naja and Luisa. At least, I hoped they'd stay long enough to change the scent palette of the place.

Ellar and Raiden came in behind us, holding their bags, and I placed Luisa on the floor. She was off like a rocket and I mentally did an inventory of hazards that could possibly hurt her. We'd have to put a baby gate near the stairs as soon as possible, but I shut the door to that hall for now and let her just explore. I'd whip something up later.

Naja was looking around with her mouth slightly open. Raiden stood beside her, his fingers brushing her hand. "Gatlin and Finlo built this place by themselves, you know. They did an amazing job." He looked at me, pride written all over his face.

I flushed slightly, and grabbed the bags off Raiden

and Ellar. "Come on, I'll show you to your room, then give you the grand tour."

Naja called for Luisa, who toddled over as fast as her legs could carry her. Ellar picked her up and pretended she was an airplane, complete with whooshing noises, and I shook my head. Poor little thing was going to forget how to walk, and probably think she could fly the way we all carried her around and threw her in the air like a football.

We'd built the place with six rooms, always hopeful that we'd have kids one day, I guess. We'd never planned for a female Omega though. I mean, how could we have? They didn't exist. And yet there was one right here, in our house, right now. It blew my mind.

I took them to the spare room, which Ellar had decorated in soft autumn colors.

"We don't have a crib, but I can run into Maxton and grab one off one of the Packs with females. I'm pretty sure my mom still has my old one in her garage. Will Luisa be okay for the night?"

Naja nodded. "She'll be fine. She hasn't had a crib for most of her life. She can just sleep in here with me."

I put her bags down near the walk-in closet. "Come on, I'll give you the rest of the tour, then you can settle in."

I showed her around the rest of the place, which was pretty open plan. We each had a room, but sometimes we all slept together in a big pile upstairs in the attic nest. I pointed out everyone's rooms, and then showed her where the bathrooms, kitchen, and laundry were. On the lowest level was the family room, with a huge memory foam-filled bean bag that really did look like a giant nest, as well as a cinema screen and a small bar. Along the back wall was an open fireplace, as well as a reading nook that had floor to ceiling bookshelves, complete with a sliding ladder. Most of the books were Gatlin's, but everyone had one or two shelves full of their own personal preferences. That side had a large, comfortable couch, and lots of throw rugs.

Luisa ran and threw herself on the bean bag, and I chuckled. You never grew out of that urge.

"This is kind of the living room, although there are televisions and couches upstairs too. But this tends to be where we congregate. It's beautiful down here in winter."

Naja didn't say anything, and I searched her face. What if she hated it? I mean, I was happy to make her her own nest wherever she wanted, especially if she needed her own privacy during the heat. But we'd made so many great memories down here as a Pack, and it would break my heart to change it.

"Don't you like it?"

She turned watery eyes to me, and I frowned. She swallowed hard. "It's perfect."

I grinned so wide my cheeks hurt, and I bundled her into my arms. "It is now." The front door opened and closed, and I guessed Gatlin was back from his perimeter check. "Let me show you the attic nest. According to everything I've read, during your heat, you'll prefer small, more protected areas."

"Plus the whole floor is a sunken couch," Raiden called over to her, waggling his eyebrows. Naja flushed, and I tried to keep from smiling. Instead, I led her upstairs.

"I'll feed the cub," Ellar said from the bottom of the stairs. "We've got some fruit and stuff in the fridge, so we'll come up with something delicious, won't we, Little Bit?"

Naja only hesitated for a second before continuing up the spiral staircase. Gatlin followed us up, and I knew it was for the same reason I took her up. I wanted to see if she liked the nest, if we were good providers. The Alpha Beast inside me was beginning to batter at its constraints.

When she got to the top, she gasped. This time I didn't bother trying to control my grin. I knew what it looked like. Fairy lights provided soft lighting, only enhanced by the huge round window on the far wall. It was just a mound of pillows and blankets of different sizes, shapes and textures, all piled into a sunken bed, like a pool, but with pillows instead of water. A padded window seat ran along the wall, as well as some pretty antique chairs toward the back. We'd put a tiny fridge up here for when the sex marathons happened; dehydration was a killer. It looked like a cozy paradise, but as I watched Naja's eyes drift around, I could spot the exact moment she noticed the gold eyelets that were hooked into the raised edges of the bed. Then the ones in the cross beams of the ceiling. Or that the ledges were the perfect height to bend someone over to fuck. It was comfortable and dirty as hell if you knew what you were looking at.

When she realized it, her cheeks went pink and her scent bloomed around the room. I groaned and turned around, squeezing my dick hard. Fuck. I needed to have a serious word to my cock because if he went this hard every time she so much as thought something dirty, I was going to die of lack of oxygen to the brain.

Raiden growled low in his throat. If my Alpha was wild, his Omega was nearly uncontrollable. It was a testament to the kind of man that Raiden was that he'd contained himself so far. The scent of a female Omega was like a drug to a male Omega. I watched his stiff shoulders as he stopped himself from launching at her.

We were fighting the inevitable, but I wanted to give her time. Let her settle in, to be comfortable.

Raiden whined. "Naja..." He gasped, buckling over,

physically in pain. To him, the scent of her need would be like having your balls in a vice.

She turned her eyes to me and Gatlin. "What's wrong with him?" she said, anxiety bleeding into her words.

I stepped forward, pulling Raiden back into my chest, tipping his head to the side with my cheek and biting the muscular column of his throat. It was primitive and primal, but it was satisfying something he needed.

It was Gatlin who answered Naja. "Your need is like a physical ache to him. He needs to, uh, copulate with you in some way. Even a taste of your slick would ease the need."

She blinked at him. "He needs to eat me out to stop feeling like he's being kicked in the balls?"

Gatlin just shrugged. "Essentially."

"And he won't feel one hundred percent better until...?"

Gatlin cleared his throat. "Until he's fucking you. If you aren't ready to impregnate him, condoms work to stop the extraction."

She was shaking her head, but not like she was saying no. More like she was befuddled by Manix physiology. I got it; it was kinda weird. Even in nature, there was only one species where the male became pregnant and gave birth. Seahorses. But we were nothing like seahorses, and even their biology differed to ours.

Naja rolled her shoulders and grinned. "Well, call me Saint Naja, because if giving me oral sex makes him feel better, I count that as a win for us all."

I gaped, my arms dropping to my sides in shock. But that was the only invitation Raiden needed. He pounced, taking her down to the soft cushions of the nest. She gasped, and I got ready to pull them apart if she needed it, but she giggled as his hair tickled her face.

It was happening, and I didn't know who was more excited.

Me, or my dick.

17

NAJA

I couldn't help but laugh as Raiden tried to lick and kiss every inch of my skin all at once. He was murmuring something under his breath, and I only picked up every other word between the kisses. Beautiful and perfect seemed to be prevalent, as well as how good I smelled, so I generally assumed it was basically all an ode to how amazing I was, which made me laugh as well.

All mirth left me though when he pushed up my shirt and began tasting his way across my skin. Wherever his mouth missed, his hands ran. It was like he was trying to consume me whole. His greedy hands pulled down the cups of my bra, exposing my breasts to the warm air. My nipples were achingly hard, and when he wrapped his lips around one, I nearly ratcheted in half. Everything was just... more. I was more sensitive, the pleasure was more intense, and my need was more urgent than ever before. I moaned and spread my thighs wider, grinding against his torso.

"Raiden..." I gasped as he bit my nipple, and he chuckled happily, moving down my body, tugging frantically at my yoga pants. When they didn't peel down easily, he growled low, tugging harder. A set of hands appeared in between us, and I looked up into Gatlin's golden eyes. He spread his huge hands, lifting my ass with one and tugging down my pants with the other, but he didn't take his gaze from mine. As soon as my pants hit the floor, all three of the guys groaned. Raiden dropped his forehead to my abdomen, his back heaving with deep breaths. I reached down and gripped his hair, tilting his head back so he was looking at me.

"Okay?"

He nodded, but his pupils were blown out. Grinning, he dove between my thighs and *holy shit*. His tongue was everywhere, flicking across my clit, sliding down my slit. He ate me like he was starving, and I didn't think I'd ever be able to have oral sex with anyone else ever again.

Then he sucked my clit between his lips and thrummed. He vibrated my damn clit with his lips, and I screeched an unholy noise like I was dying and came all over his face. I gripped his hair in my fist and rode his face. The whole time he continued to vibrate.

I was not ready for this. Orgasms like this were life-altering and if this was just the foreplay, how was I ever going to recover from full-blown sex with these guys?

Finally my orgasm subsided, and Raiden looked up at me, the expression on his face full of smug satisfaction, and his cheeks shiny with my release.

"Done?" he asked softly, and I nodded. Then he grinned and pushed back between my thighs again, stroking me to one more orgasm before I passed out, resembling a pile of mush.

I WOKE UP IN A BED, surrounded by pillows and covered in a soft blanket. I rocketed upright, wracked with guilt. Fuck, I'd passed out without a thought of leaving my kid with these guys. I was the worst parent ever.

But when I looked around, I noticed that someone had moved a giant fluffy rug into the bedroom I was using and Luisa was there, playing a game with stuffed toys and Ellar, who was stretched out in the sun beneath the window. I must have been completely wrecked if they'd been able to move me from the nest to here without waking me up.

When Ellar realized I was awake, he curled into a sitting position. "Mama's awake," he said to Luisa, who spun and ran over unsteadily, climbing onto the bed. I pulled her into my arms and she snuggled in.

"I thought you might freak less if we were here

when you woke. I promise I wasn't watching you sleep or anything creepy."

I gave him a smile. "You're right. It's not that I don't trust you guys. Well, it kind of is, but I don't trust anyone. I trust you more than most."

I didn't have this problem when I left Luisa with her babysitter, and it was probably because she was a female, even though she was a teenage girl. The notion that women are naturally more maternal or something. But the Manix had turned that whole idea on its head. Luisa was so content with them and I wasn't going to lie, the fact she was so happy definitely figured into my agreement. If she'd hated them, I would have run as far and as fast as I could, fuck them and their problems.

But Luisa liked them, and that made what I felt for them okay somehow.

Ellar climbed onto the bed beside me, staying on top of the blankets. "It's okay, Naja. No one expects you to trust us implicitly in three days. We aren't stupid." He let out an *oof* as Luisa's foot got him right in the gut. "That being said, you should know we have your back if you ever want to just let go. Trust us to be there when you need us—I promise you, we won't let you down."

I swallowed the hard lump in my throat and nodded. Ellar leaned over and kissed my forehead. "Good. Now come downstairs and try the cookies me and Little Bit made while you were otherwise occupied." He waggled his eyebrows, and I flushed. He stood, reaching out toward Luisa, who launched herself into his arms.

"Cookies, Mama!"

I grinned and stood, realizing I was in an oversized t-shirt that smelled of Finlo. I knew enough about shifters to know they were scent marking me, but I honestly didn't mind. It was actually kind of nice being surrounded by the scent of safety.

I looked at my pants, and decided against it. Finlo's shirt fell to my knees, plus three out of five of these guys had just seen my vagina on an up close and personal level. Modesty had packed her bags and left, and the only person left to man the ship was a wanton hussy.

I walked out into the kitchen to see that only Gatlin was in the open plan kitchen, dining, and living area. He had some papers spread out on the dining table, and was staring intently at a computer. I raised an eyebrow at Ellar in question.

"Finlo is outside talking to his parents on the phone and, uh, warning them about you, I guess. Seven isn't back yet but Raiden has gone to get him in the ATV." He put Luisa down and she ran like the toddler version of the Flash to Gatlin, who lifted her onto the table, talking to her softly and letting her mash his computer keys. Something about that picture made my heart seize in my chest.

Ellar wrapped an arm around my shoulders, leading me to the island counter and the fresh cookies on the wire rack. "Don't let his gruff exterior and Alpha bark fool you—Gatlin is the biggest softie of us all."

The man in question looked over his computer screen and lifted his brow. "I heard that."

Ellar grinned. "You were meant to, Alpha," he purred back, and honestly, that voice made my body go wild even though I'd gotten off like three times this afternoon already. Jesus Christ.

I looked at my watch. Three hours until the baby went down for the night.

I could wait three hours.

Ellar got some kind of casserole out of the fridge and put it in the oven. While he was bent over, the perfection of his ass was right there in grabbing distance. I wanted to get his juicy butt cheek between my teeth and bite down.

The heat was making me fucking insane. It was here and it wouldn't be ignored anymore. I could feel it like it was a living Beast, sitting there, waiting for me to unleash it and let it take whatever it wanted.

And it wanted this Pack badly. Clearing my throat like it would help the fact my panties were getting damper, I listened as Ellar gave me the grand tour of the kitchen. The fridge was well-stocked, as was the pantry. Everything was built for people who were over six feet tall, and Ellar said he'd get me a step ladder.

"Do you guys shop in town?" Now my brain had cleared a little, I wondered about the logistics of being a secret race of people who hid in the mountains. In this day and age, it must be almost impossible to stay hidden.

Ellar shook his head. "No, the main town for the Manix is Maxton. It was named for the first Alpha General, who decided that we had to secede from the greater supernatural community to safeguard the rest of our race." He passed me a glass of milk and a little plate of cookies, before pouring another glass and a sippy cup of milk, and taking them with another plate of cookies to the dining table for Gatlin and Luisa.

I watched as she gnawed on the edge of the cookie with such fervor that she was like a beaver in a time crunch.

"Slow, Luisa," I called and she gave me a dirty look, but slowed down.

Ellar shook his head, his grin wide, and walked back toward me. "The town gets shipments from the city. Fresh foods, general grocery items, all the staples. We also get fuel shipped in. It's all distributed evenly, and the Legion pays for most of it. It's definitely the perk of a small society. Some Packs choose to work as well, and use the funds for luxuries or higher education, but most of those jobs are either virtual or within the surrounding towns. We draw too much focus en masse."

I remembered seeing them when they walked into the club, right before they hit the fire alarm and tried to kidnap me. The whole club had been watching them. Some openly, but most from the corner of their eye. They were the biggest guys in the room, and for there to be five of them? Well, they weren't inconspicuous.

"You guys?"

"Gatlin is a stock market savant."

I looked over my shoulder at the huge Alpha with the gray eyes. He'd closed his computer and was now touching his glass to Luisa's as they cheersed, Luisa's favorite snack time ritual. I looked back at Ellar, and he was looking at his Alpha with such unmistakable love that it made my chest hurt.

The sliding glass door opened and Finlo stepped in, his face already stretched into a grin. "You're awake! Raiden and Seven are going to swing past my parents' place on their way back to grab the crib. My dad's bundling it all up now, and my mom is tracking down some crib sheets and linen from my sister. Cutie can have her own bed tonight."

These guys were going to make me cry and they didn't even know it. I pasted a smile on my face and thanked him, though I was pretty sure he saw through it.

Gatlin grunted. "What did you tell them?"

Finlo shrugged, ambling over so he was beside me.

He wrapped me in a hug that seemed to encompass my entire being. "The truth, to a degree. That we found a woman we could all agree on, and she came with a cub for us to spoil rotten."

Ellar laughed, kissing my cheek and moving back to the fridge to pull out the ingredients for a salad. Finlo nuzzled my hair, and I relaxed into his arms. "We'll spoil you too, if you let us."

I was warming to the idea, and that was starting to scare me.

18

GATLIN

I breathed in and out through my mouth because fuck, the scent of our new Omega was killing me. Seven and Raiden had arrived home, and with Seven's sense of smell, he knew immediately what had happened while he was gone. He'd given us all a peevish look—probably for starting without him—but hey, desperate times.

Still, he'd sidled up to Naja and then from behind his back, whipped out a full, albeit slightly battered, bouquet of flowers. I'd watched Naja melt, and then build back up her walls. But we were growing on her, that was for sure.

She'd taken the flowers and whispered a soft, "Thank you," that was entirely genuine and completely for Seven. I was jealous of my Betas again, for the second time in as many days. I'd always relied on being an Alpha to help me in life, but now, being Alpha meant nothing to Naja. She wasn't a regular Omega. She didn't see our designation, not even Raiden's. She saw us as men, as individuals. I was going to have to up my game.

We'd had dinner, which was basically the same as every night, except it now involved a beautiful woman who smelled like heaven and a little more flying food, thanks to Luisa. Now, I was putting together her crib in the spare room, the one she'd share with Naja. Maybe one day we'd turn it into a nursery for our own cubs.

I shook my head. I was getting ahead of myself. This wasn't something I would even let myself hope for yet; it still felt too good to be true. There hadn't been a female Omega even in my father's generation, so none of us knew what to expect. But caring for people? That was something I knew how to do.

I put on the linen that Finlo's mom had sent up with the crib. I loved Finlo's parents, his mom especially. She'd taken me in when I'd arrived, after my father had basically dropped me at the communal share home for orphaned Manix. I'd gone to school on the first day, and Finlo—who'd been actually tiny for a Manix kid, not that you'd know it now—had come up and basically told me we were going to be best friends. I don't know if it was fate, or the Goddess, but we'd had that fraternal bond almost immediately. So Finlo had taken me home to his parents, they'd moved me into their guest room that weekend, and I'd lived there until Finlo and I created the Huxley-Grey Pack. I was forever indebted to the Grey family, and my loyalty to them was second only to my loyalty to my Pack.

I grabbed a stuffed bear up off the floor and put it in the crib. Then I pushed that clucky feeling that was flowing through my chest right down. Emotionally aware wasn't in my wheelhouse. I stood back and eyed my handiwork. Looked good and sturdy, the antique walnut edges gnawed on by generations of little Grey babies.

I heard the soft fall of feet walking up the hall and knew instantly it was Naja. She had a sleeping Luisa in her arms, and I gave the crib one last shake to make sure it was secure before stepping away.

"All set."

She nodded, lightly placing Luisa in the crib, more like she was a bomb than a toddler, but the baby went down easily. We both sighed in relief and snuck out of the room, leaving the door slightly ajar so we could hear her if she cried.

"I'll see if we can't get a baby monitor as well. I'll call in an order tomorrow."

She squeezed my arm. "Thank you."

I didn't think she meant for the crib, but I inclined my head. "It was nothing." Dammit, I didn't know how to talk to her. I knew how to be an Alpha. Knew how to take care of my Pack. I could hit a target with a throwing knife from a hundred feet away.

But trying to convince an Omega that I was worth something when she didn't give a shit about any of that? Useless.

When we made it back to the living room, you could almost hear the tension in the room. It was a heavy silence as we all looked around the room at each other. Raiden held out a glass of wine, and Naja launched herself at him thankfully. She downed the first glass in one kind of impressive gulp, and then Raiden poured her another with a laugh.

Seven, bless his complete fucking lack of self-consciousness, stood and took off his shirt. I slid my eyes toward Naja, and her cheeks were flushed as she followed a slow path down his body. Seven was beautiful. He was broader than the average Manix. His abs were defined, and the V of his obliques looked like it'd been carved.

The smell of Naja's heat roared to life and it was like someone had dropped the starting flag. Naja closed the space between her and Seven impossibly fast. But he was ready, catching her in his arms and lifting her up so his lips could devour hers, her legs wrapping tightly around his waist. She locked her fingers in his shaggy blond hair and holy shit, I almost came. They were so fucking sexy together.

Raiden couldn't help himself, drifting closer until

Naja reached out and grabbed the front of his shirt, pulling him toward her until she tore herself from Seven's lips to kiss him. Finlo groaned beside me, and my dick was so fucking hard I felt like I was going to pass out. But I held myself back, not wanting to overwhelm her with the insanity of an Alpha in rut. Not yet anyway. Let the Betas work her up. We had days, and I wanted the Betas to feel included. The satisfaction of our Omegas was a Pack-wide responsibility, and every one of us did our duty with a fucking smile.

As if he read my mind, Ellar drifted closer as well, standing before Raiden. He grabbed Naja's chin, giving her a tentative kiss on the lips that she deepened immediately. She pulled back with a gasp, her eyes flying wildly around the room. There was no fear there now though; there was nothing but need.

"Clothes off," she growled and we all scrambled to do what she asked, except Seven, who seemed reluctant to put her down, like she wouldn't come back to him if he gave her up. But there seemed to be enough naked flesh around to appease her Omega. Ellar kissed her again, and then dropped to his knees in front of Raiden.

Ah fuck. I gripped my dick and squeezed. Naja's eyes tracked him, her forehead touching Raiden's as they both looked down at the pretty Beta on his knees. When he licked his way along Raiden's straining shaft, she let out a whispered, "Oh fuck."

Yeah, Omega. We were all in fucking trouble now.

I could see Naja rubbing herself on Seven's abs as Ellar took Raiden in his mouth, his tongue sliding out to wrap around the head of our Omega's cock, before sliding him in further. Raiden threw back his head, moaning Ellar's name as he gripped his hair and pulled him closer. Naja, no longer content just to watch, pulled his lips back to hers as Seven licked and sucked his way down her jaw.

"I'm going to blow my load so fast," Finlo grumbled, but he didn't stop stroking his dick. I didn't blame him, even though I was squeezing the base of my dick trying to stave off coming all over them. All it was doing though was working up my knot, and it wasn't time for that fucker yet. I knew we should take it to the nest but I didn't want to break up what was happening right now. It was like live porn.

Ellar's cheeks were hollow as he swallowed down Raiden, who was thrusting into his throat like he was fucking our pretty Omega already.

He dragged his lips from Naja's. "Fuck, El, I'm going to come."

Ellar kept going, until Raiden was shouting, clutching at Ellar's head as he came down his throat. Seven took the opportunity to take Naja's parted lips with his own, but she wasn't finished with these guys yet.

She looked at Seven. "I need you to fuck me."

The heat washed over us completely, mixing with the scent of Raiden's yearning. It was like a soup of pheromones designed to drive me mad, to trigger the rut. I slid my eyes to Finlo, who was gritting his teeth but holding on. I realized I was holding my jaw tight too and I suddenly worried I was going to shatter some teeth.

Seven was always the impulsive one. He took Naja at her word, moving her up his body with one arm and reaching to finally push his sweats down. He slid his cock against her dripping entrance, and they both moaned.

Fuck.

"No, wait!" I yelled, startling everyone. Reaching into my pocket, I pulled out a condom. I walked over, gripping Seven's cock in my hand, giving it a small stroke—because I was a red-blooded man and he was fucking amazing—and then rolling on the condom. Naja froze, then threw me a grateful look. Yeah, even though my Alpha was screaming at me to fill her with seed, to make her ours, my job was to protect her— even if it meant denying my baser instincts.

Seven's whole body was taut with restrained need, but he still took the moment to look at Naja. "Ready?"

In answer, she buried her face in his throat and bit down hard, making him groan and slam inside. The sound they both made snapped the last of my control.

The Beast was out and it was ready to play.

19

NAJA

You ever had one of those dicks, we'll call it a Unicorn Dick, that is just perfect? The perfect girth, length, that slight little curve to the left? Like you can already feel the instant, filling perfection of the moment when it slides inside?

Seven had that dick, and fuck me, he knew how to use it. I wrapped my arms tightly around his neck as he grabbed my thighs, dragging me up and down on his cock like he only had one shot at this and he was making it count. I wanted to tell him that his Goddess-sent dick was welcome in my lady cave anytime.

More hands appeared, running over my body, tweaking my aching nipples, squeezing the globes of my ass, all to the steady beat of Seven fucking me senseless. I squeezed my legs tighter around his hips as an orgasm more intense than anything I'd ever had in my life swept over me. If this was sex during the heat, I was going to be in a coma by the end. I dug my nails into his spine as he slammed into me harder and harder, my pussy fluttering around him until he was coming with me. His knees buckled as he pulsed inside me, but a long arm went around us both, and I looked up to see Finlo at his back, murmuring things in his ear. Strong arms lifted me away from Seven, who collapsed to his knees, panting. He looked like he'd been wrung out, and I smiled smugly at the idea that I'd done that.

The scent of Gatlin flowed over me, stoking the heat again, my slick running over his stomach where my shaking legs were wrapped around him. "We should go to the nest before this goes further," he growled, making me throw my head back and moan. How could a voice do that? He was moving toward the stairs, Raiden and Finlo racing up ahead of us.

"Ellar," he called, but the doe-eyed Beta shook his head from where he had a still kneeling Seven clutched to his side.

"I'll take care of everything down here." He stepped forward, running a hand down my spine and kissing me deeply. "I will find my way between your thighs soon, Omega, and then I'm going to make you come like that just for me," he purred, and I was about to come for him there and then, just from his words and the friction of Gatlin's body.

Gatlin grabbed his head and kissed him hard. There was love and appreciation in the caress of their lips. Then Gatlin was taking the stairs to the nest two at a time and I knew the heat—that mindless, writhing, thoughtless need—was here.

I'd be ashamed later, but I was so fucking ready right now. Gatlin climbed into the pit of cushions and soft blankets, which felt nice against my oversensitive skin. He laid me between them, these two Alphas and an Omega, and their eyes ate me up. Then their mouths.

Lips slid over my skin, Raiden's teeth on my breasts, Finlo's mouth covering mine. That meant the stubble scraping my inner thighs belonged to Gatlin, and the long tongue lapping at my lower lips was his too.

It was almost too much but I wouldn't tell them to stop even under pain of death, so when Raiden's fingers came down to roll my clit, I bucked against his hand and screamed. I slammed my thighs around Gatlin's head so hard that he probably heard the Bells of fucking Notre Dame inside his head, and I'd apologize later because right now they were driving me to insanity. Finlo moved down and took the opposite nipple to the one Raiden was teasing into his mouth. The dual sensations of them sucking at my nipples, and Gatlin fucking me with his tongue was already too much, and I soaked Gatlin's face with my slick.

Raiden moved up to kiss me, his tongue firm and insistent, and I knew he was getting crazed. He crawled down my body, his hard cock pressed to my stomach as he licked my juices from Gatlin's face.

Holy fucking shit.

Arms scooped me up and Finlo put me on his lap, facing Gatlin and Raiden. He groaned, and I could feel his dick twitching against my core. I wiggled back against him, grabbing his cock, already covered in a condom. I notched it to my entrance and slid myself down. I'd thought Seven had a Unicorn Dick, but holy fuck, maybe this was the Holy Grail of Cock. He filled me so exquisitely, and I watched Gatlin and Raiden pressed so close together, stroking each other.

"Oh, our pretty Omega likes that. You like seeing Gatlin's big dick in Raiden's hand? Or maybe it's the way Gatlin has his hand around Raiden's throat, is that what turns you on?"

Oh god. Not dirty talk too. I moaned and ground myself down on Finlo. But he stilled my hips. "Mmm, I asked you a question, Princess. Do you like Gatlin's grip around our errant Omega's pretty throat?"

I strained against his hands. "Yes," I hissed, and Finlo growled, letting go of my hips, allowing me to piston myself up and down on his lap. He slid his hand up my stomach, between the valley of my breasts, to spread around my throat. Oh fuck.

He tipped my head to the side, scraping his teeth over my neck, and I shuddered. I watched Raiden suck Gatlin's cock into his mouth and it was too much. I was panting and moaning like I was a dying animal, sweat beginning to run down my spine as I rode Finlo's cock, leaning into the hand around my throat.

"You going to come for me, Princess? Pretty, pretty Omega," he purred, and I couldn't have resisted even if I tried.

"Finlo," I panted as I came hard again. How could I have come so much in such a short amount of time? At least it felt like a short amount of time, but could have been endless for all I knew.

Gatlin held Raiden's head gently, his own head tipped back with his eyes closed as Raiden swallowed him down. They were both flushed as Gatlin gripped his hair to stop his movements.

"No, Rai. I want to fucking come inside you. I want you to take my knot. But first you have to make Naja scream for us."

Raiden slid Gatlin out of his mouth with an audible pop. He crawled over, and I could see that he was as crazed with the heat as I was. But it was called the yearning in male Omegas, according to Ellar.

Oh yeah, I yearned too. Some primordial part of me,

the Manix part, was screaming to have this sexy as fuck Omega inside me, fucking me. It was that part of me that climbed off Finlo's lap, getting on my hands and knees.

Raiden growled primally, getting behind me and running his fingers through my wet lips. But before he could do what I wanted him to do—bury himself inside me—Finlo stopped us both. Well, Finlo and Gatlin, who was holding the Omega's hip.

"Are you sure about this, Naja?"

The fact he'd stopped us to ask, breaking the rut to make sure I was still okay, cemented my decision even more.

"Yes," I breathed.

That was all Raiden needed, and he slid inside me in one long, glorious movement. He curled over my back, his hand gripping my shoulder as he slid back out and then thrust home harder.

Someone was chanting "yes" and subconsciously I recognized that it was me. My elbows buckled and I dropped forward onto my face, pushing back to meet him thrust for thrust. My brain took a back seat to the solid pound of his body into mine, the feel of his panting breaths against the sweat on my back, the absolute pleasure that was singing through my whole damn body.

Raiden's soft "Oh fuck, oh fuck, oooh fuck" let me know that he was close, and fuck I was close too.

"Baby," he panted, his hand slipping to beside my shoulder, "it's happening."

A sensation like I'd never known started deep in my womb. I wasn't sure if I'd ever be able to describe it. It was that clench of your body when something turns you on, where your pussy tenses and there's that low, aching hum of pleasure deep down in your abdomen. Except, instead of clenching and sucking around nothing, I was clenched tight around Raiden's cock and he was sucking pleasure from my body, like he had a magical button and he was mashing it constantly.

A long, low whine emitted from my throat as I curled my head up, meeting Gatlin's gray eyes. It was an orgasm so intense, so everlasting, that it was almost painful, but it was the best sort of pain. Like the burn of drowning, but in an abyss of pleasure. And if you died? You'd do it with a smile on your face and zero regrets.

"Fuck, Princess, you're so goddamn glorious. Look at you. You're the most beautiful fucking sight I've ever seen," Gatlin growled deeply, and it was too much. I burst into tears, not of fear or pain or anything like that —just overwhelming, intense ecstasy. This was it. This was what euphoria really meant.

Finally, Raiden slumped back, panting, but Finlo was there to catch him. I keened at the loss of his body from mine, my brain a jumble of confusion, but I knew

I wanted him back. I wasn't done, but also, I was broken and lost and gasping for air.

"Take care of Raiden, Fin. I've got our girl."

Raiden reached over, gripping my fingers and squeezing. He had felt it too. Had found Nirvana right along with me.

I wasn't empty for long, as Gatlin lifted me like I weighed nothing and impaled me on his cock. I let my head slump against his shoulder as I watched Finlo roll Raiden onto his stomach, parting his cheeks and pouring lube all down his crack. He lay his body along Raiden's and then slid himself inside, his thick cock stretching Raiden wide.

Gatlin's huge hands were moving me at a slow, deep pace, building my body back to the crest it had just reached. He leaned forward and nipped my earlobe. "Watch them, Omega, watch as you make all our fucking dreams come true." His hand held my chin, his fingers caressing the column of my neck. I did as the Alpha told me. I watched as Finlo buried his nose in the back of Raiden's neck, his teeth scraping, making both me and Raiden moan, his body pushing them low and hard through the cushions.

Raiden turned his face, looking at Finlo as much as possible. "Knot me, please," he gasped and Finlo grunted, kissing him hard on the lips and pounding into him harder, until Raiden was gripping the couch for traction. Finlo reared back, and buried his teeth in the firm muscles of the Omega's shoulder as he came on a shout. I watched as the base of his cock swelled as he locked with Raiden, then they both collapsed panting on the soft blankets. Gatlin ran his fingers over my too tender clit and that was it, I was coming right along with them, screaming incoherently, loud enough that I probably woke up the neighboring village. My whole body began to shake, and then I blacked out.

I watched Naja pass out, and I understood the urge. But I wasn't fucking done yet. I wasn't going to miss this opportunity. I was fucking sex-drunk or something, everything around me buzzing, my whole body a mass of tingling jello. Finlo kissed along my shoulders, my nape, the bite he'd just given me.

He showered me with love, and I was so fucking happy I could just explode. And it was all because of her. Our angel in a thong.

Finlo and I had been locked together for fifteen minutes, and I was sweaty and sticky and covered in cum and so, so, so fucking happy. His knot began to recede, freeing him from my body and as always, I was saddened by his loss.

But I didn't need to be sad for too long—no fucking

way. Gatlin gently passed the still out-to-it Naja to Finlo, who cuddled her gently on his lap. Then my Alpha stood and swaggered toward me. He was so fucking sexy that he immediately made my dick hard again. I could be dead and I would pop one last boner for a naked Gatlin.

He tugged me up until I was standing on wobbly legs, and kissed me reverently before moving behind me. "You honor us today, Omega." He made my heart race in my chest and my dick twitch against my stomach. The pheromones were riding me hard, which meant we'd all be inhaling the scent equivalent of Viagra for days.

"Put your seed in me, Alpha. I yearn," I purred, and it was like I had a link directly to the Alpha Manix who clawed inside of Gatlin. The Alpha pounced, trying to bend me but I held firm. I'd make Gatlin work for it, prove to myself again and again that this man, this Manix, was a worthy mate. A worthy Alpha.

He grabbed my cock and my knees buckled, making me fold in half to catch myself as he stroked up roughly. "Low blow, Alpha," I teased and his throaty chuckle was just as much Manix as man. He had me bent nearly in half, my ass high in the air and my forearms resting on the raised edge of the sunken couch. Grabbing his cock, he notched himself against my ass and then plunged inside, making my eyes roll back in my head. The Omega's satisfaction of breeding with my Alpha rushed through my veins, heightening my pleasure and my body's receptiveness. He felt different to Finlo, girthier but not as long, and he stretched me. His knot was bigger too—fuck, sometimes I worried that he'd split me in half—but it hurt so damn good. He continued plunging into me, his foot resting on the raised edge of the couch, like he needed more leverage. I could almost taste his cock, it was going that deep, but I loved it. He knew I loved it. I stroked my cock as it throbbed in time with my staccato heartbeat. I could feel him growing, feel his knot spreading my entrance, trapping the cum inside me, increasing the chances of fertilization. Our bodies were made for this, and thank the Goddess, it was so much fun.

Just before he locked me in tight with his knot, he withdrew, slumping down into the pillows, his back resting against the side of the sunken couch, and pulled me down onto his lap, sliding back into me easily. My muscles were too weak to move but that didn't bother Gatlin—he held me still as he fucked me just as hard from the bottom. His knot began to swell, and I let out a low, stifled moan. I wanted to roar it from the rooftops, but I also didn't want to wake Naja. She'd given us everything. She deserved her rest.

All thoughts of anything but the feel of Gatlin inside me ceased as he began to stroke my dick in time with his thrusts, until he was knotted all the way tight inside me, barely achieving small strokes. Then he squeezed the base of my cock hard, making me whimper. I soon came in long ropes that scattered across the cushions, and he came inside me in hard pulses.

My eyes rolled back in my head again, and I collapsed back against him, writhing, taking him as deep as I could.

He grabbed my hips, holding me still. "You did such a good job, Omega. I love you."

His huge hand spanned my abs, stroking gently like he was willing the Goddess for a miracle. It wasn't a miracle though, it was Manix biology. The true miracle was laying curled in Finlo's arms.

Days of being a heightened, horny mess caught up with me, and my eyes shuttered closed as I finally let oblivion take me, content that I was safe and that for the first time in my life, I'd fulfilled my role as Omega.

I woke to Ellar lifting me into his arms, which was hilarious because he was just a tad taller than me, but about as lean. If anyone was looking, it would seem like he was carrying a giant noodle down the stairs.

I looked over my shoulder at the two passed out Alphas, but no Naja. Panic lit up my chest until Ellar thrummed soothingly. "Seven has her. He's going to put her in the shower and then tuck her into bed. I'll put you in there with her, but I think you should wash in your bathroom first. Give her a little room to process."

I nodded, and snuggled into Ellar's chest. He didn't have to be He-Man to be sexy as hell, or for me to love him completely. When I got to my ensuite, I realized he'd drawn me a bath. People always went on about the prestige of Omegas, and how every Pack needed strong Alphas, but no one ever mentioned that it was the Betas who held us all together. They were the glue, and I had gotten so lucky with the two that were mine. He lowered me down into the water, and I sank into the hot bubbles with a sigh, my muscles well used. Ellar moved to his knees beside me on the cold slate tiles, picking up the washcloth floating in the water and beginning to drag it slowly over my skin. The sensation made my eyes fall closed.

"How did it go?" El murmured softly, and I opened my eyes and smiled.

No, it wasn't a smile. It was a face-splitting grin. I grabbed his hand and placed it over my abs. "It went perfectly. It was like our bodies just knew what to do."

Ellar's eyes fell to my stomach. "It's weird to think they're in there, turning into our cubs. I just..." He shook his head and looked entirely overwhelmed, a feeling I understood completely. We were not done, of course. According to my biology teacher in high school, the unfertilized eggs would last between twelve to twenty-four hours before they were absorbed back into my body. I wanted them all, and I wanted all my mates to have a chance at producing a cub.

I grabbed El's hand and tugged him closer. "Take off your clothes and get in the bath," I whispered, and his eyes lit up.

He stood, kicking off his clothes, before coming to kneel in the bath. We'd invested in a big tub because honestly, there were a lot of us and we enjoyed some bath time craziness. I rolled so I was on my hands and knees, and Ellar slid in behind me, his already hard cock rubbing between my ass cheeks.

Then he paused. "I didn't bring in any lube."

I almost laughed at my sweet, gentle Beta. I was about to tell him it was okay when Seven appeared at the door, lube in hand and a grin on his face.

"Ask and you shall receive. Literally," he laughed, swaggering into the bathroom with that cocky self-assurance that was entirely Seven. He tossed the lube to Ellar, then knelt beside the tub, right near my head, so he could lean forward and take my lips in a searing kiss. At the same time, Ellar slid his well-lubed cock inside me in a slow, delicious stroke, and I moaned into Seven's mouth.

This was nice, not the frantic insanity of the heat and the yearning all crashing together in an avalanche of pheromones. I was making love with my mates, in the hopes that we'd create a family. It was beautiful. Seven continued to kiss me, and it was at odds to El. El was making love to me with his body, but Seven? He was fucking me dirty with his tongue, nipping and biting, his hands tight in my hair.

"Harder," I groaned against Seven's lips, and Ellar began to thrust in earnest, panting.

His fingers gripped my hips harder. "But I won't last."

Seven broke away, looking over the top of my head as I rested it on the side of the bath. "That's the fucking point, El."

As if he'd gotten permission, Ellar fucked me hard until he was blowing inside of me. It didn't have the force of an Alpha and his knot, so the chances of having a cub that was his was low, but it was worth a try. The idea of a little golden-eyed, curly-haired miniature of Ellar made my heart thump.

He pulled out gently, and Seven grinned. He unbuttoned his jeans and then climbed into the tub fully clothed, kissing Ellar as he slipped out. "Let's put some cubs inside you, hey?"

Ellar grunted. "Charming, Sev."

My laugh turned into a moan as Seven slammed inside me, and I knew that if anyone could beat the odds and create Beta offspring, it was Seven.

21

ELLAR

It was a beautiful day, and it was all the more beautiful because of our house guests. While Naja was still asleep in her room, tucked in beside Raiden, Luisa had proven that she wasn't a late sleeper, up with the sun at the crack of dawn. I'd made her breakfast and Seven had fed her while they watched cartoons streamed from the satellite.

Now, I was showing her around the yard, while Gatlin was busy making safety gates in the workshop. Luisa was talking nonsensically, squatting down to pick up things that caught her attention on the ground.

She went to put a rock in her mouth and I clucked. "No, Little Bit. Yucky."

She looked up at me with big brown eyes like her sister's, and dropped the rock. Toddling back over to me with more sass than skill, she lifted her arms. "Up, El."

She knew my name. I grinned down at her, picking her up and throwing her into the air just to hear her laugh. "That's right! Lulu"—I poked her nose, then pointed to myself—"El."

She gave me a look that said *Duh!* in no uncertain terms, and we went to investigate what Seven was doing. He had one of the old bald tires we kept beneath the house, and he was hacking at it with some kind of saw. He must have heard us coming because he looked over his shoulder, grinning at us. Safe to say that the cub had made us all soft.

I booped Seven on the nose. "Sev." He frowned and fake sneezed, shaking his shaggy hair.

Then Luisa reached out and poked his nose too. "Sev!" she squealed, and he did the elaborate sneeze/shake thing again, but this time he was smiling wide. She had us wrapped around her tiny finger, and we were too smitten to struggle.

"Wanna go see if Mama is awake, Little Bit?" I said, and she bounced around.

"Mama!"

As we walked, I was looking at the yard as a parent would. We kept the surroundings of the house pretty clear because of fires, so there weren't too many hazards. There was a pool at the rear that Gatlin was already talking about fencing in, as well as putting child-proof locks on the hot tub cover on the back deck. But over in front of those big windows in front of the bottom floor would be a perfect place for a little play set and maybe a mud kitchen. Maybe we should fence off a portion for when we had three, or four, or six tiny cubs to keep track of, if we were so blessed by the Goddess. We didn't want them to be able to slip past us and end up down by the lake. I put teaching Luisa to swim on my mental list of things to do. All babies should know how to float at least. I'd suggest all this to the Pack over dinner. I walked up the steps to the deck and put Luisa down, and she raced toward the open door. When she stepped through, she saw Finlo and took off.

For some unknown reason, the kid loved Finlo. He hadn't spent any more time with her than anyone else. Hadn't bribed her with gifts. She was just mesmerised by the giant Alpha. I watched as he picked her up—his huge hand the size of her back—and spun her around as she laughed. I decided I didn't blame the toddler at all. I loved him too and he didn't have to do anything more than smile in my direction.

"Where are you going with my favorite girl?" he asked me, and I walked over, kissing him lightly on the lips.

Then I booped his nose and said, "Fin."

Luisa copied the action, though she missed his nose and got his eye. "Fin!" she shouted, and Finlo laughed, even as his eye was scrunched up and a little watery. I tried to hide my laugh, but it was hard to hide anything from Finlo. His heated look promised sweet retribution later for laughing at his misery.

"To answer your question, we are going to see if Mama is awake."

Finlo raised his eyebrows at the baby. "Is that so? Can I come too?"

I snorted. "I think you've come enough."

Finlo gasped like a 1930s matron, and covered Luisa's ear. "Ellar Belamy Huxley-Grey. Not in front of the child."

I laughed and nudged him with my hip. "Let's go and see our Omegas."

We crept through the hall, but when we made it to Naja's room, Raiden was already awake, looking down at the sleeping Omega with a soft expression. His eyes flicked to the door at our arrival.

"She's still asleep," he whispered.

But Luisa was having none of that. "Mama!"

Naja jerked awake, her eyes going straight to the baby instinctively. Her body finally relaxed as she took in the rest of us. Raiden was dressed in sleep pants, and Gatlin had left Naja one of his shirts after her shower. We'd agreed that while nudity was a part of shifter culture, including that of the Manix, out of respect we were going to be clothed whenever we were in public spaces.

Luisa wiggled out of Finlo's arms and ran to Raiden's side of the bed. Raiden leaned over and dragged her up, supermanning her across and onto her sister. Luisa snuggled down against Naja, and honestly, it made my heart simultaneously happy and hurt. Happy because they were a beautiful sight, and hurt because I knew that they couldn't be ours forever.

"Morning baby, have you been good for the Pack?" Naja cooed, kissing the baby all over her chubby, and somehow kinda sticky, face.

"Yes!" Luisa shouted, and then seemed to throw together several incomprehensible sentences that somehow Naja deciphered.

Raiden leaned over and kissed Naja's cheek before rolling out of bed. "We'll leave you guys to your girl talk," he said softly, and I knew this was important. Naja needed space. Her heat wasn't riding her as hard now that we'd satisfied some of the biological needs, but it was still there, tantalizing the edges of my senses.

That wasn't the reason I wanted to climb into bed with them though. I just wanted that beautiful domesticity. Early Sunday mornings, even though you're meant to be getting a lie-in. Baby snuggles and chatter. A beautiful woman beside me who looked at me with love. Hell, any of my Pack. Or all of them. Sunday morning puppy piles.

Instead, I followed the guys out of the room, shutting the door gently on their quiet chatter. I wrapped my arms around Raiden's waist and kissed his shoulder. "Naja and Luisa are making me even more clucky. When will we know if it worked?" I asked both Raiden and Finlo, because while this was a mystery to them, it was well and truly out of my scope of knowledge. I hadn't been Manix until way too late. I'd missed all the valuable teachings of a Manix school, and I was still playing catch-up.

"We can do an ultrasound in about five weeks, but Gatlin and Finlo should be able to pick up scent changes in two or three. Actually, Seven too probably, his sense of smell is more powerful than most Alphas," Raiden said, leaning back into me. "Fuck, I'm starving though."

"A mass orgy will do that to you," Finlo teased, but I raced into the kitchen ahead of my Omega.

Raiden raised an eyebrow at me and I waved him to the couch. "Go and sit down. I'll make you some food." He was going to be the most pampered damn Omega to ever be pregnant, and he'd probably hate every moment of it. Well, not the pregnancy itself, but the actual coddling. I couldn't help it though. A Beta's gotta Beta. It was in our makeup.

Finlo just laughed and shooed him over to the living room, laughing at Raiden's huff. Then he wandered over to the kitchen, standing behind me so he could wrap his whole body around mine. "You don't have to take on the caregiver role, El. We can help too.

No one expects you to play house servant and nursemaid."

I rested my head back against his shoulder and hungrily accepted the kiss he placed on my lips. "I know, but it feels right, you know? Like I wasn't needed before but now I have a purpose."

Finlo frowned. "That's not true. We need you more than anyone else in this Pack. You're worth ten of me."

I snorted but appreciated the sentiment. "Only in this Pack, Fin."

He nuzzled my neck. "This Pack is the only one that matters." He nipped my throat and I shuddered in pleasure. He pulled back and rested his head on my shoulder. "What are we making a hungry Omega who is possibly eating for, like, six?"

I whipped up a couple of bowls of yogurt with berries and granola, one for Raiden and one for Naja when she was ready to face the day. I hadn't been lying to Finlo—it did feel right to care for them both, especially during the heat. But the sadness that washed over me at the thought of her leaving straight after tore at my happiness.

I poured Raiden a glass of juice and looked over at Finlo, who was eating leftover yogurt and not actually being helpful at all, though that was half the reason I loved him so much. "Do you think we could convince her to stay?" I asked him quietly, though I hadn't heard Naja leave her room.

Finlo shrugged, but his brows were pulled low. "Whatever she's running from has her scared. If we can convince her she's safer here with us, she might stay. But I don't really want her to stay out of fear. I want her to stay because she wants to be here with us. Because we can build something perfect here."

He was right, and I wanted that too. But I'd be happy if she stayed out of fear as well, because whatever terrified a strong woman like that? It had to be deadly.

22

———

NAJA

How did a woman act around a group of men she'd just had a mind-blowing orgy with? Did you give them high fives and swap sex tips? Reminisce about that time you watched them pound someone into the mattress?

Was it still a walk of shame, or was it a stride of pride?

I didn't know, and I wanted to believe I was badass enough to just stroll out there and own it. I knew as well as I knew my own name that they weren't judging me for the fact I'd had sex with four different men yesterday. Or was it three? After the fourth muscle-melting orgasm, it had all gotten a little hazy.

The heat was receding, so technically I could leave soon. Just take Luisa and go. I'd given the Pack what they wanted and I'd gotten my end of the bargain too. The deal was done.

But I didn't want to go yet. And judging by the fact that Luisa kept pointing at the door and saying, "El!", she didn't want to go either. So maybe I'd just play it by ear. Have a week of more dirty sex to put in the old spank bank and then we could go. I needed a plan anyway.

Yeah, I'd go once I had a solid plan.

Decision—or justification—made, I rolled out of bed. The scent of Gatlin on the shirt I was wearing made my nipples pebble. It should be illegal for any man to smell that good. Like cedarwood and vetiver. It hung to my knees like a dress, and I was wearing my boyleg underwear, so I decided I was dressed enough. Last night Seven had scooped my jello body from the upstairs nest and put me in the shower. He'd cleaned me off, dressed me, kissed me softly and put me to bed.

The whole night had made a huge chasm in my chest open up. Like my heart was screaming for them to fill the space. They were wrapped in Christmas lights, with a big blinking sign saying 'The Thing You've Been Missing, Dumbass!' but I was ignoring it because I didn't—no, I couldn't—have the capacity to give myself over to them like that.

Luisa was standing at the door, not so patiently, and I opened it. She bolted for the living room like she owned the place, and when I made it out there, she was perched in Raiden's lap, eating his breakfast.

"Lulu, that's Raiden's breakfast," I chastised, but honestly, she stared me down with the confidence and brass balls that only a two-year-old could have. Like they knew they were too damn cute for punishment.

Raiden grinned, letting her pick out another berry from his bowl. "It's alright, Mama. We like to share, don't we?"

Luisa gave me a very solemn nod, and I shook my head in exasperation, walking over to Finlo and Ellar in the kitchen. "You guys are spoiling her rotten," I mock-grumbled, and they both grinned, not looking even a little bit contrite about it.

Ellar pulled out a bowl of bircher muesli and yogurt, topped with berries and some kind of berry compote. Okay, maybe it wasn't just Luisa getting spoiled. I sat at the breakfast bar, and Finlo leaned beside me.

"How are you feeling?"

I shrugged. "Uh, sore but pleasantly so? Less like my skin is going to crawl off my skeleton as well, so I guess I have you guys to thank for that." I flushed bright red and tried to hide it behind a mouthful of muesli.

Finlo nodded, but his grin was completely self-satisfied, like the cat who'd not only got the cream, but licked the bowl clean. Then he frowned. "I want to kiss you, but I'm not sure where you stand on that now."

I froze with my spoon halfway to my mouth. Well, fuck. I wanted him to kiss me, like a lot. But there was no *reason* for him to kiss me now. Did he need a reason? Could I cling to the heat for a little longer?

I decided on yes, so I leaned forward to kiss him softly, and he tasted like strawberries and Ellar. I thought that might be my new favorite flavor. Finlo's mouth teased mine, his tongue stroking across the seam of my lips softly but not trying to venture past. It was a promising, but still tentative, kiss.

When he pulled away, I missed his warmth immediately.

Danger, Naja, danger!

My brain was shouting at me. Well, at least the part of it that still cared about self-preservation, but my heart wasn't listening. Oh no. That traitorous fucker was thundering away like we were Seabiscuit running the damn Kentucky Derby.

His eyes traveled all over my face; he could probably hear my heart pounding, but he just stroked my cheek and stepped away. "We should talk about where we go from here after Luisa goes to bed tonight. Figure out our next steps."

I nodded dumbly and went back to eating my breakfast. They bustled around the kitchen, not crowding me or making me talk, just going about their day like I was part of the Pack. Raiden was still entertaining Luisa, and a little part of me—the part that was always drawn so tight, always ready for the next disaster—relaxed a little. I didn't need to be anywhere, or do anything. Luisa didn't need me right at this moment; she was being taken care of. I didn't need to be off to the next job, or the club, or calling the landlord to fix the leaking pipe again, or trying to work out what we had to scrimp on to make the rent this month or anything. Didn't have to worry about *him* finding me here, at least not right now.

I could just relax, and it was a feeling so foreign to me, you may as well have asked me to turn myself inside out.

Once I'd finished breakfast, washing up my bowl and putting it in the drying rack despite Ellar's protests, Raiden called me over to the couch. It was huge and gray, made to fit giant Manix. Luisa was curled up under a fluffy throw, her thumb in her mouth, as they watched a princess movie about a girl trapped in a tower with long, golden hair.

I could relate to that girl, trapped but convincing myself I was okay. Except I didn't have any long hair to save me. I did have these guys though, if I just let myself grip them and scale down the side of my wall of self-isolation.

Okay, maybe that was taking the metaphor a little too far.

Raiden patted the space between the chaise section of the couch and Luisa, and I curled up in front of him, letting him spoon me with his body.

He wrapped his arm around my waist, pressing me close, but he didn't say anything. I soaked in his warmth and comfort like I had a right to it. Like this was my life, surrounded by a Pack of hot as hell supernaturals who could make me come like a bullet train.

We got to the part where the handsome but devilish male character realized he was in love with the pretty blond girl with the long-ass hair, when Seven barreled into the room. He looked around, his eyes falling on the couch, and if I wasn't wrong, regret crossed his face.

What was that for?

When his eyes fell on Finlo, he grimaced. "Hey Fin? Your family is here," he called, and from the bowels of the house, I heard a muttered "Fuck!"

Raiden sat up, straightening his clothes. "You might want to go put on pants," he said, but he seemed more amused than worried.

Before I could take his advice, five people stepped into the room. One was Gatlin, but the other four were strangers. One woman who was older—probably Finlo's mom?—and three males, one older and two who were basically doppelgängers of Finlo.

All of their eyes snapped to me, and I gathered

Luisa up into my arm, shrinking into Raiden almost subconsciously.

The woman's eyes softened, but the males? Their eyes grew wide. Too wide.

One of the younger one's mouth fell open, before he shouted, "Holy fucking shit, Fin! There's a female Omega in your goddamn living room and she isn't wearing pants."

What a perfect way to be introduced to Finlo's family.

I loved my family. I did. They were the best people, even my brothers. Mom and Dad had taken Gatlin in when he was a kid without even hesitating. They didn't toe the genetic supremacy party line like most of the higher-ranking Manix, and they were just chilled out, loving people.

But they had shitty personal boundaries. And my brothers had no goddamn filters. Especially Trace.

My dad whacked him up the back of the head, and Trace flushed. "Shit, sorry. I mean, fuck, no I don't. I mean, uh, apologies. Ma'am."

I groaned as I ran my hand over my face. "Shut it, Trace. Guys, what are you doing here?"

My mom gave me the *are you stupid or did I actually do damage that one time I dropped you on your head* look. She had that look down to a fine art. "Son, I know you don't think you can call down for a crib one day and not expect me to come up here to see why."

I gave her a pointed look. "Uh, yeah I did, actually? I'm a grown ass man, with my own Pack. I figured you'd just let me get around to telling you the hows and whys when I was ready."

Mom snorted like I was a fool—which, granted, I apparently was—and said, "Are you going to introduce us to the *female Omega* you have in your Pack house?"

If she got any more pointed, I'd cut myself on her meaning. I looked at Gatlin for help, but he just shrugged and held up his hands. Damn traitor.

"Mom, Dad, Dumbasses. This is Naja and her daughter Luisa. They are staying with us for a little while."

My dad, who was an Alpha, firmed his jaw. "The heat?"

I don't know who flushed harder, my dad or Naja. "Yes."

Mom gasped. "Did you...?" She looked between Naja and Raiden, obviously drawing the right conclusion.

"Yes."

The squeal of joy my mother let out scared Luisa, making her cry. Mom immediately stopped, her face apologetic. "Oh, I'm sorry, sweet thing. I didn't mean to scare you," she cooed as she walked over to the couch. "I feel so rude, but you must understand—I didn't think this would ever happen again in living history for the Manix." She swallowed hard, and I knew that was step one toward 'Mom bursting into tears.' Ugh, I'd have to run interference, but Mom wasn't done yet. "I'm sorry, I've been terribly rude. I'm Selena. That is my husband Orson, and my twins, Trace and Tycen. It's wonderful to meet you."

Naja didn't look uncomfortable, but I could see she was tugging at her shirt, like she was very aware that it didn't go down to her knees.

"Mom, let Naja get changed, and we'll go out and sit on the porch. I'll explain some things without you embarrassing her to death."

Mom gave me a droll expression, but Naja looked relieved. Raiden skimmed his hand down her arm reassuringly. "I'll hold Luisa. Take as long as you need," he said softly, and she threw him a thankful smile.

"I'll be right back," she said politely, high-tailing it out of the room like her ass was on fire.

As soon as she was out of sight, Mom jumped up and down and did a happy dance, racing over to wrap me in her arms. "I'm so happy for you, son." Then she moved around my Pack, kissing their cheeks heartily until she was back at Raiden. Her eyes softened when she looked between him and Luisa. "You're going to be such a wonderful parent, Raiden."

My sexy, confident Omega swallowed hard.

"Thanks, Selena. You'll make a wonderful grandmother."

She let out another whoop of noise, softer this time, and jumped back toward my dad. "Do you hear that, Orson? We're going to be grandparents. Wait until I tell Jeff and Jack!" I noticed my other two dads weren't with her, but I wasn't surprised. They worked for the Manix Legion and had jobs in procurement. But I was surprised she wasn't calling them already. Probably waiting to grill me for all the facts.

I herded everyone to the deck, and Seven picked up a weird toy cube thing that Luisa seemed to like best. He stuck it on the outdoor table in front of Raiden, who talked to her softly, flicking switches and playing with the cube. Gah, even the sight of them like that was making me damn emotional.

Dad slapped me on the back. "You better start explaining how a physical impossibility is getting changed in your spare room."

So I did, in a low voice. From the time that Seven smelled her on the breeze, to now. I left out the more sensational parts though, because it was none of their business.

Still, Mom burst into tears. "She's an absolute miracle. I just..." She trailed off, at a loss for words, which was the true miracle.

My dad was the practical one. "You know the Legion will find out eventually."

Gatlin growled low in his chest, making my dad raise a brow. They were pretty evenly matched Alphawise, but my Dad had experience and Gatlin had youth. "Not if we all keep our mouths shut."

Tycen, the quieter, more astute twin was shaking his head. "Seven's nose is good, but this close to Maxton? The wind is going to shift and someone will work it out. We'll keep it to ourselves of course"—he nailed his twin with a look—"but you better work out what the hell you're going to say to the Legion. And if she does leave before they find out, how are you going to explain a knocked up Raiden? That shit won't make no sense. You can't hide this forever."

Gatlin shrugged. "We'll figure it out when that happens. But I'll move all of us off the mountain before we kowtow to the Legion; you know this."

My dad nodded. He knew our stance on the Legion and their archaic rules. He didn't disagree either, despite being old school. He might be a cog in the greater Legion machine, but it didn't mean that was what he wanted for his children. What any of my parents wanted for us.

"Tye is right—best to be prepared, but you do what you feel is right for your Pack. And for both your Omegas."

I sighed. "She isn't ours, Dad."

"Yet," Seven muttered, and my Mom smiled at him fondly. She had such a soft spot for Seven. She loved all my mates like they were her own flesh and blood. She'd always been the powerhouse that kept my family running, and it had everything to do with her huge heart.

Luisa decided she'd had enough of not being the center of attention and held her arms out to Seven. "Sev, up?" she asked, and my Beta complied in a heartbeat, because he was only Manix and that cuteness was just irresistible.

My mom smiled smugly. "Well, aren't you the cutest little thing to ever walk the earth? You keep all these Manix on their toes, sweetheart?" She wiggled her eyebrows like they were blonde caterpillars on her face, making Luisa laugh and try to do it herself. It mostly resulted in her chubby little face contorting weirdly, but still, it was cute as fuck.

Naja appeared on the porch, dressed in jeans and a soft pink sweater. She looked more like the girl next door and less like she'd been freshly fucked. I scooted across so there was a spot to sit between Gatlin and I, ensuring she felt as secure as possible.

I changed the subject of the conversation away from Naja and toward getting some supplies we needed to build a pool fence. Having fathers who worked in procurement sometimes came in handy, though we went through the proper channels as much as possible.

Mom then told me that my sister's oldest sons

had been caught hijacking an ATV *again,* and I tried not to laugh. I really did. But they'd apparently driven the damn thing into the lake that formed the center of town. Now they were on herd duty for the next month. Herd duty meant you had to watch that the cows didn't get eaten by predators, all day, every day. It was boring as fuck, because other than the odd bear, there just weren't that many daytime predators out here. But it was a good punishment because there weren't many thirteen-year-old boys who wanted to waste their summer holidays watching cows eat grass.

"Don't you laugh, Finlo Grey. Do you remember when you and Gatlin decided to climb the tallest tree in the woods behind the school, and got stuck at the top? Your father had to leave work to go find the biggest ladder in town to get you guys down, and you were up there clinging to the branches like scared kittens. Actually, I'm pretty sure Terra was only three branches down, so this is karma for her."

Naja laughed, and I was pretty sure she'd like my sister Terra. She had brass balls too. Actually, maybe I should hope they never met, because Terra's favorite pastime was talking shit about me and what I got up to as a teenager. I didn't need the embarrassment.

My smile fell as I realized they'd probably never meet. My mother noticed, of course. She noticed freaking everything.

"So, Naja, what will it take for you to stay with my son's Pack?"

"Mom!" I growled.

She gave me a faux innocent look. "What? You can't see how cute you all look together. The Goddess brought you into each other's lives, so it's up to you guys to make sure she is so happy that she'll never think of leaving. If you need some tips to keep her satisfied in the bedroom, I'm sure you can ask your fath—"

"Argh! La-la-la! Fucking hell, Mother. No one wants to hear that," Trace yelled.

"There are children present," Tye added.

"Yeah, your own children. I can guarantee no one wants to think about you guys doing it, let alone ask for tips. Gross," Trace said, pretending to gag.

"I just threw up a little in my mouth."

I laughed, because I agreed one billion percent. "I'm with the terrible two over here. I'll take a hard pass on the sex advice. Go home and I'll *call* you when we've come to a Pack decision. Emphasis on call."

My dad nodded, hustling my huffy mother to her feet. "Fine, fine," she grumbled. "But I'm glad I came, otherwise you'd have hidden this beauty away forever with only you five for company. It was a pleasure to meet you, Naja. I hope to see you again soon." She gave me the stink eye. "Call me," she threatened as she walked down the stairs and back to their ATV. It wasn't a request, it was an order.

I sighed with relief as they disappeared back down the track that led to Maxton. I looked over at the shell-shocked Naja.

"Well, that was my family. Welcome to the neighborhood."

24

SEVEN

I loved Finlo's family, but his mom scared the shit out of me. She was sweet as hell, but she was a force of nature. Luisa, who must have been close to her nap when Finlo's family arrived, fell asleep in my arms and I rocked her softly where I stood. Some things just seemed to come naturally, and that weird rocking motion was one of them. I'd added a gentle thrum and it put her off to sleep like magic. I could put her down in her crib, but I kind of liked holding her. Though I definitely wouldn't tell the rest of my Pack that; they'd think I'd gone soft or some fucking thing.

Gatlin motioned us inside and downstairs. I still didn't put the baby in the crib, because I knew we were about to have a Pack meeting, and what if she woke up and none of us heard?

Granted, I could literally hear a bunny burrowing

twenty yards from the house, but still. I didn't want her to wake up and be scared and alone.

We all gave a freaked out Naja some space. It was like adding more Manix to the mix had suddenly made this whole thing more real for her. I wanted to beg her to stay with us, not to run like her scent was telling me she was contemplating. We wouldn't trap her here, but I didn't think we'd be quite the same if she left. Well, we definitely wouldn't be the same, because we'd have cubs in four and a half months that contained half of her DNA. She'd forever altered us already; I just wanted her to stay so we could show her just how safe and happy life could be.

"So, that was my family," Finlo said, grimacing. "I'm so sorry. They don't understand boundaries."

I snorted softly, so as not to wake the baby, and Raiden threw me a conspiratorial smirk. He wasn't wrong. They really had no boundaries, but they were as close as a family could be and they always had our backs, no matter what. Most of us hadn't had that in our lives—Gatlin and Ellar had been half-breeds, and my family had disowned me after I got booted out of my first Pack. After the second booting, they'd pretended I was never even born.

So Finlo's family was all of our family now, no matter how wild and dysfunctional they may be. Naja gave him an amused smile. "They were interesting. Very nice too."

Finlo flopped back onto the couch. "They are bossy, nosey, and I wouldn't swap any of them for all the money in the universe." He opened one eye, looking at Gatlin and then back at Naja. "They make a good point though. We should discuss everything, after last night."

Naja looked a little pale, and I wanted to bundle her up in my arms too. I was pretty sure I could hold both the baby and the pretty Omega.

Gatlin did the next logical thing, pouring a couple of fingers of whiskey into a tumbler and handing it to her. She knocked it back with a gasp but it at least gave her a little more color in her cheeks. Seemingly more happy with how she looked, Gatlin nodded. "The heat has eased, and I am fairly certain the mating worked. If you are ready to leave, we won't stop you."

I opened my mouth to protest. Sure, we wouldn't stop her, but he was doing a shit job of telling her we *wanted* her to stay. Gatlin threw me a stern look, and I swallowed down my protests. I had to trust my Alpha, but it wasn't something that came easily to me.

Gatlin moved his gaze back to Naja. "But I know I speak for us all when I say we would really love for you to stay. You would be safe here, on Manix land. With us."

The silence in the room was heavy, with Naja looking at the floor, her eyebrows drawn tightly together. Fuck, we'd pushed too hard, too fast. We'd known her for like a week. Less than a week. Why would she stay here? We mightn't be strangers in the biblical sense anymore, but hell, we could be skinning humans in the garden shed and she wouldn't know.

Still, she hadn't said no yet, and I clung to that. I walked toward the wet bar, pouring myself a small nip, holding the baby easily in one arm and my drink in the other. Who said men couldn't multitask?

I was starting to get nervous, when she finally looked up at Gatlin, before letting her eyes drift around the room. "How would it work, exactly?"

My heart started to pound in my ears, and it was Raiden who answered. "That's up to you. We can have as little or as much physicality as you like. You can stay here just as a housemate. We'll help you with Luisa." He moved to where she was sitting, folding himself to his knees in front of her. "Or you can see if you like living with our Pack, in every sense of the word. We could be lovers. We could show you how you can be cherished and safe and happy. We'll woo the fuck out of you." He paused. "You can see our cubs being born."

I gritted my teeth. Shit, was that too far? Was she going to bolt before the babies were an unignorable fact of life?

She was silent again for a little while, before she reached out and brushed Raiden's floppy blond hair from his forehead. "I think I'd like that. Like to experience the whole thing with you guys." Her face was heartbreakingly vulnerable at that moment, then I saw her putting up her walls again. "Then when they are born and I'm sure they're okay, I can move on."

I was pretty sure she could hear my heart cracking, though I kept my face stoic. But Ellar? He had no poker face. He looked devastated that she was planning to leave, even if it was months away. But I gave him a reassuring nod. Four and a half months was long enough to make her love us. Just meant we had our work cut out for us.

Finlo whooped and bundled her up into his arms. "You won't be sorry, I promise." He kissed her hard, bending her backwards until she was gripping his shoulders. It was an old-fashioned kiss filled with Hollywood romance. Damn, my Alpha was smooth as fuck.

Gatlin cleared his throat. "She didn't agree to pursuing a physical relationship, Fin. Just to staying. Stop pressuring her." Yeah, Gatlin said the words, but his body was saying something completely different. He wanted her so bad it probably hurt.

Finlo straightened, dropping one small kiss on her forehead before stepping away. "Apologies, Omega."

Naja flushed red. "Well, I guess if I'm going to be here for so long, it couldn't hurt to, you know, explore every aspect of Pack life." Raiden fist pumped the air, and she frowned down at him. "Few rules though. No unsafe sex. I don't wanna have a baby, um, myself anytime soon, okay?"

Gatlin nodded seriously. "Of course. We'll respect your wishes completely." Ah, he was always so cool and formal, like he had no preference which way this went. All business, our Alpha, despite the fact he was as desperate for her to stay as the rest of us and just didn't know how to express it. I hoped that wouldn't stop Naja from giving him—giving us—a chance.

I thought about Naja, heavy with child. Maybe my child. Because while impregnating a male Omega was tough for a Beta, it was as natural as the birds and the bees to conceive with a female Omega. It was just the old-fashioned process. Two people who loved each other, and an hour or two of hot sex. Yeah, I meant a couple of hours; I had a reputation to uphold. Alpha, Beta, Omega, it didn't matter in single births between a man and a woman. We were all on an even playing field.

I kept all this to myself of course, because she really would fucking run as fast as she could if she could read my thoughts. But I could dream.

Naja paused, and I could hear her heartbeat start to speed up again. This made me frown. Her scent didn't say it was because she was horny. No, she smelled of fear. I looked out the windows. No scent that shouldn't be there, nothing out of place.

She kept her eyes on the floor as she said, "I feel

like I should be honest with you guys straight up. Taking me in comes with risk."

My hackles rose and I had to work hard to keep a growl from rumbling past my lips. I didn't want to scare Luisa. But the very idea of potential trouble stalking my Omega made me irrationally angry. I mean, *the* Omega. Not my Omega.

Not yet anyway, I thought and smiled to myself.

"What is it, Omega?" Gatlin asked, his voice clipped like the smell of her fear was getting to him too.

"I kidnapped Luisa from her father. He is kind of, well he *is*, the largest producer of heroin in Mexico. He's a full-blooded tiger Alpha. He's also the most violent cartel boss in the Northern Hemisphere. And he wants me back to sell me to a rival cartel boss for thirty million dollars."

Well, holy fucking shit.

25

NAJA

I wanted a hole to open up in the ground and swallow me as I blurted out my greatest secret to these perfect fucking strangers. I couldn't meet Gatlin's intense gaze so I let my eyes drop to Raiden, who was still kneeling beside my feet. The look of raw rage on the fiery Omega's face had me scooting back in my chair, though he softened it immediately. "I'm sorry, Naja. Just the idea of someone trying to *sell* you makes me feel very un-Omega."

Finlo let out a mirthless laugh. "Omega or not, we are a warrior race for a reason. You are no exception to that, Raiden." Still, Raiden rested his head on my knees and I stroked his hair, because it was impossible to resist. From what I could tell, all the full-blooded Manix were blond. I guess that was genetics for you within a small population. It must have made Gatlin and Ellar stand out even more.

Finlo sat again, steepling his fingers on his chin. "You may need to start from the beginning, Omega."

I let out a shuddering breath, and then sucked in a fortifying lungful of Raiden's calming scent. "I can only tell you what I remember, but from what I know, my mom was from the US. She fell in love with a tiger shifter, who was my dad. She moved back to Mexico with him, and he was part of the cartel too. He died in a bad deal when I was four. My uncle, Luisa's father, refused to let my mom go home. That's when things got..." I hesitated over the true extent of the horrors I'd witnessed, even as a child. "Rough. It's when things got rough."

I'd lived nearly sixteen years in my uncle's care, but I'd always had my mother as a buffer between him and I. She might have been broken and addicted to heroin by the end, though I don't think she'd started out that way, but she was a fierce protector when she could be. She must have had something over my uncle. "My uncle got my mom hooked on drugs, and then they started a relationship. He made it his mission to knock her up every chance he got—hell, I barely remember a time when she wasn't pregnant. Those babies though, they always disappeared within a week of being born." I shuddered as guilt rained down on me. Those tiny faces would forever be etched in my memory, visual representations of my help-lessness.

"Then my mom had Luisa, and it must have been like her twelfth or thirteenth pregnancy. Luisa was born, but my mom didn't make it. She was too weak, too emaciated from a long-term drug addiction. What-ever my uncle was trying to achieve by breeding my mother like a prize poodle didn't happen with Luisa, but I refused to let the last vestige of my mom disap-pear into the night, never to be seen again like the rest of my half-siblings. I fought for her, and my uncle gave in, letting me keep her. I was so stricken with grief that I failed to see he'd given himself a weapon, a tool he could now use to keep me in line and make me do what he wanted me to do." I shook my head about how foolish I'd been, though I had no regrets. I'd been grieving for my mother, sleep-deprived from trying to keep a heroin baby alive, and I was so dreadfully, painfully alone.

"He told me I was going to make him a shit ton of money and cement his position in North America. I couldn't understand why I was worth anything at all. I'd seen hundreds of beautiful women come in and out the doors of the mansion, although some came and never left. But he held Luisa over me like a proverbial gun to my head. Said I could take her with me, but if I didn't do what he asked, he would shoot her in the head himself."

I shuddered as the memories surged back to the surface, the raw wounds that would never heal, the residual fear that would plague me forever.

"He knew you were Manix," Gatlin growled, and I nodded.

"He must have, though if he told me or even said the word, I must have blocked it out. I guess, from what you guys told me, my mom must have been Manix too, but she never said anything about it. I saw her in her tiger form hundreds of times."

Now it was Raiden's turn to frown. "That can't be right. Luisa isn't Manix, she's one hundred percent tiger shifter." He paused, his brows pulling even more tightly together. "Your uncle, he's tiger shifter too?"

I nodded. I'd seen his Beast more times than I'd have liked.

"Your father? Did you ever see him shift?"

I shook my head, though I only had vague memories of the man. He'd had dark, sad eyes, like mine. His front tooth was slightly crooked. Other than that, he was a blur. I couldn't even tell you what the rest of his face looked like. Only those two small details.

Ellar, who'd been silent up until this point, looked between me and Raiden. "You think the father was Manix?"

Raiden shrugged. "At least in part. Even if it was a recessive gene, he could have passed it on to Naja."

I wanted to cry. All those years of fucking pain and

suffering as my uncle had tried to breed another *me* from my mother, and she hadn't been the special one at all. My exhale was choppy and I could feel myself losing it. I should go, hide, not bring this bullshit to the doorstep of these men who'd been nothing but kind to me. Anxiety made my chest feel too tight as I panted to draw air, and suddenly I was in a lap, my head pressed tightly to a chest as it vibrated softly against my cheek.

"Hush, Omega. Hush." Gatlin's voice was just as soothing. Normally I'd be outraged at being hushed like a child, but whatever he was doing was chasing away the panic attack. "You have us now. We will protect you both."

I wanted to laugh in his face because he didn't understand. Maybe the cartel's reach didn't spread this far up, but he'd already found me. "He knows where I am."

Seven growled, then hushed himself as Luisa stirred. "The fucking flower."

I nodded. The fucking flower. "Mexican marigold. It symbolises grief and despair. He said my mother was the embodiment of the marigold. Only celebrated when she was dead."

My body began to shake, and Gatlin held me tighter. Tears threatened to leak from my eyes but I held them back with sheer lady balls. I was tougher than this fucking shaking mess. But being safe and happy for once had made me realize how generally miserable the rest of my life truly was.

Finlo was pacing back and forth now. "We'll have to tell the Legion."

I froze in Gatlin's arms, already shaking my head. "You can't, Finlo. You don't understand—this is not someone to fuck with."

Finlo gave me a truly predatory smile. "You don't understand, baby. You are the last living Omega female. The Manix will fight for you even if they don't know you. *We'd* fight for you, even if we didn't know and respect you already."

"You don't stand a chance."

Finlo grinned, looking at Gatlin for something. Gatlin tensed, shifting me on his lap. "Show her."

Finlo began to strip, shedding all his clothes except his boxers that I definitely didn't stare at. But in the end, he shed those too. He started to shift, his bones stretching and morphing. He got taller, though I didn't know how that was possible considering he was huge already. His flesh sprouted fur, and I'd seen this camouflaged form before, but the dappled calico shade of his fur kept darkening and hardening, until he had what appeared to be scales, or maybe armored plates. Fangs dropped and pressed into his full lower lip. Ears which were kind of round, fluffy Mickey Mouse ears popped out of his head, and a laugh burst from my mouth.

Finlo looked outraged. "Is she laughing at the most fearsome predator on the planet?" he growled. His voice had dropped so low that I could almost feel it more than I could hear it.

I swallowed my laugh and swiped my arm across my eyes, removing the stray tears. "I'm sorry, but the cute fluffy ears kind of detract from the scary exterior."

I could imagine how this eight foot tall, armored, fanged Beast charging at me would be absolutely terrifying. I looked at his hands and noticed that barbed spikes had erupted from each knuckle.

"He also has training that is the equivalent of Special Forces training in the human world," Gatlin whispered.

Seven snorted. "Only better."

Gatlin nodded. "Indeed. We are a weapon, Naja. We've been trained like warriors since the time we could walk. Trust me when I say that threats have come against us, but none have survived yet, and they were a lot scarier than humans with guns."

I stood and walked toward Finlo. I recognized I should be terrified, but when I put my hand out and touched his—I wasn't sure what the hell they were, scales? Plates? They reminded me of a pangolin maybe, the scales smooth and small, overlapping to create an impenetrable armor. They were shades of brown and black, like a wild dog or something, something designed to blend into the scenery. I stroked my hand down his arm to his fists, to the sharp claws and those barbed knuckles. Then I looked at his cock because the guy was like eight feet tall in this form, and I was barely five on a good day. I was basically at perfect blowjob height, so yeah, I was going to look.

His dick had gotten bigger too, and while it didn't have scales, it did seem to have two rows of ridges that ran up his shaft, a little like a Jacob's ladder. It looked... intriguing.

"Omega, you have to stop looking at my dick like that, or I'm going to bend you over the couch and fuck you."

A shiver ran down my spine, pure lust, and I very nearly climbed him like a tree and screamed, "Yes please!"

Instead, I dropped his hand, running my fingers over his hip and walking around his body. Up his back were more barbs, or maybe spikes, that ran along his spine. I stepped back in front of him and motioned him down. He stooped obligingly and I lifted my hand up to trace his face. It was still covered in the same soft fur from his half-form. He twitched his large ears, and honestly, I was done. The laughter bubbled up from my belly, and my shoulders shook as I giggled silently, letting out a snort. I held onto his face with both hands as I hissed with laughter, and he let out a warning rumble.

"Are you laughing at me, Omega?" But I could see

the twinkle of mirth in eyes that were exactly the same shade as his human eyes, only his pupils were wider.

"It's just they're so big, and it's cute when they twitch." I giggled, and he bundled me up in his arms, pressing me to his hard chest. He nuzzled his face into my neck, and I still didn't feel fear, even though those huge fangs traced lines down my throat.

"Want to see what else gets bigger and more dexterous in this form?" His tongue flicked out, and the answer was yes. I really, really, *really* wanted to see.

Gatlin cleared his throat. "Perhaps we can solve our problems before we fall back into more sex?" he suggested, but his eyes held enough heat to cook an egg.

Dammit, he was probably right. But soon, I was going to ride Finlo in this form and see if his scales were waterproof as well.

26

I fucking hated The Legion. They were archaic, pompous and worst of all, my father was their leader. I avoided them where I could, and if it was a choice between visiting them and pulling out a toenail, well, I'd have no nails left in no time.

But of one thing I was very, very sure—if the Legion knew that Naja existed and was under threat, they would move heaven and earth to protect her. But would they also try to take her from us?

Well, they could try.

I realized my lips were curled into a savage grin when Naja's eyes widened. I quickly schooled my features into something less feral. The way she was perusing Finlo in his full Manix form was making my dick hard, but we really did have things to discuss.

"Do you want to stay with us? If not here, then in

Maxton. Because once we tell the Legion of your existence, they will not let you run away again so easily."

She narrowed her eyes. "I'm not swapping one prison for another."

Raiden gave me an exasperated look. "No one is saying you can't leave. But they'd want you to stay in touch, and check in. Like family. They'd want to know you're safe. *We'd* want to know that you're safe," he said, making a sweeping gesture to all of us. He looked at me and raised a brow. "If you felt trapped, we'd help you leave."

And we'd go with you, his eyes said, but he kept that bit to himself. Mostly, because I'd probably argue the point. He was my Omega; I'd keep him where he was safest. I just had to hope it wouldn't come to that, because this woman? She'd worked her way under my skin real fast.

"Fuck yes we would. We do not love this town enough to make you stay if you're uncomfortable. I think the bigger problem is that they will try and persuade you to pick another Pack," Seven said.

The low growl that started in my chest wouldn't be contained behind my lips. "No one makes Naja do anything she doesn't want," I snarled, and Seven held up a hand.

"Of course not, Alpha. I'll fight any fucker who thinks he has a right to take her from us." He cleared his throat. "If she doesn't want to go, I mean. But a battalion of Manix, especially ones who haven't had a good fight in like a damn century, would be like having a human army at your back. We could get rid of your problem once and for all."

Naja looked so torn. It was a lot to think about, I got that. I didn't push her, but also, I was already thinking of ways to fortify the perimeter of our Pack lands. No one knew an area like its native inhabitants, and given that several generations of Manix had been trapped on this small stretch of land for centuries, there was hardly a rock that hadn't been charted.

"We'd have to tell the Legion eventually anyway, because Raiden is going to be big with cub soon enough. But we have the weekend, at least. You can make any decision you need to make and we'll support you. But don't run from us out of fear," I said one last time, just so she knew we were serious.

Ellar, who had been silent up until now, clapped his hands together. "Let's make pizza and watch movies. That's enough craziness for one day."

I nodded, taking in every member of my Pack. I would lay down my life gladly for any of them, and my Beast included Naja in that. Luisa too. He already thought of them as his to love and protect. The man questioned, but the Beast? He just went with his gut every time.

Seven went up first, finally going to put the baby down in its crib. He thought he was playing it so cool, thinking we wouldn't notice that he was clutching that baby like it was a lifeline. He was going to be a great father. They all were.

Raiden was literally made for this life, and for the last few years, his yearnings had been getting harder to satisfy, making him more and more irate, and then depressed once a year. I'd thought we were going to have to find a female for the Pack just so we could appease his Beast.

Ellar was such a nurturer naturally, it was a no-brainer that he would be an amazing parent to our cubs.

Seven though? He liked to pretend that he didn't care about what people thought of him. That he was tough, strong and emotionless. I got that too. Manix society had smacked the poor guy down to what they'd decided his place in the world should be, until he didn't know *who* he was supposed to be. I just wanted him to be whoever he wanted to be. I didn't need him to fit into a preordained slot. I just needed him to be happy.

Finlo was good at whatever he did, and I had no doubt he'd be a great sire. He had such good role models.

Me? I had no fucking idea. My sire had been a piece of shit, and still was. I had no good example of parenting to emulate. I could only rely on my Pack to show me what to do.

I walked up the stairs, catching Naja sneaking off with Ellar in the corner of my eye. I decided to pretend I didn't see it. She needed to confide in someone, and Ellar was the best of us really.

But as much as I tried not to, I couldn't *not* hear her words.

"I wanted to ask you something," she whispered. "If I have to go, will you keep Luisa here with you? I'll come back for her, I swear." There was raw anguish beneath the steel of her words. "But she is collateral to him, not the prize."

"Naja—" Ellar started, but she cut him off.

"Ellar, please. Yes or no?"

I could hear his sigh, the undertone of frustrated helplessness in his voice. "Of course I will. I will take care of her like she's my own child, but it won't come to that. You won't have to run. I swear it."

Her voice got muffled and I thought maybe she was speaking as she hugged him, so I tuned them out as much as I could. I walked toward Raiden, whose eyes were worried. We'd all heard—there were no secrets in a Pack, mainly because Manix had the best hearing of any supernatural on the planet. Well, maybe not the vamps. Those dead fucks heard everything.

But we all pretended to be oblivious when they reappeared moments later. Raiden was making dough like he'd been at it for hours rather than moments, and

I leaned against the countertop sipping a beer that had just appeared in my hand.

She gave us a shaky smile, like she hadn't just offered Ellar her very heart for safekeeping.

I hated the Legion, but I would supplicate myself at their feet for her. That scared me. She wasn't meant to mean this much to me this quickly. She was a means to an end—a way to finally fulfil my Pack's greatest wish. But I wanted her, and not just for the crazy fucking.

Finlo said I had a savior complex, and perhaps I did. Perhaps I needed to be needed, or maybe I was addicted to that look of relief that I saw as they realized the bad times were finally over.

Yeah, okay. Maybe I did have a hero complex, but that wasn't really a bad thing.

"Can I have the week to decide?" Naja asked quietly, and I nodded.

"Take all the time you need."

My Beast though? He was glaringly in control right now. I walked over and picked her up, holding her hesitantly until she wrapped her thighs around my hips. It just felt so fucking right. "Pizza first. Then a movie. Then, if you are amiable, I thought I'd eat you out until you can't feel your thighs."

She froze in my arms, her eyes wide like prey, but quickly relaxed into my embrace, nuzzling her nose into my neck. "I think I'd find that satisfactory."

I rumbled low in my chest, spinning her until she

was sitting on the bench. She spread her thighs and I leaned over her, my hands either side of her hips. "We could skip the pizza and the movie," I purred, and she made a low humming noise.

Then something whacked my knuckles. "Ow!"

I looked around Naja's shoulders at a stern Raiden. "No. First we feed our Omega, then we get to eat. You know this shit. That's a bad Alpha. *Bad Alpha!*"

I gave him a mock growl and darted around the bench top. Raiden yelped and ran, his grin wide.

The little fucker was fast though, always had been. I chased him around the open plan living room but he was still a step or two ahead of me. He dodged around the couch, and I jumped and cleared it easily. I barrelled into his body, the force of my momentum catching him up in my path until he was slammed between the wall and my body. But I lifted my hand to catch the back of his head so it didn't hit the wall. I'd never cause him injury.

He was panting hard. My wild Omega loved a bit of primal play. He liked to be chased—liked to be caught even better though. I lifted my other hand and wrapped it around his throat, and his lips parted. I licked over his pulse point and then along the curve of his jaw, a primal claiming. His life was mine right now, and I could take it with a squeeze of my hand. Instead, I nipped his lip and then plunged my tongue into his mouth, making him moan and grip at my shoulders.

Someone moaned behind us. "This is making me so wet. Should this be making me this wet? Fuck, do you think they'll do it again if I ask nicely?" Naja was asking in a low voice, and whoever she was talking to chuckled low.

"Definitely," Finlo said. "Now tell me what you want on your pizza."

"Sausage. A lot of sausage."

I laughed against Raiden's lips. "Love you, Omega, even if you don't know your place."

He ran a hand up the back of my head, twisting my hair in his fingers and tugging. "Alpha, you love me *because* I don't know my place."

I chuckled low because he was so fucking right.

27

ELLAR

The times when the Pack were all together were my favorites. We would be one large pile of arms and legs, laughter and kisses. I hadn't thought I could enjoy anything more than I enjoyed those moments, but I'd been wrong. Naja made them better. She lay beside me, her head on my arm as we watched some mindless chick flick. She still smelled so good, but it was less of the primal reaction to her heat and more because she just smelled good. Like violets.

It wasn't just me either. Everyone was in touching distance, even if they weren't openly touching her. Well, Raiden had no qualms whatsoever. He had his head on her stomach, his hands wrapped around her thigh like it was his favorite teddy.

I was no longer watching the movie; instead, I was watching her. Her long lashes brushed her cheeks as she blinked sleepily at the television, her lips slightly parted and looking so damn kissable.

She turned toward me. Oops, busted... "Are you going to kiss me already?"

Someone laughed softly, but I didn't care. I wasn't going to argue. I caught her lips with mine, and she let out a soft sigh as she kissed me back. This was better. It wasn't the insanity of the heat, and I knew she was kissing me because she wanted me, not because she had the biological urge to mate.

I deepened the kiss, tracing her lips with my tongue as my hand traced down her ribs and splayed across the soft rise of her stomach. She felt like heaven. We continued to kiss, until I felt Raiden shift beside her, his hands tugging at her soft sweats. She lifted her ass, and I didn't protest Raiden joining in. Everything was more fun together, and that included sex. Once he'd freed her from the confines of her pants, I rolled her onto my body, so her breasts pressed to my chest. Fuck, she felt like she was made for me, but I was beginning to think we all felt that way. I felt Raiden kneel between my thighs, leaning up to prop up her hips, and then she hissed against my lips, her body bucking.

It didn't take a genius to know what he was doing,

especially not with my sense of smell. Her need perfumed the air, and Raiden could probably feel the hard line of my dick against his stomach too. The height difference between us all would be hilarious if I didn't love that I could throw her around like a doll.

I felt Raiden's hand reach down to the waistband of my pants and tug at them too. My greedy Omega wanted us all naked apparently. I lifted my ass, making it easier for him to drag them down my legs while he ate out our girl.

See, multitasking.

Naja was panting against my lips now, and I kneaded her ass because it was fucking glorious. "Oh fuck, I'm going to come," she gasped, and I growled low in my chest, a sound that echoed around the room. Raiden pulled back, and I saw a condom flying through the air. Thinking Raiden was going to ride her, I was surprised when I felt his hands grab my straining dick and sheathe it. If I wasn't obsessed with kissing Naja right then, I'd thank Raiden from the bottom of my heart. As it was, I dragged my lips away.

"Baby, I'm going to let you ride me now. Do you want that? Do you want to come around my dick, or do you want Raiden to keep eating that delicious little pussy?"

I felt her convulse beneath my hands. "Dirty mouth," she moaned. "I want you inside me, Ellar."

Oh, she used my name, and I was going to make her scream it again and again before we were done. I felt Raiden's hand line me up against the sweet clutch of her core and then I slid her down slowly, my eyes crossing as I scrunched my lids closed. Jesus, she felt amazing. She curled herself up until she was seated on me like a damn queen. So beautiful. We were all watching her as she rolled against me, and she must have known. It didn't make her shy, oh no. She fucking soaked up our attention like she knew she was perfection.

I gripped her hips tightly, holding her as she pistoned up and down on my dick. I gritted my teeth because I refused to be a two pump chump. Holding her tightly, I tried not to think about how glorious she felt on my cock. Or the soft little moans she was making. Goddammit. I slid my thumb around to her clit and tapped it in time with her movements.

She threw her head back as she came on a moan. She collapsed back onto my chest, but I wasn't done yet, oh no. I'd promised myself that she would scream my name before we were done. I'd vowed to.

I rolled her onto her back, not even withdrawing from the warmth of her body. Then I slowly rolled my hips, deep and hard, and her thighs slammed around my hips so hard that I knew I was hitting the right spot. I quickened just a touch, my rhythm fluid, until her heels were pressed so hard into my ass I was probably going to have bruises. She was now chanting my name like a plea. I grabbed her thigh, slipping it over my shoulder, not changing my pace or angle, just going deeper.

"Oh god, fuck, Ellar," she moaned, and it was the sweetest thing I'd ever heard. "Don't stop, I'm close again, oh god!"

She came on my cock once more, clenching around me like a fist until I was coming right behind her. I slammed my way home through her orgasm and mine until I collapsed on top of her, completely spent.

I curled down, kissing her lips as I withdrew. Her cheeks were flushed, her hair everywhere, and I'd never seen anything more beautiful.

I couldn't help myself. "I hope you can stay," I said softly, and I felt her tense. *Idiot Beta. Can't fucking help yourself,* I chastised myself.

Instead of pulling away though, she wrapped her arms around my ribs and pulled me down, so I was blanketing her, hiding her from the world.

"I hope so too."

THE NEXT MORNING, my mouth was dry and my body was sore. Last night had just been a warm-up, because as soon as I'd climbed off Naja, Finlo had picked her up and dragged her back to his room, first to sleep but

I soon heard her muffled moans. Footsteps padded up and down the hall all night as we swapped her between beds, but if we kept that up, we were all going to be zombies with insomnia.

This morning, I was making everyone a massive breakfast, with Luisa sitting in a highchair beside me, eating fruit while I cooked something more substantial. Muffins, bacon, eggs, and sausages were definite, but I should really ask Naja what she enjoyed. Maybe call down and get a delivery. Hell, maybe I could go into town.

I looked over at Luisa. "What about you, Little Bit? What do you like?"

"Scream!" she yelled.

I snorted. "You got that right. Hmm, scream.." Deciphering toddler-speak was hard. "Ice cream?"

She went off on an excited tangent of gibberish with the word yes interspersed in there, so I was taking that as an affirmative. "Okay, Little Bit. I'm putting ice cream down on the list."

I turned toward the hall to grab the notepad. I'd make a list and then email it. Spinning back to the kitchen, I noticed a scent that shouldn't be there.

Then I spotted a figure on the porch.

"Gatlin!" I roared, shifting to my Manix Beast form as I raced back to Luisa, lifting her out of her highchair and into my arms.

Gatlin, Finlo and Seven all appeared nearly

instantly. I couldn't find Naja or Raiden, but I assumed they were still further in the house. I held Luisa safe in my arms, and now that the panic had lessened, I realized it was Wilkie and his primary Beta.

Fucking Wilkie.

I realized the baby was stiff in my arms and I drew back to look at her. "Sorry, Little Bit. It's just me, but kind of fluffy. Like a mouse, see?" I twitched my ears, and she lifted a tentative hand to stroke the soft fur on my face. She still looked a little pale and her face was scrunched in consternation, but she didn't cry or freak out the way you'd expect a child to react to what was essentially a monster holding her. Maybe she still knew it was me?

"Take the baby to the back," Finlo rumbled, already fully shifted too. I did what I was told, my scaled arms around Luisa protectively. As I made it to the door of Raiden's room, it was pulled open and Raiden dragged me inside. Naja grabbed Luisa, her face pale.

"It's okay, Omega. I'm sorry for scaring you. It's just Wilkie. I just acted instinctively." I held out my hand to her. "I'm sorry."

She grabbed it and squeezed. "Better to be too careful, right?"

Raiden nodded, but his face went really red. Uh oh. "Fucking Wilkie. I'm going to tear him another asshole."

He slammed out of the room, and for once, I was torn. Well, not really. Raiden could handle himself, and I didn't think Wilkie's Pack were actually a threat. They were showboaters and assholes, but wouldn't act out in violence. Well, probably not until my hot-headed Omega started throwing punches. Then it would be a brawl. I could talk him down, but I couldn't leave Naja and Luisa either on the off chance I was wrong. That Wilkie's Pack was more desperate than I thought. Without the pheromones of the heat, I liked to think that most of my kind would be civilized. But you could never be sure.

I opened the door and I could already hear the snarls. Naja put her hand between my shoulder blades. "Are they a threat to Luisa?"

I shook my head. Wilkie was a dick, but he was an old school dick, which meant he wholeheartedly believed that hurting a child should have the punishment of death. Manix were do or die when it came to that. But they also considered you eligible for the Legion Force—our army—at fourteen, so it was a bit of a grey area. But a girl, and a toddler at that? There was nowhere on earth she would be safer than in Manix territory.

Naja shifted Luisa onto her hip. The baby, despite the drama of being whisked away, didn't seem as perturbed as last time, like she already knew we would keep her safe.

Naja waved a hand at the door. "Well, let's go shut this shit down then?" She pushed me through the door and marched down the hall. The Goddess had apparently blessed me with two fiery Omegas. Lucky me.

At the end of the hall was a cacophony of growls and snarls, and I pushed her slightly behind me. I wasn't much of a fighter but I was still shifted. When we strode into the room, all snarling and conversation stopped.

Wilkie scented the air, and I knew what he was sensing. The lack of heat. There was only one way that happened, and it was when the female Omega's body had completed its physiological purpose and handed off her eggs.

Wilkie was old school; he knew what the lack of heat meant. His eyes whipped between Finlo and Raiden—he always refused to acknowledge Gatlin as Alpha due to his mixed heritage—then back to Naja.

"You did it? It worked?"

Raiden looked at him, wild-eyed. "That's none of your fucking business. Leave."

I looked at Wilkie's Betas, because Wilkie only ever had Betas. I understood their forlorn look of longing. They didn't have a male Omega, although Raiden's sister, who was part of their Pack, was a Beta. She provided the softness to their hard edges. Gatlin hated her, but I saw her for what she was. Sad. She knew she was a substitute for what the Pack really wanted. Wilkie had always made that known in no uncertain terms. The man was an asshole.

Stephan, Wilkie's second in command, murmured softly in his ear, "We should go."

Wilkie gave Naja a hard-eyed glare. "With her, we could attract another Omega male. I could have a litter of cubs. Pass on my genetics to the next generation."

Ew.

Naja, bless her heart, screwed up her nose. "Ew. Unlikely, asshole."

Apparently, it was now too much for Gatlin because he roared, his fangs bared and his chest heaving. "Get out!"

I implored Stephan with my eyes to do the right thing. He was a nice guy when he wasn't under Wilkie's thumb. He'd cleaned me up that first week after I'd arrived in Maxton, after the other kids had kicked me into the dirt and stomped me to make sure I stayed down. He motioned for the two other Betas to move, which they did, but they remained in their fully shifted forms.

Wilkie was the last to leave, and he eyed both Raiden and Naja hungrily. "The Legion will hear of this. They'll pass the Omegas over to a more worthy Pack. A Pack that will strengthen the Manix bloodlines rather than weakening it."

With that, he strode out the doors, jumped the porch railing and landed effortlessly on the ground. He was right about one thing—he did have good bloodlines.

But he was crazy if he thought we'd give her up without a fight.

Fuck. I tried to not be *that* person, the one who bemoans her life and wallows in self-pity. I knew for a fact there were people out there who had it worse than I did. The ones who were at the bottom of a barrel of misery from which there was no return, and that was their reality day after day. Fuck, I'd met some of those people.

But I couldn't help but think that maybe Fate liked to kick me around a little. I'd obviously done something to piss her off, so that whenever I got the tiniest ray of happiness, she made sure to snuff it out as soon as possible.

Or maybe she just wouldn't let me wallow on the fence. Maybe she liked to drive me to hard decisions so I got to my happiness quicker. I was going to go with that because the other option was too depressing to consider.

I was sitting out on the porch swing, moving backward and forwards softly while Luisa played beside me. She was already more secure here, happier. She wasn't even overtly perturbed by the terrifying visage of the guys in their Manix forms.

I liked it here too. And it wasn't just the orgasms, though they were pretty amazing. I liked the company. The safety. I liked that they were a family, though I wasn't sure I even knew what that was supposed to feel like.

If I ran, I'd be running forever. I wanted to pretend that I could circle back in a few years and grab Luisa. That I could offer her any sort of life except one of transience. But I knew if I left, I'd never see her again because I could never be that selfish.

If I took what they were offering, I could be free... Or I could be dead. And so could they. And Luisa.

I leaned my head back against the swing, and pushed us gently. The guys had left me alone to make my choice, so I didn't feel pressured, I guess. I knew what they wanted me to do.

A figure blocked out the sun and I realized it was Seven. He was looking down at us, his shirt long since gone. He made my mouth water, like he was a feast and I was just on the other side of the glass window looking in. He could be mine, if only I had the balls to open the door. He gave me a half-smile. "May I sit?"

I nodded and shuffled Luisa into the center of the swing so Seven could sit on the other side. The whole apparatus groaned under his weight but held. He took over the gentle swinging motion. "You should stay."

I opened my mouth to tell him all the reasons I couldn't stay, including endangering them all, but he held up a hand to stop me. "But if you want to leave, you need to do it now and never return. Even if you leave Luisa, don't come back."

So many emotions stole my breath. Anger, outrage, fear, desolation. How dare he tell me I couldn't come back for Luisa? Who the hell did he think he was?

"I know what you're thinking, but you don't know my Pack—you can't see the effect you're having already. You fit with us like you were made to be here, like you were meant to be one of us. Raiden is absolutely smitten, and Ellar? I'm pretty sure if you left today, his heart would break anyway." His eyes turned sad. "The longer you wait, the more attached we all get, and the more your leaving will break us."

I shook my head like I could shake his words from my brain. "I barely know you. You can't say that; you may hate me in a month. You can't know that they will feel anything for me."

The look he gave me would have made weaker women quake in their boots. I was being purposefully obtuse, because I couldn't take the responsibility of one more person's happiness on my shoulders, let alone five.

Seven picked up Luisa, shifting her onto his knee and scooting closer to me. "Don't run. Stay and explore this thing we have. Build something with us. It's a risk—we know it too." He gripped my hand. "You're worth the risk."

We sat in silence for a little longer, and eventually Luisa got bored and began to explore the porch on her own. Like any true shifter child, she loved being outdoors, being one with nature. She loved it here.

I snorted internally. I loved it here, I just refused to admit it to myself. I felt like I was home. Maybe that was the feelings of the inner Manix I never knew I had, or maybe it was just because it smelled like freedom, I don't know.

Seven didn't say anything else, but I found myself moving into him, borrowing his strength as my brain whirled with 'what-ifs.' The uncertainty of the future was plaguing me. I rested my head against his arm, closing my eyes because for once in my life, I was sure that there would be someone else there to watch Luisa.

I could rest. I was barely twenty-one and I was exhausted. Seven brushed my hair off my face, but didn't try to manhandle me any more than that. He was just an anchor. I blinked my eyes open and looked up at him. He'd told me that *they* wanted me to stay. That they would suffer if I left.

"Do you want me to stay?"

He took his eyes off the baby for a moment to meet and hold my eyes. "More than I've wanted anything in my whole life."

I swallowed hard, nodding and dragging my eyes away in case he saw how much his words meant. "Then I'll stay."

The low thrum in his chest was the only reason I knew he'd heard my words, and that he was happy as we fell back into an easy silence.

WHILE SEVEN'S RESPONSE TO my decision had been subtle, Raiden's was the exact opposite. He'd whooped for joy and gathered me in a hug that threatened to crack ribs. He'd kissed me hard and I'd kissed him back. Finlo had grinned and bundled me up into a hug of his own, and Ellar had kissed me with a heart-breaking tenderness. Gatlin had smiled and looked pleased, and I had a feeling that was something significant. He was a man of action though.

"We should get ahead of Wilkie. He'll be getting his shit all figured out so he can present himself as the best possible candidate for the last female Omega, but if we walk into the Legion as a *fait accompli*, then it'll be harder for them to find a reason to protest," he said, as we sat around the dining table that night.

I nodded, watching Finlo take a sleeping Luisa off to her crib. At this rate, I was going to lose my Mom-biceps. The ones you get from deadlifting thirty pounds twelve hours a day. It was nice though, almost too nice. I felt guilty, though I didn't know if I was guilty that they had to do my job for me, or guilty that Luisa wasn't getting the same one on one time with me she used to get.

On second thoughts, probably not, considering normally I'd be at work twelve hours of the day. Still, residual guilt was a bitch.

"Okay, so we go and see them tomorrow. What do I need to know?"

Everyone looked at Finlo as he walked back into the room, and he sighed. "I hated high school. Why do I always get stuck with the academic questions?" he whined, then he grabbed me and dragged me to the couch, settling me on his lap. "On second thoughts, I'd be okay with these studying arrangements." His big hand wrapped around my thigh, and I silently willed him higher. Gatlin cleared his throat pointedly, and Finlo stuck out his tongue.

"Always the killjoy, that one. Okay, so the Manix are governed by the Legion. They were the Manix army in the old days, and were separate to the Alpha ruling family. When the ruling family was killed during an attack a couple of centuries ago, the Legion took control. They make the decisions, dole out the punishments and generally see to the day-to-day running and defense of Maxton. They are run by an Alpha General, who is our Alpha now, I guess." He slid a look to Gatlin, whose face looked stony. Ah, there was history there, but now was not the time to mine that secret. "There's only a couple of thousand of us left, so it isn't a taxing job. But we keep a specialist elite force of warriors on hand, the Legion Force, and everyone gets combat training from child-hood. Generally, we are just like a normal Pack of supernaturals. We follow the same social hierarchy as, say, wolves."

"Except we are stuck a hundred years in the past with our social values," Raiden growled from where he'd flopped down on the other end of the couch.

Finlo squeezed me harder. "Yes, except that. With us all being separate from the greater part of human or supernatural society, our views tend to be conservative to the point of detrimental. Half-caste Manix are treated with general disdain by some elements of the community, irrespective of their strength. Omegas are like the 1930s housewives, intended to be seen and not heard. Anything out of the ordinary is viewed with suspicion, and basically it's open season for the strong to prey on the weak."

I wanted to be outraged at the barbarism, which I

was, but wasn't human society still like this in some places? It wasn't just a Manix condition, that's for sure.

I looked around at them all and suddenly understood them better. They were the ones that were cast outside the mold. The different ones. It was what made them so unique, so special.

"And what'll happen tomorrow?"

Gatlin gave me a purely crocodile grin. "Tomorrow we blow their tiny little minds."

I'd wanted to stay home with Luisa, but Gatlin had put his foot down. We needed to show a united front, and if the cub and I stayed home, he'd have to leave Finlo and Seven with us for protection. I got it. He hated the idea of splitting up his Omegas right now, but still, this sucked.

This morning, Gatlin had smelled the change in my physiology that meant that at least one of the zygotes had taken. I was pregnant.

I'd never thought I could be so happy.

Or so scared.

It was like a switch had flicked in my brain now, and the people and places I'd known my whole life were suddenly potential threats to my cubs. I eyed them all warily, knowing that they'd pick up the change in my scent too, if they focused on it hard enough. Maybe the sight of Naja would distract them enough they'd miss it.

It wouldn't fool the Legion though.

Finlo was on the phone to his dads, who'd all meet us at the Legion headquarters. It sounded like it would be something impressive, but really it was just an ordinary wooden building. Behind it were barracks for single men in the Legion Force and some of the peripheral workers of the Legion. Families had homes around the outskirts, some provided by the town, and others—like us—had built on land bought and annexed from the Legion, a benefit granted for Manix who formed their own Packs.

We pulled the ATVs up to the front steps of the Legion HQ, and I helped Naja down. Ellar climbed off with Luisa in his arms, and already I could feel eyes on us from every direction. Finlo's parents, all four of them, walked down the steps to meet us. They were there for support, and given the wideness of their eyes, they were taking in all the new scents, including my pregnancy.

Selena's grin got impossibly wider. "Congratulations again," she murmured to Finlo under her breath, though I could tell what she actually wanted to do was yell it so every person in Maxton would know she was going to be a grandma.

"Thanks, Mom." He gave the older Manix woman a hug. He looked at his dads, the ones who hadn't come around the other day—Jeff and Jack. "Did Wilkie make it here first?"

Jack shook his head. "No, and you can bet we would have heard about it by now. Come on, the Alpha General will be having his daily update with the rest of the Legion Generals. Can't think of a better time to spring this on them," he said with a grin. Jack was a rabble-rouser, that was for sure. Finlo was definitely his kid.

Gatlin held his head high as he walked inside. It was an average-looking building, but the men inside held our future in their hands.

Selena stopped Naja with a hand on her arm. "Would you like me to watch the little one for you?" She asked it softly, her face reassuring and open. I watched Naja hesitate, her natural suspicion of people warring with the warm sense of rightness that Selena naturally gave off. I could have reassured Naja, but it had to be her choice.

Naja finally nodded, although she left it up to Luisa. Selena wasn't a dumb woman; she reached into her purse and pulled out a chocolate bar. Luisa reached out with grabby hands and Naja let out a soft laugh. She let the baby go into the arms of Finlo's mother. As if she'd been prepared for this moment, Selena also pulled out a giraffe toy.

Finlo chuckled. "Really, Mom? Bribery already?"

Selena just raised a brow. "I take my role as a

grandmother very seriously, son." With that, she plopped down onto the ground of the foyer with Luisa to play giraffes and eat chocolate.

Orson looked down at them fondly. "I'll watch over them," he promised Naja. It was a reassuring statement. Orson was built like a hundred-year-old tree. Giant and immovable.

Naja nodded and swallowed hard. "Thank you."

Orson shook his head. "No, child. Thank *you*."

Finlo put his hand on Naja's lower back and urged her further into the building, with the guys reflexively forming a barrier around us. We stopped at the huge double doors that led to the Alpha General's office. Radic, the Alpha General's secretary, looked between us all. Radic was a Beta and a nice guy. He was efficient and took no shit, but he was the more empathetic arm of the Legion, and although he was only a secretary, he wielded a fair amount of clout. If you want to appeal to someone for a favor, you didn't ask the Legion Generals. You asked Radic, and Rad would either give you what you wanted on the down-low, or pass it up the chain.

He frowned at his computer and then back at us. "You guys don't have an appointment." His eyes lingered on Gatlin, because just the appearance of Gatlin meant drama. There was a reason we avoided Maxton like the plague most of the time.

"No."

"The Alpha General is in a meeting," Radic said hesitantly.

Gatlin stepped to the side and revealed Naja. "Take a deep breath, Beta." Radic did as instructed and his jaw dropped. He looked at Naja, then back at me, then back at Naja.

"She's... and Raiden is..."

Gatlin smiled. Well, less of a smile and more baring his teeth. "They're going to want to see us, now."

Radic nodded, and I could see the small grin on his face. "I believe you're right." He picked up the phone and pressed some buttons. "Sorry for the interruption, Sir, but there's something you need to see." He went silent. "I promise this is important. I'm sending them in."

Then he just hung up. On the Alpha General. Rad had balls of steel, and I grinned. He motioned us toward the door. "Go in."

The guys formed a tight diamond around us again, with Finlo and his dads bringing up the rear. Gatlin would lead our Pack and Finlo would guard our backs. It was how we'd always worked as a team. In the beginning, it had irked me that they always placed me in the center; I was just as capable of saving our asses as they were. After a while, I realized it was because I was their heart, their nucleus. I was the thing that held them together, and there was honor in that. It was something to be proud of.

The Alpha General's office was a large room, and there were six Alphas in there—the Legion Generals. They all looked basically the same, all through the different generations. Big, blocky and blond. If they didn't loosen the reins soon and let in some new blood, we'd be looking down the barrel of extinction sooner rather than later, purely from inbreeding.

The Alpha General stood. I'd forgotten how intimidating he was, even though I jutted out my chin. I caught my own father's eyes, and he just raised a single brow at me. He wasn't a bad man. He was just a Legion General through and through. He'd done what he could for his Omega son, given me the freedom I needed, taught me to focus the anger I had. He didn't treat me any different to my Alpha brothers or my Beta sister. My mother had died in childbirth when I was a cub, so he'd had no idea of what to do otherwise. Even my sister was an expert marksman and could shoot an arrow through a wedding ring.

I gave him an imploring look, as the Alpha General flushed.

"What's the meaning of this, Gatlin? Just because you are my offspring doesn't mean you have the right to barge in like you own the damn place," he growled, which made all the hairs on my body stand up.

Naja threw me a look, and I winced, apologizing silently. We should have told her that Gatlin was the only son of the Alpha General, but Gatlin hated the man with a passion. We never mentioned their connection, and the fact that the Alpha General was insinuating that Gatlin was trading on it was outrageous.

Instead, Gatlin half-stepped to the side, just enough to reveal Naja. The Legion Generals were arguably the strongest of our kind, so it didn't take them long to decipher her scent. And then even less time to figure out that I was pregnant.

My father jumped to his feet, his shock written all over his face. "How?" he gasped. He looked pale, and I kind of hoped that we hadn't given him a heart attack. I wasn't as close to him as Finlo was to his parents, but I didn't wish him dead, that was for sure.

I grinned, ready to give him the birds and the bees talk, but he waved a hand to cut me off. Yeah, he knew me well enough. "Not that. How is she possible?"

Gatlin growled. "She has a name. This is Naja, last of the female Omegas. You want to throw her out because she's not a pureblood, Father?"

I winced, because the Alpha General deserved it, but damn, we needed him on our side right now. I put my hand out to soothe Gatlin, but Naja got there first. See, I knew she was perfect for us. She gripped his fingers and he squeezed hers back. The movement wasn't missed by the Alpha either.

"What do you want, Gatlin? I'm assuming this magical reveal has a point?"

"Naja belongs to the Huxley-Grey Pack. She is the mother of our future cubs. She is ours." The last bit was more Beast than man, the Alpha power in his statement making my skin prickle.

Ah, there was the glaringly unmistakable truth that came up any time Gatlin and the Alpha General were in a room together—the elephant if you will—that no one wanted to mention. That if Gatlin hadn't been a half-blood, he would have been Alpha General. He would have been the most powerful Alpha Manix to ever live, and his father hated it. Hated that his half-blood son was almost as powerful as him. Gatlin hiding in the hills worked for him too, because it would never be too obvious that he was a strong Manix, despite the 'watering down' of his Manix blood.

The Alpha General gritted his teeth as he stared down his son. "You do not get to choose who the Omega female bonds with, Gatlin. And you do not get to make the decisions in this office."

Naja straightened. "He's right. You don't get to choose, Gatlin Huxley. I do."

My heart stopped when Naja contradicted Gatlin and agreed with the Alpha General. Fuck, maybe she wanted a different Pack. Hell, maybe she didn't want any Pack. Had we thought to ask her if she wanted to stay, but not with us? I couldn't remember.

She cleared her throat. "Gatlin doesn't get to choose for me, and neither do you, Alpha," she said with steel in her voice. "I make my own decisions, decide on my own path in life, and no one—not Gatlin, not you, no one—gets to tell me otherwise."

Gah, she was so fucking hot as she stared down a room of Alphas, this sexy as fuck Omega. Raiden's father inclined his head. "Of course, Omega. It is one of our oldest traditions that Omegas choose their own Pack. We wouldn't consider interfering, even if their decision isn't one we approve of. The Goddess decides."

She gave him a soft smile, and I was glad we'd warned her that Raiden's father was a member of the Legion Generals. It was easy to tell he was Raiden's father too; he was a carbon copy of his son.

"I'm glad," she said softly. "Then you will respect my decision when I say I choose the Huxley-Grey Pack. As you say, the Goddess decides, and to say that their finding me was anything less than divine intervention would be to spit in her eye."

Yep. I'd popped a boner. Fuck, she was gorgeous. My dad cleared his throat, frowning at me, and I shrugged sheepishly.

Theodore, one of the younger Legion Generals, frowned. "You haven't even met any of the other Omegas or Packs, how can you know that the Huxley-Grey Pack is the right one for you?"

Theodore was an entirely reasonable guy with a lot of ambition, and a good heart. I hated him. I knew exactly what Pack he meant—he wanted her to consider his Pack. I was about to get myself thrown in lock-up for hurdling a table and smashing my fist into the pretty face of a Legion General.

Naja, obviously seeing the same hopefulness, gave him a soft look. "I've met Wilkie several times now, as well as his Pack, and I'm not inspired." Theodore winced. Yeah, Wilkie wasn't known for his tact and not exactly a poster boy for the Manix either. Naja chewed her lip. "Look, I understand what I represent. But I won't be a broodmare, or a baby maker, for anyone."

"Anyone but the Huxley-Grey Pack. Hardly strong stock to continue our legacy with," Legion General Eldridge grumbled, and I snarled loudly. My dad reached out to grab my arm, but he was snarling too.

"Let's get one thing straight. I don't give a fuck about your legacy, and honestly, if the rest of the Manix are like you, then good riddance," Naja said coldly. "This Pack is full of males of worth, who would have protected me without expecting anything in return. They are my choice."

Theodore threw Eldridge a cold look. "We appreciate that, Omega. We aren't trying to change your mind." He looked around at the other Alphas, but no one seemed to be willing to back him. "Perhaps you'd consent to our medical staff running some tests to see why you are an Omega, since this is a trait that disappeared from our own females generations ago? Also, congratulations to your Pack on the successful breeding. Our race will celebrate the birth of your cubs."

Naja nodded, and I felt relief for my people. Test tube Omegas were going to be no good to this generation, but perhaps the next generation may be able to experience the joy we were feeling.

I cleared my throat. "That brings us to our second point. Naja is being hunted by a tiger shifter who is the head honcho of a cartel that wants to sell her to the highest bidder." I paused as I watched that sink in. "My Pack would appreciate any aid the Legion could give us in protecting her."

I could see the Alpha General wanted to tell us to fuck off, but Raiden's father, a man who was just as decorated and strong as the Alpha General, nodded. "Of course we will help you protect the last remaining female Omega. She possibly holds the key to our future in her DNA. We wouldn't be so short-sighted as to let her fend for herself." He grinned at Naja and Raiden. "Besides, it's been a decade since we've had a good fight, and the men are getting disgruntled."

I rolled my eyes, but Naja smiled. "Thank you, Sir."

Silence fell over the room, and I took that as our cue to leave. Apparently, so did the Alpha General. "You've rubbed all our noses in it now, Gatlin. You can leave. We will send up Murphy and Merrick tomorrow to work out what defenses you will need. You are dismissed."

I saw Gatlin's whole body vibrating with tension, but Naja tugged on his hand and he followed us out, his eyes never leaving the other Alphas in the room.

Joshua, Raiden's father, caught up with us in the hall. "Wait a second, I'd like a word." We all stopped except Naja, who met Mom further down the hall and took Luisa back into her arms. Joshua stood in front of Raiden. "Son. I'm so... "

"Excited, ecstatic, over the moon, proud. Any of those would work, Joshua," my mom snarked, and Joshua rolled his eyes.

"All of those things and so much more. You've created a miracle." He grabbed Raiden's shoulders and dragged him into a hug.

That was the real miracle of the day. Joshua wasn't a hugger. He was a man of very little outward emotion.

Raiden stood there stunned, before lifting a hand to pat his father's back. "Hopefully there's more than one miracle in there, though we'd be ecstatic with just one."

Joshua stepped back, and if I didn't know the man, I'd say he was a little misty. "Of course. If you need anything, please let me know. Your brothers and I would be only too happy to help."

He didn't mention Raiden's sister, who was truly under Wilkie's thumb. He looked over at Naja, suddenly spotting Luisa in her arms. "Who is this?"

Oh shit, yeah, we'd kinda forgotten to mention she already had a kid.

"My sister, Luisa. I have raised her as my child since our mother died during childbirth."

Joshua swallowed hard. Naja couldn't have known that it reflected so closely what had happened to his mate. He gave a sharp nod. "You're a good sibling. I best get back in there before they decide on something ridiculous. I hope to see you again soon?"

Raiden nodded. "Of course, Father."

Joshua turned on his heel with military precision, and then it was just us left. "Let's do a quick tour of the town and then you can take your pretty Omega home. What do you say?" Mom said softly. One of my dads must have caught her up on what happened in the Alpha General's office.

Maxton wasn't a big town. It had twelve square blocks of housing, a store that was more like a commissary, the Legion barracks and building, and then surrounding farms, mostly livestock. It was too hard to stay off the map and plant full crops. The town itself was built on the banks of a large mountain lake that was carefully fished so that it could provide a source of food for years to come.

But there was a cafe to get coffee, plus a small park for children. A bar to play pool and find a warm body for the night. A school and a mechanic. Maxton's population was generally happy with small town life, and most people stayed, either because they formed a Pack when they were young, they were scared, or they were just generally happy maintaining the status quo. Some left, and I couldn't blame them. Some people had ambitions bigger than what Maxton could provide. The Legion stayed in constant contact with them, and if you didn't check in once a week, they'd send the Legion Force down to kick your ass for worrying them.

I shook my head. "Just the commissary, then I want to take my Omegas back to my territory."

Raiden punched him in the arm. "Enough of this 'my Omegas' business. You are beginning to sound like a General." I grimaced and he laughed. "I'd like to stop at the commissary though, to order some baby things for Luisa and for the cubs."

My mom squealed again, and I rolled my eyes. I didn't think she was going to stop doing that until she held a cub in her arms. We headed out of the building and down the steps, crossing the road to head toward the commissary. We got so many looks that it was getting hard to ignore, but my dad had been right—the news of Naja, and of Raiden's pregnancy, would have spread through town even before we stepped through our front door this afternoon.

31

NAJA

Two weeks later, it was easy to forget that life had ever been uncertain. We settled into a routine that was so comfortable, it was easy to lull myself into complacency. It didn't hurt that there were now extra patrols on our quadrant. The stern-faced men who were with the Legion Force had visited, as promised, and openly gazed at me like I was a miracle. I was like a beacon of hope, but these guys weren't looking at me like I might provide them heirs. They were looking at me like I was the return of the Goddess' blessing. Like I was heralding the return of the female Omega.

It was disconcerting, even though they'd been perfectly respectful. I'd been glad once they left and it was back to being just me and the guys. Now that I'd committed to staying, they seemed happy to let our relationship progress at a more natural pace. Which meant no more orgies.

Honestly, I was a little put out.

Now that the heat was gone, I couldn't use that as an excuse anymore, and had to actually admit to myself that I just wanted to ride them all like I was the only cowgirl in the rodeo.

Everyone was pretty giddy with excitement today though, because the guys had sunk an absolute shit ton of money into an at-home, medical grade ultrasound machine. I mean, I was antisocial, but buying your own ultrasound machine so you didn't have to travel to town was next level.

We all huddled around Raiden's bed as Gatlin worked his way through the instructions. Finally, he plugged it into his smartphone with a humph, and pulled up the program. I leaned back against Ellar, who kissed my cheek. "Isn't it too soon to hear heartbeats? It's been what, like a couple of weeks?"

Ellar nuzzled my hair; he was easily the most physically affectionate of the guys. It was like he couldn't help but touch me, and I wasn't complaining. Despite having been groped every night at the club, I'd come to realize I was touch starved. "Manix gestation is quicker. Given there are usually multiple cubs, they tend to be smaller when they are born, but just as strong as normal human children. So we should be able to hear heartbeats, though I don't think we'll get a clear picture of them yet."

Excitement was written over all their faces. I was nervous. What if my eggs were defective because I was half tiger? What if Gatlin's nose was broken and they hadn't actually conceived? Would they still want me if I couldn't give them babies?

Raiden must have sensed my anxiety, because he reached out a hand. "Come and lie with me."

I crawled up the bed and lay beside him, my head pillowed on the crook of his arm. He leaned down, kissing me softly. "It'll be okay, baby. I *know* I'm with cub, but even if I'm not, it changes nothing. I promise."

Hands stroked soothingly down my back and arms as they all reassured me. I was going to cry, but I swallowed hard. Gatlin leaned down to kiss Raiden, and then me. "Let's do this."

He handed it over to Seven, who'd become designated ultrasound technician. They'd decided his videogame skills were basically transferable, which had made me laugh my ass off. We all held our breath as he slid the wand over Raiden's abdominal muscles, the sound of silence dragging on and on until I wouldn't have heard anything over the sound of my own pounding heart. Seven continued to move it around until a frenetic sound boomed out of Gatlin's smartphone. Not just one heartbeat, but several.

I let out a relieved laugh as we all looked at the

screen. Honestly, I was looking at a Rorschach painting or something because I had no idea what I was seeing, but Seven had taken his new role very seriously. He moved the wand over the blobs, and there was a bunch of tiny distinct shapes. Like... five, with fluttering movements.

"Holy shit, are they heartbeats?" Finlo gasped, leaning closer to the screen. He had Luisa in his arms, and she looked just as interested in the grainy images on the tiny screen.

Seven squinted. "I think so. Let me see if I can pick up how many there are. I learned what I could, but our physiology isn't the same as the people these machines were created for." He hummed under his breath as he moved the probe around, staring at the screen. "One, and there is two just to the left of him. Three down here, and wait... No, there's four over there. I think we're having four cubs. Oh wait, no, five."

I flopped back onto the bed and stared at the ceiling. I should have run, because right there, in the pseudo-womb of the man beside me, were my kids. This was so fucking weird. I was going to be a mom, or like a dad, or something.

Ellar noted down all the things Seven was reading out so we could keep tabs on their growth and progress, and Gatlin squatted down beside me. "Doing okay?"

I shook my head, and then I nodded. And then I

shook my head again. I didn't know what I felt right now. Overwhelmed mostly.

I gave Gatlin a weak smile. "Just seems real now, I guess. In... like a hundred or so days, we'll be cutting Raiden open to deliver my kids. I mean, our kids."

Gatlin nodded. "Our kids. It's a beautiful thing, but terrifying. I know." There was stress around the corners of his eyes, and I knew he wasn't giving me lip service. He was legit terrified. I squeezed his fingers.

"You'll figure it out. You'll be a great parent."

He squeezed them back and smiled. "We'll be great parents, Naja. You too, if you want to be." I swallowed hard and nodded. This conversation was too much, too intense to have when I could literally hear the heartbeats of the cubs.

I needed to sort my shit out as soon as possible, because I refused to bring five innocent lives into a world that was still being haunted but the ghosts of my past. I wanted to run away, but I knew if I left the room, one of them would follow me, and I refused to bring down the joy of the moment.

So I nestled further into Raiden, closed my eyes and listened to the sounds of my future.

I WASN'T surprised when it was Ellar who found me in the attic nest, sitting in front of the big round window looking out over the mountains. After they'd recorded a small sample of the ultrasound to send to the Manix doctors, they'd put away the ultrasound and celebrated. I'd snuck away under the guise of putting Luisa down for her nap, which I did, but instead of heading back out to the celebrations, I snuck away to the attic nest. It was a beautiful room, and someone had put a lot of thought into making it the most inviting, comforting place in the entire world.

"May I come and sit?"

Ugh. He was really the sweetest. "Of course. It's your house."

He walked around the sunken couch. "Yes, but it's your space." He sat down beside me, and I could see him fighting not to pull me into his arms. So I did us both a favor and just climbed into his lap. He wrapped me up, and he smelled so comforting, like fresh linen and sunshine. I rested my head against his chest, listening to his heartbeat, which was considerably slower than the ones from earlier.

"Do you want to talk about it?"

I closed my eyes. "No. Yes. I don't mean to bring down the mood."

He stroked my hair and I nearly purred. "We've had a lifetime to understand and come to terms about how things happen in Manix culture. This is all new to you. We understand."

Yeah, him being understanding? It made me feel even more like an asshole. "I don't know. Is this how men feel? Like connected but disconnected? I guess I'm conditioned to think that if I had children, I'd be the one growing them inside me, and now I kind of feel like I've been robbed." I sighed, and my cheeks flushed red. "I think I'm jealous."

Ellar burst out laughing. "Wait until he's so huge that he waddles. You won't be so jealous then." I snorted but I didn't agree. He grabbed my chin and lifted my face until I was looking at him. "You will definitely have that too, Naja. As soon as you want, but you shouldn't let your crazy hormones decide." He raised an eyebrow. "Though if it's not your hormones and it's really what you want, I'm happy to provide you with a solution right now," he purred, waggling his eyebrows.

I slapped his arm, but the idea didn't horrify me as much as it had three weeks ago. It was the fact that it *didn't* horrify me that actually made me scared. I was getting too comfortable, and my heart was all like, why not? They are sweet, protective, and loyal. My vagina felt the need to get in on the argument and add that they were also hot as fuck. They were all different, but all had the same underlying values that matched mine.

They were perfect, and I was worried that one day, after they'd had all the kids they wanted, they'd wake up and realize I was a fucking mess. Even my baggage had baggage. I was one of those Russian dolls, but with issues. There were issues inside my issues. One day the Pack would decide that I wasn't worth the drama.

"Ah, Omega, stop it. I can see your mind working overtime. I can even guess what you're thinking because I've been there too. You know what it was like to be a half-blood Beta in one of the most powerful Manix packs ever to exist? Gatlin is a crazy strong Alpha, and Finlo is his match in every way. Seven is such an overpowered Beta that it took two of the strongest Alphas in Maxton to accept him. Raiden? The Omega son of a General? May as well have been a fucking Prince." He shook his head, like he still couldn't believe Raiden had chosen their Pack. "Then there is me? I'm such a weak Beta that I'd be a liability in a fight. I'm a half-blood. I don't know if you noticed, but Maxton is like the whitest place in the universe because they basically bred within the species for the last century. There are old timers who hate me, just because I'm proof that not all Manix hold to their high standards. I understand what its like to feel like you bring nothing but problems to a Pack, but I'm here to tell you, Naja, we don't fucking care." He kissed me softly. "We don't care that you have a past that's chasing you." Another kiss. "We don't care about your heritage, or your status as an Omega, or that you have a kid." He kissed me between each statement. "The fact you are a female Omega is what led us to you, but it isn't why we want you to stay. We want you to stay because of you. Because you are funny."

A throat cleared at the door. "And sexy." Seven was here too, apparently.

"Fierce," someone yelled from downstairs. Raiden, I thought.

"Intelligent," Finlo shouted from outside, and it hit me how fantastic their hearing really was.

"You're the queen we've been searching for. The missing piece in our Pack. That's why we want you to stay," Gatlin said from behind Seven.

Ellar wiped at my cheeks, and I realized I was crying. "Thank you."

Seven strode into the nest. "Okay, El, you made her cry. I think I can do this thing with my tongue that will make her happy again.'

I laughed even as I sniffed, but Seven made good on his statement as he fell to his knees in front of me, his lips tilted up into a cheeky grin. I cupped his cheeks. "I mean it. Thank you," I said to Seven, but I met all their eyes.

Seven rested his cheek against my palm, then turned his face and nipped at my thumb. "You can thank me by screaming my name. Now lie back and enjoy the ride."

32

SEVEN

I didn't often think about death, except in an abstract way. Like, if I was going to die, it was going to be in battle, in a blaze of glory, blood on my claws and victory in my heart.

I'd changed my mind, though. Now if I was going to die, I was going to die because I suffocated while my girl rode my face, panting my name like she couldn't draw enough air. I gripped her thighs, pulling her down so I could go deeper.

Fucking heaven. I'm pretty sure if there was a Valhalla, the VIP area was set aside for people who died fucking. Finally, her release spread across my face and I lapped it up like it was the true elixir of life. Ellar was sucking my cock, and the combination of her taste on my tongue and Ellar's lips suctioning around my dick was enough to give a man an aneurysm. Someone plucked Naja off my face and I heard the distinct sound of Gatlin's groan. I turned my head to see him pulling her onto his lap, impaling her on his dick, chasing her orgasm and coaxing her into another. I wrapped my hand in Ellar's hair, those fucking glorious locks that were made to be fisted. I tugged him off before I blew, because I wasn't done yet, no matter how amazing El's blowjobs were.

He looked up, his lips swollen and his grin self-satisfied. The cheeky fuck knew how wild he drove me and made it his mission in life to swallow my sanity down his pretty throat. I turned his head so we could both watch Gatlin slide our pretty Omega up and down his dick.

He had her hair bundled up and fisted in his hand, her neck bare so he could suck the skin on the column of her throat. His eyes flashed to mine and I could see his Beast just there, riding him hard.

He wanted to mark her, wanted to bite her and make her part of our Pack forever. His control was tenuous, and I scooted back up the couch and crawled over to him. I grabbed his chin and pulled his lips toward me, kissing him hard. He couldn't do something he'd regret if he was too busy trying to top me with his tongue. I bit his lip and he growled, making me grin against his mouth.

"Holy fuck, that is so damn hot," Naja gasped, riding Gatlin faster, her perfect tits bouncing. I dragged my lips from Gatlin and stuck my face between their bodies, taking her nipple in my mouth and sucking hard. "Oh fuck, oh god, I'm coming," she squealed, and I bit down so there was a little bit of pain with all that pleasure.

Gatlin grunted, probably from the grip of her perfect little pussy. He buried his face in her neck and wrapped both arms around her waist, holding her hard to his body, his body shaking as he came.

They both collapsed, and Ellar and I searched her neck for a mate mark but it seemed our Alpha had resisted. Thank fuck. That would be hard as hell to explain. Gatlin slumped back against the cushions, Naja pressed to his chest. I curled myself around their hip, so I was eye to eye with Naja and eye to, well nipple, with Gatlin.

"Feeling better?" Ellar asked, his dick achingly hard, though he didn't seem to mind. That was Ellar in a nutshell. A giver until the end. I'd heard what he'd said earlier to Naja, about how he felt in the beginning. I know he didn't still feel like that, because you'd have to be blind and stupid not to see how much we loved him. He was the one person we all felt comfortable being vulnerable with, where we were all free to be ourselves. I mean, we were like that with the whole Pack, but Ellar had no expectations for your designation, your Alpha level, nothing. When you were with Ellar, you were just a man, not a Manix.

I grabbed him into my arms so we were chest to chest, kissing him softly. I filled it with all the love I'd always struggled to express, but I knew Ellar understood. He kissed me back with just as much tenderness.

Naja reached out and wrapped her arm around his waist, and soon we were all pressed together in a puppy pile.

A throat cleared from the doorway. "You guys started without us? Rude."

I looked around El's shoulder at Raiden in the doorway, a grinning Finlo just behind him holding a baby monitor. At least we hadn't woken up Luisa. We were going to have to soundproof this room.

Raiden yawned. "Never thought I'd say this, but I think I'm too tired for sex."

Finlo gasped, and felt our Omega's forehead. "Have you been body snatched? Remember that one time we fucked for twenty-four hours? I thought my dick was going to fall off during that yearning."

Raiden flipped him the bird. "Growing people is hard work. Now come over here and spoon me. I need a nap."

We all shuffled over, Gatlin refusing to let Naja move from his chest. Ellar climbed off me and removed Gatlin's condom, knotting it and tossing it in the trash like he was shooting hoops. Show-off. He came back and lay down beside me, and Raiden tugged Naja onto the cushions, ignoring Gatlin's mock growl.

"Hush, Alpha. You had a fourway and didn't invite me. You're in my bad books," he chastised, despite just telling us he was too exhausted. I couldn't have imagined being this happy five years ago. I was on my second Pack back then, and they would never have done this.

I had my arm around Ellar, my hand pressed to Gatlin's abs. My feet were tangled with Raiden's and Finlo's.

So fucking happy. "You know, neither of my other Packs did this."

Raiden lifted his head a little so he could look at me. "Napped?"

I shook my head. "Had this connection. We fucked, but it was like eating after starving all day or taking a piss in the woods after holding it for too long. It felt good because it had been awhile since the last time, but we didn't do it because of affection. Never would have lain like this after either, spooning and shit."

Finlo grunted. "Knowing your past Packs, I don't doubt it."

Naja squeezed my hand. "Other Packs aren't like yours?"

Gatlin hummed low in his chest. "Some are. Finlo's parents definitely are, and a few others. It helps when you have an Omega. We got really lucky when Raiden chose us."

Raiden rubbed his foot along my calf. "That's bullshit. You and Finlo were a Pack before I came along, and Seven and Ellar completed that. I was just the icing on the pizza."

Naja screwed up her nose. "That is gross. No icing on pizza. Do you get cravings like humans?"

Raiden shrugged. "I don't think so. But I wouldn't mind some pickles."

Naja laughed again, leaning into Finlo's hand as he stroked her hair. "Every Manix is different. Some decide to have monogamous relationships like Raiden's parents had, and some have all male Packs that are based more on convenience and blending of assets than love. I think our way is best though," Finlo said softly, and I nodded.

"Me too," I seconded.

Naja looked at me across Gatlin's chest. "Me three. I'm glad you guys have let me into your family."

I paused but threw caution to the wind. "You could become permanently Pack, so you would know that we didn't just want you for what you can give us, but because we want *you*. You could mate the Alphas and become ours forever."

"Seven," Gatlin warned.

Well, as long as I was saying 'fuck it' I may as well go all in. "You know as well as I do that your Beast wants it. So does Naja's, though I don't think she recognizes it for what it is yet. But you will. You will want him to bite you during sex. You'll feel incomplete without it."

Ellar stroked my chest, his eyes big with understanding, but also a hint of warning. "It's too early to be talking about that, Sev. Let Naja settle in before you start talking matebonds, hey?"

Raiden rolled his eyes. "You have no chill, Seven. You're so lucky we love you."

I snuggled down, burrowing my nose in the back of Ellar's neck. "Don't I know it."

"**A**re we sure he can't cross the wards into our territory?" I asked Merrick, and he nodded solemnly. I puffed out a tiny breath of relief. Because this? This was a whole new level of insane.

Row after row of Mexican marigolds had been planted along the fire road that formed the edges of Manix territory. It would have taken all day to plant these, and that level of dedication to causing someone terror? That spoke of a psychopath, an obsessive one at that. Seven hadn't stopped growling since Merrick and Murphy had called us down here to look at it. I understood—it made my Beast claw at my chest with the urge to shift.

"Are we going to tell her?" my Beta asked, and I shook my head immediately. She was finally happy, secure in our situation and our growing feelings for her. This display? It would send her running as far and as fast as she could. That was unacceptable to both sides of me.

Murphy came over, his eyes on the area outside our wards. I could feel that fucker's eyes on me too. Seven said he couldn't smell him on the wind, but I could sense it. He was out there.

So I gave the mountains the finger, and hoped he could see it. Then I turned and walked back to my ATV, Murphy and Merrick beside me.

Seven continued to growl at those fucking flowers, plucking one out of the ground and throwing it in the river that ran along the other side of the road. "Fuck you! She's ours now, you fucking psycho," he yelled to seemingly no one, then stomped back toward me.

I looked back at Merrick and Murphy. "We might have to get the witches in to strengthen our wards, just in case. This shit? It's unhinged. It makes me sick to contemplate what he might do to the Omega if he gets his hands on her. You need to make doubly sure that anyone leaving Maxton is vigilant as well."

Merrick nodded. "I suggest we take this fight to him, Gatlin. Sitting around is just giving him time to find our weaknesses."

I shrugged. Our numbers were so limited that the loss of even one Manix would be a blow to our future. But Merrick was right—we were sitting ducks out here unless we took some proactive measures. I was going to have to go and see my father, and that idea grated along my skin. I hated that fucker.

There'd been a time I'd idolised him, before I came into my full Alpha power. He'd changed then, showing me the cold, heartless, methodical man he was. He wasn't a bad leader—he had the good of the Manix at heart; it was all he thought about. But the man had been a shitty father, especially considering he'd left me for so long with my mother before she'd died. Sometimes I wondered what would have happened if she'd lived, if he'd have just let me stay with her forever. I would have been as oblivious about my heritage as Naja had been. Maybe I would have had a happier childhood, but I wouldn't give up my Pack for anything.

I gritted my teeth. "I'll talk to the Alpha General, see what we can convince him to do."

Murphy slapped my back. "We'll see what we can do from our end too. She's worth it, even if she wasn't the last Omega female. She's one of us and we don't leave our own to die." He looked over at Merrick. I was pretty sure that if they ever quit the Legion Force, they'd form a Pack together. They were both Alpha, definitely lovers, and they'd make good Packmates. "Besides, god knows what this psycho fuck was doing down there with all those kids he bred off that poor woman. Hell, maybe there are more Omega females down there. It's worth checking out, right?"

We'd shared Naja's history with them, because they couldn't adequately protect her if they didn't know the truth. Naja didn't seem overly worried about it. She didn't take any of the responsibility for her shitty past, didn't feel any guilt over anything but those kids. But she'd saved Luisa, and that would have been hard for a girl stuck in a world of violence and pain. She was so fucking brave.

Murphy made a good point, and I was interested to know what had happened to those kids too, even if they were buried in that fucking sociopath's backyard. If they had died, they deserved a proper burial. I nodded my agreement, and climbed back onto my ATV with Seven. I wanted to be home with my Pack now, and wanted to show them how much they meant to me. Instead, I was heading to Maxton to see my father.

Seven was silent, but I could see his simmering rage in the tension of his muscles.

"We will get him, Beta, and we will end him."

Seven nodded once, but that was the only indication he'd heard me. We drove into Maxton, and without Raiden and Naja, we were less of a spectacle for the townspeople. But I could still see people staring and whispering. Obviously word of Naja's designation had gotten around the town, and I put on my scariest Alpha *fuck off* face so no one came up to ask questions.

I pulled into the parking lot of the Legion building

this time, and Seven stood with me, just a step behind like we'd been taught since childhood. Alphas at the front, Betas to the rear. I didn't ascribe to any of that elitist bullshit, but sometimes we fell back into old habits.

I stopped at the top of the stairs. "Go pick up Ellar's stuff from the commissary, so we can get the hell out of here as soon as possible."

Seven frowned. "You need someone at your back."

One side of my mouth pulled up in a smile. "I'm pretty sure I'll be fine. But I promise not to piss him off, Beta."

Seven grumbled something about bringing Ellar, but I slapped him on the back and handed him the keys to the ATV. It was better to do this alone; my father and I understood each other better if he didn't have to worry about losing face in front of the people who were meant to respect him above all else. I could have told him that my Pack already thought he was a douche-canoe, but it hardly seemed conducive to a civil conversation. No, diplomacy was needed, so that he'd give me the resources I'd require to catch the bastard who threatened my Pack.

Seven gave me a pointed look but skipped back down the stairs toward the ATV. I strode through the hallways of the office to the double doors of the Alpha General's office.

Radic looked up and raised a brow. "Twice in as many weeks? This has to be a record, Gatlin."

I gave him a polite smile—or hell, maybe I bared my teeth, I don't know—but I didn't enter into pleasantries. Radic was nice enough, and I knew my Pack liked him, but he worked too close to my father for me to truly like him.

"I need to see the Alpha General."

Radic looked skeptical, searching behind me, probably for the rest of my Pack. He sighed. "I'm a Beta, Gatlin."

Now it was my turn to frown. "Yeah, I'm aware."

"If you make me wade into that office to break up a fight, I'm doing it with a taser set to 'crispy balls,' and I swear, I'll zap you until your pubes catch on fire. Got it?"

This time I really did smile. "Got it."

He lifted the phone and called my father's office. "Sir, I have Gatlin here to see you. I'm unsure, Sir, but I imagine it has something to do with his Omegas considering he avoids you like the plague otherwise. Yes, Sir." Radic hung up the phone and tilted his head toward the doors. "Go in. Remember though, fire crotch," he said sternly, waving a taser at me.

Yeah, okay, maybe he was alright.

I straightened my shoulders and pushed open the door to my father's office. He was facing the window that looked down over the main street of Maxton. "What can I do for you, Gatlin?"

I ground my molars as my silence sat heavily in the room. "The psycho after my Omega is getting bolder, making a statement around the edges of Manix territory."

Father titled his head. "Making a statement, how?"

"Planting flowers."

My father raised an eyebrow and let out a mirthless laugh. "Well, what a monster. Planting flowers. Someone send out the assassins."

I was pretty sure he could hear the scrape of me grinding my teeth to dust now. "They are funeral flowers. The kind you put on someone's grave. Part of her culture."

Father grunted and turned from the window. "Then I suggest you protect your Omega. I already have the Legion Force doing extra patrols. If you can't keep your Omega safe within a ward, with an elite force at your beck and call, and your ragtag Pack watching over her, then I suggest you hand her over to a Pack that can."

I curled my fists, trying to remember my promise to Radic. I liked my balls, and he didn't seem like the kind of Manix prone to empty threats.

"I can protect her just fine. Someone getting so close to the border with a malicious intent is a problem for us all, and *that* is your job. Protect your fucking people."

The power in the room ratcheted up a notch as we held each other's eyes. It was something we did every-time we were alone together, like my Beast wanted to remind him that I could take this all from him. He was getting older, and I was in my prime. Despite being a half-breed, I could take him, and he hated it. It would be bloody, and there was a chance that neither of us would survive, but still, it was impossible to ignore.

He growled. "You brought the threat to this town. You don't get to lecture me on protecting my people."

"I brought them hope."

He snorted. "Hope for yourself and your Pack maybe. Don't think your girl is going to agree to be a broodmare for the entire town, do you?"

I should have known better than to try and reason with this dick. "Do what you do best, Father. The bare fucking minimum." I turned and left. I caught Radic's eyes on the way past, nodding my goodbye. He was frowning but lifted his hand in a wave.

I'd come up with another solution. I could protect my Pack. Whoever was at the end of my claws would regret the fucking day they were even born.

I GENTLY GLUED and clamped the two pieces of pine together, setting it off to the side to set. My brain was whirring a million miles an hour about all the things I had to do before the cubs came, what I could do to keep Naja safe, how to deal with the Legion, whether I should sell the stocks in that sinking retailer whose CEO had just been accused of being an alien or wait it out... My brain was a mess. It was my father, of course—that old fuck got in my head every single time.

A soft knock against the door had me looking over my shoulder. Naja's tentative face was in the doorway. "Can I come in?"

If I had ninety-nine problems, she wasn't one. I would take all the issues that came with having her here with us, times them by a thousand, and still thank the Goddess we found her.

"Of course." I cleared off the stool that sat in the corner and dragged it closer to the workbench.

She climbed up, because she was fucking tiny, but all the better to throw her against the wall and fuck her senseless.

No, bad dick. Down.

I cleared my throat. "How are you feeling, Omega?"

She rested her elbows on the bench and cupped her chin. "Better. You guys really know how to make a girl feel special."

I gave her a crooked smile. "Naja, you are the very definition of special."

"Seven told Raiden that you had a meeting with

your dad? I'm still mad you guys didn't tell me that your father was the Supreme Ruler."

"Alpha General," I corrected, my lips twitching.

"Same thing. Totally walked into that one blind, and I hate walking into things blind." She frowned at me, and I realized she was actually pissed.

I blew out a long breath. "Apologies, Omega. It's just that my father makes me fairly irrational so we don't tend to talk about him." She kept frowning, and I quickly continued because I didn't want her to think I was a violent asshole who wasn't in control of his temper. "Not that I would ever lash out at you guys or anything."

She smiled and gripped my forearm tightly. "I know that, Gatlin. Not one part of me doubts that you would lay down your life before you hurt anyone in your Pack."

"Or you or Luisa," I insisted. I wanted to tell her I considered her Pack already, despite the lack of bonding marks.

She nodded. "Of course, Alpha. I know the type of men who like to inflict violence on those who are help-less. You aren't one of them."

I snorted, because she was right. I would never hurt anyone who was weaker than me. But during my teenage years, I'd enjoyed the violence of putting other Alphas in their place, usually with my fists. Seven and I were a lot alike in that respect.

I went back to cutting the timber, not focusing on Naja as I said this next bit. "I lived with my mother until she died when I was twelve. I have that in common with Ellar—we both grew up human. But when you grow up human and you're Manix, no matter where you are or what you do, you just feel wrong."

I swallowed hard, grabbing some sandpaper and stroking it along the wood in long, even swipes. "After she died, my father came and collected me. I'd never met the man before, and his power threatened to swamp me completely. He brought me back, and for a little while, he was happy to have a son. I was just happy to finally fit in somewhere. I believed him when he said he hadn't known that I existed. Then I hit puberty, and my Alpha power manifested. And he went from loving me to hating me overnight. I went from beloved son to pariah. I got kicked to the boarding rooms at the high school, at least until Finlo's parents took me in." I stopped and looked at her, and her eyes were so filled with sympathy that I hated myself. I didn't want her to look at me like that. I'd accept love, or lust, or happiness. But not pity. "I don't want your sympathy, Omega. I just want you to know why my father is a touchy subject."

She nodded, shifting up so she was kneeling on the stool and we were the same height. She gripped my cheeks hard. "The only thing I feel for you right now is overwhelmingly horny." She leaned in and bit my nose gently. "And if I did feel anything else, it's regret over not kicking your dad in the nuts when I had the chance."

I kissed her then, picking her up by the waist and putting her on the workbench. I plunged my tongue into her mouth and she kissed me back with the same ferocity. Pulling away, I grinned at her, marvelling at her ability to make me feel better even though I was airing my fucking *feelings*.

"I can help with the former feeling, but the latter might have to wait."

She grinned and it stole my breath. "Don't worry Alpha, I've got a long memory."

Then she kissed me until I forgot about everything but her.

34

NAJA

I was going to have to ease up on the orgies otherwise I was going to be walking like a cowboy, all bowlegged. Worth it though. This whole thing had been worth it.

I hadn't heard from *him,* and I was hopeful that we were safe here now. Though Gatlin looked stressed out, and it didn't take a rocket scientist to work out they were hiding stuff from me.

But you know what? I. Did. Not. Care.

I was happy to live in blissful ignorance just for a little while, like a vacation from the harsh reality of my life. I assumed they'd tell me if it got too bad, and then I'd deal with it. But if they wanted to play big bad Alpha and take care of everything, then I was happy to play damsel in distress for the first time in my life. I'd been strong for long enough. I'd been the brave badass who threw herself into danger.

Right now, I just wanted to revel in the knowledge that there was someone else here who was as capable as me, who could take care of this shit for me.

It was a heady and addictive feeling, this co-dependence.

I knew eventually reality would creep back in, and the stress would come tumbling down on top of me, probably worse than ever because I was no longer living in that heightened sense of fight or flight mode, but it was worth it. These moments would be the ones that would get me through dark days.

Lying with Raiden on the couch, I rested my hand on what was now a tiny baby bump. It blew my mind. I turned my head in his lap and kissed it. Raiden watched me, stroking my hair.

"You guys have made me lazy, you know? Ellar gets me all my meals, you all do baby duty, Finlo or Gatlin are there to lift anything heavy, or hell, lift me."

"And give you that good dick," Raiden added, and I flushed pink.

"You all do that."

Raiden tilted his head, as if he was listening to something in another room. His whole body stiffened. "Hey, let's go and check on Luisa, see if she's awake from her nap."

I frowned because I wasn't an idiot; I knew something was wrong. "Raiden, what is it?"

Had I been wrong? Had he found us? I knew I shouldn't have even insinuated that I was happy, because if there was a way for Karma to kick me in the box, she'd find it, and she didn't need suggestions.

"It's just another Pack, not Luisa's father."

I chewed my lower lip. "Then I'm not hiding." He looked vexed, and I raised an eyebrow. "Maybe you should go and check Luisa. You're the one carrying the precious cargo."

He gave me a grumpy look, and I knew he was just going to drop me in Luisa's room and run back out to figure out what the other Pack needed.

Nope. That wasn't going to fly with me.

I held out my hand and he grabbed it, uncurling himself from the couch with agility that I envied. We walked toward the deck and I looked down at the courtyard, and more importantly, at the two fully shifted Manix Packs that were snarling at each other. There was only one stranger who remained in his human form. He was rubbing his temples, and when he noticed Raiden, he raised his hands.

"A little help?"

Raiden chuckled low under his breath. Out loud he said, "Depends. What are you doing here, Darius?"

The guy, Darius, sighed and went back to rubbing

his temples. "We've come to speak to the female Omega."

Raiden curled his lip. "Then you can turn the fuck around and go home, because there's nothing here for you."

Woah, woah. Hold up. "The *female Omega* can speak for herself." I gave them all the stink eye. "If we could stop growling and comparing dick sizes for a moment, and maybe switch back to a form that can hold a beer can without Hulk-smashing, maybe we could have a conversation?"

I heard someone say, "Do you think she actually wants us to compare dick sizes?"

Darius, who given his slightly leaner physique was either a Beta or an Omega, shook his head furiously. I bit my lip so I didn't laugh.

I looked sternly at my guys. Yeah, *my* guys. That felt nice. I found Finlo and Gatlin, who were scary as fuck in their Beast forms, and pointed at them. "That's enough. Are they likely to be a threat?"

Darius was shaking his head, but Raiden growled. "Everyone is a threat."

I frowned at him again. "That can't be true. You must have been raised with these men. Have you ever seen them do anything that would make you doubt their character?"

Raiden gritted his teeth, and I could tell he desperately wanted to lie. "No."

I clapped my hands together. "Well, that solves that. Everyone put on some goddamn pants and come inside. It's getting cold out here."

I turned and went back inside, Raiden on my heels. "Gatlin is going to spank you so hard for speaking to him like that in front of other Alphas," he cooed, and honestly he sounded delighted. Given the clench in my lower body, it was hard to deny that maybe I was delighted by the idea too.

Raiden must have scented my desire because he pulled me to his body, the thrumming of his chest both soothing and arousing all at once, and that was an insane power to have. "You should send the Wiley-Fletcher-Reid Pack away so we can get to the fun S&M portion of this evening," he purred against my ear. His hand stroked down my spine and I curled into him instinctively. I leaned in and kissed his full lips. Then I bit him, which made him moan.

Which made me hornier.

Someone cleared their throat behind us and I looked over at a wall of hot guys. Seriously, there was something to be said about this breeding within the gene pool because they were all sexy as fuck.

Wait. Did I just condone hillbillies and inbreeding? Finlo explained they hadn't quite gotten to the I'm-A-European-Royal stage of inbreeding, and there were still enough Manix who said 'fuck you' to the Legion and found lovers outside of Maxton. But if something didn't change soon, the twang of a banjo would start to play as soon as you crossed the ward into Maxton.

Ellar skirted around the edges of them, walking over to me and kissing me hard. It was pure possession, and I moaned softly into his mouth. He pulled back, and grinned down at me. "I'll get beers."

I shook my head as I watched him walk to the kitchen, because that man had a fine ass, then turned back to the four strangers in front of me. "Pack Wiley-Fletcher-Reid. Three Alphas?"

Darius nodded. "And little old Omega me."

I raised my eyebrows. "That seems like a whole lot of machismo to handle."

Darius threw back his head and laughed. "You have no idea." Ellar returned with beers, handing one to Darius. "Thanks, El."

Huh. So they weren't strangers. They were friends. I gave Raiden the stink eye.

"You guys are friends, and yet you carried on like that? Like they were here to cause me mortal peril?" I turned my disapproving look on them all, and even the other Alphas looked a little ashamed of themselves.

Darius threw his hands up in the air. "Oh, you're gonna need to tell me your tricks, because I said the same thing outside and they ignored me."

Seven just grunted, strode over and picked me up bodily, before moving to the couch and placing me down on his lap. I gave him a stern look, but didn't move. He had those strong thighs that you just wanted to ride, so I mean, they made a good seat. Everyone seemed to relax onto the couch, and judging the way the other Alphas just collapsed back into the cushions like they'd done it a million times before, I could tell they were close friends.

"So, you better introduce yourselves. I'm Naja."

The biggest one had deep red hair, and muscles for days. "Corvin." He pointed to a blond guy with hair that sat in messy waves to his shoulder. "That's Cooper, and the guy with the perpetual pout on the end is Beckett. You've met Darius, our Omega." He looked at the slighter man with such wholehearted love, it made me smile. "We were hoping that perhaps, you would act as a donor for us."

My guys all started yelling at once, each with variations of 'fuck no.' I looked at Darius, whose eyes were pleading, which broke my heart as I shook my head.

"I can't."

Cooper leaned forward, his eyes imploring me. "I promise, if it's because you aren't interested in us, it would just be Darius. We'd wine you and dine you and I swear, that's all we need from you. If there was a way to do it without the act, we would. The next heat, you guys will be loaded down with cubs already, it would be such a waste..." I was still shaking my head, because I was devastated for them, I was. But I wasn't an egg machine, and the implication that I was wasting my eggs since they were such a rare commodity made me feel all sorts of weird.

"I know, I do. But I can't. It's not in me to just make children and leave them. Plus, like, if you guys have a litter of cubs each, won't that really fuck with the next generation? They'll all be like half siblings or something." I winced. "I'm sorry, but I promised to let the physicians study me and see if they can't work out a way to give you what you need."

Beckett snorted. "Sure, if these fuckers ever let you off their damn mountain."

"Fuck off, Beckett," Gatlin growled, but it was friendly, if cursing someone out could be considered friendly.

I really didn't know what to say. They were obviously desperate, but they were strangers, and I could only impregnate one set of hot strangers in my lifetime. "I really... I'm sorry."

Darius reached over and squeezed my hand, looking between me and Seven. "I understand. These guys will just have to put up with my ass when I go through the yearning. It won't kill them, theoretically." He winked.

Dammit, I liked Darius, and I felt all sorts of guilt, which was ridiculous. "Do you guys want to stay for dinner?" I asked quietly, and it was the fire-haired Corvin that answered.

"We'd love that, thank you."

35

ELLAR

fter the visit from the WFR Pack, Naja had been adamant that we take her down to Maxton to fulfill her obligations. That sent everyone into freakout mode, and it had taken us all nearly a week to figure out logistics.

Seven and Gatlin were staying with Raiden and Luisa at the Pack house. I tried not to grin at the level of trust Naja now had in us that she was happy for us to watch the most important person in her life. Trusted us to keep her young safe. I'd never felt so proud of my Pack.

She leaned her head on my shoulder now we were off the rockier mountain trails and on the well-worn road to Maxton. "What's to stop hikers just wandering into Maxton? I mean, you must be able to see it on a satellite."

I shrugged, and rested my cheek against the crown of her head. "Combination of things. We are so small and uninteresting that people don't really make it here unless they're hiking. We get the occasional hiker, but the folks who live in Maxton are naturally private and a little suspicious, so it's never very comfortable for outsiders." Didn't I know that one from personal experience. "If someone wants to stay, then there is no real estate for sale, no houses for rent, no rooms for boarding. We once had a guy try and wait out the winter in a tent, but eventually the cold and unfriendliness of the people chased him out." I shook my head.

"If there are people with more malicious intentions, they are kept out by the wards," Finlo added. "We had it constructed to keep out murderous Packs of shifters, but it works for all people who know what we are and have an intent to do someone within the wards harm. Gatlin is negotiating with the witches to send someone out and strengthen the wards. They should be here in a couple of weeks."

Witches gave me the creeps, but I'd put aside my prejudices to ensure the safety of my Pack. Still, one day soon, we'd have to do something about the fucker still haunting the edges of our territory. He'd recently constructed a cross, and added a shrine, right on the banks of the river. I wanted to find him and drown him in those crystal clear waters.

I ignored the curious gazes of the people out and

about in town, doing whatever it was that people did on a day-to-day basis. I'd been here nearly a decade and it was still a mystery to me. It might have been different if my father had given an actual shit about me, but he hadn't.

My Pack filled in the gaps of my knowledge wherever they could, and we would do the same for Naja.

We pulled up in front of the small demountable building that was the office of the town doctor. Doc was a nice old guy, very unusual in the Manix community because he didn't have a Pack or family. He was a lifelong bachelor, and I personally thought it might be partially due to his pickled body part collection that he kept in the waiting room. That shit was creepy as hell if you didn't know the man. He'd lived a really long time too; he'd been around when the last female Alpha had died of old age decades ago. But Doc stayed up-to-date with all the current medical practices and technologies, played a mean game of chess, and had a wit so acerbic he could use it to cut instead of a scalpel. I predicted he'd be on his best behavior today though because what Naja giveth, Naja could taketh away.

"What the hell...?" Naja breathed, and I knew she'd just seen the jars. You see, the Doc didn't collect hearts or lungs or spleens. No, he collected weird reproductive systems. Which made sense considering how unique ours was, but there were dicks from almost every species you would find in the area. He never said where he got them, but he'd assured us they were all dead before he'd lopped off their dick, which was vaguely reassuring.

"Does that jar say 'mouse penis' or do I need glasses?" she asked Finlo, who just laughed.

Before he could answer, Doc appeared. He suited his name; he kind of looked like a stereotypical little old man. He just happened to like collecting cock. Everyone needed a hobby.

He smiled wide, his cheeks dimpling. Naja stared at him, then back at the dicks in a jar, then back to the Doc. "That's a lot of D."

Doc grinned. "Same could be said for you, Naja." He gave a pointed look between me and Finlo, and I laughed. Naja gaped before she laughed too.

"Touché, Santa. Let's get this show on the road."

"Come on back," Doc offered, and both Finlo and I stuttered. Did we go with her? Would she even want us with her? Did we actually trust Doc?

Probably, considering he'd delivered both Finlo and Raiden. Finlo and I stood awkwardly around the waiting room, until Naja looked over her shoulder. "Are you guys coming?"

I grinned because that was the second huge step of the day. She wanted us in there, with her, during a medical procedure. We made her feel safe.

Doc led us back to an examination room that hadn't really been updated since the sixties, but the medical equipment was all state-of-the-art. Doc loved his techno-toys.

He sat at his huge, cluttered desk, indicating we should all find a seat where we could. "Let's start with a brief medical history, shall we?"

Over the next forty minutes, the Doc poked and prodded, questioned and theorized, and my girl? She was gracious the whole way through it. She really did want to make it better for Packs like the Wiley-Fletcher-Reid Pack. To give them hope.

Finally, Doc had taken all the notes he could take today. "When you go into heat next, I'd like to take a blood panel to see the difference." Finlo growled, and Doc just raised an eyebrow. "Finlo Grey, I delivered your squawling backside after thirty-six hours of labor. Do not make that noise at me. I couldn't possibly be less interested in your Omega. If I must, I will teach Ellar here how to draw blood and he can bring it to me here in Maxton, or you can use your forebrain and stop being a Neanderthal."

The Doc wasn't an Alpha, but he took no shit and I respected the hell out of him for it. Plus it was really funny. When it came to having sway over the people of Maxton, Doc was right up there with the Alpha General. But he didn't have the same stick up his ass about it.

Naja smiled at him and nodded. "Sure thing."

We exchanged a few more pleasantries as Doc led

us toward the door. I noticed his secretary was back from lunch, and he didn't even try to hide the fact he was gawping.

Doc ignored him though; it was probably why he'd sent him away to start with. "Tell Raiden that he needs to come down and see me too. Your scans look good, but I'd like to do a few more of my own."

Finlo hesitated, and this time I was with him. Raiden was beginning to nest hard, and soon getting him to leave the house would be nearly impossible. "I'll try, Doc, but if not, you might have to come up and visit us."

Doc nodded, even if he did give us a put-upon sigh. He turned back to Naja. "I can't thank you enough for your time today. We've made the first steps in improving the longevity of the Manix race and that's all down to you."

Naja swallowed hard and gave a feeble smile. "But no pressure, right?"

He patted her on the back in a fatherly manner. "None whatsoever. Now, off you go before your Alpha has a coronary. I have no other clients today, and thought I might sit down to have a coffee and a donut. I'll be super peeved if he shits a kitten on my floor because I've held you up too long."

That was it. I couldn't hold it in anymore. I laughed so hard my abs hurt, and Finlo had to half carry both me and Naja out the door. He stuffed me into the passenger seat of the ATV, a cackling Naja beside me.

"Laugh it up, assholes. Now I need a donut," he grumbled, but I could see the mirth in his eyes. He drove us over a couple of streets and pulled up out the front of the bakery. He hustled us both inside, and I wrapped my arm around Naja's waist. It was a possessive move but I wanted all these bigots to know she was mine. She'd chosen me, and my Pack. Directing her toward the cake display, I watched her eyes bug out of her head when she saw the selection of pastries.

"I've never seen this much cake in one place."

I wanted to buy her one of everything. Still, we settled on a couple of cream donuts, one iced pink donut for Luisa, and a small box of other pastries. We'd have them for dessert, or maybe I'd eat them off Naja's stomach.

Finlo moved around the bakery, talking to random people. Having grown up here, he had connections with a lot of people. It was hard to walk down the street of Maxton without either Raiden, Seven or Finlo being stopped by multiple people to chat. Gatlin gave too much of a *fuck off* vibe, which suited me fine. I usually went with Gatlin because then I could at least pretend people didn't ignore me for my heritage, like I was somehow lesser just because my dad had gone into a human town and impregnated a college girl.

Naja was beginning to frown as we finished up our

order, and I bustled her out of the bakery before she asked questions. But I should have known she wouldn't let it go unremarked.

"What was that?"

Finlo looked at me, then away again. "What was what?"

Ah, we were going with the ignore it tactic. In the early years of our Pack, both Finlo and Gatlin used to beat the shit out of anyone who so much as made a snide comment. Add in Seven, and we were brawlers for a long while. But we'd settled down before Raiden arrived, once we realized you couldn't beat good sense or tolerance into people. So we'd retreated to the Pack house and avoided town ever since. It had worked for us, mostly.

She gave Finlo a disapproving look. "You know what. The girl at the counter only addressed you, like Ellar didn't even exist. No one made eye contact with him, or waved, or anything. What the hell?"

"There's a lot of history there, but in a nutshell, when Ellar arrived and his father didn't claim him, he became—for a lack of a better word—defective. They viewed him as too different, too lesser to even associate with. We probably didn't do him any favors taking him into our Pack; people already viewed us as some kind of abomination."

I snorted. "I wouldn't change you guys for a single one of those assholes."

Finlo gave me a loving gaze. "Me either, El."

Naja frowned, and I could sense her angry outrage simmering just beneath the surface, but she didn't ask anymore questions.

I pulled out a small brownie and handed it to her as we bounced down the road. "Try this. It's my favorite."

She opened her lips obediently, her small pink tongue darting out to lick the crumbs off my fingers. She moaned and her eyes went wide. "Holy shit. I was ready to write this whole town off, but that might be worth sticking around for. We'll keep the brownies, but I'll make these fucking people better, by force if necessary."

I could see the cogs turning in her brain.

Something caught my eye in the woods beyond the road, and I turned my senses to it. I couldn't see or smell anything unusual, and Finlo seemed unperturbed; he had sharper vision than I did, so it was probably just a deer.

Still, I'd tell Gatlin when we got home and see what he said. I switched my gaze back to watching Naja finish eating the brownie, and wondered if I could make her moan like that later.

I stood in front of the bathroom mirror, staring at my protruding stomach. If I held my gut now, I could feel them kicking, or sliding around each other doing gymnastics. I couldn't believe how huge I'd gotten in such a short time. The cubs were growing like weeds and by extension, so was I. I climbed into the shower and stood beneath the scalding hot water. I was halfway there, two months along, and I wouldn't tell this to the guys or Naja, but I was exhausted already.

The bathroom door opened and closed, and Gatlin walked in, already removing his shirt. He slid off his pants and was gloriously naked before he even stopped in front of the shower screen.

"Need me to wash your back, Omega?"

I looked at his amazing body. He had deep olive skin, from his mother's heritage I guess, and while most Manix were hairless, Gatlin had a faint spray of curls over his chest and down his abs. Chest hair that had tickled my cheeks more than once. Hell, probably more than a million times. I couldn't get enough of him. I looked back at his face. "Always, Alpha."

He stepped beneath the warm water, stepping up behind me, and I leaned back into his body with a sigh.

He kissed my shoulder, his arms coming around my waist. "How are you feeling, Raiden?"

I closed my eyes and let myself relax. "I'm fine. Exactly the same as an hour ago when Seven asked me, and thirty mins before that when Finlo asked."

Gatlin chuckled low in his chest. "We have been a bit overprotective."

I smiled softly. "It's fine, Gatlin. We're all excited and worried and terrified. But my body knows what it's doing."

Gatlin nudged my head with his cheek and I obligingly tilted it to the side, shivering at the feel of his stubbly beard against the sensitive skin of my throat. He ran his lips over my skin, kissing and licking at the water droplets. I could feel the hard press of his cock against my ass and his hand stroked over my hip. He gripped my hard cock in his fist.

"What's your body doing now, Omega?" he growled against my ear, and my whole body shivered in his hands. He stroked my cock once, twice, and I let my head fall back against his shoulder. But I should have known that Gatlin wouldn't have settled for the easy tease. He spun me around so I was facing him, kissing me hard. He tasted like sin and chocolate, and I couldn't get enough. I'd never been able to get enough, not since the first time he kissed me.

He fell to his knees, and I openly gawked. "Gatlin, what are you doing?" He looked up at me, and I stopped breathing. Alphas? They didn't kneel before anyone, and especially not Omegas. And they definitely didn't suck cock.

But Jesus, as he slid his lips around mine, he was proving me wrong. He sucked me down his throat and I didn't know what to do with my hands. I didn't want to grab his hair but I needed to hold myself up, so I slapped my hands against the tiles. It made me go deeper into his throat, making us both fucking moan.

He pulled his mouth away, continuing to gaze up at me. "If you are going to watch, you may as well join in," he said softly.

I frowned, until I realized he wasn't talking to me at all. Beside the vanity was Naja, her eyes hooded, her lips parted. She cleared her throat.

"I didn't want to intrude."

I grinned. "Get in here."

She pulled off her tank top and peeled down her pants until she was gloriously naked. Holy shit, she had a body to die for, all soft curves. The past month of not working two jobs, plus me and Ellar making it our duty to feed her whenever possible, had softened the muscles she'd gained from dancing, but her core strength was still there beneath the softness. Her and Gatlin together were a visual orgasm.

She stepped into the shower, and I would hug Finlo later for thinking of making a walk-in shower with only one screen. We could fit at least five of us in here if a couple didn't mind being cold. And I knew none of us would mind the chill.

I reached out and grabbed Naja as soon as she got close enough, dragging her into a messy, wet kiss. Gatlin ran his tongue over the head of my cock, and this time I did grab his face.

"If you keep doing that, I'm going to come."

He chuckled, his lips brushing the sensitive tip of my dick. "That's the idea, Omega."

I tilted his head back so he was looking at me. "I don't want it over that quick. I think there are far better places to come."

He growled again and turned his head, gripping one of Naja's thighs and putting it over his shoulder. Oh yeah, that was what I was talking about. I kissed her as he ate her out, and she was soon a writhing, wet mess in my arms. I would never, ever get sick of the sound of her moans, and the urge to make her ours permanently hit me again.

We needed to make her our mate, make her Pack

officially. But now was not the time to talk about mate-bonds. I drew back so I could watch Gatlin suck and lick at Naja, until she was weak in my arms and I was holding her up as I kissed her, echoing Gatlin's technique.

My Alpha surged to his feet, spinning Naja around until her hands were braced against the tiles, and he slammed inside her.

She screamed her appreciation, the orgasm he'd been coaxing with his tongue exploding out from her in the most beautiful cries I'd ever heard. Capturing her lips again, I turned them both until I was kissing her as Gatlin held her, slowly sliding her up and down his cock. I supported her chest, her hard nipples scraping against my chest.

"Bedroom," Gatlin moaned, and I had to agree. There were things I wanted to do that couldn't be done defying gravity in the shower.

I turned off the shower and watched as Gatlin threw Naja over his shoulder, marching out of the ensuite and into my room.

Dropping her onto the bed on her hands and knees, he didn't even waste a single second before thrusting back into her. I knelt on the bed and just watched because they were like choreographed art—the roll of Gatlin's abs, the push of Naja's hips. It was a thing of beauty.

But then Naja's hands were gripping at my legs,

dragging me closer, and I went willingly. When I was close enough, she grabbed my dick and put it to her lips. Then she slid me deep down into her throat, and I threw my head back and cursed.

"Holy fucking Goddess."

Gatlin upped his pace, setting Naja's rhythm on my cock, and he was fucking us both in true Alpha fashion. Every thrust slid me further down her throat and I was going to come undone, despite what I said to Gatlin.

I watched her, not even blinking as her pretty red lips went up and down my cock, and then it was too much. I gripped her hair, rocking my hips in time with Gatlin's, fucking our girl.

A resounding slap had her moaning on my cock. "I haven't forgotten about the little incident with the other Pack, Omega. Ordering me around like you were the Alpha." He slapped the other cheek, and she moaned around my dick, arching her back.

Oh shit, I was definitely going to blow. But I could tell Gatlin wasn't done. I gritted my teeth as she hummed around me, which turned into a moan as my Alpha smacked the first cheek again. Nope, I couldn't hold back. "I'm going to come," I panted, giving her the chance to move away, but she just swallowed me deeper. Gatlin slapped her ass so hard she squealed, and that was it. I came down that pretty throat and she swallowed every drop.

Pretty sure I was in love with her. I looked up at Gatlin and he was looking down at her with the same level of reverence. I wasn't the only one.

"Do you know what you did was bad, Little Omega?" *Slap.* "Do you know your place? I will revere the very ground you walk on, but I am the Alpha, the protector in this Pack. Understand?" She was nodding furiously, her face as pink as her ass, and she kept moving closer to Gatlin. I lay back on the pillows, watching Gatlin work. I'd been at the other end of his palm one too many times so I knew the pleasure and pain combination she was enduring right now.

He slapped both cheeks in quick succession. "I asked you a question, Omega, and I expect a verbal answer. Do you understand?"

"Yes Alpha," she squealed, and then he gripped her hips, fucking her into the mattress until she came on a scream.

He was close behind her, his hands clenching around her hips. "Good girl." He pulled out and came all over her back, his satisfied groan echoing around the room. I slid from the bed and walked to the bathroom for a towel, dampening it and returning to see them both collapsed on the bed. Slowly cleaning Naja up, I peppered kisses on the reddened globes of her ass cheeks, making her sigh happily.

Once I was happy she was clean, I lay down beside her, my hand still soothing her ass. I wanted to tell her that I loved her, but I didn't think she was ready yet. Maybe I had to let her come to the conclusion first, let her choose us. So I swallowed down the words and wrapped myself around her body as best as I could.

Gatlin flung his long arm over us both, and I knew this was pure bliss.

There was a knock at the door, and Ellar poked his head through. "Uh, if you guys are done, we have guests that you might want to come and see." His eyes took in the scene and I could *see* the desire in his eyes, like he wanted to climb into bed with us.

"Who?" Gatlin barked, his nose already in the air.

"The witch has arrived."

Holy shit. I flew out of bed, Gatlin flying out the other side. The witch was here, and we had literally been caught with our pants down.

Naja frowned. "What's wrong?"

Ellar came in, passing her some clothes. "The witches are a notoriously formal and easily offended race."

"And we were in here fucking. We were lucky that we didn't get our balls fried for the insult," Gatlin groaned.

Yep, we'd fucked up.

When we were dressed, we walked into the living room, only to see a single red-haired woman drinking tea from a mug. I flushed as red as her hair as she curled an eyebrow at me, obviously knowing exactly what we'd been up to while we kept her waiting.

Finlo and Seven were close but not too close, obviously keeping an eye on our guest without being too obvious. Well, they were trying at least.

Gatlin strode into the room like he had no regrets. "Apologies, Ma'am. If we'd known you were coming or that you'd arrived, we wouldn't have keptyou waiting." Gatlin threw a slightly annoyed look at Finlo, who just shrugged.

"It's no problem. I told them to leave you be. You were obviously having a very important meeting." She grinned, and it turned her almost stern face into something arrestingly beautiful. "I'm in no hurry and honestly, being inside the Manix stronghold is a rare treat." She screwed up her nose. "Though your taste in tea is not fantastic."

Seven grumbled something about no one drinking tea anyway, and Gatlin threw him a warning look, but the witch just smiled.

"I should introduce myself. I am Miranda, representative of Wilde, Member for the Convocation."

Gatlin nodded. "Welcome to our home. I'm Gatlin, Alpha of the Huxley-Grey Pack, and this is my co-Alpha, Finlo. Our Betas, Ellar and Seven, and our Omega, Raiden." He paused, pulling me closer to his body in a possessive gesture that I didn't miss. "This is Naja. She's Omega and our very special guest."

Miranda took a sip of tea, and I was fairly sure she was hiding a grin. "Indeed. Is your very special guest the reason the wards need to be renewed? They are abysmal, by the way. A kitten with an Uzi could have stepped over those wards like they didn't exist."

A what now?

But the witch wasn't done. "You need to tell me what exactly we are keeping out, and then I will give you my price. This will have to be an expansive ward, unless you intend to be a prisoner in this house forever?" I shook my head vehemently. "I didn't think so. So we will need to talk to your Council—uh, what do you refer to them as? Yes, the Legion. We'll have to talk to them and get the proper permission to drop the wards completely and build them back up."

The guys all frowned about that and I didn't blame them. Having met the Legion once, I'd decided that was more than enough.

Finlo nodded finally. "We can do that. How long will it take you to put up the ward?"

Miranda shrugged. "I'll dismantle yours first, and build up a far better one. About half a day? I'm going to need the proper supplies and the right phase of the moon." She looked out the window like she could see the moon in the bright sunlight. "I'm thinking we should do it Thursday next week, if we can get permission from your powers that be."

They talked more about the logistics, and she listed a staggering amount of money as a fee, before standing. She smiled as she stepped toward me, making everyone tense. "Congratulations, Naja. You've brought a little more magic back into the world."

As I stood there gaping, she opened some kind of glowing red portal and stepped through it casually, like she hadn't just bent space and time for funsies.

I turned to the rest of the guys, who were equally gobsmacked. It was Seven that shook himself out of it first.

"Witches are so fucking weird."

Well, a-fucking-men to that.

.   .   .

THE WITCH's list of things that needed to happen meant that another trip to Maxton was necessary. Finlo's mother had also decided we'd been hiding up in the hills for long enough, so the day in town had resulted in an invitation to a family barbecue, which terrified the absolute fuck out of me. Not the scariest thing to ever happen to me, of course, but it made my heart pound like a bass drum for half a day leading up to it. I'd already met Finlo's parents and the twins, but I was meeting his sister and older brother this time, as well as Raiden's family. The numbers had blown right out. And I was freaking out.

The plan was that Gatlin, Ellar and Raiden would go to the Legion and request that they allow Miranda to put up stronger wards. Raiden and Ellar would ground Gatlin and hopefully prevent him from pounding his dad into dust, and if that didn't work, they were going to play the pregnant Omega card. While they were there convincing a crusty old guy that protecting us was necessary, Finlo would be showing me and Luisa off to his family, or so he put it with a grin.

When I'd asked if Seven's family would be there too, Seven had scoffed. "I hope the fuck not."

Now, he sat beside me, holding Luisa who was excited to be in the ATV again. She was snuggled tightly in Seven's arms, more than content to be there. Hell, she was utterly besotted with the Pack, like they were her real flesh and blood.

It was nearly painful to admit that I was too. Besotted, I mean. When we reached the edge of town, both ATVs stopped. Everyone from the other ATV climbed out and came over. Raiden kissed me hard. "Have fun. We'll be there soon enough."

Ellar kissed me next, before blowing a raspberry on Luisa's cheek, making her giggle. "See you guys soon, I promise to keep these hotheads in line." That last bit was directed at Finlo, who looked kind of unconvinced. That was worrying.

Finally, Gatlin came over and kissed me softly. "See you soon."

I grinned at him. "We're only going to be apart for like an hour, not forever, Gatlin."

He gave me an intense look. "Doesn't matter to the Beast. Or to me," he said softly.

My heart fluttered in my chest. "In that case, be good and get back to me ASAP," I whispered back, and he kissed me again.

Then they were back in their ATV and moving off in the opposite direction. "My family owns a big house on the other side of town," Finlo said as we drove off. "They weren't the townie kind of people either."

I was thankful for that. The road up to Finlo's parents house was beautiful, the mountains gorgeous this time of the year. It would be even more beautiful in winter, and I couldn't wait to see it.

I paused. I was really staying. I knew in my heart that was what I wanted. Not just for a few months, or a year or two. Forever. I wanted to stay with the Huxley-Grey Pack *forever* and I wanted to be a real part of the Pack.

I looked at Finlo and Seven. Would they want me to be with them forever? To intrinsically tie themselves to me and all my bullshit? The look in Raiden's eye when he was fucking me yesterday said yes, but maybe he looked at everyone he was fucking like that.

I gasped when we pulled up in front of Finlo's family home. Holy shit. I'd thought the Pack house was impressive, but Finlo's parents' house was an architectural confection. It butted right up to a cliff face, and was made of steel and glass, yet somehow blended beautifully into the surrounding landscape.

"Wow."

Seven grumbled as he stood, shifting Luisa to his hip. "All the houses are this ostentatious if you have a large Pack. A six-income family has a lot of spare cash to throw around."

Finlo slapped his back. "Yours included."

Seven frowned. "Mine especially."

If I ever met Seven's parents, I had a mental note to thank them for bringing such an amazing person into the world, and then I was going to junk punch them both.

I could hear the sound of voices and laughter from what seemed to be the back of the house. Finlo grinned at me, and I could tell he was happy to be here. I felt a little guilty then. It was because of me he'd been trapped up at the Pack house. He wrapped his long arm around my shoulders. "Come on, pretty girl. Let's go meet the madness."

Seven groaned, looking down at a wide-eyed Luisa. "Save me, Little Bit!"

She planted a big kiss on his cheek and I saw the surly Beta melt. Then she pointed at the house. "Hot dogs, please."

Finlo laughed, ushering us all through the front door. Raiden had mentioned that they'd probably have hot dogs at the barbecue and she'd been insanely excited about these tubes of processed meat. It was a kid thing.

I barely had an opportunity to take in the beautiful foyer with its polished stone floors and high ceiling, as Finlo led us straight through and then out the back door. There must have been two dozen people back there, and every head turned toward us.

Selena quickly made her way over, her face alight with joy. Behind her was a younger woman who looked so much like her that she could only have been a daughter. Selena wrapped me up into a hug as soon as she was in grabbing distance. "Naja, it's so good to see you. Thank you for coming!"

The other woman, however, made a beeline for Finlo. When she was close, instead of hugging him, she punched him in the pec. "Hey, Shithead, would it have killed you to pick up the phone and say, oh hey, I knocked up Raiden and found a pretty Omega who is way too good for me?" She turned to me. "I can already tell you are way too good for this ragtag bunch of assholes."

Finlo held up both his hands. "Terra, it's not like you check in with me every time you and your mates get pregnant." Terra hit him again, and he whined, "Mom, make her stop hitting me."

Selena rolled her eyes at me. "Terra, stop hitting your brother."

Terra crossed her arms over her chest. "Well, tell him to stop making false equivalencies. Me having another baby, and you finding the last damn female Omega and having the first male Omega pregnancy in a century are different goddamn levels of importance." She smiled at me. "I'm Terra, by the way. Nice to meet you."

I waved lightly, and Finlo rolled his eyes. "*So* sorry I didn't call my sister and inform her of my sex life, I'll do better. Like this morning, Ellar gave me a blow—"

Selena snapped her fingers. "That's quite enough from the both of you. Terra, have you met my new grand-cub, Luisa? She's almost the same age as Leisel, maybe a year or so younger?"

Terra's face morphed into one of pure joy when she saw Luisa in Seven's arms. "Hey Sev," she said to my grinning Beta, before looking down at Luisa. "Hello, Angel! You want to come and meet my baby, Leisel? She's about your age, and likes fairies and brawling."

I snorted, and Terra winked at me. Seven looked to me for permission, which I loved about him entirely, and when I nodded, he allowed Luisa to shift into the waiting arms of Terra. I didn't know what it was about the Manix, or if her animal just knew she was safe now, but my baby had really come out of her shell these last few weeks.

You would never know of the rough start that she'd had, or the violence she'd witnessed. As Finlo pulled me along to meet more of his family, Seven reassuringly bringing up the rear, I realized that my shoulders weren't tense anymore. I wasn't coiled and ready to run or fight at any moment. I staggered a step at the realization that it wasn't just Luisa who felt safe and happy here. I did too.

Seeing Naja with my family did something to my chest. She talked with my brothers and brothers-in-laws easily. Terra was a whirlwind in herself and it was hard not to like her, but they got on like two peas in a pod once Naja relaxed around all the people. I hovered over her and Seven took up guard over near Luisa. My niece Leisel was basically a miniature version of Terra, but with a shorter fuse. She'd be brawling and throwing fists at the boys if they so much as insulted her Barbie, let alone her new friend Luisa. She was going to be a handful in her teenage years, and judging by the way Luisa hovered behind her, she was going to take our new cub with her into mischief.

I rested my hand gently on Naja's hip and she leaned into me as she spoke to my brother Jock about gardening. Jock was the head horticulturist in town, employed by the Legion to keep the parks and gardens Pleasantville-perfect. He had a natural green thumb, and I was a little jealous that he could relate with her about one of her passions. I made a mental note to myself to look into planting a garden at the Pack house. Or maybe a glasshouse so she could still do something she enjoyed in the winter. Oh, or a solarium off the back of the house. Perfect.

I was mentally constructing plans, occasionally kissing the top of Naja's head in case she forgot I was there, when the rest of my Pack walked in, plus Raiden's dad. Their faces gave nothing away but when Gatlin met my eyes, he gave a slight nod. I let out a relieved breath, but I was guessing it hadn't been as simple as a 'Yeah, sure. Take down the wards and drain the Legion coffers of a hefty chunk of funds, son' conversation.

The party died down again, everyone turning to look as Gatlin, Raiden and Ellar entered the party. No, scratch that—they were all looking at Raiden and his stomach.

My mother swooped to the rescue one more time. "Come in! It's food time so you guys are right on schedule. Raiden, sweet child, look at you! You look absolutely the picture of contentment." She wrapped her arms around him, whispering something in his ear that made him chuckle and blush a little. God knows what it was. She went and kissed Ellar and then Gatlin's cheek too, and ushered them all over to where we were standing. Each of them came up and kissed our girl, and she smiled up at them softly, her cheeks flushed. I guess she probably wasn't used to the idea of polyamorous relationships; it was probably awkward as hell in a group of strangers. But the Manix had been a polyamorous society by necessity for a century, and no one here would judge her for being with more than one of us. They would applaud it, especially being who she was.

A whirlwind of terror came barreling up from the garden. Leisel, with Luisa close behind her, was tearing through the crowd of legs. "Uncle Raiden!" Leisel screamed, and I winced. Yeah, Raiden was the favorite, even though I was her flesh and blood.

Raiden squatted down and caught the little girl, peppering her cheeks with kisses. "How's my girl?"

"I'm good. I have a new cousin. Have you met her? She's great. She doesn't talk much but that's okay because she's a bit younger than me and I can look after her."

He scruffed her hair. "I've met Luisa. She's staying with us up in the Pack house. She's my other favoritest girl."

Leisel frowned. "So I'm not your favorite anymore."

Oops. I didn't know how Raiden was going to talk himself out of this one. But then I remembered my brilliant Omega handled us four with ease every single day.

"You are still my favorite, but we have big hearts and I have the room in there for lots of favorites. Like your Mommy loves all your Daddys and I love all your uncles. Love isn't a competition, Lees. There's plenty to go around, because it's endless."

Leisel thought about it. Then she wrapped her arm around Luisa's shoulders, which made the little girl freeze. "We can share. Luisa needs me."

She said it with such conviction that I paused, but then Leisel was talking about how she had to punch one of the boys, and Gatlin was trying not to laugh. Ellar bent down and rescued a wide-eyed Luisa, hefting her into his arms. "Having fun, Little Bit?"

She nodded. "Leez. Friend." Well, she said a bunch of other stuff, but I was still learning toddler speak. I could see she was a little awed, and I wondered if she'd ever had one before—a friend, I mean.

Ellar nodded and kissed the top of her head. "You're lucky then. You'll never have a more loyal or ferocious friend than Leisel." He put her back down on the ground and she ran away after her new friend. Naja's eyes were big and a little shiny, so I held her closer. I wanted to tell her that they both had family now. A family that was just as loyal and ferocious.

Instead, dinner was served and everyone dived for the food. Nothing like a Manix barbecue to bring out the Beast in us all. It was a bit of a feeding frenzy, but Gatlin threw his Alpha power around like a dick and came back with two plates piled high, one for Raiden and one for Naja. Ellar had dived in to get a hot dog for Luisa, and was currently smothering it in a small pool of ketchup at her request.

As Gatlin went back to get his own plate, I walked with him. "What did the Legion Alpha say?" I said in a low voice, and Gatlin gave me a fiery look that never meant good things. "Is he still alive?"

He rolled his eyes but nodded. "Barely. If the other Legion Generals hadn't stepped in and outvoted him, he would have sent us packing happily, rubbing his hands with glee at the thought of finally being rid of me." He grabbed us both a beer from the cooler. "But it is hard for them to look at Raiden and not do something to safeguard our future. Plus they were a little disturbed by the ease of the witch's entrance onto Manix lands. There were the expected protests about trusting a witch we didn't know, and the cost, but in the end, they all saw the necessity to update the wards and pay the money, not just to protect Naja but to protect us all. All of them except my father, I mean."

I slapped him on the back in a supportive way. "Doesn't matter what that cockhole thinks, Gat. We got what we needed to keep our girl safe. We'll message the witch and get her back here ASAP." I paused and lowered my voice a fraction more. What I was about to say was a group decision, but I wanted to see where Gatlin stood first. "I want her to be our mate. Officially."

Gatlin's whole head swivelled to mine, and he did that thing with his bottomless gray eyes where he searched your entire soul. "Why?"

I groaned, but I should have expected he wouldn't make it easy. Gatlin had never made anything *easy,* but he always made everything worth it. "She fits. No, that's not even right. She isn't like a round peg we've stuffed into a square hole. She more than fits. It's like the hole has always been Naja-shaped. She was meant to be there, and we've been waiting for her without even knowing it."

Gatlin was silent, piling salads on his plate, though judging by the mound of potato salad he wasn't actually focused on it. Finally, he dropped the spoon and looked at me. "I agree. I don't think she's ready to mate into the Pack for life yet though. That kind of commitment will make her run."

I shrugged. "So we get her the equivalent of a human engagement ring. Something so she knows that we are serious and willing to wait for her, forever if need be."

He nodded. "After we tighten the wards, and deal with her problem, then we'll... propose?"

I nodded because it was such a weird idea. Manix didn't propose. We usually lived together as a Pack, and within the Pack some of the members mated, or they all mated, or none did. There was no promise of mating in the future. It was a natural progression, a short sprint from point A to point B. But Naja wasn't raised by Manix, and I had to trust the Beast she had inside her to lead her right, to let her know that we were perfect for her, just as mine knew she was perfect for us.

When I got back to the long table we were all sitting at, I didn't trust the gleam in my sister's eye. She'd had one too many wines and that usually meant she lost the last of her social niceties.

But I was too slow to head her off.

"So, Raiden, how many babies are you having and will you name one of them after me?"

That set off an absolute barrage of questions that Raiden fielded, some that Gatlin shut down, and some that put Naja under an insane amount of scrutiny. She stammered over her answers, trying to dodge questions that were way too personal, even for my family. By the end, even Terra looked a little guilty.

Finally, it got too much for even me. "That's enough. I know everyone is excited, and you all have questions, but it's as much of a mystery to us as it is to you. Now, stop stressing out my Omegas," I growled, more Beast than man for a moment.

Raiden looked more amused than anxious, but Naja twined her fingers with mine and squeezed.

"Thank you, Alpha," she whispered in my ear. My whole body shivered at the feel of her breath on my neck. Yeah, it was definitely time to go.

"Thanks for the food, Parentals. Terra, you're a dick. We're out."

I reached down and hoisted Naja into my arms, putting her over my shoulder and striding out of the backyard. I vaguely heard Ellar thanking my parents for having us, and Gatlin doing all the polite things. Seven, though? He was right on my heels. I paused near the door, spinning to look over my shoulder, checking where everyone was. Has someone grabbed Luisa? We weren't used to having a cub. Naja punched me in the asscheek, and I swear she corked the muscle.

"The blood is rushing to my head, you Neanderthal." I stepped out onto the front step, dropping her to her feet as Seven shut the door behind us. He was laughing.

Pain was still shooting down my thigh. "Holy fuck, that hurts!"

She grinned, and I was definitely fucking that pretty mouth later on; we'd see who'd be laughing then. I ushered her to the ATV just in time to see Gatlin exiting the house with Luisa in his arms, Raiden and Ellar behind them.

"Let's go!" I shouted at them. "Naja punched me in the ass and I intend to make her kiss it better."

SEVEN

My Packmates had, on occasion, accused me of being pessimistic. I wasn't a glass half empty, half full kind of guy. No, I believed that the glass was completely full. Full of piss. Life just didn't hand you happiness. You had to work for it every fucking day.

I don't think anyone got that the way Naja did. And sure, I was probably being a whiny bitch, considering her life before she'd come here had been one long hardship. Mine had been... okay. Until I'd met my Pack, that is, and now I was so fucking happy. But it still took work. I had to try hard to control my anger, to watch that I didn't speak before I thought and ruined everything.

I sat with Naja outside in the sun, a large picnic blanket on the grass, and Luisa off exploring under the watchful gaze of Finlo. It was idyllic, like the kind of moment you daydreamed about.

Naja looked up from where her head was in my lap. She was reading a book from Gatlin's library, and now she rested it on her chest as her eyes appraised my face. "I want to know more about you, Sev. All of you."

"What do you want to know?"

She sucked her lower lip between her teeth, which made me kind of want to do the same thing. "Tell me about your life before you joined the Pack."

Ugh. We were going straight for the scabbed over wounds then? Didn't matter, I would tell her whatever she wanted to know if it would make us closer, and convince her to stay forever. "It was a kind of basic existence."

She narrowed her eyes. "Really? Just run of the mill, hey?"

I snorted. "Fine. My parents didn't have a family Pack. They were one of the monogamous couples, but they had a lot of sons. Six, to be exact—two Alphas and the rest were Betas like me. That's a lot of cubs for a Manix Beta female. Anyway, I was the third oldest, but I was Beta. I wasn't the heir to the family—that went to my oldest brother, or the oldest Beta, who was my second oldest brother. I was just... middle of the line. I was treated as such. My parents, despite their ability to breed well, weren't very nurturing. They just did what good Manix couples did, bred until it was too dangerous to breed more." I couldn't keep the disgust out of my voice, but I shook it off and continued. "Anyway, after being basically ignored for sixteen years, I went out on my own. No, that's not quite true. I struck out with my best friend. His name was Casey. Anyway, Casey was the perfect Beta; a little bit subservient, but with a strong Beast and a nurturing nature. I'm pretty sure that's why we became friends in the first place, because I needed the softness and he couldn't help himself." I smiled at the memories playing in my brain, but they were the bittersweet kind.

"Long story short, we petitioned to join a Pack, and we were accepted almost immediately, probably because Casey did most of the talking. I was just the strong, silent type. A year in, I realized that the Alphas of my new Pack didn't want Betas. They wanted servants. Their idea of where a Beta should fit in a Pack was somewhere above paid help but miles below an Alpha. There was a fight when I refused to clean up after their dirty asses anymore. They tried to bend me to their will using their Alpha power, I resisted, and that's when we all realized that I was a strong Beta. Not a desirable quality for a Pack." This time the bitterness leaked into my tone like acid.

Naja gripped my hand and squeezed. "Yet you're perfect for this Pack," she said soothingly.

"So are you." It came out before I could stop it, and her eyes widened. I decided to ignore my little slip and pretend like it was nothing, continuing quickly with my story.

"So I got booted from the Pack. I begged Casey to come with me, but he wouldn't." The pain of losing my best friend was far worse than the pain of being booted from a Pack. I begged and begged, told him we were worth more than what they were offering, despite the prestige of their Pack, but Casey just shook his head over and over until I left. "We stopped being friends that day. I don't think we've ever spoken again." I cleared out the emotions that threatened to clog my throat. When we passed each other on the street now, we never made eye contact. Maxton wasn't a big place, so avoiding someone completely was nearly impossible, but I still mourned the loss of the only person who'd known and loved the Seven I was before... everything.

"Anyway, I was aimless for a bit, until another Pack decided to drag me out of the bottom of a bottle. Their Alpha said they didn't care that I was a strong Beta—hell, that they wanted that in their Betas. Sounded too good to be true. It *was* too good to be true but I was too stupid it see it." Disgust at the next part of the story made my stomach roil, but I carried on, determined to give Naja my truth. "Turns out that their Alpha did like strong Betas, because his favorite pastime was breaking them. Dominating them. Either through physical strength, Alpha power or... sexual domination." My voice broke a bit and I cursed myself for the weakness.

"Another long story short, he tried to force me, I bit off his left testicle, and ran as far from that toxic bull-shit as I could. The Alpha said I was too strong to follow Pack hierarchy, that it was my fault I was exiled from a second Pack in so many years, and that I was defective. I didn't need to worry about being in a Pack after that, because I was a pariah. My parents were so ashamed, they ostracised me from my family. Wrote me out of their will. To them, I don't exist."

Naja sat up and climbed into my lap, wrapping every part of her body around mine until I was encompassed in her warmth and scent.

"I'm going to kill him," she whispered in my ear, and I swear to god, my dick went from soft to punch-a-hole-through-drywall hard in a second.

I buried my face in her neck and inhaled deeply, drawing her into my lungs like she was nicotine and I was an addict. "No need, Princess. I have a happy ending, right here, right now, with you wrapped around me like a vice. Gatlin and Finlo were the Alphas I was meant to have; I just had to have a few false starts on the way."

She pulled back. "What he did was not okay. It was sexual assault."

I smiled wanly. "I know, baby. But I kept the testicle I bit off. It's in a jar in the family room downstairs." She let out a choked laugh. "When Gatlin found out why I'd been exiled from my second pack, he tracked down the Alpha. He beat him until his front teeth fell out, then kept them too. We can heal most things, but we can't regrow teeth. Now he looks like Gappy Joe, only has one ball and probably hasn't eaten a good steak in years. I've been plenty vindicated."

She laughed, resting her chin on my shoulder and not attempting to move out of my arms. Fuck, this was so nice. I loved our time altogether as a Pack, in one huge puppy pile, but this, wrapped in this creature that was too perfect for me or anyone else, was just more perfect than I'd ever hoped for.

"What about your brothers?"

I shrugged. "I see them from time to time, but we were never really close, you know? I'd chosen Casey as my brother, and he'd turned his back on me. My oldest brothers didn't approve of our parents' actions, but there's little they can do when they are firmly under my father's thumb."

She kissed my neck, scraping her teeth down the muscle there. "You know I wouldn't want you any other way, right? Scars and all. You had to go through all that shit to become the amazing man you are today. Fate, that fickle bitch, put you through all that so you could be the Manix this Pack needs and loves."

I tilted her chin towards me so I could kiss her properly. So I could pour all my appreciation and my hopes and yeah, my love, into the kiss. She kissed me back and ground against my dick, making me growl. But as much as I wanted to lay her down and fuck her right here under the wide blue sky, I resisted. I didn't want to end the perfection of this moment.

"Later on, you are in so much trouble, Princess."

She chuckled softly against my lips. "You and your promises."

I nipped her lips softly, making her give a little yip of surprise, and I didn't think it was possible to love another person the way I loved her right now. I couldn't tell her yet though. Later however, I would show her with my body just how much.

We were silent for a little bit longer, then I squeezed her tight. "I want to know everything about you too." She tensed in my arms, and I held her closer. "But your history doesn't need to taint this moment. Surely, there were a few good memories amongst the bad? Before Luisa, I mean."

She was silent for a long time, and if it was taking her this long to think of one happy moment... Well, my heart shattered into a thousand pieces and was reconstructed with rage as the glue. I tried to keep my emotions in check, but I was going to have to beat the fuck out of someone and soon.

Finally, she spoke. "When I was eight or nine, *he* went away for a month on business, taking a lot of his higher-level cronies with him. No one was there, and my Mom tried to detox. Tried to come back to me for just a little while. We couldn't leave, of course—there were still guards everywhere—but she locked herself in her bedroom, made me padlock the door from the outside, and went cold turkey for five days. I'd slip her granola bars and food under her door. When she came out, she looked like death but her eyes were clear for the first time in as long as I could remember. It was like having my mom back, the one I remembered from before, but had convinced myself was really just a dream. We baked. Created a succulent garden in the backyard. Watched old movies. It was the best three weeks of my life. Then he came back and she went back to being strung out all the time, until the end. But I remember that she went through that torture just to have a couple of weeks with me."

She buried her face back in my neck, and I could feel the hot slide of her tears against my skin. I didn't say anything, feeling like shit that I'd even brought it up, but sometimes you had to rip the scabs off old wounds so they had a chance to heal properly. I held her tightly, my chest thrumming in a purr, as I comforted her the best I could.

When her tears dried a little, and my legs were well and truly dead, I pulled her back slightly. "I swear that Luisa will only know happiness here. There'll only be laughter and light. We can't go back and erase your childhood, but we can give her the one you should have had. If you let us, we'll chase away all your pain too."

She nodded softly, burrowing back into me. I lay back, still holding her against my chest, thinking maybe she was right. Maybe my past was just what I needed to get here. It was a trial, but now I was the man who would protect her and Luisa until my final breath.

Seven had a really shitty opinion about the Universe and Fate. The ones you say with Capital letters like they were living entities. Sometimes I thought they must really be goddesses, because they could be cruel bitches when they wanted to be.

Two days before the witch was scheduled to return to fix the ward, the perimeter alarms blared to life. It sounded like a smoke alarm, an ear-piercing whooping noise waking us all from our sleep. I was wrapped in Gatlin's arms, with Raiden pressed against my back. Seven and Finlo were in bed with Naja.

Luisa had moved to the nursery we'd been painstakingly constructing over the last two weeks. Gatlin sat straight up, on his feet and in sweats faster than my eyes could track. Raiden wasn't far behind me, and I scrabbled off the bed, shucking myself quickly into sweats and heading to Luisa's room. The little girl was standing in her crib, her eyes wide with fear. I picked her up, and she wrapped her arms around my neck so tightly that I could feel her trembling.

"Don't worry, Little Bit. It's just the alarm. Everything is okay," I cooed softly, and she relaxed a little in my arms. The alarm cut out, but none of the lights came on. We didn't need lights; it would just make us easy targets in case this wasn't a false alarm. But I knew it wasn't, could feel it deep in my gut.

Naja appeared, holding out her arms, and I passed her Luisa. Although she had a small smile on her face, I could see the absolute fear in her eyes. She was keeping it locked down for the cub, but she was terrified.

Raiden came into the nursery, and I could see from the bulges beneath his clothes that he was armed. "Gatlin, Finlo and Seven are going to check it out. They've called the Legion Force, and they are on their way. We should head up to the nest."

We'd come up with a plan for this. In the case of an incursion, Raiden, Naja, Luisa, and I needed to head up to the nest. It had a reinforced door, and we could escape across the roof if we needed to. I was the last line of defense for them. That fucking terrified the shit out of me. I didn't have the combat training the others had, but what I did have was an extreme protective instinct. If it came to it, my Beast would tear apart anyone who came for our Omegas and cub. I had to trust the Beast.

I ushered them all up the stairs, and I could tell Raiden was annoyed that he couldn't be out there too. But he carried our future, and he needed to worry about protecting them first. I bolted the door in three places. We'd replaced it with reinforced steel and bolt slides. It wouldn't be easy to kick in, even for a super-natural. Unless you were a vampire, of course.

Raiden walked straight over to the window and looked out into the darkness. I couldn't tell if it was my mind playing tricks on me, or if I could really see movement in the trees. I willed the Legion to hurry the fuck up.

Then the gunshots started. Distant at first, but each one ratcheted up my anxiety. Naja sat on the side of the sunken couch, Luisa clutched to her chest, and she flinched with every shot. I sat beside her, pressing her to my side. "It's gonna be okay, baby. We were literally bred for this."

She nodded, but I didn't think much was sinking in.

Raiden looked back over his shoulder at me. "There are dozens of them out there. The Legion Force isn't going to make it in time. We're already surrounded."

Naja's breathing became ragged. Raiden came over

and knelt in front of her, one hand on Luisa's back as he sent his calming Omega power through her body. "I promise you, Naja, that this ends tonight. He will die. You will be safe."

She shook her head. "You don't even know he's out there."

Raiden growled. "He's out there. That psycho fuck has been here the whole time, watching and waiting. I'll kill him myself."

I growled low in my chest too. "I'll spit on his corpse."

He kissed her head and stood, heading back to the window. More gunshots echoed, but I refused to think that one of my family might be out there catching those bullets. I believed what I'd told Naja—we were made for this. They would be okay.

My eyes moved to Raiden, and I saw him tense. He threw me a meaningful look and I knew what it meant. They'd breached the yard and were heading to the house. How had they gotten so close without tripping the perimeter wards?

"Any sign of the guys?" I asked softly, but Raiden shook his head. Naja let out a sob, and I squeezed her closer. Raiden handed me a gun, and I took it.

"Baby, I need you to come over here and sit with Luisa behind this cupboard, okay?" I moved the wardrobe as silently as I could, so there was only a little space between the wall and the wardrobe. It would stop any stray bullets and protect them both.

Naja came over and sat behind it, and I hated the blank looks on both their faces. I knew she was reliving the past, they both were, and I wanted to roar in rage.

Instead, I moved to the other side of the room and waited. We didn't have to wait long. There was a thump on the door as they tried to get into the nest.

"Locked," I heard someone yell, and another voice came through the door eerily clearly.

"I know you're in there. Come out and this all ends. The rest of your boyfriends don't have to die, and you can even leave the brat here with them. I just want you."

Raiden held his fingers to Naja's lips as she opened her mouth in a silent scream. Her eyes were squeezed shut but somehow the tears were still falling down her cheeks.

He was full of shit though. We were all mated. I would know if one of the guys was dead, but Naja didn't know that and I couldn't reassure her without giving us away.

We should have mated her when we had the chance. Should have told her we loved her.

The chilling voice on the other side chuckled. "It's always the hard way with you, Marigold... Burn the place to the ground. We'll smoke the foxes out of their little hole."

I could hear the stomping of feet down the stairs. It wasn't long until the smell of smoke drifted up though. They'd lit something on fire, probably the stairs themselves, forcing us to go out through the window. We had to act fast.

"I'll go out, draw their fire toward me, and then you guys can head for the woods. Try to get to Maxton."

Raiden was shaking his head. "Fuck no. Ellar." He walked over to me and gripped my chin. "I will go. I have better aim and can take some of those fuckers out." He dropped his voice low. "If the worst happens, I can't carry her out of here, man. This?" He pointed to his protruding stomach. "It makes me weaker, makes us more vulnerable. You need to protect her. She is the most important thing right now, do you understand me?"

I was shaking my head. No. That was not how it worked. "You can't. The cubs."

Raiden swallowed hard. "There can be more cubs without me, El. But not without her. You have to protect her at all costs." He stepped away. "I'm going to head back across the roof and back through Finlo's window. Maybe I can put out the fire and buy us some time until the Legion Force arrives. If you hear gunfire, go. Don't look for me, just go." He walked toward Naja, crouching in front of them. "I'm going to put out the fire, Princess." She looked up at him and he kissed her so tenderly that it could only be construed as a goodbye. "I love you—you know that, right?"

Raiden didn't wait for her reply, instead kissing the top of Luisa's head and sprinting to the window. Unlatching the round panel, he swung it open on squeaky hinges. Raiden let out his Beast, scales covering his body and his ears twitching. He didn't switch to his stealth form, which was better at hiding but more vulnerable to bullets.

He stopped and kissed me. "Look after her, Ellar. I love you." Then he was gone.

I shut and locked the window, even though I desperately wanted to climb out there after him. The smoke was getting stronger, and I didn't know if Raiden would even be able to put it out if he got down there.

I paced back and forth, my ears straining to hear anything, any hint of rescue. But all I heard was the crackle of the fire taking hold and the sound of gunshots further away.

When those shots sounded closer, I knew we had to move.

"Naja, baby, we gotta go." I ran over and stroked her face, bringing her out of whatever terror she was in. "We have to go."

I would protect them; it was the only thing I could do. The alternative was unthinkable. I dragged her to her feet, and that seemed to bring her out of her own head. She stepped up to the window and I opened it quietly, not that I thought anyone would hear it.

I shifted forms, my hands elongating to claws, the barbs of my knuckles piercing my skin as the scales ran across my body. Everything was clearer in this form, but it made Luisa whimper and I hated that.

"It's okay, Little Bit. It's still me, El. But with fluffy ears." She'd been fine with it before, but the situation was making her more frightened, the darkness making me more of a monster than her friend. I climbed out the window first, looking down to see if there was anyone down there to take pot shots at us.

All clear from what I could tell, so I ushered Naja out onto the roof. I put myself between her and the open space, hemming her in against the wall. We walked swiftly under the eaves, but when we rounded the corner, I froze. Four men, all dressed in black, were stuffing an unconscious Raiden into the back of a van.

"No," Naja whispered. "No, no, no." She peeled Luisa off her body and stuffed her in my arms. I reflexively grabbed the cub but it meant I was too slow to stop what happened next. She looked me dead in the eye, all her previous fear gone, an iron determination replacing it. "Take care of her, Ellar. She's my whole world."

Then she turned and jumped off the roof.

"No!"

One minute I was landing painfully on the dirt, and the next I was on my back staring up into the face of my worst nightmare. Him. Iago, my uncle. He smiled down at me, but it was a sharp-toothed expression. Cruel in the extreme. I also realized I wasn't in Manix territory anymore. I was in a room, the walls concrete and cold. I was on a dirty concrete floor, and Iago had his boot to my neck.

"Hello, Marigold. I'm glad you woke; I couldn't sell a lifeless corpse. Though, there is a market for that." I swallowed bile as he laughed at his own joke. "In my opinion, you would be preferable in a permanent coma. I am fairly sure you can provide what the buyer wants without consciousness."

The bile surged back up and I turned my head,

vomiting on the ground beside me. It was hard with his boot on my neck but I wasn't going to die choking on my own vomit. Iago screwed his nose up in distaste.

"What do you want, Iago? I'm just a fucking mongrel half-blood tigress. What the fuck do you want?" I screamed, but it came out more as a gasp as he increased the pressure.

He sneered at me. "Oh, Marigold, we both know you are more than that."

I began to struggle as the oxygen got less and less. I clawed at his leg and he laughed, black spots dancing in my vision. This was how I died then—beneath my uncle's boot heel, just how I'd lived. At the last moment, just before blackness consumed me, he lifted his boot and I heaved in oxygen.

Iago wandered away, talking to the room like he was some great orator rather than a piece of shit. "I'm an intelligent enough person to admit when I was wrong. I always thought that it was your mother who supplied the Manix genes, but I have since learned that it wasn't her at all. All those years and useless offspring wasted. It wasn't her—it was your father who was the Manix. Apparently, my mother was a whore too. I should have guessed." He paused. "But you were Manix, a female at that, and I needed more. Most in the supernatural world think your species is dead. Extinct. Thank you for leading me right to an entire colony of them. Bad for supply and demand, but it's always nice to have a farm." His grin widened and I tried not to flinch at the expression. "Imagine my surprise when I realized I had the last remaining female Omega Manix just living under my roof. Your value skyrocketed. Hell, I could name my price and my buyer would take it." He was practically gleeful, and I shuddered.

"I don't know what the fuck you're talking about, you psycho piece of shit."

Iago frowned. "You are a lot more mouthy when I don't have the brat to keep you in line. Luckily for me, I brought along some new insurance. Bring in our guest," he yelled to whoever was watching the door

Ice flooded my veins. No. He couldn't mean…

They dragged in a nearly unconscious Raiden, and I screamed. Scrabbling to my feet, I rushed over to him. He was shirtless and bleeding from what seemed to be dozens of knife wounds. His face was absolutely battered, but they'd left his torso alone.

I leaned over him, hissing at the men who held him. Men I'd feared my whole life.

Raiden opened one battered eye and looked at me. "Naja." Then he passed out again. Blood loss? Head injury?

I checked him over and could see he had a couple of broken fingers, the wounds and gashes across his chest and back, and his face was a mess, but they hadn't touched his stomach.

"Oh, don't look so relieved, Marigold. I wouldn't hurt the future merchandise. Do you think I'll get another female Omega from the litter? This is like one of those surprise unboxings." He actually sounded gleeful.

His phone rang, and he pulled it out of his jacket pocket to answer. His face lit up at whoever's name was on the screen.

"Ah, it's nice to hear from you, old friend. Yes, I have retrieved the merchandise." He was silent for a moment and then his brows rose. "I see. And where did you hear that? Hmm, interesting."

I was dying to know who was on the phone but it didn't take a genius to realize it was my buyer. "I'm afraid I am reluctant to part with the new stock. Perhaps after he's..." His eyes grew wide. "How much? Oh, well then, we might just have a deal, friend. Always best to get a breeding pair. I'm afraid that the new stock had a bit of a rough time in transit though, he doesn't look the prettiest." Whatever the other guy said made Iago laugh. "Fair enough. I shall see you soon."

Iago pocketed his phone and turned to grin at me. "Marigold. You have just made me the richest fucker on the planet."

He gave orders for someone to clean up Raiden, but I kicked and scratched any person who even came close to him. I was feral, my long-dormant Beast riding me. I could feel her moving under my skin, frustrated that we weren't Manix enough to burst out and put these fuckers down like the rabid dogs they were.

Someone dropped a bucket and a cloth at my feet, plus a first aid kit. "You do it then, you psycho bitch." He called me a string of vile names as he walked away, but I took the kit and opened it up. It was basic, but it would do. I ignored the water, which could be full of god knows what. I wouldn't trust these fuckers as far as I could throw them. I closed up the wounds I could with bandaids, relying on Raiden's supernatural healing. There was nothing I could do for his face though. I cleaned it up as best I could, wiping the dirt and fuck knows what else from his skin. He flinched away, and I softened my touch. I'd caused him enough pain now. I wouldn't cause him any more.

"Raiden, baby," I whispered, choking back a sob that caught in my throat and expanded so big I was worried I'd choke on it.

This was all my fucking fault. I should have left Luisa with them and run. Instead, I was selfish, so fucking selfish, and now Raiden was paying for it. I'd started to believe I could have it all, and could be happy. What a fucking joke. Some people weren't destined for happiness and I was one of them.

I stroked Raiden's hair from his face gently, but it was tacky with blood and that made me cry harder.

I looked at the predators in the room, turning so I

could keep them all in my line of sight. They were drinking tequila and laughing like they hadn't nearly beaten Raiden to death, like they weren't selling me to some freaking psycho who wanted... who wanted to... My mind shied away from the thought. Instead I crouched beside Raiden, my hand on his stomach, the only uninjured part of him.

The cubs kicking against my hand just made me want to cry and cry and cry. My selfishness had prevented them from having a life too. *I'm so sorry, little ones. I've fucked it all up before you even had a chance to enter the world. I'm so sorry.*

The sound of a helicopter landing outside made the guards whoop, because I guessed it was their payday landing, and my stomach threatened to revolt again. My uncle stood, straightening his jacket, which told me that he wanted to impress the man who was about to arrive. It meant he was either super rich or super powerful. Definitely one hundred percent evil.

Something snapped inside me, and I scrubbed my cheeks on my forearm. If this fucker thought I was going to come easily, he was insane. No, I knew if they managed to get me onto that helicopter, I was better off dead. I looked around the warehouse we were in. It was obvious that it was a warehouse because it was filled with shipping containers. It was definitely remote, because until that helicopter had landed, there hadn't been a single sound.

I had to pay attention. If I was going to get us out of this, I couldn't be fucking weepy. I had to be tough. Smart like I used to be. I'd fucking learned how to make the best forgeries south of the goddamn border. I'd navigated the dark web and saved Luisa. I was a badass. This shit wasn't over yet.

My inner pep talk managed to chase back some of the fear, and I searched for a potential weapon. It was a fucking warehouse though; it wasn't like they were just going to have Uzis lying around.

My uncle moved to the door of the warehouse, his guards flanking him. I could see my buyer, and he was younger than I'd expected. He was in a three piece suit, and looked like he had the whole fucking world in the palm of his hand. But the cruel twist of his lips told me he wanted more, and he wanted to make it bleed.

We couldn't leave with him. I searched harder and saw a crowbar lying discarded beside some crates. Nothing like bringing a crowbar to a gunfight, but it was better than nothing. Keeping an eye on the group near the huge sliding doors of the warehouse, I crab-walked backwards toward the crowbar. I hated to leave Raiden unprotected, but I couldn't make sudden movements otherwise I'd attract the attention of the guards.

When my hand finally hit the cold metal of the crowbar, I gripped it. Fuck, it was heavy. But that was a good thing—maybe I could cave in a few skulls before they killed me.

A soft sound behind me had me whipping my head around. Someone was hiding in the shadows. I strained my eyes, and who I saw made my jaw drop open.

The very last person I ever expected to see soft-walked toward me. He looked at me, and I saw the shock in his eyes too. "You," he mouthed softly, his eyes wide.

I couldn't even form words. Why would the guy who'd smuggled me out of Mexico be here lurking in the shadows? I never even knew his name, but I didn't think he'd been working for my uncle.

I opened my mouth to demand answers, but he shook his head violently, lifting his finger to his lips. He reached behind his back, and pulled out a gun. He silently passed it to me, and I gripped the warm metal in my hand.

He tilted his head back toward Raiden. "Go," he mouthed.

I didn't want to go back to being a sitting duck, but for some reason, I trusted this guy. He'd saved me once, and I had to believe he'd do it again. I checked the safety was on, and then stuffed the gun down between my breasts. I moved faster toward Raiden this time, and breathed a sigh of relief when I was able to touch him again.

He was awake now, and his eyes were full of questions, but I shook my head. I didn't have any answers for him, even if I had the chance to speak right now. The solid weight of the gun against my chest was like a security blanket, and I vowed that even if I didn't escape, I'd put a bullet between the eyes of my uncle, and kill my monsters forever.

42

GATLIN

There were too many of them. They'd swarmed from the trees in the dozens and it was statistically impossible to hold them back. But we'd fucking tried and now the woods around our home, our Pack house, was littered with bodies.

But it had been for nothing. They'd taken Naja. They'd taken Raiden. Seven had taken some kind of armor-piercing bullet to the gut and was in surgery. I had failed my Pack. I'd failed them as an Alpha, as a protector.

Finlo was bloody in the corner, his back against the wall, his head hanging low. The Legion were here, in the Doc's office, conferring. Too fucking late. Everything they did was too fucking late. The Legion Force had been too late. The witch had been too late. Everything was too late, and now they were gone.

Raiden's dad was nearly hysterical. "I say we get the Legion Force together and get my son back," he growled, but my father was shaking his head.

"And what? Where do we send them? We don't know where they've taken them. We need to get our best trackers out there and get on their trail."

"Our best tracker is in surgery," Finlo's dad shouted.

It went on like that, everyone talking but no one making any decisions. I didn't know what to do. I'd lost two great loves of my life because I hadn't been good enough.

"If we'd given her to a proper Pack, we'd still have the last female Omega," someone said, and I stiffened. I was on my feet, but not as fast as Finlo was, and he had the Legion General on the floor and was pounding his face. The General might have been powerful, but he was old. Finlo was young and powerful in his own right, and I had no intention of dragging him off the cocksucking piece of shit.

His dads unfortunately had better sense, pulling their son off before he did permanent damage. I didn't care anymore.

But everyone stopped when a glowing portal opened in the middle of the doctor's office and the Witch Miranda stepped out. Everyone gaped, most of them having never seen the weird portalling thing she did before, and I dropped my head.

"What the fuck happened?" she said in a low voice that made all the hairs on my body stand on end. On the outside, she might be a pretty woman in a peasant blouse, but on the inside there was power that far outranked anything I, or any Manix, could counter. I knew that in my soul.

Still, I didn't fucking care. "Your schedule meant that the wards were still weak when they attacked. They just walked straight through them, like you said. They are gone." My voice broke, and I didn't care. I didn't want to be the toughest Alpha in the room anymore. I didn't want to be anything.

She turned her angry glare on my father. "You. Squabbling over pennies and look what has happened. You are a disgrace." An Eastern European accent made itself known, and I wondered absently if it only came out when she was angry. She looked back at me, her glare like an inescapable snare. "You. Tell me what happened. Everything."

So I went through the whole thing, from the moment the alarms blared, to fighting a Kevlar-protected army as I uselessly watched Naja throw herself off the roof, and the enemy scooping her up, tossing her into the back of a van. The glimpse I saw of Raiden in that same van. Of finding an absolutely devastated Ellar clutching a traumatised Luisa in the woods halfway to Maxton.

They were at Finlo's parents house now, as ours had been reduced to rubble. All those memories. Gone. It was painful, but not as painful as not knowing what was happening to my Omegas right now.

No, not *my* Omegas. I didn't deserve them.

Miranda clucked her tongue. "Enough of the pity party, Alpha. You lost the battle but the war is far from over." She gave my father another disgusted look and then pulled a phone from the pockets of her voluminous skirt.

She clicked the number 2, holding it down. I could hear the grumble of a voice down the line. "Alexander. I need to call in a favor." Whatever the person at the other end of the line said made her lips twitch. "Not now, Alexander. This is a time sensitive matter." She quickly outlined the events of the last few hours. "I want your super special team on it. Don't bullshit me and say that they don't exist—we both know they do." She paused, her eyebrows rising, until they nearly met the auburn of her hairline. "Indeed. Is that so? Well, isn't that fortuitous. I have two Alphas who would like to join that operation. No, they aren't liabilities, you pompous fucking lizard. They are Manix." She sighed and squeezed the bridge of her nose. "Obviously not, Alexander, because I am literally standing in a room filled with them. Can we discuss this later, when the last female fucking Omega Manix isn't about to die? Yes? Okay." More silence. "No need, I'll bring them to you." Whatever he said next made the witch's cheeks flush, and a small smile turned up her lips. "Only in your dreams, Dragon."

Then she hung up. If you believed her words, she hung up on a fucking dragon. This bitch was terrifying, and one look at the rest of the Manix in the room told me that we all knew it.

She turned back to me. "You shifters are all so dismissive of that Moon Goddess of yours, but sometimes she truly does smile on you. It just so happens that the Convocation Member for the Shifters has been doing a sting on this Iago for nearly two decades."

Iago. The name that Naja had refused to speak, but a little bit of digging had made it easy to find out information on him. He was brutal. A sociopath. Little better than a rabid animal. He was wanted in the US on drugs and trafficking charges, but the human FBI agents kept getting shipped back to FBI headquarters in pieces. Sometimes in a box with a ribbon. Because they were dealing with shifters and not normal drug dealers. He was every bit the monster that Naja had said he was. And now he had her and Raiden.

"Long story short, he reached out to one of Alexander's assets and said he had the last Manix available for sale. The asset jumped on it. They're going to take this piece of shit down tonight, and you're going to get back your Omegas." Fuck, I needed my guns, but Miranda was hurrying me. "Let's go, they'll have the weapons you need and we don't want to miss it."

"I'll get my car," Finlo said, and the witch shook her head.

She grinned at us, and it was just as predatory as any shifter. "No need." She waved her arm and a slit in reality that glowed a real weird red, appeared again. "Get in the portal. We are wasting time and it's been a while since I've shed a little blood. I don't want to miss it."

Well, that was as reassuring as a red balloon down a storm drain. But I had nothing left to lose. I stepped through the portal, Finlo close on my heels. It was like walking through quicksand, but when I came out the other side, I was somewhere less mountainous and far clearly from home. I couldn't even see our mountains from here.

They'd moved them so far in such a short time. Three huge dudes turned, and it wasn't often we met anyone else of our stature. But I stood eye to eye with the guy who was obviously the leader. He grinned at me.

"Holy shit, you guys are big fuckers. Alexander wasn't fucking with me when he said that two Manix were coming to help out. No offense man, but I thought you guys were all dead. Functionally extinct except the little Omega in there."

I curled my top lip. "Mine."

The huge guy lifted both hands. "Definitely yours, bro. I have my own little Omega at home, and she's more than a handful." He thrust out a hand. "Name's Vance, Alpha of the Cold River Sleuth. These are my Packmates Talbot and Franklin. Bear shifters. My team and I operate to rescue shifters from dangerous or undesirable situations."

Well, that would explain the size of these guys and the army around us. With that, the guy morphed back into soldier mode, and outlined the plan. It was simple as far as plans went: get in, extract the hostages, and get back out again. I looked at the assembled people, inhaling deeply. Mostly shifters of various species, but damn, were those two guys human? What the hell were humans doing in this fight? No one seemed overly worried about them though, and one handled the automatic rifle like he was born with it in his hand, so I wouldn't begrudge his help.

Fuck, I would take anyone's help right now.

Vance's phone chirped and he looked at the screen. "Asset is here in T minus twenty. Everyone move out and into position."

I looked at Finlo, at the determined set of his jaw. We were getting them back, or we weren't coming back at all.

The minutes dragged on as my uncle talked, and I tried to keep my breathing under control. I wanted to pant in panic, but I couldn't. I needed to stay alert. Something was about to go down, and I didn't want to be having a panic attack in the corner when it happened. They finally quit talking, and the buyer pulled out his phone. Probably the funds transfer. Whatever he'd done had put a huge smile on my uncle's face.

Iago waved his hand and stepped aside, like we were a prize on a gameshow that he'd won.

The man strode over like my uncle was beneath him, his shoulders tight and his face impassive. You wouldn't think he had just spent what I assumed was tens of millions of dollars on buying actual living people.

His guards were huge, and they held their finger on the triggers of their AK's. They never stopped scanning the room for threats. Looking for a trap maybe? A double-cross? I wouldn't put it past my uncle.

The man stopped in front of me, his face still cool. "Naja. It is a pleasure to finally meet you." There was nothing lecherous in his tone, nothing to insinuate that he'd bought me for any kind of sexual proclivities.

I set my jaw. "I won't go with you quietly."

Big guy to his left cleared his throat, and then he winked at me. Again, not in a lecherous way, more like we were both in on a secret. Oh shit... The guy from Mexico hiding between the containers. They weren't looking for a double-cross—they were *executing* the double-cross.

The man, my new owner, reached out a perfectly manicured hand. "Let us go."

I shook my head. Double-cross or not, I wasn't going anywhere with these fuckers. "I won't leave Raiden."

The man gave me a look laden with meaning, but maybe I'd done more damage than I thought with my swan dive from the roof of the house, because I couldn't decipher what he was trying to tell me. His jaw flexed. "We won't leave the Omega either, Naja. Please, let's go."

But it was too late when I finally understood his meaning.

Someone shouted that it was an ambush, and then all hell broke loose. Bullets flew, and the man bent and scooped me up. I whimpered as he ran toward the containers for cover. I looked back to see one of his big guards had grabbed Raiden while the other provided cover.

"Fuck!" The man growled, dropping me unceremoniously to the ground behind one of the shipping containers.

As if summoned by the curse word, the guy from my past reappeared. My original savior. One of the big guys pointed at him. "Kell, watch them." Then they all disappeared, leaving me with my Omega and the fucking mystery man.

"Kell. Nice to finally have a name."

Kell grinned as he lined up a guy who was trying to climb the gangway and pulled the trigger. The guy fell over the edge, and I had no doubt he was dead. "Nice to meet you too—Naja, right? How's the kid?"

I swallowed hard at the thought of Luisa in Ellar's arms. "Safe, I hope."

Kell gave me a sympathetic look. "We'll get you back to her soon." Then his eyes were back on target, ducking around the corner to shoot anyone who got too close. I dropped to my knees and covered Raiden.

He'd fallen into unconsciousness once more, and now I was worried. But I wouldn't allow us to be saved only to lose him. I wouldn't. The presence of Kell—the guy who'd delivered me to safety—eased something inside of me. I hugged myself around Raiden's head, protecting it from the stray bullets pinging against the container we were hiding behind.

Finally, the gunfire stopped, and strong hands grabbed me. A scent that I craved as much as oxygen filled my lungs. "Gatlin," I gasped, and I was spun and encompassed in strong arms. Finlo was right behind him, and he fell to his knees beside Raiden, sucking in a breath at his injuries. "How long has he been out?"

I shook my head, because I didn't know. This ordeal felt like it had taken months, but it could have been only an hour. "Forty minutes maybe? I don't know, he's been in and out of consciousness." The panic that I'd kept locked down now threatened to rise up and consume me.

Gatlin squeezed me tightly and passed me into Finlo's arms as he bent down to check out Raiden. Finlo enveloped me completely in his arms, like he was trying to merge us into one person. "God, I've never been more scared, Princess. Terrified."

I swallowed hard and suddenly realized I was crying. "Luisa? Ellar and Seven?"

FInlo squeezed me harder. "All fine. Seven was shot, but Doc is patching him up. Luisa and Ellar are at my parents' house now, and they couldn't possibly be more protected, I swear to you."

Guilt washed over me. The Pack house. "The house?"

Finlo hushed me, kissing my face and hair. "We'll talk about it later. Nothing we can do about it now."

The shouts of my uncle had me tensing in Finlo's arms. He was swearing, and I stepped out of Finlo's arms to look back into the open space. My eyes skittered over the pool of blood where Raiden had been lying and over to my uncle, who was on his knees in front of the man who'd bought me. I was so fucking confused right now.

Finlo must have gleaned the direction of my thoughts. "We're as surprised as you are, but apparently there's some super secret task force that's been watching your uncle for decades."

Thank the Goddess. I desperately wanted to watch him taken away in cuffs.

Actually, no I didn't. I walked toward my uncle, handcuffed on the ground. I walked toward the man who had been a waking nightmare to me for as long as I could remember. He had the fucking audacity to smile up at me, the evil shining brightly in his eyes.

"Ah, Naja. I will be seeing you."

Calm came over me. Calm like nothing I'd ever felt. I was floating in a sea of nothingness, no sound, no emotion. Just all perfectly blank. I looked down at my uncle and shook my head.

"No, you won't. Enjoy Hell, you piece of shit."

I whipped the gun out from between my breasts so fast, sliding off the safety in the same movement, that no one had time to react before I put it to his head, blowing his brains all over the concrete floor.

I had conquered my monster and he'd haunt me no more.

Someone was laughing. I looked up to see one of the big guys pointing and laughing at the other one. Actually, staring at them now, I was fairly sure they were twins.

"Franklin, you've got brains on your shoes," he chortled, like it was the funniest thing ever. Franklin shook his boot, dislodging the chunk of my uncle's brain until it slid onto the floor. "Gross. A little warning next time so I can get out of the splash zone, hey?" he said to me, and seemed more amused than pissed off.

I looked between them all. The only ones who looked concerned were my Alphas, and I was pretty sure that was because I'd just murdered someone in cold blood.

The biggest guy shrugged again. "Eh, he deserved it, and it's less paperwork this way. We're going to have to get clean-up in here though."

"Leave it to me." The Witch Miranda appeared from somewhere, completely bathed in blood, and grinning. The actual fuck?

The big guy rolled his eyes. "You know this is why we don't invite witches to these things normally,

Miranda. You guys always have to play with your food. It's hell on stealth missions."

Miranda continued to grin completely unapologetically. She murmured something beneath her breath, waving a finger, and then everything disappeared. The bodies, the blood, all of it.

"Waste not, want not, young Alpha," she said to the big guy, before turning to us. "Are you guys ready to go? I'll give you a lift home."

Gatlin was nodding, but someone cleared their throat. It was the guy who'd bought me. I froze. "I'd like a word with Naja, if I may?"

I could sense my Alphas preparing to say no, so I stepped toward him and nodded. The more I stared at him, the more familiar he looked, but I couldn't work out why. Oh, he was still cold, dead behind his eyes, and yet there was something about those eyes that my brain was furiously trying to remember.

We were silent for a long time, and I was wondering if he was ever going to speak when he finally said, "All your siblings are safe. The babies. I bought them from Iago every time one came up for sale. He thought he was scamming me out of money, but the truth is, I would have paid a lot more to save their lives."

Of all the things I'd expected him to say, that wasn't it. "What?" I shook my head, not understanding. "Why? I mean, thank you, but why?"

He sucked in a deep breath. "Because they were innocent. Because they were your siblings. Because they deserved the happiness I couldn't give you."

I could hear Gatlin's low grumble behind me, but he made no move to pull me back to him. "But why? Why do I matter enough that you'd pay to save my siblings?"

None of that shit made sense to me. None of it.

He sucked in another deep breath, and for the first time an emotion entered his eyes. Anguish. "I should start again. My name is Courtland." He paused for a moment. "I am your half-brother. I failed you, failed your mother. The children—your siblings—were penance for my failure."

A high-pitched sound started quietly in my ear, and grew until it was all I could hear. "You're my brother? I don't understand. Are you…?"

It was Finlo who answered my question. "He is Manix."

It was too fucking much. This whole thing was too fucking much. Blackness curtained my vision, and I heard Finlo's yelp of alarm just before I went lights out.

If I'd died and gone to hell, it was soft and smelled really good. I pried open an eye and reached out a hand, searching through the softness for something, anything. When I hit the warm hip of a person, my eyes shot open. Seven lay beside me and he looked rough. His pallor was grey, and his lips were dry. I'd have thought he was dead if it wasn't for the rough wheeze of his breath.

I sat up, wincing as wounds on my chest pulled and tugged.

"Easy, Omega." Finlo was there, pushing me back down onto the pillows gently. On the other side of Seven, I'd seen a sleeping Naja, and something in my chest loosened.

"Gatlin? Ellar and Luisa?"

Finlo's big hand stroked over my head. "All

perfectly fine. Ellar had Luisa halfway back to Maxton by the time we found him. He did such a great job."

I let myself relax, letting go of the tension that had held my body in a vice. "Tell me the rest."

I remembered too much of the night. The pain. The helplessness. But the last thing I remembered was Naja looking down at me, tears streaming down her cheeks.

Finlo hesitated. "You should rest, Rai. We can talk about this later."

I shook my head. "Tell me."

He sighed, and I could tell he wanted to be in bed with me, holding me in his arms but there wasn't enough room. Instead, I felt a soft hand on my chest and realized that we'd woken Naja. I gripped her hand in mine, lifting it to my lips to kiss her knuckles.

Finlo let out another long sigh. "Turns out that Iago, Naja's uncle, was already on the radar of some very powerful people. Gatlin and I muscled our way into their rescue attempt. You were unconscious and looked like you'd gone ten rounds with a fucking gorilla shifter. We brought you back here and you've been out for forty-eight hours. Doc said your vitals were all fine but your body needed time to heal."

The strain on his face, the desperation in his tone, all tugged at my heart. I reached down and smoothed a hand over my swollen abdomen. "The cubs?"

Finally, Finlo smiled. "Healthy, happy, and wildly oblivious to the turmoil."

A relieved breath whooshed out of me. We were all okay, or almost all okay. I turned on my side, facing Seven. He hadn't woken up even with all the chatter.

"What happened to Sev?" I ran my hand over his chest, pausing when I hit the gauze covering half of his stomach.

Finlo stood, coming closer to kneel beside Naja, so he could put a hand on our Beta himself. "Got hit by an armor-piercing bullet. It took a long time for them to fish out all the pieces, and his body has shut down until it finishes healing. Doc says he'll be fine and should wake up anytime now. I've never wanted to kiss the surly bastard as much as I do right now."

So much anguish. So much pain.

I looked over at Finlo and Naja, their heads close together as they watched me intently. "It's over, right?"

Naja nodded. "I put our tormentor in his grave myself. No one hurts what's mine."

I blinked, looking at Finlo for confirmation. Naja had killed her uncle? My sweet, soft Naja? No—she was sweet and soft with us, but I'd seen the steel beneath the surface.

I wanted to ask more questions and fill in the gaps that were missing from my memory, but exhaustion was dragging me down again. My eyes fluttered closed but this time, my body could actually rest.

. . .

THE NEXT TIME I woke up it was to the piercing blue of Seven's eyes. "Hey," he whispered, and I leaned forward, kissing him.

He kissed me back, his lips dry but soft now. I pressed myself against him, though it was hard given his gunshot wound and my stomach. Finally, he drew away, and I rested my head against his arm. "How are you doing?" His voice was always rough, like he'd smoked a cigar a day, and I loved it.

"I should be asking you that, Sev. You were the one that was shot."

He thrummed low in his throat, the look on his face murderous. "I saw you when you came in, Rai." He didn't expand on that, which I was happy about. I was going to avoid the memories as best I could. The cuts on my chest had scabbed and soon enough there'd be no trace of them at all. On the outside, anyway.

"I'm fine. Happy to be home. Relieved it's all over."

Seven's hand rubbed my belly and the cubs kicked against the pressure. We sat there in silence a little longer, just appreciating the quiet moments and the fact we were both alive.

Finally, Seven stood stiffly. "I'm sick of being in a fucking bed." He shuffled to the ensuite, and I crawled out of bed too. Struggling to drag my sweats up my legs, I grunted with effort until Seven returned, and together we got dressed.

I knew we were at Finlo's parents house—I recognized the decor—and that brought up something I'd purposefully not been thinking about. Our beautiful home was gone, the one my two Alphas had built with their own hands. The first place we'd made love, where we'd taken our matebond vows, where the cubs were conceived. Where we were all so fucking happy. I swallowed hard, and the scent of my sadness had Seven slowing. He turned and wrapped me in his arms and I rested my forehead against his chest.

He was more intuitive than any of us gave him credit for though. He kissed my head. "We'll rebuild it, Omega. As a Pack. It'll be our home, with little touches of us all. A big playroom for the cubs, and that fancy kitchen you've always wanted. Maybe a conservatory for our Omega. A proper workshop for Gatlin, and the best nest you can think of, Rai. It will be our dream home, all the more because the Pack that is living there is a dream come true for me."

Big fucking romantic. "Love you, Sev."

He kissed my forehead and wrapped his arm around my shoulder. "Love you too, Omega. Now, let's get out of this fucking room. I'm so done with being an invalid."

We walked out of the spare room and down the big marble halls of Finlo's family home. I could hear the soft murmur of voices and as we walked past what was the family room, I noticed Leisel and Luisa playing on the floor. Leisel heard our approach first, jumping up to stand in front of Luisa like a little protector. It made me smile.

But as soon as Luisa saw us, she was on her feet and sprinting toward us. She slammed into my thighs, and I wrapped her up in a one-armed hug. "Hey, Little Bit. I've missed you."

She just nodded against my knees. I wanted to pick her up and snuggle her but I knew my body would protest.

Seven however, didn't seem to have the same worries, or maybe he just didn't care. He leaned down and scooped the cub up into his arms. She burrowed her head into his chest and squeezed him back.

"Mommy said you're a sleeping princess," Leisel said in a small voice, and it made me smile. I could imagine Seven as Sleeping Beauty.

He shifted Luisa to one hip and I saw him grimace in pain, but he didn't put her down. I held out a hand to Leisel, and she grabbed it. "You look better, Uncle Raiden," she said softly. "I snuck in to look at you and I was worried you were going to die."

Her lip wobbled, and I squeezed her to my side. "I'm tougher than that, I promise." I ruffled her hair. "Thanks for looking after Luisa for me."

Leisel shrugged like it was no big deal. "Mommy

says she's my cousin now. That you are going to make her mommy your mate because you all make the kissy face at each other."

I raised an eyebrow. "The what?"

She clasped her hands under her chin, opened her eyes real wide and puckered her lips. It was a ridiculous expression, and I burst out laughing. Terra was ridiculous, but her kid was cute as hell. "You really are the best kid, Lees. You know that, right?"

"Yep." She even popped the P. She skipped ahead of us as we entered the huge informal sitting room, and there were people everywhere. As soon as Ellar saw Seven holding Luisa, he strode over. "Seven Huxley-Grey! You've just had surgery," he chastised softly, reaching out and grabbing Luisa with soft hands. He pulled a funny face at her. "Naughty Papa Sev."

Everyone in the room stilled, looking at Naja. She just gave us a soft smile and raised an eyebrow.

Ellar cleared his throat and ushered us further into the room. "It's good to see you guys out of bed, but you have to take it easy."

I grabbed his hand and pulled him to me, kissing him softly. "I was scared too, El. It's okay now. You did the right thing."

He froze and his whole body shuddered with emotion. "You almost died, Raiden. I would never have forgiven you if you'd done that."

I pulled him tighter against me. "Never again, Beta. Never."

He stepped back, his hand brushing my stomach, like he was saying hello to our cubs. He stepped away. "Go and sit down, the both of you. We're going over plans for the new house."

Seven gave him a grumbling kiss on the cheek. "Don't fuss."

"Eat a dick, Sev. You almost died, so I get to be as fussy as I like."

Seven leaned forward and murmured something in his ear that made Ellar flush. I was almost positive he said, "I'll make you eat my dick, Beta.". I walked over to sit down between Gatlin and Naja, and they both shifted closer to me like they needed comfort.

Seven was right. Our house may have burned down, but our home? It was safe and sound right here.

45

FINLO

I was so fucking nervous. In the weeks since the attack, we'd all healed physically. The mental scars would take longer to heal. Raiden still flinched at loud noises, and Ellar needed to have the Omegas and Luisa in sight at all times. Gatlin was still drowning in guilt but he was coming around. It helped that the Witch Miranda had come back a few days after Naja had woken up, and redone the wards.

But only after she completely chewed out the Legion. Even the Legion Alpha had got the sharp side of her tongue and honestly, it was the greatest thing I'd ever seen. The wards were now impenetrable to anyone who had any ill intent against the Manix or anyone who lived in Maxton. I wasn't sure how you even tested that, but I had faith she knew her shit.

Seven was still a little stiff, but worse than that, he

got pricklier and pricklier as Raiden's pregnancy advanced. Some of it was due to his natural Beta instincts—hell, we were all a little more closed off as Raiden got closer to the birth. But Seven hadn't been more than ten feet from him at all times. I was pretty sure he slept outside his door if he wasn't in bed with him.

The only person who seemed to have healed inside and out was Naja. Killing her tormentor had freed something inside her, and it was fucking beautiful. She laughed easier, and trusted more quickly. She was like the bright, golden version of the woman I'd fallen in love with, and even though I hadn't thought I could ever love her more, here we were.

"Stop pacing, Fin. You're making me nervous," Gatlin growled, and I flipped him the bird.

I continued to pace up and down the hall of our newly completed house. Everyone was here except Raiden, Seven and Naja. Terra had taken them all baby shopping in the next big city over to replace what had been burned in the fires. I would have been freaking out, but all of Terra's mates had gone with them, and they were scary as hell as a group. The kids went too, so honestly it sounded like hell, but I knew Naja was excited. Finally, she could live freely. It was a beautiful thing to see.

I tilted my head, hearing the low whir of an engine. Yeah, that was definitely coming up the road toward us.

Even with the dust from the road obscuring the ATV, I could see it was Seven driving up, Naja and Raiden in the back. I held my breath as he pulled the vehicle up on the drive and climbed out, helping Raiden out. I wouldn't say it to his face, but Raiden's stomach was so fucking huge. When he turned to the side, I wondered how the hell he remained upright.

Raiden looked up at the house, his mouth hanging open. Naja came to stand beside him, her mouth equally as agape.

I locked eyes with Naja, tilting my chin to beckon them both up. "Want to come and see your new nests?"

"Yes!" they said in unison, Naja racing up to the deck, Raiden waddling up a little slower. Yeah, we didn't use the W word out loud around him. And we weren't allowed to make any comparisons to any creatures of the sea or penguins at all.

Naja launched herself into my arms. "Holy shit, Finlo! It's gorgeous."

She was gorgeous, but there was something else that needed to happen before we stepped foot inside the new house. I looked at Raiden, my eyes loaded with meaning. He nodded, and I let my eyes move over the rest of my Packmates before settling back on Naja.

"Finlo, what's wrong?"

I laughed. "What's wrong? What's wrong is that you waltzed in here and stole our hearts. You completed our Pack even though we didn't know anything was missing. What's wrong is that you made us all fall hopelessly in love with you." I paused and dropped to my knee in the human gesture. "What's wrong is that you aren't our mate yet, but that's something I want to change right now."

Rings weren't usually a Manix custom either. It was a good way to lose a finger when you shifted, but because Naja had no Beast form, we'd deemed it safe. I pulled a ring from my pocket and held it up to her. "Naja, will you be our mate? A part of our Pack forever? Our love will be yours, and Luisa's, forever. Our protection is yours. Our home, our hearts. All yours."

Her eyes were so wide, her mouth opening and closing repeatedly. The silence dragged on for centuries, until she finally whispered, "Are you sure?"

The quietly hopeful note to her voice slayed me. "I've never been more sure of anything in my life. None of us have."

She looked around at the other guys, holding each of their eyes, and then back down to me.

"Yes."

My hands shook as she took the ring and put it on her finger, then I jumped to my feet and dragged her into a hug. Within seconds, my entire Pack was squashed into the embrace, truly one. One by one, my Packmates gathered her into their arms and kissed her until her lips were swollen and her cheeks were pink.

Gatlin picked her up, and she wrapped her legs

around his waist. "Wanna see your new home? Maybe I could interest you in seeing your nest?"

She squealed, and I grinned, wrapping an arm around Raiden's shoulders. "Where's our cub?"

He raised an eyebrow. "Having a sleepover with Leisel, at Terra's insistence."

I looked over at Seven, and he just gave me a small smug smile back. *Oh, I see.* Seven had his own plans, and I can't say I didn't wholeheartedly approve.

Raiden huffed beside me. "I can't believe we are going to have an orgy when I'm so fucking huge I can't even see my dick."

I kissed his temple. "You are the sexiest thing I've ever laid my eyes on. Besides, I can see your dick just fine."

He shoved my shoulder but was back to smiling again. "I'm fucking exhausted. I think I might just watch this one from the sidelines."

I frowned but I let it go. He was birthing five freaking baby Manix in less than three weeks; that would be exhausting. A human would be hospitalized by now.

We followed the rest of the Pack inside, and I looked around at our handiwork. Not much had been able to be salvaged in the actual structure of the building, though when we'd gone through the rubble we realized that while the original house had collapsed, the lower living room had been saved from most of the fire damage. That meant that a lot of little mementos had survived, as well as Gatlin's library. We'd extended the top floor and put the library up there now. It was also where the nests were. The bedrooms were all on the second floor, and the kitchen and living room were on the ground. We'd planned for more space this time around, extra rooms for nursery and spare rooms so our family could grow.

Raiden looked around, his smile one of contentment and happiness. "I'm going to start up the stairs, otherwise I'll only be on the second floor landing by the time the orgy starts," he whispered conspiratorially.

"Are you sure you don't want to look around first? We would never start without you, Rai. You're our heart," I chastised gently.

He waved me away. "Baby, I have an entire lifetime to check out every nook and cranny of this house, but the first time we make love to our new mate? That's once in a lifetime and I'm not going to miss a second."

With that, he headed up the stairs, Seven on his heels. I went in search of the others and found them in the nursery on the second floor. It was the largest room in the house, outside of the living room. Already there were five cribs set up, along with a princess bed.

I wished Raiden had seen this first, but I was glad he was heading up to the nest. Naja was touching the gauzy curtains over Luisa's bed. I leaned against the doorjamb and tried not to launch myself across the room to hug her as the scent of her happiness flavored the air.

"Do you think she'll like it?" Ellar asked softly, and Naja nodded so hard I thought she'd dislocate something.

"It's the most beautiful bed I've ever seen. She's going to love it." She walked around the room a little longer, touching little trinkets we'd gathered for the cubs. As she passed closer to me, it got too much and I grabbed her, dragging her back into my arms. I swooped down and caught her lips, kissing her hard. I poured everything I was feeling in that moment into that kiss, and it was excitement and fear and so much damn lust.

"So, my beautiful Omega mate-to-be, we can show you your new bedroom, or..." I kissed my way down her throat. "We can go up to the nest and strip you naked and make love to you until you're wrung out and hoarse from screaming our names."

Her eyes hooded immediately. "The tour can wait."

I hooted a probably unattractive noise, and picked her up in my arms like she was a bride. By the time I made it to the top step, hearing the pound of Gatlin and Ellar's steps behind me, I was harder than granite. I followed my nose to the nest where Raiden had gone. We'd set up two nests because having two Omegas meant they'd each need their own space from Pack life occasionally. Naja's was filled with greenery, painted white and all the furniture stained ash. There were mounds of pillows and blankets, and an Alaskan king-sized bed.

Raiden's was more sumptuous and decadent, like the inside of a tent in the Sahara Desert, filled with silks and velvets in dark colors with pops of jewel tones. The floor was one giant cushion. There was nowhere you could step that wasn't soft. We could roll around in here for hours.

I lowered Naja to her feet and just kept going, until she was on her back surrounded by jewel-colored velvet cushions. However, I did a double take as I noticed Raiden in the corner, naked with Seven sucking his cock. Apparently, our Beta was affronted by the idea of Raiden sitting out.

Naja followed my gaze and her mouth popped open. "Apparently they started without us, Princess. We better catch up." With that, I started stripping her and myself at a rate that probably wasn't possible to see with the naked eye. She smelled like heaven, the sweet scent of her arousal filling my senses.

"You better slow down, Finlo, or you're going to embarrass yourself," Gatlin said teasingly, and I flipped him the bird over my shoulder. I'd rest when I'd wrung at least two orgasms out of her personally. Then I'd take my own pleasure.

She tugged at my shirt, and I happily abandoned it.

I didn't need or want it. The sooner we were all naked, the happier I'd be.

When she was naked in front of me, her knees splayed onto the mattress, open and dripping for me, I almost swallowed my tongue. So fucking beautiful, and the warmth of her skin was complemented perfectly by the colors of the bedding. She looked like a painting.

"I love you, Naja. You know that, right?"

She nodded. "I know. I love you too. But especially your tongue, so if you could…" she joked, and I growled at her softly. She stroked her hands through my hair, scraping her nails against my scalp until I purred.

"This mate thing—what do we need to do?"

I froze, the blood pounding in my ears. Surely, she wasn't suggesting… "Uh, it's super simple really, there isn't a big ritual around it, unlike everything else with the Manix. It's a bit different between the different designations. There's a bite and vows for the Betas, there's a blood exchange between Alphas, and uh, for Omegas, basically we bite you while you're taking our knot. It's the strongest of bonds, really."

Her eyes widened, and I could almost see the different cogs turning her head. After a moment where no one breathed, she nodded. "Let's do it. I want to be Pack Huxley-Grey by sunrise tomorrow."

Well, holy shit.

46

NAJA

Despite my bravado, the idea of tying myself to the Pack forever caused me equal parts anxiety and excitement. The look of absolute elation on Finlo's face chased away any doubt though. He gathered me up into his arms and kissed me again, and I wrapped my legs around his now naked waist. No one could get undressed at the speed of Finlo; it was basically a superpower. I ran my palms over the flexing muscles of his back as he fucked me with his mouth. Ellar came up behind me, kissing down my spine as he gently pushed on Finlo's shoulders, until he collapsed onto his back and I was straddling his waist. Ellar's hands smoothed over the globes of my ass before gripping my hips and raising them a little higher. Then I felt the hot puffs of his breath on my soaked core, and moaned against Finlo's lips.

"If you're taking the knot for the first time, we'll have to get you properly wet and ready," Ellar crooned against my pussy, and I wasn't sure if he was talking to me or my vagina. Probably both. He made good on his promise though, as he licked me from my clit to my taint.

Finlo's hands dropped down to rub my breasts, and I knew at that moment I was never going to leave these guys. How could I go back to one-on-one sex every time? Being worshiped by so many hands and mouths like I was some hedonistic Greek sex goddess was an amazingly addictive feeling.

Ellar swirled his tongue inside my entrance, his finger rubbing a circle on my clit in time with it. The pressure was growing already in my lower body, and I knew I was going to be wrung out by the time tonight was over. I grinned against Finlo's lips. I couldn't fucking wait. He pulled his mouth away, and I dropped my head to his chest as Ellar thrust two fingers into me. I didn't know how Ellar knew his way around a pussy the way he did, but he set the perfect pace, his fingers curling just right to make my thighs clench and shake.

"Get in there, Ellar. Make love to our mate," Finlo growled. I could sense the Beast inside him on the rise, and it excited me. There was no fear with these guys now, only trust. As a special surprise for the guys, I'd gotten Doc to put in an IUD, because as much as I loved them, I figured five newborns was going to be enough for a little while.

Ellar slid his cock inside me, and we both groaned. "Fuck me, Ellar," I whispered, and I don't know who growled, or if they all did, but some switch flicked over inside my sweet, beautiful Ellar. He fucked me into Finlo's body like he was possessed, his hard thrusts making me pant as he hit the good spot over and over. He curled over my back, gripping my hair so he could turn my head and kiss me, his thrusts short and shallow until I was crying out in ecstasy. Ellar wasn't far behind me, as he gripped my hip tight in one hand, slamming us together as he filled me with his seed. But he never stopped kissing me.

Finlo watched as Ellar moved back up my spine, squeezing my ass as he pulled out. His hand dipped back between my thighs, and I lifted myself up on shaky arms to look between my body and Finlo's. Ellar was stroking Finlo's dick, lining it up with my still pulsing core. Then he leaned down and bit my asscheek—*hard.*

"Ah!" I said, looking over my shoulder to see he was wearing a goofy, happy expression.

"Welcome to the Pack, Princess. When we mate, this is where I'm going to put my mark," he said smugly as he rubbed the indented flesh where his teeth had been.

I lifted my eyebrows but couldn't resist the smile I

gave him in return. I mouthed "Love you," and he winked back.

Then Finlo was notching against me, and sliding his cock into my pussy deliciously slowly. I forgot about everything but the feel of his body in mine. Jesus Christ, did they have to be so in proportion? I was so full, I felt him everywhere. He slid me up and down his cock with hands that spanned almost my entire waist, and my whole world narrowed down to sensations. The stretch, the slide, the pressure of his fingertips.

Minutes—or centuries—later, I was shaking and sweating, coming again, and Finlo groaned as my pussy milked his cock.

"Aw, Princess. God, you take my cock so good," he grunted. "Are you going to take my knot just as good, Naja?" I nodded. Hell, I'd promise him just about anything as long as he continued to fuck me like this. He made a low growl in my ear and rolled me onto my back. "Get ready, baby. This might feel... different."

He spread me wider, and I felt the slow swell of the base of his cock pressing at my entrance, making me squirm. As it got bigger and the pressure turned almost painful, he thrust into me hard, locking his cock inside me.

"Oh my fuck!" I shouted as he continued to expand inside me, and I clawed at his chest, trying to pull him closer and push him away at the same time.

"Easy baby," he crooned, and suddenly there were

hands on my torso, lips on my breasts and someone was kissing me. I knew Raiden's taste, the feel of his lips. Finlo's knot pressed into me harder and then it was throbbing against my G-spot and I was coming over and over.

I bit Raiden's lip, and he groaned. "It feels like too much but not enough, doesn't it?"

I nodded as Finlo started to move again—short sharp thrusts that just stimulated more than making him go any deeper. I didn't think he could get deeper. I was full.

Finlo's head was thrown back, and he was thrumming so hard that I could feel it through his cock. "Oh, fuck, Angel. I'm going to come. It's... well, it's a lot."

That was all the warning I got before he was exploding inside me. And I mean, *explode*. I could feel the hot pulse of his seed as it released inside of me, and I sent up a godspeed to my IUD. I didn't fucking care in that moment though because I felt amazing. Finlo lowered himself down, his lips on the curve of my neck. "Are you ready? Last chance to back out, Princess."

"There's no pressure to do this now. It can wait," Gatlin rumbled from somewhere in the room, but I couldn't see him from the bulk of Finlo against me.

"I want this. I'm ready." I'd never been more sure that I wanted something, and honestly, their constant need for consent just soothed away the last of my anxiety. Since the moment I met them, these guys had prioritised what was best for me, making sure that I was safe, happy and satisfied. How could I not want to spend forever with them, ensuring the same?

I tensed as Finlo's teeth pierced my skin, hissing in a breath as the pain combined with the pleasure of Finlo's still pulsing knot. He held me tight, stopping me from tugging away instinctively to escape the sharp sting, but soon the sting turned to pleasure and I was coming around his cock yet again. Fuck. That had to be like my tenth orgasm, and my brain was starting to short-circuit.

Finally, Finlo released me, lapping at the wound on my neck as his hands stroked up and down my side. "Love you, Naja," he whispered beside my cheek.

I was like a limp doll as he rolled onto his back, his body still locked with mine, and I rested against his chest, listening to the steady pounding of his heart beneath the slow vibration of his chest.

I turned my face and bit him too, glorying in the small hiss of pain which turned into a moan. "Mine," I murmured as blood filled my mouth, and he thrummed harder.

"Always yours, Princess."

Seven's face was suddenly in my vision as he leaned in to kiss me tenderly, not even worrying about the taste of Finlo's blood on my lips. "Love you, mate."

I mouthed, "Love you," because I wasn't sure I

could actually get my vocal chords to cooperate right now. Seven lay down beside Finlo, curling his body close to both of ours.

Ellar was there then, kissing my cheek. "Mate," he whispered reverently before lying down beside Seven, his cheek pressed against his spine. Raiden kissed my hair, curling up on the other side, no words needed. I knew how he felt—he showed me so often—and I hoped he knew how I felt about him. If he didn't, I'd gladly spend decades showing him.

Finally, a big, warm hand stroked down my spine. "Sleep, little mate. Soon you'll have to wake up and do this all again." There was a dark tease in his tone that made my body clench, and Finlo groaned.

"Cut it out, Gatlin, or her clenching pussy is going to inflate my knot again and we'll be stuck here all day." He looked down at me and grinned. "Not that I have any problem with that at all," he purred with a wink.

I huffed a laugh. Hopefully I didn't need reconstructive vaginal surgery after I was done.

Sleep slowly started to creep in as my exhausted body decided enough was enough. But curled up here, amongst these men, I knew that I was home.

The Beast had consumed my body. I snarled at every person who entered the room if they weren't part of my Pack. I'd shifted hours ago, and no one was sure how they were going to force me back so they could use a scalpel to do the Caesarean incision, but my Beast didn't care.

A wave of pain across my abdomen made me want to howl, and the only thing that soothed both me and the Beast was the soft hand stroking across my face. "Shh, Rai. You're doing so fucking good right now. I'm so proud of you," came Naja's soft voice, and my Beast let go of some of its tension.

Finlo and Gatlin were talking to the Doc, and Ellar was somewhere fussing about with blankets and cribs and god knows what else. He needed to stay busy, to feel needed. Hell, I needed him to be busy, to be doing the nesting that my Beast craved. He wanted to crawl into his nest and hide from the world until the cubs were stronger.

Seven, on the other hand, refused to leave my side. He stood in the corner, out of the way, and bared his teeth at anyone who walked through the door. He had my back; he would defend me from rival Packs while I was at my weakest.

The logical, normal Raiden knew that there was no chance that any other Manix would try and take my cubs, or kill me while I was vulnerable, but it was a primal part of me that was in control right now.

I vaguely tuned back into the conversation between my Alphas and the Doc. "You're going to have to do it, Gatlin. He won't shift back to human with outsiders in the room, even if I'm a doctor. Unless you want me to try and open him up with a chainsaw, there's no way we can get through those scales."

I growled low and menacingly at the very idea. Finlo looked over his shoulder and gave me a reas-suring expression. "Of course we don't want that, but I think what Gatlin meant when he said 'no fucking way' is that he doesn't have any medical training what-soever. None of us do."

I heard Naja huff out a laugh, but she didn't stop stroking my forehead. Another clenching pain gripped me, causing me to shout. Everyone turned to stare at me with wide eyes, and I gritted my teeth.

"Hurry the fuck up," Seven growled, and I knew that my pain was making him short-tempered. I didn't have it in me to both deal with this and soothe him though.

I should have known my mate would take care of us all though. "Come here, Sev. Our strong Omega needs us."

Seven kicked off the wall and dropped to his knees beside the bed. They'd laid down plastic-backed sheets, and made the room as sterile as possible. The Alphas and Doc left the room, and I breathed a little easier. Normal Manix women didn't have this issue, so I knew it was an Omega male thing.

They were gone for ten more minutes, which was like three contractions, and I started cursing everyone I'd ever met. Fuck the Manix. Fuck the Doc. Fuck whoever thought this was a good idea. I didn't even give a shit that it had been me.

The pains weren't really contractions, because my womb didn't actually have an exit. From what Gatlin had read and told me, it was my womb contracting to compel the cubs into movement. Eventually, if I didn't get intervention from my Pack, the contractions would force the cubs to shift and they would attempt to claw their way from my body and we'd probably both die. Omega mortality had been very high until we started cutting them out while praying to the Moon Goddess hundreds of years ago. I shuddered at the thought of tiny little claws slicing my flesh from the inside. Nature was a cruel wench sometimes.

Finally, Gatlin returned with Finlo, and I tensed. But Doc wasn't with them, only Ellar. He had a stack of warm blankets and a tub of shiny metal instruments. Finlo came to stand on my other side, gripping my hand.

"How are you doing, Omega?" His low rumbling voice let me know his Beast was riding him too.

I gritted my teeth. "Out now. Please," I begged, and he stroked my face.

Gatlin cleared his throat and he looked a little pale, but his jaw was clamped determinedly. "Do you trust me, Omega?"

I grimaced through the pain. "With my life, Alpha."

He nodded, swallowing hard. "Then shift back, Rai, so we can meet our cubs."

I nodded, imagining myself in my other form, but my Beast was stubborn. It was also scared.

Finlo squeezed my hand. "Shift, Omega." He put all his Alpha power into those two words and my Omega obeyed, my body receding into my softer human form. Someone breathed out a relieved sigh.

"Okay, Rai, I'm going to give you a local anesthetic. I don't trust myself to poke anything into your spine. This will help, but it might still be uncomfortable." He grabbed a needle from Ellar and gave me several injections I didn't feel over the next contraction.

"Can you feel this?" Gatlin asked, and I shook my head. I could feel the dull pressure of whatever he was poking me with, but no pain.

Finlo squeezed my hand. "Goddess, watch over our Omega and our cubs as we deliver these lives into the world in your honor." I looked over at him questioningly, and he shrugged. "I figured we needed all the help we could get. Gatlin, you've got this. Let's go."

I watched as Gatlin swallowed hard, and I gave him a reassuring smile. At least, I hoped it was reassuring. "I trust you, Alpha."

He gave me a look so filled with fear and love that I knew this would be as hard for him as it was for me. "Don't do anything stupid like die because so help me, Raiden, I will track you down in the afterlife and drag you back. You got that?"

I snorted a laugh, but another contraction stole my air. "It's time."

Gatlin nodded. "Do me a favor and don't look, okay?"

I nodded and closed my eyes, but I didn't need to, because Naja was there, kissing my face. The waves of her calm Omega power washed over me, and it still blew my mind that she'd had no idea she was Manix when we found her.

I could feel the weird sensation of the scalpel slicing my skin, but it didn't hurt. "We haven't thought of names," Naja murmured softly.

Well, we had thought of names, but we hadn't agreed on any yet. It was like giving the cubs names would have meant we'd love them even more, and if this went badly, I wasn't sure I could ever recover if they'd already been named.

She rubbed her nose up and down my cheek. "You know, now's the time you can put your foot down and demand they be named whatever you want. No one can argue with you when you are doing all the hard work."

"Seven," Gatlin called, and my Beta stood quickly, moving down the end of the bed. Naja looked over her shoulder and then back at me.

"It's okay, though I think I might not pursue a career as a surgeon." She looked a little green, but she smiled. "We did it, Raiden. We have one healthy beautiful cub. Only four more to go."

The soft cry of a baby was the best thing I'd ever heard. Seven came back with a white gunk-coated perfect little Manix, in its human form. He knelt by the bed and held it out to show me, and the noise that came from my throat was more animal than human. Sev grinned. "It's a boy, baby."

I felt the wet splashes of Naja's tears on my face as we both looked at our firstborn. A baby made of her DNA, born of my body. I heard a happy rumbling noise and looked up at Finlo, who was crying hard.

"Hand that one to Finlo, Sev. We've got more."

Seven handed the tiny cub to Finlo, and the baby wasn't even as big as his hand. "Is it okay?"

"He's doing just fine, Rai. He's perfect," Finlo gushed, and then Sev was back with another baby. It had a different colored blanket, and had a shock of dark hair. No guesses whose Daddy this one was. This little one went up into the crook of Finlo's other arm, and then Seven was back down the business end.

"You are so perfect, Rai. Look what you've created," Naja said, burrowing her head into my neck, and the smell of her hair was almost like a drug. Another baby came up to meet me, and I kissed its tiny cheek. Naja held out her hands, and Seven passed the baby to her.

"Another boy," he cooed, and I smiled down at the pale, scrunched little face. I was mesmerized as another baby appeared in my arms. One more to Naja. Five. Five beautiful boy cubs. A perfect blend of us all.

"Sev," Gatlin said sharply, and Seven looked to our Alpha. The panic in Gatlin's voice had me defying his earlier request not to look. But the splayed open wound of my stomach was nothing compared to the tiny little unmoving baby in his hands. "This one goes to Doc. Now, Beta!"

Seven didn't hesitate. My eyes couldn't track him as he left the room.

"Alpha?" I said in a broken voice.

He gave me a tight smile that was probably supposed to be reassuring, but just made me panic more. "The boys were protecting their sister, apparently. Doc has her, Rai. She'll be okay."

Panic rose up in my chest, making it hard to breathe. We were all silent as our ears strained to hear what was going on in the other room. I could hear Doc muttering to the baby, sounding like he was checking off a list but also like he was talking to the baby.

Finally, the tiniest cry sounded, and I huffed out a breath of relief that was closely followed by tears. Seven and Doc reappeared in the room, Seven holding the baby which was good because as relieved as I was that Doc had been here, he was still a stranger in my Pack house to my Beast.

Seven dropped to his knees beside us. "Our baby girl."

I reached up and touched her tiny head, not even half the size of my palm. She blinked an eye open, looked at me, and then closed it again.

I'd done it. I felt like I'd been through a blender, but I'd done it.

I looked around at my Pack. No, we'd done it. I closed my eyes and let exhaustion wash me away into oblivion.

N aja

"THE NATIVES ARE GETTING RESTLESS, OMEGAS." Gatlin's slightly amused whisper came from the doorway of Raiden's nest. Against the walls were six Moses baskets, each with a tiny cub swaddled tightly inside. They were finally all sleeping at once, which was a small miracle. They'd almost doubled in size in the last week, which was equally miraculous.

The last week had been the best, most joyous, but also intense week of my life. After Raiden had passed out, Doc had come in and sewed him up properly, and the relief on Gatlin's face would have been hilarious if we weren't all feeling that way.

Raiden's recovery had been nothing short of unbelievable. His body had healed the C-section scar in days and he even had his abs back. You wouldn't have even known that a week ago, he'd been so huge that going up and down the stairs had been a challenge. Still, we'd been holed up in his nest during recovery, and I'd stayed with him. Mostly because I couldn't bear to be away from him and the cubs.

Six. Five boys and a tiny baby girl. I couldn't believe it. We'd decided to name them after virtues, because they were going to love matching names when they were teens. I grinned as I thought about it; I would be here to watch them grow and be happy. The thought made my throat thick with emotion.

Hale, Noble, August, Sage and Chance. Our precious baby girl was Amity Jane. They were perfect, and when Luisa had come in to visit, she'd been absolutely besotted with her new siblings.

Raiden huffed. "Tell them to come back tomorrow."

I almost agreed because I was loath to end the perfection of this moment. But these cubs? They weren't just a miracle to us. They were the herald of hope for the rest of the Manix race, and they wanted to see them too.

Gatlin snorted. "Sure thing, but you can go down

and tell Selena that she can't see her grandcubs for another day. That woman is scary. Amazing, but scary."

I snorted because I just didn't see the scariness. Selena had been amazing, watching Luisa during the birth, and making sure we were all fed and happy. Generally just taking care of things. She'd left us alone to bond as a Pack for a week, despite how excited she'd been, but I could imagine she'd be beside herself with excitement now.

I crawled over to Raiden and snuggled his face. "Come on, Rai. It's time to introduce the cubs to the big wide world."

He huffed but stood. He was only in a pair of sweats, but Gatlin walked in to kiss him softly. "Such a Papa Bear." He handed him a t-shirt I hadn't noticed until then. He also handed me a dress, because I was still in Finlo's shirt from yesterday.

"Thanks, Alpha." I pulled the shirt off and slipped the dress on over my head, before stepping into his arms for a kiss. He delivered it in abundance, with tongue. I grabbed the front of his shirt and curled my body against his. He ran his tongue over the small pink scar that was his mate mark on my neck, on the opposite side to Finlo's.

I shivered, and the smell of my arousal flooded the room.

"Maybe we can stop at my bedroom first...?"

Gatlin shook his head and stepped away. "No way,

mate. There's a whole party waiting for you guys and the little stars of the show." His eyes hooded. "But tonight? You're on, Omega."

Goosebumps ran over my skin, and I grinned.

Looking over my shoulder at Raiden, I noticed his eyes were also filled with lust. He switched his gaze to Gatlin. "I think you're right, Gatlin. It's definitely time to leave the nest."

Yeah, he was going to end up in my bed tonight too.

Gatlin walked over to the Moses baskets and lifted out Amity Jane, cradling her gently in his arms. She was smaller than the boys, but she was growing well, drinking just as much as the boys. She was going to be thoroughly spoiled.

There was a knock at the door and the rest of my Pack appeared. Finlo had Luisa on his hip, and I wandered over, placing baby Hale in his arms. Luisa looked down at the baby with such love it made my heart swell.

Raiden juggled August into one arm, and I gave Chance to Seven. Finally, Ellar delicately lifted Sage from his basket, and I reached down and scooped up Noble.

We trooped down the stairs, keeping Raiden in the center of us. This would be hard with his Omega instincts, but the Beast had gone back in his box over the last day or two. Raiden was running less on instinct now. Finlo told me that historically, the Omegas would be holed up with the female Betas for a month before they'd emerge. Apparently, in the olden days before formula, female Betas lactated to feed the young. But there weren't enough female Manix at all for that now.

I could hear the noise of so many voices drifting up the stairs. Gatlin had promised no one would touch the babies without permission, and I think that eased all of our more primal natures. When we got to the landing, my mouth swung open. Holy shit—there were dozens of people down here.

I could see all of Finlo's family, Raiden's dad, and even Gatlin's father standing at the very back of the crowd. Terra and her husbands, as well as all of her kids, were there in a tight bunch. Surprisingly, the Legion Force soldiers Merrick and Murphy were there, as well as the Fletcher-Wiley-Reid Pack. They looked at us longingly, and it broke my fucking heart.

I nearly tripped over my feet when my eyes fell on Courtland. My brother. My brother Courtland.

"Easy, Omega," Gatlin said, his hand shooting out to grab me. "He asked if he could come and see the cubs. He's your last remaining family, outside of our Pack. He's the reason you are here with us now. I thought you wouldn't mind."

I didn't mind, but hey, a heads up would have been nice. Courtland dipped his chin and I gave him a half-smile back. It wasn't that I didn't want to see him, it was just that I'd firmly shut away that moment of my life while I healed, and whilst we had bigger things to worry about like taking care of new life.

Beside Courtland was a pretty teenage girl with dark brown eyes, long straight hair and my mother's nose.

Holy shit. He'd brought one of my siblings.

I concentrated on getting down the stairs without falling on my face or dropping the cub in my arms. When we all reached the foot of the stairs, Gatlin cleared his throat. "Meet the newest members of Pack Huxley-Grey."

Everyone cooed and spoke at once. I noticed the giant mound of presents. Damn. These guys went all out.

The next hour was fending off touching hands, making sure Raiden was coping, and mingling within the crowd. Eventually, I ended up in front of Courtland and the girl who was my sibling. Seven appeared behind me, not saying anything but just offering support. He was no longer holding Chance, but I wasn't worried. One of the others would have him.

"You look well, Naja," Courtland said, though he could have been talking to a complete stranger. There was something odd about Courtland, like he was broken, but when he looked at me, I could see the hint of guilt that sat behind his eyes. There was something more to Courtland, and I honestly didn't know if I had the fortitude to discover what it was. I just wanted to be happy. That Scooby Doo Mystery Machine bullshit was for someone else. I was done.

"Thank you, Courtland."

The girl beside him huffed. "For fuck's sake, Court. Introduce us so I can finally meet my damn sister."

Courtland's eyes flashed with irritation, but still, he did what he was asked. "Naja, this is Rosa. She's your half-sister. The first of your mother's offspring with Iago." He said it so coolly, like it didn't matter that she was the product of something horrible, or that I'd killed her dad. For her part, she didn't seem to care either.

"I kinda killed your father. I'm sorry."

She snorted. "No you're not, and neither am I. Scum," she said, fake spitting on the ground.

I laughed, and she laughed with me. But the sound, the sweet tinkling joy made my heart hurt. It sounded just like my mother's laugh, back when she hadn't been a shell of herself.

"So you're...?" Seven asked. I elbowed him in the ribs, because that was kinda rude, but he shrugged. "Every person in this room is waiting to hear with bated breath. That guy is a Manix. What if she is too? I can't tell over all the scents in here."

Courtland gave Seven a narrow-eyed stare, but Rosa just laughed. "Sorry, big guy. Full-blooded tigress from what I can tell, as are the rest of my siblings. No systematic savior of the Manix race here, but I gotta say, these little cuties must give them hope. Hey, little guy," she cooed at Noble.

We talked about the cubs for a while until Courtland cleared his throat. "We should go. We have to return to your siblings, and then I must return to my business."

I swallowed hard, remembering the last time I'd seen most of them, the last time I'd seen Rosa. She hadn't been named Rosa; she hadn't had any name at all. She'd been a tiny, squawling infant torn from my mother's dazed arms.

"Did you really save them all?"

Courtland nodded. "Yes, all eleven, including Rosa."

I shook my head, refusing to believe it was true. "But why?"

Courtland's face gave nothing away. "I failed you and your mother. It was the only promise my father asked of me—that I protect you both, and I failed. It was my atonement to your mother, and to you until I could save you from Iago himself."

I looked at the man in front of me. He had to be thirty, but not much more. "You were what, ten? Twelve? You can't hold a child to that kind of promise, Courtland."

He shrugged. "They say evil prevails when good men do nothing, Naja. I am not good, but I could not let this stand." He cleared his throat. "Should you wish to meet the remainder of your siblings, I have left my number with your Alpha. They are all with loving families, and some of them have even grown up together."

Rosa rolled her eyes. "What he means to say is that the first five of us were raised by his Abuela. Your Abuela."

I shook my head, looking between them both. "Thank you. Both of you. I just... I thought they were all in a mass grave in the compound, or that he sold them for drugs or something."

Courtland's jaw clenched. "He did sell them. He was reprehensible." He looked at my sister. "We need to go."

Rosa gave me a quick hug. "Don't be a stranger."

With that, they melted back into the crowd. I shook my head, looking up at Sev, who pulled me tightly back against his chest. "That guy sets off all my alarms," he grumbled and I shrugged.

"Mine too, but I don't think he's a threat to us."

He harrumphed and moved us back through the crowd. Looks like he was done with show and tell for the day. He made a hand gesture to Gatlin, and he nodded. I didn't even get to say goodbye before he was herding me up the stairs. When I reached the nursery, I realized Raiden was already here, as were Amity Jane and Hale, who were in their cribs. Apparently, they'd been squirelling the babies up here for a while. When

Ellar appeared with another two cubs, I knew that we'd all had enough of having people in the Pack house.

Raiden flopped down into a rocking chair, and Ellar placed a baby against his chest. He rocked back and forth, humming. "Why didn't anyone tell me this whole parenthood thing was exhausting?" He looked at us all accusingly.

I laughed, because I couldn't argue. I walked over and kissed him on the lips. "Raiden? Parenthood is exhausting," I said against his lips, giggling as he slapped my ass. I gave him a stern look. "If you'd let me finish, I was going to say, we're all here to help. These cubs have the most amazing parents ever. And who knows... maybe next year, we'll have six more?"

"No!" everyone yelled at once, and I collapsed into Raiden's lap with a laugh, carefully curling myself around the tiny life we'd created that was sleeping against his chest.

So maybe no more cubs for a while yet, because what we had right here and right now? It was perfect.

ABOUT THE AUTHOR

Grace McGinty is eclectic. She has worked as a choco-latier, a librarian, a forensic accountant and finally a writer. Like her professional career, the genres she writes are also eclectic. She writes romance, reverse harem romance, fantasy, contemporary young adult and new adult books.

She lives in rural Australia with her crazy family, an entire menagerie of pets, and will one day be crushed by her giant piles of books that litter every room.

Head over to www.gracemcginty.com and join my mailing list for sneak previews into what I am working on and to stay up-to-date with new releases and giveaways!

Join my Facebook group Grace's Bookish Angels to stay up to date!

Want to go back to the (sort-of) beginning? Check out Newly Undead in Dark River, book one of the Dark River Days series.

NEWLY UNDEAD IN DARK RIVER

DARK RIVER DAYS
Book 1

GRACE MCGINTY

NEWLY UNDEAD IN DARK RIVER
CHAPTER ONE

I woke to a rat scuttling across my chest, its tiny nose twitching as it paused to stare at me before scurrying off. Damn, I was hungry.

The fact that my initial reaction to a rat was hunger and not disgust was the first sign that something was very, very wrong. The second clue was that I was lying in a drainpipe in the middle of the night. Although it was hard to concentrate on anything but the hunger clawing at my stomach, I could hear the nocturnal animals shuffling around in the silence and smell the stale water that now soaked my clothes.

I tried to sit up and banged my head on the slimy concrete. Groaning, I rolled over and crawled my way out into the open. My body felt like I'd climbed Everest. Twice. I couldn't see my backpack anywhere. Panic began to fill my chest. Everything was in that pack. But it was pitch black, the moon not even visible behind the clouds. I became acutely aware that I was standing in the middle of the wilderness, at night, alone. I was a serial killer's wet dream right now.

I stared down the road, looking for the oncoming lights of a car or truck or something. Maybe I could hitch a ride into the nearest town. It was probably hitchhiking that had put me in this predicament to start with. My mom was going to be pissed that I'd been so irresponsible.

I felt dazed like I'd been tranquilized, but I patted down my clothing with sluggish movements. Nothing was torn, and all my clothes were still on. I didn't feel violated in any way. My brain was cloudy, and I tried to sift through the fog to remember why I was lying in a ditch, outside of...

I looked up at the road sign. *Welcome to Dark River.* Where the hell was Dark River?

Hunger tore at my belly again, a burning ache so painful I moaned into the darkness like a wounded animal. First, I needed to eat something. Maybe then I'd be able to work out what the hell was going on.

I stumbled down the side of the road, and I could see the muted glow of the town lights once I was over the small rise.

Electricity surged up through my chest, and the edges of my vision dimmed. The last thing I felt when my body buckled was the rough gravel scraping my cheek.

I snapped back to consciousness all at once, like when you dream you're falling. My head felt too full, and panic was beginning to mingle with the overwhelming hunger.

I was now in town, beneath the striped awning of Bert and Beatrice's Old Fashioned Diner. How the fuck did I get here? Everything was completely blank as if someone had plucked the memory from my brain like a bad apple. A clock tower sat in the middle of town, proclaiming it to be almost midnight.

I pushed through the glass door, and a little bell tinkled above my head. The place was filled to the brim, which was unusual seeing how it was basically the middle of the night.

Every set of eyes turned to look at me, and the old guy behind the counter dropped the soda glass he was drying, the smashing sound shooting pain into my skull. I must've really looked like hell. An elderly woman bustled out of the swinging doors, which probably led to the kitchen.

"What's goin' on out..." she trailed off when she saw me standing in the doorway. She nudged the old man out of the way.

"Lass, are you feelin' alright? Bertie, get the girl a drink. The house special," she said slowly, her accent a thick Scottish brogue. "Tilda, call the Sheriff, please. Get him down here, quick smart." She was rounding the counter now. "Here, Lass, take a seat."

I obediently took the stool she indicated. She had a no-nonsense, matronly tone that soothed my panicked nerves.

"I lost my money and my passport." My voice sounded so weak that I hardly recognized it as my own.

The elderly lady just patted my shoulder.

"Not to worry, Sweet. It's on the house."

I could hear the sound of Tilda murmuring quietly into the phone down the other end of the diner.

"Yes Sheriff, just stumbled in the door. Looking like death, if you know what I mean."

The old man, Bertie I guess, slid a cardboard milkshake cup in front of me, complete with red and white straw. It smelled so good that I fell on it like a half-starved animal. When I'd sucked down the last drop, I looked up, embarrassed.

"Sorry. I was really hungry." Bertie just took away my empty cup and put a fresh one in front of me.

"Don't worry about it, Darlin'. Have another one." I was struggling to concentrate on her words. I found it hard to concentrate on anything but the milkshake in front of me.

The bell over the door tinkled, and everyone's eyes shifted in that direction again, even mine. A tall man in a chocolate brown uniform walked into the place, and everyone started talking at once. The cacophony after the complete absence of noise was hell on my eardrums. I pushed my palms over my ears to try and muffle some of the sounds.

"Quiet!" The guy was obviously the Sheriff, judging by the way that everyone's flapping jaws snapped shut with almost perfect synchronization. Silence again. The man strode over, his every movement elegant, to where I was sitting and gaping in his direction.

The man was hot. Like, spontaneous combustion, three-alarm, call in the National Guard, hot. He had sandy brown hair and deep green eyes. The uniform hugged his muscular body. He was so attractive it made my teeth hurt. Literally.

"Ma'am, my name is Sheriff Walker Walton. Do you need some help?" His deep voice was gentle, almost as if he didn't want to startle me.

"I don't know how I got here," I whispered. It was all a blank.

I'd been backpacking my way through Canada with my friends, but they had gone home last week, while I continued to travel up through Alberta by myself. I'd missed my bus to Yukon, so had decided to hitchhike my way through the last stretch to the border of British Columbia. After all, what's life without a little adventure? I'd been picked up by a family with teenage sons, but they'd let me off near Grande Prairie. I'd walked down the highway a bit more, and then poof, every-thing else was blank.

"Do you remember your name?" the Sheriff asked in the same soft voice.

"Mika McKellan. From Boston."

"That's good, Mika. I'd like you to come down to the station with me, so we can get this all sorted out. The town doctor will meet us there, just to check you over."

I nodded absently, and followed Sheriff Walton out of the diner, clutching my cardboard cup to my chest like a lifebuoy. He walked me over to the squad car, and let me sit in the passenger seat, instead of the back.

We drove in silence around the block, and I took the town in. It was actually quite beautiful. Not the cemetery stillness of most small towns after dark. Fairy lights were strung around the town square, and people milled about. The lights were on in all the shops, and small clumps of people were talking to each other on well-lit sidewalks.

"Is there a festival going on or something?" I asked Sheriff Walton.

"Or something," he replied, letting silence fill the car.

Within a minute, we'd pulled up in front of a skinny brick building. There were shiny bars on the windows, and a Police sign hanging over the front lawn.

Sheriff Walton moved around the front of the car and opened the passenger door. I heaved myself out of the seat. Moving wasn't as painful as it had been when I first woke up, but I still felt sluggish.

A plain woman with sparkling eyes met us at the front door. She looked me over and then sent a pointed expression to Sheriff Walton.

"Mika, this is Doctor Alice Sommer. I'm gonna get the Doc to check you for any signs of, uh, injury."

He held open the door of the station for me, and I gave him a polite smile.

"Let's go into the conference room. We need to have a chat after the Doc has looked you over. I'll be out here doing some paperwork."

He opened the door to an interrogation room. No windows, just a metal table with two chairs. Conference room, my ass.

"Thanks, Walker. I'll give you a shout when we're done," the doctor said softly.

The door closed with a click. The doctor sat a leather doctor's bag on the metal table. "Have a seat, Miss McKellan."

"Mika."

"Okay, Mika it is. But you have to call me Alice. Now, let me have a look at you." She shone one of those penlights in my eyes, and I let out a little squeal.

"Ouch."

"Hmm, light sensitivity. You have a little bruising

on your throat too." She got out a measuring instrument and measured the width of the bruise. "Anything else feel off to you?"

"Except for the starving feeling, the aching muscles, the weird blank spots and the passing out?" My sarcasm was obnoxious, but I couldn't seem to help it. "Other than all that, I'm as healthy as a horse."

The doctor clicked her tongue and wrote down the measurements. "Walker, can you get the cooler from the backseat of my car and come in here please?" She barely raised her voice, but the Sheriff must have heard because the front door of the station slammed.

"Don't worry, Mika. Your symptoms should lessen in a few days."

"Lessen?"

But the Sheriff was striding into the room, cooler in hand. Damn, he was fast.

"It's confirmed, Walker. Though let's face it, it was obvious to everyone as soon as she walked through the door of the diner. You can smell it just as well as I can."

The Sheriff ran a hand down his face and sighed. "I know, but I didn't want to believe it. I didn't want to think someone we know could have done this."

What the hell were they talking about? I sniffed my armpit stealthily. I didn't think I smelled that bad, considering I'd been sleeping in a ditch. My nose twitched. A tangy metallic smell was coming from the cooler. A smell that was so familiar, but I couldn't quite put my finger on what it was.

"You know, I'm still in the room. Do you think someone could take me out to the ditch and see if I can find my wallet and my backpack? Everything I have is in that pack."

"Ditch?"

"The one I woke up in. Under the welcome sign."

The Sheriff's eyebrows knitted together, and I could basically see the cogs turning. "Sure. We'll go take a look out there first thing tomorrow night."

"Why can't we go in the morning?"

Alice laid a hand on my arm and rested her butt on the table. She was looking down at me sympathetically. In my experience, that was never a good sign.

"Mika, we have something to tell you. This is going to sound outrageous and frightening, but I want you to know that we're here for you."

My heart started to race. Something in the back of my mind screamed that in a minute, nothing was ever going to be the same.

"Did my pet goldfish die? Are you two getting a divorce?" I deflected awkward situations with sarcasm. My therapist and I were working through it back home.

It was the Sheriff that answered. "No. Well, maybe, I don't know. I've never seen your pet goldfish, but I understand they die quite frequently." Walker ran his hand through his hair, and my hands itched to follow suit. "Look, Mika, I know this is going to sound strange, but it's our opinion that last night, you, well uh, you died."

I laughed. Maybe I'd stumbled into one of those reality TV shows. The producer was going to jump out any minute and make me sign a media release and a Non-Disclosure Agreement.

But the door never opened, and the two people opposite me never cracked a smile. "In case you guys didn't notice, I'm sitting right here, conversing with you. I haven't seen many dead people in my life, but I went to Great-Aunt Milly's funeral when I was twelve, and she didn't talk back to me from the coffin."

Alice gripped my hand. There was something off-putting about a doctor holding your hand like you were about to get really bad news.

"What Walker is trying to say, Mika"—they kept saying my name over and over like I'd suddenly forgotten it—"is that you are the undead. We believe you have been turned into a vampire. I should say, we *know* you've been turned into a vampire. It's the *how* that we don't understand yet."

I blinked. And then blinked again. They were actually serious. They thought I was a vampire. I'd definitely stumbled onto a TV set. It sounded like something the SyFy channel would come up with. But my heart was thudding, and I felt like I was going to throw up. It was like my body knew they weren't kidding, and it was just waiting for my mind to catch up.

"A vampire?"

Walker nodded sympathetically. "The hunger, the light sensitivity, even the blank spots, are all symptoms of the Turning."

"And you guys know this because..." No, this couldn't be right. My mind rebelled.

"Because we are vampires. The whole town is populated by vampires."

I stared at them dumbly, expecting something, I wasn't sure what. For them to turn into bats, or broodingly sparkle in the overhead fluorescent lights. But nothing happened. They just looked like ordinary people. Not overly pale, their eyes weren't glowing red, they didn't have crooked, needle-like teeth. Nothing.

Alice had mocha-colored skin and smooth blond hair that went all the way down her back. She wasn't extraordinarily attractive by any means. She was pleasant and professional; exactly what you'd want in a physician. Okay, so Walker was hot, but from what I remembered of the diner, it wasn't like I'd stepped onto the stage at Milan Fashion Week or anything out of the ordinary.

"Do you have any questions?" Walker asked. Uh, yeah, I had a few. Like could he pinch me so I would wake the hell up from this bad acid trip?

"So, I'm a vampire, and you're a vampire. And she's a vampire." He nodded. "Do you, I mean I, have fangs?"

Walker bared his teeth, and there, gleaming white against his pink lips, were two pointed fangs. They were actually quite sharp, and I wondered how he didn't cut his mouth up with them. I looked at Alice, and she too was baring her fangs, which weren't quite as long as Walker's and sat in her mouth with more ease. I eased my tongue over my own canines and found they'd elongated. I cut my tongue on them, and the blood dripped into my mouth.

Blood.

Hunger clawed at my stomach like a ravenous beast. Suddenly, I understood what the smell coming from the cooler was.

"Please." It was a half yell, half sob, as I dived for the cooler. Walker was around the table in a flash, his arms like iron bands around my body.

"Calm down. Alice is going to get you something to eat right now." As he said it, the Doc was getting a blood bag out of the cooler, like the ones you saw in hospitals. She unscrewed the cap on the tube and handed it to me.

Walker released me from his hold, and I closed off the part of my mind that was grossed out at the thought of drinking blood, and let my body take over. I sucked that baby like it was my first cocktail on spring break in Cabo. All that was missing was the little umbrella and the frat boys trying to convince me to come to a snow party.

All too soon, the bag was empty. "I want some more." My voice wasn't weak anymore, but it sounded slurred like I was drunk. Alice shook her head.

"With the two you had at the diner, and now this one, you've had enough. If you gorge yourself, you'll be vomiting for the rest of the night. I'll come see you tomorrow and we'll discuss how everything works. For the remainder of the night, you need to rest." She picked up the cooler and her doctor's bag. "Are you taking her to your place?" she asked Walker.

He nodded. "I'll find somewhere more permanent for her to live tomorrow." He walked the doctor out, leaving me alone in the windowless room.

The shock settled over me like a numbing cloak. My mind spun as I tried to process, well, everything. I placed my hand on my chest, and felt my heart slowly beating in there. Somehow, that made me feel better. I may have been dead, but my heart was still beating. The illogicality of that statement was something I'd deal with another day.

Walker was suddenly back, and his warm hand was on my shoulder. "There are a lot of things we have to discuss. We can do it here, or back at my place. I know that sounds almost creepy, but I promise you'll be safe." He shifted from foot to foot, almost uncomfortably. "You are new to this world, and I wouldn't feel right about leaving you on your own. There are rules, life or death rules that you need to know. But, if you'd like, we could do it somewhere a bit more comfortable."

I nodded absently, every warning my mother uttered about going home with strange men now defunct. What was the worst that could happen? I was already dead. Plus the guy was the Sheriff of a vampire town. If I couldn't trust him, who could a girl, err vampire, trust?

We hopped back into the squad car. I looked at the town through the window in a new light. I really studied the people, their inhuman grace, the fact that there were no children around. A guy stood on the pavement waiting to cross the road, and then magically was on the other side. I didn't even see him move in front of the car.

"Did that guy just teleport? Can we do that?" The thought was exciting. To just close my eyes and picture anywhere I wanted to be in the world, it would be amazing. Such freedom!

"I'm afraid not. He just moved really fast. As your vampirism settles into your body, you'll see him move as slow as a human. We can all move that quickly."

I was disappointed, though moving at super-speed was still pretty cool. "If we can move that fast, why the hell are we driving? Wouldn't we be wherever we are going almost instantly? Unless your house is in Alaska."

"Two reasons. Firstly, I didn't want to freak you out, plus you'll need a bit of time to get used to moving at that speed. Secondly, I enjoy the slower pace that a vehicle has to offer. Just because you can go at break-neck speed, doesn't mean you should." He sounded like my dad teaching me to drive. Thoughts of my parents made me feel homesick.

"I need to call my parents and tell them I'm okay. Sort of."

Walker looked uncomfortable. "If you want, but just wait until tomorrow. Give everything you'll learn tonight time to process first."

He pulled up in front of a cute little whitewashed cottage, with a wrap-around porch and a perfectly manicured hedge. I looked at the man in the driver's seat and then back at the house. I saw him as the log cabin type of guy, not the gingerbread vibe that this place had going on.

I followed Walker up to the front door. I don't know when I started to think of him as Walker instead of Sheriff Walton, but it was probably around my third dirty fantasy.

When we walked in, the space had a bit more of a masculine feel. Leather couches, a big-screen TV, and a scarred wooden coffee table occupied the living room. A large breakfast bar separated the living area from the kitchen, with three old diner stools tucked under the overhang.

Walker went over to the kitchen counter and poured two glasses of scotch into crystal tumblers.

"I can still drink?"

"Sure. You won't get drunk, but sometimes it's nice just to indulge in the nostalgia. You can also eat and go out in the sun. Though I wouldn't suggest going out in the daytime just yet. The increased sensitivity to light makes daylight extremely painful. It's something to work up to over time. Please, have a seat."

I walked over to the big scarred leather armchair. There was a burgundy throw rug over the arm, and I pulled it over my lap, even though I wasn't cold. The softness of the mohair was amazing. I could see the intricate pattern of the weave, the tiny flyaway fibers on each of the strands of wool. It was like my sight had become microscopic.

Walker handed me my drink and sat across from me, his elbows on his knees.

"I know this has been a lot to take in, but you have some serious decisions to make, Mika. This is a whole new world, with all new rules. Especially Dark River. We aren't your average community, as you know."

"Because everyone is the undead."

"Right, because we're all vampires. But it's not just that. Even within our own race, Dark River is rather unique. I'll explain the rules, and then it's up to you if you stay or you go. We can't keep you here against your will."

Well, that sounded ominous.

"Rule number one, there is absolutely no drinking from humans. Blood is delivered and distributed around the town by the Town Council, and no one goes hungry. The penalty is banishment from Dark River, forever."

That didn't sound so bad. It's not like I wanted to go around munching on people, giving them the hickeys from hell. I nodded for him to continue.

"Rule number two, you can never, ever, turn a human. The Town Council has decreed that the penalty for disobeying this rule is death. Because, in our eyes, turning a human is essentially murder." He looked at me imploringly. "This is what has happened to you, Mika. Someone has murdered you, and it's my job to find out who and bring them to justice. You are young, beautiful, and full of life. You should have had the opportunity to do everything you wanted to do. The opportunity to have children, get married, grow old with a loved one, live out in the light. You deserve retribution." His eyes lit up, and I don't mean sparkled with fervor, I mean literally started to glow.

"Uh, Walker, what's going on with your eyes?"

"Sorry. I didn't mean to freak you out. That sometimes happens when I get worked up. Plus I need to feed."

He walked over to the fridge and pulled out a bag of O positive. I knew it was O positive because there was a huge sticker on the side. He poured it into his tumbler on top of his Scotch. Ew.

He sat back down in front of me.

"Okay, the third rule is usually the most problematic for new vampires who want to join our community. You must cut all ties with your old life, both for our safety and the safety of the people from before. You wouldn't know this yet, but being around humans is..."—he let out a shaky sigh—"an overwhelming temptation. Especially when you are only just learning to control your new body."

I collapsed back on the couch. I'd have to cut ties with my family? Never see my mom smile again, or hear my dad tell a lame joke? Never watch my youngest brother graduate high school? Tears welled in my eyes as my death sunk in. My mind was in the denial stage of grief, apparently. I mean, I felt fine now that I'd drank that blood bag. Maybe I could go home and become a goth or something. I lived alone in my apartment, so I could keep the blood hidden.

"I know what you're thinking. Really, I do. But think about it. You will never look older than you do today. You will live hundreds, if not thousands of years. If you go home, you'll watch your parents die, and your siblings, and their children, and then their children's children. Trust me when I say that it is a soul-shattering experience to watch everyone you have ever loved wither and die." The level of pain in his eyes told me that he knew from experience.

I couldn't decide this now; I needed time to think it over.

"What if I choose to leave?"

Walker bit his lip, his fangs pressing into his full lower lip. "If you choose to leave, then you are subject to the rules of the Vampire Nation. No telling humans what you are, or revealing your nature in a way that could bring vampires as a whole into the limelight. If you feed on humans, you must do it in a way that they do not suspect your true nature. Which basically means that unless you have the ability to wipe memories—which some vampires do—you'll have to kill them and dispose of their bodies discreetly. If you break these rules, Enforcers will come, and you will die. Trust me when I say that Vampire Nation always finds out if you break the rules."

Well, okay then.

Walker's shaggy hair slipped over his eyes, and he combed it back with his fingers. The move made his shirt pull taut against his chest, and a completely different kind of hunger overtook me. The need to lean over and rip open his shirt was almost impossible to resist.

Walker's eyes met mine, and whatever he saw in

them made him look nervous all of a sudden. He stood quickly and took a step away.

"Okay, I'll let you think it over. The guest room is the second door on the left, and the bathroom is right next door. Make yourself at home. If you need anything, just give me a yell." With that, Sheriff Walker Walton hot-footed it out of the room, faster than my eyes could follow.

NEWLY UNDEAD IN DARK RIVER
CHAPTER TWO

When I was little, I was one of those curious kids. I needed to know the whys and hows of everything. It wasn't enough that my parents told me that the sky was blue, I wanted to know *why* it was blue. When my parents told me that little girls couldn't fly like birds, I'd had to test the theory myself, and broke my wrist jumping off my mother's kitchen counter.

Apparently, I hadn't grown out of this need to test every theory, because when I woke up the next day, I had to pull apart the heavy velvet curtains and check if being in the daylight really hurt as much as Walker had said.

It did.

The searing pain that burned at my eyeballs was excruciating, and I let out a loud shriek. Well, I just had to know, didn't I? And apparently, Walker was a master of understatement because this was beyond extremely painful. Getting a tattoo was extremely painful. Childbirth was extremely painful. The pain I felt when I fell back against the floorboards was beyond that. It felt like someone had plucked out my eyeballs and set them on fire.

I thought I was going to vomit as I curled into the fetal position on the floor and moaned in pain. Everything was black, and panic overcame me. Had I just done irreparable damage to my eyes? Would I spend eternity blind because I was a foolish idiot who couldn't take anyone at their word?

The door crashed open, and the scent of Walker permeated throughout the room. "What happened? Oh. You opened the curtains." I looked in the direction of his voice and let out a choked sob. He picked me up off the ground and placed me back in the bed. "The pain will subside in a couple of hours, just relax. I'll get a cool washcloth for your eyes, it helps." His presence was gone from the room and then returned so quickly, there was a slight breeze across my face. He laid the wet washcloth across my eyes, making tutting noises. His disapproval wasn't necessary; I already felt like an idiot.

He pulled the blankets up around me, tucking me in like a child. My moans of pain had subsided to pitiful whimpers.

"I should have known you were going to be one of those vampires. You turn up, against the odds, in what I'm sure was a terrible situation, but you aren't a hysterical mess. No, you were all bravado and sass. You have a courageous heart and a stubborn chin. But you have to trust that what I'm telling you is the truth; otherwise, you're going to end up dead. And I don't want that for you."

All I could do was nod and try to stem the flow of tears from my eyes.

"Just rest. I have to go out and run some errands and check the spot where you said you woke up for clues. I'll be back at dusk, and then I'll take you out for dinner to meet the rest of the town."

"How can you go out in the daytime?" It came out like an accusation.

"I'm far older than you, and I have some damn good sunglasses. And a really big hat." I couldn't see his face, but the amusement in his voice led me to believe he was laughing at me.

I huffed as another whisper of wind told me he left the room.

My sight started to return around four in the afternoon. Although my eyes still stung, I could see enough to make my way out of the room and into the shower. Having a shower with my new senses was beyond divine. I felt each droplet of water pulse against my skin like a lover's caress. When the water eventually ran cold, I reluctantly left the bathroom.

With the exception of my sight at this particular moment, all of my senses had increased tenfold. I could hear someone laughing in the house down the lane. I could smell the roses in Walker's front garden from my bedroom, without a window open. I found myself running my fingertips against every surface because the range of textures had changed so dramatically.

But the inevitable downside was that I was bombarded with stimuli my brain had no chance of processing. I couldn't block anything out. The perfume of the soap in the shower nearly knocked me out. The pipes rattling in the walls was a cacophony. If I couldn't learn to control my senses, I was going to have to live my days in a padded, soundproof room.

I was still wrapped in a towel when the front door opened and closed.

"Mika?" Walker called from the living room.

"In the bedroom," I yelled back.

I eyed my filthy clothes that smelled musty and dirty from lying in a ditch. The smell made me want to heave. There was no way I could put those back on.

Walker strode into the bedroom and stopped dead when he saw me in just a towel. He quickly turned his back.

"Sorry. I see you found the shower." He sounded a

little flabbergasted, and for some reason, that made me smile. "I bought you a change of clothes from the boutique in town. Tonight we'll go and pick you up some more, but I thought you'd appreciate a fresh set sooner." He held out the plastic shopping bag and placed it on the floor near the door. "I'll leave you to it. When you're ready, we'll head into town and get you acquainted with the place, and grab a bite to eat."

The mention of food made my stomach growl loudly. I was ravenous again, and even Walker's slow heartbeat sounded enticing. I finally realized what he was trying to tell me yesterday about the temptation of humans. If Walker, another vamp, made my mouth water, then I shuddered to think about my reaction to a human.

Walker left and shut the door, and I picked up the plastic boutique bag. Inside was a soft cotton T-shirt, a cashmere sweater and a pair of jeans, in exactly my size. I briefly wondered how he'd known my size, and decided that it didn't matter. For all I knew, it was a special vampire ability. There was no underwear, which was fine with me because that just would have been weird, but the idea of putting on dirty ones also repulsed me. I decided to go commando, at least until I could pick up some new ones myself. I pulled on the t-shirt and then slipped the sweater over my head. Its softness was unbelievable.

I lost fifteen minutes just standing there, stroking

my sweater like an idiot.

I quickly pulled my hair into an elastic and brushed my teeth with one of the new toothbrushes Walker had in the bathroom cabinet. I looked at myself with my newly sharpened eyesight. My wild hair was still a riot of blond waves, and my skin was still creamy-white with a few freckles across my nose. If only vampirism had gotten rid of my freckles. The biggest change, I guess, was my eyes. My greenish-blue eyes seemed wider, and the pupils were abnormally large, like a cat at night, or a dancer at a rave party.

I didn't look different, or any more perfect, as Hollywood would have you believe. I still looked like me.

I walked out into the living room to see Walker relaxing in the armchair, his eyes closed and his head tipped back, exposing the long line of his throat. The slow thump of his heartbeat made my limbs tingle, and my stomach churn. It wasn't as lively as a normal heartbeat. It only beat every few seconds, but that was enough to stir a new primal need deep within me. I felt the caged predator that now resided in my blood raise its head and whisper to me.

I let out a cry as my fangs slid down and cut my lower lip. Ouch, dammit!

Walker's eyes snapped open, and he took a deep

breath in. Something wild appeared in his eyes, and he inhaled deeply. Holy crap, he could smell my blood. He stood and walked toward the window, and I could see his back heaving as he took several deep, steadying breaths.

"What would happen if you were to drink from me?" My voice sounded too loud in the room.

Walker's shoulders stilled. He turned to look at me, but I could still see him struggling with his nature. "We can drink from each other, but it's not something that should be done without ample preparation. Extra sustenance would have to be taken, control would have to be firmly in place. It is possible for a vampire to be killed if another takes all the blood in their body." He shifted uncomfortably from foot to foot. "Plus, it usually isn't done unless the two vampires are in some kind of relationship. Taking blood can be an extremely intimate act." A blush lit his cheeks, and I resisted the urge to laugh. I had the feeling he was giving me the vampire version of the birds and the bees talk.

"Good to know," I said, trying to keep the smirk off my face. "I'm ready to go now."

Walker looked relieved that that line of questioning was over, and picked up his hat from the floor beside the armchair.

The trip to town was quiet, as I took in everything I could in the fading light. Not that the lack of light seemed to be a problem for me; I could see everything with a clarity that startled me. It was like watching high definition after a lifetime of the fuzzy goodness of Betamax.

"Did you find my stuff?" I was hopeful. My camera, my passport, my life, was all in the backpack.

He shook his head.

"There was no sign of it. I got a few scraps of material, and a shoe print from the area, but otherwise it was clean. I have no idea how you ended up in a drain outside the town limits." He sounded frustrated. Well, that made two of us.

I still hadn't decided what to do about my... uh, death. The thought of never seeing my family again tore at my heart. However, the thought of literally tearing at their hearts with my fangs was even worse. So I was doing what I did best. I was stalling until the last possible moment. It was an innate talent. Instead of choosing someone to go to prom with, I'd gone stag. Instead of choosing a major in college, I'd set out to backpack my way around Canada. Look how well that ended.

He eased the car into a spot outside Bert and Beatrice's Diner. "Let's go grab something to eat, then we'll figure out the rest." He pushed open the diner door and stood to the side to let me through.

Every set of eyes turned to look at me, and I got a

strange sense of déjà vu. Beatrice was manning the counter today, and she gave me a warm smile.

"Evenin' Mika, Sheriff. Just grab any table, I'll be over to get your order in a minute." She bustled down the other end of the counter to refill the coffee of a man in a tight cable knit sweater with shoulder-length black hair. He was the only person in the room not staring at me.

Walker placed a hand on my lower back and directed me to an empty booth. There were some hushed murmurs, and then everyone descended at once.

People were in my space, shaking my hand and introducing themselves in a blur of names and faces that I'd have no chance of remembering. Walker was equally as bombarded with questions: who made me, were there any leads in my murder case, did he think it was one of the townspeople?

Two women, who looked to be in their late thirties, were hanging off Walker like two extra limbs.

"Well, I think it's that drifter. When I watch CSI, it's always the drifter." One, I think her name was Lynette, said to the people surrounding our table.

"I thought it was always the husband? Are you married, honey?" Lynette's shadow asked. I dazedly shook my head. "Well then, maybe you're right. Maybe it is the Drifter." Both of their eyes swung to look at the guy in the cable knit. I could see his shoulders were tense, and I was guessing that a) he was the Drifter and b) he'd heard every word Lynette and her parrot had said.

I stared at his back and wondered if that was the truth. Was he my murderer?

In a town full of carnivores, anyone could be the person who stole my life. The people crowded around me now seemed a lot more ominous.

"Ladies, please. What the town doesn't need is idle gossip pointing the finger at innocent people. I will do a thorough investigation, and only when I have found hard evidence, will anyone be charged. This isn't the Wild West, where you string up the new guy first and ask questions later." He gave them a stern look. "Now, if you'll excuse us, I think Mika would like to eat in peace. There's no need to overwhelm her on her first day."

Everyone left us alone for the time being, though I could still feel their collective gaze like a weight on my skin. Beatrice finally made her way over to take our orders.

"Don't worry about it, Lass. By next week, you'll be old news. Now, what can I get you two?" I hadn't even had time to look at the menu in all the hubbub, so when Walker ordered a burger with fries and a Type-O float, I ordered that too.

I was glad I could still eat food. The idea of sustaining myself entirely on blood gave me the heebie-jeebies. I'd always loved food, and you could tell by the snug way I fit into my size twelve jeans. My motto had always been why deny yourself dessert, when there was a chance you'd be hit by a bus the following day? Luckily, I loved to go running nearly as much as I loved chocolate, so I was still more fit than flab.

"So if I'm immortal, can I still get fat?" It was a shallow question, but there had to be a silver lining to the dead thing, right? If I couldn't grow older, or get sick, surely I couldn't put on weight?

"You'll remain exactly the way you were when you were turned. Your body ceases to grow at a normal rate. Alice would be better explaining all the medical mumbo-jumbo though."

I resisted the urge to do a little happy dance. Instead, I waved my hand at Beatrice. "Could I get an extra serving of cheese fries and a piece of lemon meringue pie as well please?" Beatrice nodded and scribbled it on her notepad.

I grinned from ear to ear, and Walker shook his head. "You can still get stomach aches, you know."

I didn't care. I felt free for the first time since I hit puberty. No longer did I have to worry about the cheerleaders at school mocking my puppy fat, or being unattractive to the freshman class boys. I didn't have to worry about diabetes, heart disease, obesity. All my food guilt was gone.

When Beatrice placed the bowl of cheese fries on the table in front of me, I fell on it like a demon unchained. It was the most glorious meal I'd ever had, partly because calories didn't matter anymore, and partly because my sense of taste had heightened. It was like a mouth orgasm.

The tall milkshake glass had a deep ruby red liquid in it, and a hard ball of ice cream floating on top.

It was simultaneously the funniest and most disturbing beverage I'd ever seen. Considering I'd recently seen a hipster with a lumberjack beard have a flaming Sambuca shot mishap, well, let's just say, that my Type-O float was really something.

I tried a sip, and then another. I wished I could explain the taste of blood to someone who wasn't a vamp. It was like the very best wine, coffee, and chocolate fondue all rolled into one. I let out a little moan, and Walker's eyes widened. Whoops.

"That's really, really good."

"That's 'cause Beatrice does the best Type-O floats in North America." A deep voice said from over my shoulder. His voice was gravelly, somewhere between a rumble and a growl, and he had a thick Southern accent. I turned and looked into the darkest blue eyes I'd ever seen. They were like the night sky right on dusk. My mouth seemed to unhinge, and a little Type-O float dribbled over my lip. The night blue eyes dropped to my lips, and then back to my eyes.

Walker cleared his throat. "Judge. What can I help you with?"

Once my eyes got past his, I realized he was the man the townspeople called the Drifter. His shaggy black hair hung in waves to his shoulders and looked as if it had been hacked in a restroom mirror. His chest was broad, and the knit sweater wrapped around his shoulders like a present on Christmas morning. He made me salivate.

I gaped. "You're a judge?" That was almost harder to comprehend than the existence of vampires.

"Just in name, Sugar. I just wanted to set the record straight. I've never seen this girl in my life. Though, I wouldn't mind seein' more of her now." He smirked at me, his pearly white teeth glistening in the fluorescent lights. The smile made something tingle.

"I have no suspects in this matter yet. I am following up all the evidence I've gathered and then I'll interview people."

Uh-huh. What evidence?

Judge nodded. "Well, if the little lady needs a hand with anything, anything at all, don't hesitate to ask. I am more than willin' to show Mika the perks of being a vampire, and help meet any needs she may have." His eyes twinkled with mischief, and I could understand why everyone automatically went to him as the primary suspect in my murder/rebirth. He just oozed bad-boy troublemaker.

If only that didn't make me so damn hot.

"She'll be fine." Walker gave him a hard look, and my back arched up a little. Did I suddenly become unable to make my own decisions? Sure, I'd obviously made some bad ones because, hey, I was dead. But generally speaking, I was a good judge of character. I knew that Judge was trouble, but I didn't like being treated like a child.

"Luckily for everyone here, I have a voice of my own. Thanks for the offer Judge, I'll keep it in mind."

Judge grinned and touched two fingers to his forehead as he left. It was an old-world gesture, and it made me wonder what age Judge actually was. He didn't look more than twenty-five, but if we stopped aging, he could be centuries old, millennia even. I watched his ass as he left, and if there was ever a finer butt in the world, I had yet to see it. He must have been some kind of laborer when he was turned because his body was that lean musculature you could only get through hard, physical work. I sighed as he melted into the darkness beyond the streetlights.

"If you are quite done, we're late to meet Alice, and I still want to take you out to where you woke up, to see if you can remember anything."

Walker sounded pissed, but he could just eat me. I made my own damn decisions. I raised one eyebrow challengingly, as I slurped down the rest of my float. When Walker threw down a twenty, I again felt bad.

"Is there a way I can get at my money? I can't keep letting you pay for stuff."

"We'll figure it out later. It's no big deal." Walker held the door open for me, and we stepped out onto the brightly lit pavement. The light posts were the town's originals, ornate gas lamp style, and they emitted a warm golden glow. The night sky was so beautiful this far into the wilderness.

"Alice's practice is on the other side of the town square. We'll walk if you like." We crossed the road, although there was no traffic. Why bother when you could super speed everywhere?

"Have you made a decision about staying?"

I heaved out a sigh. Giving up my family, my life back home, it would be like dying all over again. "I'm not sure. What would I have to do, exactly?"

"Cut off all ties with your old life, change your identity, swear to uphold the values of the town. We have people that help you with the transition, of course. People who will work you up some new documents and help you adjust to our lifestyle. There are three months of compulsory therapy, as well. We'll set you up with a job within the town, so you can earn a living. You can go on trips and leave town of course, this isn't a prison, but you have to have an escort for the first six months until you have the initial thirst under control. We learned that one the hard way."

There was a sadness in his voice, and I sensed a story around that.

"How long has the town been here? I assume it didn't start out a vampire colony." Getting tradespeople in would have been a nightmare.

"It was abandoned by humans about a hundred and fifty years ago after the gold boom was over. Five or so vampires bought it with a vision of a better life for us, one out of the shadows. So far, it has worked well. Every year we have one or two new vampires petition to join the town."

We walked the rest of the way in silence. I had a lot to think over, and I was getting hungry again. And not just for blood. I was going to have to ask Alice if this overwhelming need to rip off Walker's clothes and ravish him was something to do with being a vampire or just my normal hormones. Let's face it, I probably would've had a hard time resisting him if I'd stumbled into town human.

"What happens when humans come through? Surely they must realize something is off?"

He nodded. "It's been known to happen, even though we are completely off the beaten track up here. We aren't on the road to anywhere, and we have no accommodation. So in most cases, they come into the gas station, fuel up and move on. Or they'll stop in at the diner and Bert will make them something absolutely abhorrent and they'll leave. This isn't an inviting town for the weary traveler."

It wasn't an inviting town for anyone with a normal heart rate and their mortality intact. There was probably a good chance you wouldn't get out alive.